It's tne Second Hand Man

Alan Tansley

Author Alan Tansley. © 2009

All rights reserved. No part of this book may be reproduced, stored in a retrieval system or transmitted in any form or by any means without the prior written permission of the publishers, except by a reviewer who may quote brief passages in a review to be printed in a newspaper, magazine or journal.

Names, reference to places and events are purely fictional.

ISBN 978-0-9561568-0-8

Cover photos are of the West Riding Square Normanton West Yorkshire. Provided by Alan Tansley

Chapter 1

In a small town on the outskirts of Leeds in the old West Riding of Yorkshire just before the outbreak of the Second World War, Jessie Harper, now twenty years of age, married Colin Mathews was a year older.

With Colin's brother David as best man, who was courting Doreen Pritchard, and acted as Jessie's only bridesmaid, they attended a plain simple ceremony which was paid for by Jessie's grandmother. There were very few presents because this moment in time nobody had any money, so most gifts were mainly homemade or hand-me-downs.

Their ceremony, as their opportunist vicar cheekily stated, was to promote not only theirs but everyone's Christian unification to bring happiness together and throughout their religion, even though the nation congregations was dwindling fast.

That evening, the drinks didn't flow because of lack of funds however, and as usual, the older end always found a few bottles of Mackison from somewhere which they normally spiked with a red hot poker gingerly taken out of a good old coal fire. Why? Well really nobody knew the reason, but the most popular answer was that it tasted better.

Unfortunately news of another world war was rife being now everyday conversation, and now the wedding after living with Colin's parents for three weeks, Colin and Jessie dropped lucky because eight streets away they were granted then began to privately rent next but one to an end terraced house, in a row of fifteen on an estate of five hundred.

Their house was one of many in the industrial north of England, set in row-upon-row, and always leading off a main road, just a typical northern working class area.

Jessie and Colin always thought they were very fortunate not to have been allocated a one-up one-down, similar to three streets away which were very cramped. Their house was a two-up, two-down, had good sliding sash windows, with an outside toilet next to a coal store.

To bathe, you used a galvanized tin bath, and when not in use this was always hung on the washing line hook outside and near the kitchen window for safety. After the weekly washing of clothes it was normally filled with hot water from a copper boiler situated in the corner of the kitchen adjacent to a big black-leaded coal fireplace, regularly used for baking, cooking, and provided heating.

There was also a smaller fireplace in the front room, and in the locality when all the fires were lit, usually first thing in the morning, with their chimneys combined, this gave off a heavy thick sooty atmosphere. Everyone coughed and spluttered, but nobody complained, as they were only trying their best to keep warm and clean.

Three months after their wedding, Jessie's grandparents died within weeks of each other, and as usual amongst families at this unfortunate time, their furniture was shared out. Jessie obtained a table and four chairs for their front room, and of course the only way to get them to their house was to carry them.

Their downstairs lighting was provided by gas mantle and upstairs had to use candles. It was a bleak existence for the working classes, who just plodded along didn't know anything better, but the main thing was, trying to keep good health, when many children died young with differing ailments with the main cause being lack of nourishment.

Every week there was at least one funeral for the local undertaker who always wore a black morning suit with top hat. Always walking in front of the horse drawn hearse, which had a removable top so later that afternoon, he would probably be delivering coal or groceries with it.

Horse and cart was the main source of transport at this moment in time, and while the cortege slowly continued down the main road and on towards the cemetery, the local folk would stand outside their front doors with heads bowed paying their respects.

When the Second World War was declared, Jessie began work in a clothing factory in Leeds, travelling daily on the tram with Colin who worked in an iron foundry nearby. Because of the nature of his job he was exempt from joining the army; however, his firm was soon allocated to make tank parts for them.

This exemption also meant he had to have a part time job, so Colin volunteered for the fire service. Discipline was harsh, and you had to be dying to dare miss the rigorous twice a week practice. Eventually when fully trained, he was now on permanent call out to attend bombing raids from the enemy, which as of yet hadn't materialized.

Throughout this time, both Colin and Jessie saved like hell, as their objective was to try and buy a house when the war was over. While courting they often discussed their future, and decided the main objective was to improve their standard of living not only for them but their children. Unfortunately both knew it was against all odds, so first on the agenda was to put back, and desperately tried not to start a family.

During the war years, and after the death of Colin's grandparents, this meant the family had to scrimp and scrape to bury them. Times were very hard and again could save very little. The nature of their employment had also changed dramatically when the firm Jessie worked for now made service uniforms for the armed forces, and with Colin, like the rest of the workers with any spare money they were now encouraged to buy war bonds.

Luckily because of his straight talking business attitude, Colin received promotion and became a manager within the firm. This was also the boost they needed which enabled them to begin their savings again so obviously raised their moral.

When the war ended, Colin and Jessie joined the rest of their locality to attend the many street carnivals and parades with jubilation. However, to the older generation, most wondered what would happen next, when there seemed to be far fewer commodities than before the war started as now nearly everything was rationed.

Still saving like hell, including the odd shilling or florin, deposited weekly in the local post office. In March nineteen forty seven, at home with the aid of an unqualified but experienced aunt, Jessie had a son and they named him Gordon, unfortunately both never realized you had to pay for the local doctor to visit.

Not calling much anyway because the weather was shocking, with at least three feet of snow so freezing temperatures lasting many months, the worst for many years. Colin did his utmost to keep them all warm, by collecting firewood or chopping down bushes. Again, their savings went on hold hoping Gordon could stave off the most serious of infant ailments, and with proper nourishment, luckily he did.

Always satisfied with their privately rented living accommodation now sixty years old, and decorated best they could to their liking, Colin also maintained the outside of the house. Some neighbor's frowned while watched when he repaired a leaky roof, however, Colin would scorn, "If you want to live in a pig sty, go live with pigs. I don't."

Colin's brother, David, a carpenter by trade, soon as the war ended married Doreen Pritchard who was from Garforth. Realizing housing was cheaper in Colin's area, and better than the hovel they lived in now, decided to move nearer the city.

Eventually, and thought themselves to be very lucky, had obtained the house next door to Colin and Jessie, so obviously all the family helped them to move.

Unfortunately throughout the following year, rumours became rife, that their local council, under new government legislation, was to compulsory purchase all the old houses, knock them down and build new dwellings in the area.

Ruffled by the news David maintained his job as a cabinet maker, but knowing this would affect their future began to do home repairs, renovating furniture for friends and relations for the extra money. Doreen discussed the problem with him so decided to do the same began to take in washing, and both began to save like mad, hoping very much they were approved one.

One night in early April nineteen forty nine, relaxing in Colin's front room, all discussed their future while sharing two jugs of ale from the local off-license. Debating plans now published, the council was to commandeer all the privately owned houses, knock them down and build new. "So what are they going to do with over a hundred and fifty families near us while they do it?" asked David, while stared at Colin because he thought it was impossible.

"That's up to them brother; anyway, did you finish that wardrobe for Mrs Whitaker?" he asked before had a drink.

"Yes the varnish is drying, don't worry it'll be ready tomorrow," he replied while sat up to pour out the rest of the beer.

"What did the doctor say then?" asked Jessie, to purposely change the subject.

"He said there was no medical reason, just keep on trying," replied Doreen looking disappointed. Unfortunately she was having difficulty in conceiving, suddenly smiled when Gordon roused, stood up, picked him up out of his hand-made wooden crib and smiled saying, "Hasn't he a lovely head of hair."

When she sat on the sofa nursing him, "You have in here nice now, it'll be a shame to knock it down," said David, before had a drink.

"We've discussed that, and you know them that moved into number twelve last week? Well, Jessie felt so sorry for the poor buggers she gave them a set of draws and some bedding," replied Colin, and smiled while watched Doreen.

"I think most of the street gave them something, anyway at least they have something to eat off now," said David, then stood up and stretched.

Colin smiled saying, "Yes but how long will they be in there to use anything."

Jessie smirked saying, "Go on tell them."

David didn't understand, and pulled a face asking, "Such as?"

"Right then, we've been thinking about buying the next two houses on the end, with the intentions of opening a second hand shop in there," replied Colin while smiling at Jessie.

David sat down and rest back asked, "Oh I, so go on then?"

"I'm going to the council offices on Wednesday because I want a look at their plans. If they will let us buy the end houses, we'll knock them into a shop, and sell second hand furniture in there, then we could extend to use the above rooms," he replied, then smiled before cheekily raised his eyebrows as if to goad him.

Looking gob-smacked, "Well, you bugger. You kept that quiet," said David looking bewildered.

"You should know him by now," said Jessie then grinned watching Gordon looking round while Doreen tickled his chin tormenting him.

"The only thing is we have to modernize them. Knock the outside toilets down and build a workshop there. You could do up furniture in it and sell it at the front. We'll do a bomb mate," said Colin, and laughed as if to ease his proposal.

David didn't, just stared at him. "What if it flops?" asked Doreen then nuzzled Gordon's chin making him smile.

"We move out and get a council house," replied Jessie, and grinned watched them.

"At least we have had a go mate," said Colin, before finished his drink.

Looking unsure David asked, "So, you mean me to do the repairs for you?"

With an enthusiastic smile on his face, "No I mean we as partners. Come on our kid let's have a go. What can we lose? A couple of hundred pounds is a fortune I know but furniture is expensive and a necessity for all. If we can buy it in, do it up, and sell it at a profit, then we split it fifty-fifty."

"It's a big thing though starting a business," said David, and frowned at the thought.

"Will he want a feed yet?" asked Doreen, noticed Gordon bad become restless.

Still smiling, "Shortly," replied Jessie.

"Any business is a risk. Anyway it all depends on the council plans. Let's see what they have to say first. If these houses have to come down, all well and good, we will just have to look round and see if there are others we can buy," replied Colin then smiled when seeing him study.

David, as if in a quandary slowly stood up asking, "If you don't mind Colin, I'll have a think about it first. Anyway are we ready Doreen?"

Three months later, the council published their building plans. Soon as he found out, Colin approached them to be notified they were on display in the public library so he walked round there to a study them. Now knowing where the new estates where to be built, and especially taking note the position of roads and shops, he returned to the council offices, to arrange a meeting with the councilors in charge.

The following week, in a town hall side chamber, Colin began to outline his proposition to three councilors, and noticed none looked impressed. Quickly deciding to change his approach he stressed, "So you are going to knock everything flat with no consideration to our history. I have photos of three thatched houses on the end of our street turn of the century that looked magnificent, and all the council did was knock them down. It is disgusting that all you are bothered about is concrete," and shook his head in disgust to make the point.

"That is progress, and don't forget we've just fought a bloody world war for it," said one, turned and smiled sarcastically at his mates.

Colin stared at him then snapped, "We might have, but what have our kids got to help educate them in our local history, nothing?"

"Point taken lad and I must stress this we do have alternative plans for this area. Anyway we have to go now so many thanks for your assistance," said another while closed his folder.

"Before you go, will you at least call and have a look at our houses? I know I haven't anything in writing, but I soon can have," asked Colin then purposely looked at each councilor in turn.

"Again, point taken lad, and we might," said one, who seemed to be the chairman of the three. Colin acknowledged them before leaving with mixed emotions didn't know what their future would be. Still paying rent to the owner of his house, and as the weeks dragged by, heard nothing from either party.

Colin's spirits suddenly lifted when three months later, he received a letter from the council to attend another meeting in two weeks time. It also stated their rent would be due to them from the first of June nineteen fifty, so he now knew their compulsory purchase order had gone through.

That night, sat in the front room with Jessie while she fed Gordon. "If only I knew what they were thinking," Colin moaned, was now running out of patience.

Jessie smiled while reassuring at him, "We'll soon find out love."

As prior arranged Saturday night before the meeting, in their front room with David and Doreen, Colin stood in front of the fireplace before disclosed the amount of their savings, then politely asked how much they could contribute towards a business.

Looking surprised at the total amount, David said, "Listen mate, first I've been thinking this. As you suggest, if we could buy these end two houses, live in our two and knock the end two into one shop. We could buy the best timber off the old houses that are being knocked down to build our workshop, and if we use our heads when families move away, buy whatever furniture they don't want to take with them. We could store it in there, and renovate it at will."

Colin smiled had noted his enthusiasm, quickly replied, "Right mate. I will propose it and see if they agree. It's unfortunate we don't know what they are going to do yet, so for now let's wait and see." He also noticed their women were uncannily quiet, and suddenly winced could see by his size that Gordon was growing up fast. Smiling at Doreen and knew she doted on him; David had quietly informed him she badly wanted a child, but all the doctor would continuously say was go away and keep on trying.

When Colin attended the council meeting, to his surprise, when in principal, the councilors after studying his plans accepted them, but with restrictions to future maintenance of the buildings. However, first they wanted to see proper architect's plans, and gave him two weeks to produce them.

Quickly taking measurements with David and with the aid of a draughtsman from work, after a lot of alterations then adjustments, a week later, Colin arranged a meeting to present them.

Not knowing he had to wait a further two weeks for a reply, Colin was on tender-hooks until early Monday morning when the letterbox rattled. After opening a letter from the council, instant celebrations began when read his plans had been approved. "What the hell-fire do we do now?" asked David, looking bewildered.

"Well partner. I should say this is where the work begins, wouldn't you?" replied Colin then heartily laughed.

Over the next six months, with the end four houses bought, and now with the deeds in their respective names, after paying their rates for six months, work began on the outside. The only problem was they cut off the gas, but really were glad as it was coal gas and smelled awful.

The council did provide Tilley lamps with white spirit for fuel, but as they could not work much in the dark were now also minus street gas lamps to help, so wherever possible, every bit of daylight was spent working and renovating.

The women helped best they could, same as the men were used to hard work, but their main problem was food. Shopkeepers were one of the first to move away from the area, mainly into the city market to save their businesses. So now having to travel into the city for certain commodities Doreen and Jessie took it in turns, however, they still favoured the travelling fruiter with his horse and cart, visiting twice a week.

Jessie had applied for her old job back at the sewing factory, was now making gents shirts and was over the moon when she was accepted. So now with everyone working full time, Doreen was not feeling left out because she was untrained for today's piecework methods. She looked after Gordon during the day and prepared dinner for the evening. However, Wednesday became known as a red letter day, as it was always the day when the bills came in, or the day when something went wrong.

Another set-back, again on a Wednesday evening, while working on the two houses they were living in, Colin and David discussed a letter that stated they had to pay for architect and solicitor's fees before could make permanent alterations. Knowing money was tight, David frowned moaning, "Well, that's bloody marvelous."

Colin smiled saying, "They'll run out of rules to send us before long."

"Either that or paper brother," moaned David then both laughed.

Two weeks later, and as they thought with everything paid, this left them with a healthy balance, but knew it wouldn't last long much longer. Both Colin and David always grimaced when they received regular visits from the council inspector however, luckily unlike today, rules and regulations were less stringent, so usually they had worked near enough to their plans.

Always on the cards, and now through lack of money for materials to renovate the inside of their houses, eventually Colin and David had to cash in their war bonds. When this process was eventually done they deposited the money with their savings in the post office knowing it would be one of the last buildings to be knocked down. At the time the GPO was one of the largest saving institutions in the land and seeing as they had plans to build a new office in a proposed adjacent street, they didn't fancy drawing it all out and depositing in a bank, would have to travel into Leeds to do it.

With adjacent houses being readily knocked down and now nearly on their own in the area; they had their block re-wired for electricity by a qualified electrician from the foundry. All waited impatiently for the electricity board to lay the mains, then they could be connected up. When this eventually happened, Jessie continued to switch the light on and off, could not believe it was so bright and easy.

It was also a sign of the times, when Jessie was regularly put on short time while machinery at their mill was changed over to make gentlemen's suits. She frowned at receiving her fifth short weekly wage, decided to pack her job in to help the men at home.

After a family discussion, this she did, and after working a week's notice, now with Doreen, they worked together, began to take in washing. However, when more families began to move away, their business soon dwindled.

They discussed what to do, decide to knit, and one Saturday visited Leeds market. They approached a trader with samples, who, after bartering, agreed to buy their wares then arranged to call weekly to their house, but the main thing was he would pay by cash.

While travelling home they discussed various styles and patterns. Each discussed then arranged to do the ones they liked the best, knew they were onto a winner, because over the years had seen many friends start then stop knitting with lack of incentive or boredom.

With a pile of second hand timber in their back yard from demolished houses, David began to knock down the old outside toilets, when they now had them inside. One day, he suddenly stopped, and glanced round at a derelict landscape thought, *oh boy, it looks like we are the only families on this planet.* Studying if they had done right or not, and with their money going out far quicker than it was coming in, he suddenly grimaced then took his apprehension out of some bricks while demolishing a wall.

Chapter 2

Twelve months later, with the shop, their houses modernized, David had completed the workshop at the rear. So with both Mathews families settled in; David and Colin still maintained their jobs and were lucky to have enough money left over for when the last of the families began to move away into temporary accommodation. Both always classed themselves to be in a fortunate position, could buy whatever furniture the families wanted to dispose of, unfortunately they always had the problem of carrying it home.

Another major set-back was, Jessie's parents suddenly died within months of each other, and this caused problems with the rest of her family. Two of her brothers had died very young, and from then on her eldest brother always took command, so with Colin, they just attended the funeral before returned straight home to save any arguments.

With the workshop finished and stacked to the rafters with furniture of every description, David began to renovate and repair. He was very good at his job, whereas Colin, with a more technical mind had done the footings, bricklaying, plastering, and then decorated their extensions.

One pleasant evening, while stood outside drinking tea, and admiring their work. "All we want now is some customers," said David half-smiling.

"They'll be here and don't worry mate, many of them will be moving back into the area soon. They will have nothing and now have more rooms to fill. Our only problem is managing to survive with what we have left from now on," replied Colin, knew they were nearly rock bottom and soon had more bills to pay.

Another problem instantly arose when the diggers moved nearer their site causing clouds of dust. They had to put up with it and two months later, with roads nearly complete, footings for the new council estate began rising. Now being the only families in the area, most weekends their only visitors were the local tradesman to collect knitted garments. The coalman, who still used horse and cart, and of course their position was always a burden for the dustbin men, had to water and feed their horses before slowly trudged back towards the old main road.

Meanwhile on an evening, David taught Colin various aspects of his work while slowly they filled the shop to make a display. Jessie and Doreen were very pleased with their accommodation, same as before, two up and two down, only now with less draughty window frames. Sporting modern fireplaces, level concrete floors and of course had electricity in every room. Not once did they criticize their men, knew they did it for their future, which didn't matter anyway because everyone's was still uncertain.

The men had completed extensions on the rear of each house, and downstairs this gave them a proper separate kitchen, while upstairs, off the rear bedroom, was now a toilet with bathroom. Top of the shop, one bedroom was earmarked for an office, and another a toilet. This left two rooms spare, and Jessie had plans for one if she had another child.

Bricks for their extensions had never been a problem, having dressed and re-used the best from the demolition site. Their biggest problem was cleaning out joints for re-pointing, and neither relished it because of the dust. Sewers and drainage were dug out ready; however, the council insisted all connections were inspected by them. When realized they also had to be properly tested, Colin smirked when informed, they wouldn't be a charge, just a small increase in their general rates.

One Wednesday, during a visit by two councilors, both seemed impressed with the work done, especially the shop front, now had a green rectangular sign over the front, and in gold lettering displayed, Mathew's Furnishings. David looked well pleased when they signed forms which gave them their approval. Winking at Colin, he knew all they had to do now was sell furniture, and that would prove difficult being on their own in the area.

The day Gordon began nursery school, which was two miles away and had to walk there, they officially opened the shop. Twenty new houses had been allocated to families, but what made Colin and David smile more, was the fact that the council had released plans for five hundred more houses to be built north side of town.

Obviously at first trade were slow, they mainly sold second hand beds and wardrobes. While the men retained their day jobs, the women tried their best to keep the shop clean, polished furniture, and in between serving looked after Gordon.

Two months later, and because trade had increased that much, after a family meeting, the men decided to leave their jobs. This gave David more time to spend renovating, which he loved, and Colin more time to buy in, now even took old furniture in part exchange.

One morning while reading the morning post, Colin smiled with relief when found out plans had been passed to build two more new smaller housing estates with a shopping complex nearby. Informing David, who slowly smiled had always seemed sceptical; however, he didn't have time to moan with such a backlog of work.

Jessie with Doreen still knitted, now had more time, and with a twin tub washer and electric iron each, these commodities saved them both a lot of extra work. With downstairs floors damp proofed, and better than the old stone paving flags, this gave more warmth in the houses. However, because they still used coal for heating, Colin wasn't satisfied with it but as of yet there wasn't anything better.

The only chore for Jessie was walking to school twice a day with Gordon, who unfortunately was growing up in an adult world. The only children he saw was at school, and there weren't many, however, when he returned home, after tea, would listen to the wireless then sketch, or paint which was his favorite hobby.

Approaching May nineteen fifty five, with the new estate half full and the other half still being built, the shop was always busy so business healthy. Colin would always ask a fair price, hoped for a knock on effect to increase trade. This worked, and word soon spread giving them more customers.

It also gave them a good lifestyle, and when Jessie announced she was pregnant again, not many days later, Doreen enthusiastically announced she was as well so it led to a very big celebration.

Unfortunately for everyone it was constant work, and since neither family ever had a holiday they never missed one. In fact during all their lives none had strayed far from their houses since moving in. This was a typical northern way of life; however, it was all about to change for them.

Start of the nineteen sixties, and with both council estates nearly finished, trade at the shop had improved every year. Colin decided to drive and learned with a taxi driver friend in Leeds he used to work with at the foundry. Luckily he passed, and with advice, bought a second hand Bedford van. He had their name painted on the side, and on a weekend while travelling to sales or demolitions in other towns, began to take Gordon with him.

While they were away David would serve in the shop, and soon as they returned, began to grade, renovate and update their purchases. He was very good at his job, and at this moment in time with coffee tables all the rage, began to make various styles by the dozen.

Having to smile at all the fads people had when another quickly became popular, having wooden pelmets over their interior windows. Obviously knowing materials were expensive; David always kept plenty in stock, of varying sizes and all made out of scrap wood.

Jessie had a girl and same as Gordon, the birth was at home, only this time attended by the local midwife. Luckily with no complications, they decided to call her Tracy, and instantly knew there was going to be a problem because their house just wasn't big enough.

Now short of a bedroom for when she grew up, three weeks later, Jessie smiled while began to outline her plans. The very next day, and without question, Colin knocked through a hole in their bedroom wall, began fitting a door frame, giving them access into a bedroom above the shop.

He knew it was a necessity, would greatly improve their accommodation, and was all preparation for when Tracy grew up. While painting it, Colin also decided, that now with all the extra paperwork required for running a business, it was time to make one of the rooms above the shop into an office then furnish it accordingly.

Two weeks later, and because if complications, now resting in hospital, Doreen was over the moon after giving birth to a girl and they decided to call her Barbara. Even though she had a bad time during labour, their outlook in life was now complete. Unfortunately all this was too much for Gordon, who would often draw or paint, as he didn't like girls much and kept out of their way.

Encouraged by both parents to read, they always gave Gordon their spare time to improve his education, so everyone was rewarded and pleased when he sat his eleven plus and passed. At the age of twelve, off he went to Grammar school and unfortunately it became a bind. Gordon didn't like travelling there when it took an hour on the bus each way. It became a long day for him especially with homework he was given. Of course with assignments and projects, this also took up most of his weekend, so couldn't go with his dad to the salerooms.

In his second year, with more pupils on the bus, Gordon took particular note of two girls, and one was Andrea Hastings. She was small, petite, always sat prim and proper and was always reading a book.

While pretending to read, Gordon would eye her because she had a very nice figure and always wore clean clothes. Other than the usual, hello, they hardly conversed, and when departed the bus, he would smile in acknowledgement before they went in different directions.

The other was Caroline Blakemore, who was more boisterous, and often played hell up with the other lads, occasionally clouted them when they messed around. Gordon would smile, and even though she also had a good figure, thought her a tomboy.

Unfortunately as the years passed by, Gordon proved to be just average at school; however, painting had become his forte. Now wanting to become an artiste he bought loads of books about the old masters, and certain new painters. Religiously he studied them and practiced hours on end, just to hone a skill.

Each Saturday evening, Gordon would eagerly await his dad to return from the salerooms or house clearance, where he would buy paintings for him, damaged or not. Colin would hand them over, then smile content while watched Gordon inspect them, knowing they would keep him occupied for a few days.

Gordon would renovate them in a spare room over the shop, now known as his studio, and when finished would hang them in the shop for sale. Colin allowed him have the proceeds, and frowned one day noticed he had sold six so far and made over two hundred pounds.

When asked him what he was going to do with the money, using present day teenage body language, Gordon pulled a face at all the interruptions, then politely informed him he was going to buy a house at Otley and move away from everyone just so he could paint to his heart's content.

"All I have to say to that then is just hurry up pal, it'll be one less mouth to feed," joked Colin, and watched him spin round as if angry.

Gordon moaned, "Don't temp me," while set off upstairs being fed up of constantly reminded to do his homework, and even more, interrupted by banging or sawing from the workshop when concentrating during renovating a painting.

The following Saturday morning, Colin was in for a surprise when an old school friend of his came into the shop. He frowned when she seemed nervous however, smiled asked, "Hello Enid, how are you going on love?"

"Fine thanks apart from a few aches and pains, but I've called for a favour, well, that's if it's possible," she replied then bowed her head.

"Go on then love, what can we do for you?" he asked, but studied her face thought she didn't look well.

"It's our Caroline. You know she passed to go to high school with your Gordon? Well, I feel such a fool but since her dad died I have no spare money. She needs another new uniform soon and its thirty pounds," she replied looking very near to tears.

"Well now," said Colin, and rubbed his chin as if knew what was coming.

Eventually she pulled her wedding rings off, and holding them towards him asked, "I don't know how they expect us to manage these days, so could you pawn me these please?"

Colin had no idea of their value, and didn't want to take them anyway smiled saying, "Just a minute love," turned and set off into the back room.

Doing this on purpose so Enid would not see him take the money out of his wallet, Colin glanced over his shoulder and noticed her looking round the furniture. Returning he quietly said, "Here take this. I don't know what the rules are on doing it, but go on," passed her forty pounds in fivers, and noticed her eyes opened wide.

Enid looked up, and staring into his eyes asked, "Are you sure Colin?"

Grinning he replied, "Take it, and when you win the pools you can give me it back."

"Nonsense Colin, I haven't any money for bus fares never mind the pools," she moaned, took the money then handed him her rings.

Pushing her hand away, "No, you keep them."

"No, a deal is a deal. When I can I'll be back for them," she snapped, smiled while placed them on a sideboard nearby then quickly turned continuing towards the door.

While watched her continue out of the shop, "Okay then Enid but look after yourself," he replied.

There and then, Colin made up his mind it was time to have a telephone installed, not only to aid their business, but he could also ring for advice on such matters. Giving her the money out of his own pocket, he decided not to inform David about the transaction, having noticed Enid was dressed shabby so knowing she must be rock bottom. Not being like that at school he also knew she was never a liar so the money must have been for her daughter, placed the rings in his wallet, and when the time was right, would give them back.

Unfortunately Colin never knew if Enid had informed others about his help so having had a phone installed in the office, with party lines into his house and David's who at first was reluctant when it was another bill to pay. However, over the next few years, occasionally Colin continued the business of pawning goods, even for furniture, but only with people he knew. He would not do it with strangers in case they used stolen goods, always referred them to a broker near the new bus station in Leeds.

At the first opportunity, he also bought an old safe, and had it bolted to the wall in the workshop. David would wait while Colin opened it then would take the Mickey, when all it contained was junk, never had any cash in it. "That's not the point, it looks good," said Colin while locked it.

Enid never returned for her rings had died, and after finding out, one day while going through the safe, Colin frowned noticed watches, jewellery, cameras and strings of pearls. All pawned over the years, he didn't know if they were real or not, and was undecided how to get rid of it all.

Gordon left school at sixteen with six o-levels, and it caused a big row when said he wanted to go to technical college to learn and study painting. "Over my dead body," shouted his dad.

"So you want me to go to university to do it? Well, it's not on. I just don't want to go there," shouted Gordon standing his ground was fed up of learning something that he was not interested in.

"Bloody painters," moaned Colin, looking annoyed.

"They might be, but it's earned me nearly a thousand pounds so far," snapped Gordon quickly standing up.

"And what's that bloke calling for tomorrow?" growled his dad staring at him.

"Why don't you be here and find out?" asked Gordon staring back.

"You are getting too big for your boots my lad. Do not push your luck with me, because I can still clout you one," he replied raising his hand. "Dad, I don't know if you have noticed or not? I'm the same size as you now. It's alright raising your hand it's bringing it down. I can assure you I will catch it," said Gordon, and laughing walked off.

Colin stared in shock. He suddenly realized he was looking at a man and not a boy. Later that night in bed, he began to discuss him with Jessie. "If he's happy and is still broadening his education, why not?" she asked.

"That's not the point woman," he snapped.

"Keep your voice down you'll wake Tracy? And besides he's only doing what you did, isn't he."

"Oh hell, I'm fighting two now," he moaned, and rolled over.

Saturday morning in the shop, Colin was dusting furniture, noticed Gordon unlock the shop door to welcome a chap inside who struggled to carry large paintings under his arms. After carefully leaning them against the wall he shook Gordon's hand and introduced himself. The way he was dressed looking more like someone from MI5 wearing a long tawny colored raincoat and brown trilby made Colin frown but he didn't interfere just pretend to dust a tallboy but quickly raised his eyebrows when heard him ask, "How much do you think will be the overall cost?"

Picking one up and inspecting it, "First I will have to go through some catalogue's to find out the artist and see if they are genuine," replied Gordon, and after inspecting another said, "This is a copy, a good one though."

Nodding his head as if knew, "You are right about that lad. What about the other?"

"This is a shame," replied Gordon, while examined a tear. Turning it round he knelt down to examine it further saying, "At least forty pounds for the canvas, and touching up another twenty."

Frowning he asked, "Come on lad, you've done others for me so just tell me the overall damage?"

Gordon stood upright saying, "One hundred and fifty pounds, and ring on Thursday to see if I've finished them. I am rather busy at the moment."

"Right lad will do. I'll have to be on my way now, so I'll contact you later," and raising his hat, waved before walked out. Soon as the door closed, Colin glanced out of the shop window watching the chap get into an old ford car. Spinning round he continued up to Gordon asking, "Where's he from?"

"He's from that famous auction house in Leeds. Don't worry, he thinks he's getting a bargain, well, in a way he is, because there is no one else round here can do it," he replied, while inspected another painting.

Colin studied, watched when Gordon pick up the paintings and continued upstairs into his studio above. Glancing round before continuing into the workshop to give David a hand, Colin smiled thinking, *well, let's hope he can make a career out of painting; he's no bloody good at anything else.*

That evening, Gordon was in his studio painting, while Tracy was in her room with Barbara playing records on her new Dansette player, a gift for both passing their eleven plus. There was very little conversation between them, other than the usual brother and sister constant petty arguing. Whereas Gordon was reserved and gave respect, Tracy was outlandish, had to have the best of everything, and also had to show it off.

With the shop closed and books done, their parents relaxed in Jessie's front room and drank wine while discussed them. Colin rest back moaning, "I wouldn't mind but our Gordon's first uniform was only fifteen pounds."

"They are Sixty five now and you know very well the cost will never come down," said Jessie smiling at him.

"I'm really pleased both girls passed their eleven plus, they can go to school together," said Doreen, sat up, and held out her glass.

"I wish dad was alive to see all this, instead of being buried down pit for a shilling a shift," said David, while filled her glass. "Your mum didn't last much after, did she?" asked Jessie while holding out her glass.

"What do you expect when folk are knocking on your door for money every hour of the day? By God they drove her underground," moaned David now shaking his head in disgust.

"The poor bugger never let on though, and he always said it would never happen to us," said Jessie, and nodded to Colin while had a drink.

"There's one thing about these two, no one can ever say they wouldn't work, they've put their heart and soul into here," said Doreen now looking a little tipsy.

David turned to Colin asking, "That reminds me, what you think about that bloke that called from that furniture warehouse?"

"I said yes and he's bringing some furniture out on Monday for you to inspect. Well, let's be fair mate, you're not getting any younger so we might as well sell some new stuff as well," he replied then laughed.

"Yes, then it's time for a holiday," said Jessie, and suddenly smiled when they all looked at her.

"Your right there and I want to go to Spain," said Doreen pretending to look adamant.

Colin frowned asking, "What about the shop?"

Jessie stared at him snapped, "We have a son haven't we?"

"Maybe next year," he replied, knew he was more interested in painting.

"Right Doreen, you heard him, let's go get prepared. We are off to sunny Spain," shouted Jessie, and heartily laughed.

Soon after his seventeenth birthday, Colin applied for a provisional driving license for Gordon had decided to give him lessons in the van. Deciding if he passed, it was time for a new one, never thought that two months later, Gordon did. As the old van was unreliable and now bad at starting, after negotiations with the local dealer he traded it in, and bought a brand new Bedford van.

With trade at the shop still brisk, now selling new and second hand furniture, turnover and profits remained stable. Procedure was now reversed, and Colin went with Gordon when they made deliveries or visited nearby auctions or sale-rooms.

One thing Colin had noticed over last couple of years, even though he was in a fortunate position, and only bought good second hand furniture to renovate, Gordon distanced himself from it, and only inspected paintings. Trying hard even asking him his opinion or value even state condition of particular items, but Gordon just shrugged his shoulders then turned away.

While in one town, Colin asked him to wait while he went inside the gas showrooms, and when he returned, Gordon asked, "What did you call in there for?"

"Because next is gas central heating, and don't tell your mum yet," he replied smiling at him.

"The soul of discretion, that's me," said Gordon, and grinned while started the engine.

Gordon, now nearly six foot tall, slim with thick curly black hair, same as his dad in his younger day, who now had a receding hair line, never went to college also thought that was a waste of time. At this moment he was happy making money renovating paintings. Always with that inkling to paint for himself, Gordon considered when his style developed more and had enough money to open a studio near Otley, he would move over there, having once visited with the school and fell in love with the place.

Girls never entered his head, until one late evening. Now working a delivery rota, and this week it was Gordon's. When he did the last delivery on the far side of the estate, after pulled up outside the front door and knocked on it, a young woman opened it. Wearing a brief pink nightie and barefoot, she cheekily smiled asking, "Yes my darling?"

"Mathew's furniture store love. I have a sideboard and a set of draws for you," replied Gordon while eyed her top to bottom.

"Oh, well, you had better put them in the hallway. Mum never said anything to me about a delivery," she replied opening the door wide.

"Two minutes," he said while continued round the rear of the van.

Gordon opened the back doors, and taking out the draws, carried them inside the house placing them in the hallway. Tongue in cheek she asked, "Are they paid for?"

"Oh yes," he replied while set off for the sideboard.

Struggling with it, he managed to get it inside, and now with a sweat on, Gordon rested on it while made out the receipt. "I bet one of my uncles has paid for it," she said taking it from him and read it.

"Would you like me to put it in elsewhere?" he asked.

"Oh you are cheeky, that's my mum's favorite saying," she replied, and heartily laughed.

Gordon watched thinking, *she hasn't a bra on, and I can see her tits*. Raising his eyebrows he murmured, "Is it indeed?"

"Well, it's nearly as good as asking do you want a cock-up?" she asked, and smirked held her hand up to her mouth raising her nightie slightly.

"And do you?" he asked, glanced down, noticed a dark shadowy triangle through her nightie thought she hasn't any pants on either.

"Not this week love, maybe next," she replied the sexily winked.

"Right then, must be off now, see you later," said Gordon, but had to smirk when set off to the van.

This banter between Gordon, and the women customers he delivered to, began to increase, and it sometimes continued to extremes. Gordon became cheeky with it, however, always had an excuse to leave, usually saying he had left the van engine running.

One woman took his attitude completely the wrong way, thought he meant it and she trapped him blocking his exit to the door. Sexily stating what she was going to do with him she suddenly noticed the colour of his face, and was looking really embarrassed.

Laughing in devilment when he maneuvered himself behind a sofa Gordon had delivered. The trouble was the lady was well into her forties, and he really didn't fancy her, thought she was too wrinkly, then suddenly gasped when she vaulted the sofa and grabbed him between the legs. While trying to escape, she greedily kissed him, forced her tongue in his mouth and like a man possessed, Gordon made a dash for the door and eventually escaped.

With a sweat on, Gordon sat in the van, wiped his brow, and gasping for breath moaned, "Good God, I am not going in there again." With a crafty look out of the window he set off, however, suddenly smirked because he had enjoyed the experience.

There were a couple of lady customers that did take his fancy, but unfortunately they were also a lot older than him, and this always put him off. Although Gordon had many a chance to improve his sex education, he never dabbled, mainly because of two reasons. First, he was frightened his parents would find out, and second, being caught by their husbands, didn't know if anyone was listening to them or waiting in another room to trap him.

Early April nineteen sixty seven, approaching Gordon's twentieth birthday, and with their house now fitted with gas central heating. Having finished redecorating throughout, his parents dropped it they were going to Spain for a fortnight's holiday. "Oh thanks very much mum and dad," he replied staring at them sarcastically.

"You're all old enough to look after the shop aren't you? You know the ropes. Tracy or Barbara don't won't to go with us and we can't force them, anyway it's time we had a bit of pleasure for a change," said Colin was pushing the situation because of pressure from Jessie.

Pulling a face of disgust Gordon snapped, "You mean you're going with David and Doreen and leaving Tracy and Barbara with me?"

Trying not to smile because knew he had him cornered, "Oh yes. Don't forget we have worked very hard for this mate, and if you save up enough, maybe next year you could do the same."

As if losing his patience Gordon stared him asking, "And who would I go with?"

"That's not my problem it's yours lad. Don't you think it's time to live a little, you know begin to sow a few seeds?" replied Colin smirking at him.

"Oh I, and if I did you'll kick my head in."

While staring at him, "Have we ever said anything wrong to you?" Suddenly recalled pressure from Jessie, when she stressed it was time he started courting.

"Well, no," he replied, really in fairness.

"So go out and find yourself a bloody woman," snapped his dad then spun round walked out.

Chapter 3

Saturday morning, a week before his parents flew to Spain, Gordon was in the shop waiting, had four paintings ready for the chap from the auction rooms ready for him to collect. Suddenly the shop door opened and in walked a girl he thought recognized. "What can we do for you my love?"

"Oh sorry, you won't remember me. I've called to see if you have a small white set of draws for my shop? About so high," she asked, and smiled while gestured the size.

Recalling her face but not her name he smiled asking, "How do you mean, remember me?"

"I was at the high school when you were at the grammar school," she replied.

Eyeing her while she browsed furniture he asked, "Sorry, what do they call you?"

Smiling at him she replied, "Caroline Blakemore."

"Oh yes, I do now, and yes we have some somewhere," said Gordon turned and glanced round.

"There are only for my shop, and they must be white because the rest of it is," she said while watched him.

"What sort of shop is it?"

"I'm a hairdresser," and watched when he reached over and lifted up a set from behind a sofa.

"Will these do?" he asked placing them on the floor in front of her.

Smiling she asked, "Very nice, and how much are they?"

Gordon recalled her travelling on the bus, and fancied her then. Standing up straight he studied while scanned a lovely face. Thinking she hadn't changed much he smiled replied, "Fifteen pounds to you."

"Could you deliver them please? Unfortunately I don't drive and carrying them there is out of the question," then cheekily raised her shoulders smiling at him.

Frowning he replied, "Well, normally we charge a fiver for delivery."

"Go on then," said Caroline opening her handbag.

Beginning to write out a receipt he asked, "Please leave me your address and delivery will be around six tonight. Will that be alright?"

Smiling she held out the money saying, "Oh, go on then I'll wait for you."

Eyeing her when she walked out of the shop, Gordon smiled thought, *I wonder if she's free*, suddenly spun round when his dad said, "I hope you do better than this when we're away or else we will go bankrupt."

"That'll be the day," he replied.

Raising his eyebrows he asked, "And who was that?"

"Caroline Blakemore, she's bought those draws there," he replied pointing to them.

"Oh, that must be Enid's girl, and that reminds me," said Colin, studied, then turned and walked into the workshop.

"Gordon, your lunch is ready," shouted Jessie.

"Right mum," he shouted.

Just before closing, Gordon loaded the van with the draws then a sideboard and a double bed he had sold earlier, was to deliver them first. Looking round when his dad approached, he passed him a little blue velvet pouch asking, "Give Caroline these, they belonged to her mother."

"What are they?" he asked.

"She pawned her rings years ago for her a school uniform, anyway just give them to her," said Colin while closed the van doors.

Gordon's first delivery was to a young couple just moved onto the estate, and after finding the street he pulled up outside. Continuing down the path he knocked on the front door. "Oh hello, oh its Gordon, how are you?" asked a tall slim brunette.

He recognized her from school saying, "Hello Christine, and sorry I didn't recognize the name on the delivery note."

"It's my married name that's why. We've been living with my mum for over a year and just moved in here."

"Well, I'd better go get the bed in first then," said Gordon, and spun round.

Leaving the mattress while last, and with everything all piled up in the hallway, "You couldn't do me a favour will you could you help take it upstairs for me? Mind you the place is in a mess just yet we haven't finished decorating," she asked while flashing her big green eyes at him.

"Well, really I haven't time, I've some more deliveries yet," he replied really didn't want to be late.

"Please? I'll give you a hand," she asked seductively pursing her lips at him.

"Oh go on then," replied Gordon, and sighed while picked up the mattress then began to drag it upstairs.

"Second on the left," she shouted while followed carrying the headboard.

"Where's your husband then?" he asked propping it up against the wall.

"He's on afternoons, he finishes at ten," she replied then turned walked downstairs.

Gordon followed, glanced round, and thought they hadn't much. Taking hold of the bed while Christine held the end, and together they carried it upstairs. Managing to ease it into the bedroom without scraping the paintwork, eventually resting it on the wall, "Are you wed yet?" she asked.

"Me? Oh no, still footloose and fancy free," he replied smiling at her.

"I wish I'd never married now. I had a good job but you know what men are like, they want their women at home and it's as boring as hell," she said, leant forwards and quickly kissed him saying, "Thanks for your help love, I'll put it up later."

"That's what they all say," said Gordon and laughed continued out of the bedroom.

"You cheeky bugger," she gasped while followed.

In the hallway Gordon gave her a receipt saying, "Thanks love."

Waving when she closed the door, sat inside the van he started the engine, and had to smile at the banter between them while he carried on to the next delivery. There an elderly chap helped him inside with a sideboard, and after positioned it for them Gordon refused a cup of tea saying, "Thank you for the offer but no thanks, however, thank you for your custom," then gave him a receipt, before set off to the hairdressers.

Gordon was fifteen minutes early when pulled up outside the hairdressers, noticed Caroline had a coat on and was sat in a chair reading a magazine. After sounding the horn, Gordon got out and opened the van doors. Taking the draws inside he asked where she wanted them. "Over there please," replied Caroline pointing.

Gordon positioned the draws then had a quick glance round saying, "Nice shop."

Smiling she replied, "It's not bad and thanks you're early."

Admiring her smile he plucked up the courage asking, "Right then, a week on Sunday do you fancy a ride to Otley?"

Looking surprised she asked, "Whatever for?"

"I just want to go there and have a look round," he replied, however, thought, *well she hasn't reused me yet.*

Pulling a face of surprise as if didn't believe him she asked, "You mean, on a date?"

"Well, sort of," replied Gordon, was taken aback at her questioning.

Caroline began to tease him, and smiling said, "Well now, Gordon Mathews asking me out."

Mainly to change the subject and watched when she opened the top draw began to fill it with combs and brushes he asked, "How long have you been in here?"

"This is my first year," she replied, while began filled the second draw with towels.

Gordon eyed her then suddenly realized he was staring quickly turned and glanced out of the window asking, "Are you courting?"

"More to the point are you?" she asked while turned to face him then tried to read his face.

Looking serious, he replied, "No, I've never met anyone good enough yet."

Smirking she asked, "So I'll take that as a compliment then?"

Thinking he had put his foot in it, Gordon slipped his hands in his pockets suddenly felt the pouch, took it out, and holding it out towards her said, "Oh, by the way, Dad told me to give these to you."

Caroline frowned, took it, opened it and emptied the contents into her hand. "These are my mum's wedding rings. Where the hell did you get them from?"

Gordon was in a dilemma and didn't want to insult her. Quietly he replied, "According to my dad, she pawned them to get you a school uniform."

"Oh did she? Well, I'm very sorry but I must go now," snapped Caroline, quickly turned and switched off the lights.

Gordon watched but didn't understand her change of attitude. Opening the door he continued outside then turned asked, "Do you want a lift? I'll drop you off home."

"I'm alright thanks," she snapped while locked the door, tried the handle then marched off up the street.

Gordon watched Caroline, with head bowed quickly walking up the street. Reluctantly he turned, opened the van door and inspected the shop front before sat inside. Starting the engine, he glanced through the mirror watching her march up the street. Knowing she was upset by her body language he moaned; "Bloody hellfire and I really fancy her. What a way to try and start a relationship," indicated, turned, drove the opposite way and continued home.

A week later, with their parents on holiday, seemingly celebrating an early twenty fifth wedding anniversary, Gordon, Tracy, and Barbara, stayed at home looked after the business. The girls were growing up into fine young women, and their schooling was going well. Both were due to leave in two years time, and subject to what qualifications they received, as of yet both were undecided what to do.

Unfortunately Gordon didn't get on with either of them, and so he could do two jobs at once, brought his easel and painting materials downstairs. Working in the shop he could attend to customers in between painting, and one afternoon, looked up when Christine walked inside. Smiling she closed the door behind her, and cheekily smiled said, "I have called to make a complaint."

"And what is that?" he asked, put down his brush then walked towards her.

"That bed you sold me squeaks like hell," she replied, and laughed.

"So rub a bit of butter on it," he replied, reaching round her to check if the door was closed properly.

Sexily winking at him she replied, "I do, and regularly."

"So what can we really do for you?" he asked while smirking at her.

"I want a nice sideboard, but it's got to be cheap mind you," she replied, while glanced round.

"That's a nice second-hand one over there," said Gordon and pointed.

"Can I have a look at it?" she asked while sauntered over.

"Anytime, you know that my love," he replied and grinning followed.

After a quick inspection, and deciding to have it, at the rear of the shop, Christine inspected the painting on the easel while Gordon made out a receipt. She turned, peered round a half open door asking, "What's in there?"

Noticing he stood in the doorway he replied, "It's our workshop."

Turning to face him she smirked said, "So in there you do the business, as it were?"

"As I said earlier, anytime my love," he replied and smiled passed her the receipt.

"Better go lock the shop door then, and let business begin," she said, pushed the workshop door open and continued inside looking round.

Ten minutes later, Christine was sat on an old chest of draws, had her knickers round one ankle and both legs wrapped tight around him. Gordon was stood in front of her with trousers round his ankles and his arms tight around her waist while his arse was banging away fifty to the dozen.

Christine didn't have to give him any encouragement as it was Gordon's first time having sex; however, her main problem was keeping up the pace. In the end, Christine pushed him off gasping, "Bloody hell Gordon let's have a rest love."

The end product for Christine was to obtain furniture on the cheap, and it worked. Gordon gave her extra discount, and over the two weeks while his parents were on holiday, Christine visited the shop four times, allowed him to have his way, and then made a purchase. Gordon knew what she was doing, however, when she wanted to buy a set of chairs and a dining table at a quarter of the price, he refused. "And why not?" she snapped, defiantly staring at him.

"Because they are new and we can't do them so cheaply," he replied.

Christine got the huff on, spun round and stormed out. At first Gordon became worried, thought she might start to spread rumours about him, but when she didn't call in the shop again, in a way he was relieved.

Because of this experience Gordon never went to Otley, and when his parents returned home, while handing round presents, Colin was more interested in what he had sold in the shop, and quickly examined the books.

Not making more than he should have, Colin questioned him about certain sales, however when Gordon explained Tracy and Barbara never helped him was more concerned with playing records then quickly changed the subject asking for a wage instead of pocket money.

Colin stared, however, did have him on the books as a salesperson had never informed him. He had also opened a pension plan for both his children's future, and gave them what was left over as pocket money. Although the business was sound, Colin reluctantly agreed, and later that afternoon, explained to Gordon, how to work out his own wage, pay national insurance stamps and income tax.

From then on Gordon worked out his own wage, and after paying his board now with slightly more pocket money, still relied on his painting for extra income. The restoration work for the auction house continued on a regular basis, and so did his experience.

The following week, when the chap from the auction house brought him more paintings to renovate, one was Victorian, a nude woman kneeling on a chase lounge. Gordon examined it closely had noticed excessive damage to the top half. Purposely moaning, "This is a shame," however, he had to smile when the torso remind him of Caroline.

"It's only a cheap copy, but the frame seems alright. It might come in handy in the near future," said the chap while inspecting the ones he had done then smiled took out his wallet and paid for them.

When he left, Gordon took them up to his studio, put the damaged painting on the easel and examined it further. Wincing he noticed the face had been purposely destroyed right through to the canvas and was beyond repair. Standing back, he smiled, admired the torso knelt provocatively on a plush studded sofa against a backdrop of maroon velvet curtains and was similar in stature to Caroline. Imagining her face on it, he studied saying, "Right then, let's get it cleaned up first and give it a go."

Two hours later, with the painting cleaned and looking a lot brighter, after repaired the canvas, Gordon began to paint on Caroline's face. He studied, recalled the shape of her head, carried on, and did his best to keep it in perspective then suddenly jumped when heard, "Dinners ready," shouted Jessie.

"Right mum," he shouted, smiled, put down the brush, stood back and admired his work before going downstairs.

In the kitchen, while they ate, Gordon sensed friction with his parents didn't know Tracy had informed them; with Barbara they were going into Leeds later that evening to meet some school friends. "Male or female?" asked Colin.

"Mixed," snapped Tracy.

"Just watch what you are doing love," said Jessie smiling at her.

"Well, I say you can't, your too young for a start," moaned Colin purposely staring at her.

"Don't be daft dad. We won't be all that late in," but really wanted to smile now knew they had got away with it but daren't.

"How come no bugger takes any notice of me anymore?" moaned Colin before rest with his hands on the table staring at her.

"Because you're too old fashioned," said Gordon then laughed.

"Don't push your luck. You have three deliveries to make tonight," he replied was now staring at him.

"And you have to wash up," said Jessie, and purposely stood up to ease the tension.

"Oh bloody hell, talk about being master in your own house," moaned Colin, rest back in his chair and folded his arms.

That night when Gordon returned with the van, he locked it up, went straight up into his studio and continued with his painting. He smiled, heard his dad in his office occasionally answered the phone while did the paperwork. However, one hour later, after heard his dad laughing out loud, "Oh hell," moaned Gordon, decided to rest his aching arms, went downstairs and made them all a cup of tea.

Two days later, the painting was finished, and rather proud of his work, Gordon hung it in his studio. He had kept with the same original size brush strokes, colours and style used with the previous artiste, thought it was easy, and it did look as fresh as when originally painted. "Better get cracking on the rest now," he moaned, had wasted a lot of time on it so instantly began the others.

Wednesday, when the chap from the auction house called, Gordon gave him discount for the frame, stating the painting was beyond repair. Without question he accepted his word, had brought two more. After he left, Gordon took them upstairs into his studio, stared at the painting of Caroline, and the more he did, the more he fell in love with her.

Next it was Gordon's twentieth first birthday. Jessie prepared a family party in the front room, with Barbara, David and Doreen. However, Colin had a big smile on his face, was sat with Tracy, who had been accepted at Sheffield University and was going to study graphic design.

Gordon knew the party was mainly for her, and after they all ate, while drinking wine, his parents began to reflect in years past, brought up their struggles and hardship.

Barbara intervened and moaned she hadn't been accepted at a University yet. "Don't worry love you will be," said Doreen, and lovingly smiled at her.

Gordon asked, "What's that to do with riding on the trams to work?" then heartily laughed.

"Nothing," snapped Barbara, and with Tracy both went upstairs to her room.

Picking up his glass but about to have a drink Colin moaned, "Bloody kids of today, they have no respect for nothing. When I was young half the buggers died before they started school."

"That's true," agreed David, frowning at the thought.

"Those days have gone thank God, anyway tell him what your plans are now," said Jessie, stood up, replenished their glasses, and nodded to Gordon.

"What are you doing now?" he moaned.

"Moving out," replied his dad laughing.

"You know that new private housing estate being built down near the river. Well, we are buying one of them," said Jessie rather proud.

Raising his eyebrows Gordon asked, "That much in the bank?"

"Mind your own business. So that means in future you could be living in here on your own," said Colin and grinned before had drink.

Looking shocked when thought Tracy might be staying with him, he nodded towards upstairs moaning, "What about Tracy?"

"She'll be at Sheffield University then. Don't worry you will be here all on your little own," replied Jessie then laughed.

"And what about the business?" gasped Gordon when it now seemed they didn't care about it.

"Oh don't worry lad, I'll still be here to wake you up on a morning."

"Thanks, it must be nice to semi retire," moaned Gordon, and drank up, didn't know David and Doreen, were going to do the same as well.

"What do you think about it all then?" asked his mum trying to test his patience.

"I think this, just hurry up and get out and let me have some peace," he replied, walked out and continued up to his studio.

In the shop two weeks later, Gordon wrote out delivery notes for later that evening, suddenly looked up when the door opened. Staring at Caroline when she walked inside, he quickly stood up straight and smiled saying, "Hello."

"Hello, and am I disturbing you?" she asked, seemed nervous.

Gordon gestured saying, "Not at all and please close the door its cold."

She did, and slowly walked towards him asked, "I've called to see if you have another set of draws?"

"Of course," he replied, quickly looked round asking, "White again?"

"Please."

After sorting out a set and dusting them off, Gordon smiled asking, "Are these alright for you?"

"Fine and I must say this. I'm very sorry for my outburst when we last met but you took me by surprise," said Caroline eyeing the draws.

"No problem love," he replied while admiring her profile.

"It's just that you said it really smug and I thought you took the Mickey, anyway, how much are these?" she asked while pulled round her handbag began to open it.

"Twenty five pounds and I most certainly did not," he replied.

"It seemed it. Does that include delivery?" she asked taking out and opened her purse.

"Of course and if you think for one minute I would ever take the Mickey out of you. Please, come with me a minute, I want to show you something," said Gordon, reached out, took hold of her hand and nearly dragged her towards the stairs.

"Where are we going?" she asked looking round while walking up them.

"In here," he replied, opened his studio door, stopped and pointed to the picture on the wall.

Staring at it she gasped, "That's me."

It suddenly went quiet, and now wondering whether or not he had done right showing her it, Gordon began to blush. Watching when Caroline slowly walked towards it, then when she leant forward as if inspected the painting he moaned, "Sorry, it wasn't meant to offend you."

"I should bloody well think not," she replied, turned and quickly walked out.

Gordon slowly followed and grimaced knew she was angry. When he entered the shop, Caroline turned, paid him then snapped, "I will be in the shop until six thirty," spun round, opened the door, walked out and quickly closed it after her.

"Oh bloody hell, I can't do anything right," moaned Gordon, while added to the delivery note.

Jessie walked inside, carried a cup of tea asking, "What's that love?"

"Nothing mum, just me being stupid again," he replied while took it from her.

Chapter 4

Again, leaving Caroline's delivery while last, Gordon set off and slowly pulled up outside the shop. Noticing her sweeping up, he got out to open the van's rear doors. Taking out the draws, he carried them inside, and placed them on the floor asking, "Where would you like them?"

Pointing she replied. "Over there please."

Looking sheepish Gordon set off towards the door saying, "Right then and sorry about this afternoon. So...right then, I'll be off now."

Caroline asked, "Hang on a minute, you can run me home if you will please?" However because she didn't look at him her body language gave it away that she was embarrassed.

"Of course," he replied, had noticed and smiled continued to the van. Gordon closed the rear doors and sat inside waiting. Five minutes later when Caroline got in and closed the door he asked, "You'll have to direct me?"

Smiling she replied, "Turn round first then I will."

After doing so they travelled in silence, but approaching her flat, "I didn't know they had built these here," said Gordon, stopped, and looked round.

"I moved in two years ago. Its rented that's all I can afford, but the business is doing alright, well, I think so. I can't get my head round that damn paperwork yet it drives you balmy. Anyway all-well-and-good so far, maybe next year I might be able to buy a house nearer to the shop," she replied.

Gordon stared out of the window saying, "I must own up and say this Caroline; I didn't do all that painting you saw. The top half was damaged and as the figure was similar to yours I just painted on your face."

"Did you indeed, but it looked like new," she said, and studied because really didn't believe him.

Facing her he stared into her eyes saying, "I must be good then."

"Was it really an old one?" she asked, and now smiled thought he would tell her the truth.

"Oh yes, it would be late Victorian, around the late eighteen hundreds at a good guess," he replied, sounded confidant.

"Oh, right then, well, many thanks for the lift and see you later," said Caroline opening the door. Gordon waited while she closed it, waved then slowly set off. Studying about her he suddenly wished he had asked her out on a date but really daren't.

Continuing home round the back of the shop, Gordon parked the van then locked it up. Later that night when he went to bed, he studied what his dad had said about them buying a house, knew his routine would change if he had to work in the shop full time so knew his painting would suffer more.

Over the years he had bought various reference books, religiously studied the old painter's ways and techniques. Knowing this type of work would eventually ruin his own style, he was determined to earn a living and that was the most important thing.

Never owning a camera, Gordon decided to buy one, and on his rounds would take photos of anything interesting, in other words increase his perception of still life knowing at this moment in time it was mundane, better still knew it was non-existent.

With nothing present day for reference, only a few old photos of his mum's depicting scenes where they grew up or where they had worked. Gordon often thought how to put them on canvas had only the experience of portraits, cleaning and touching up, then decided to read up to broaden his range.

Having old postcard photos of his grandparents depicting how they dressed at that time, this spurred him on, and when the chap from the auction house called and informed him it would be three weeks before called again because he was going on holiday. Gordon took advantage of this spare time, decided to make a start, and if possible sketch out an industrial scene, then paint one.

The following morning, while his dad and David adjusted furniture for a better display then dusted in the shop, upstairs in his studio, from old photos, Gordon decided to give his industrial scene realism, and added some relations from memory.

An hour later, when his mum brought him a cup of tea, she eyed the easel asking, "What are you up to now?"

"The usual, and by the way, grandma's dress in that photo what colour would it be?" asked Gordon, as it was black and white.

"That dress she wore was dark brown, and her apron white, well, near enough," she replied, and smiled when he picked up his palette.

"And granddad?" he asked then blew some dust off it.

"How come you never painted me and your dad?" she asked, and wafted her hand.

Laughing he replied, "I will if you pay me."

"Get out you daft bugger. Anyway in that era all the blokes wore black trousers, black hob nailed boots, and again, white shirts near enough with a black waistcoat" she replied then waved while walked downstairs.

Gordon sarcastically smiled saying, "See you later mum."

Present day it was hard for Gordon to imagine smoke, grime and soot pouring out of the chimneys, however, he had a rough idea when glanced out of the window across the estate, knew where all the colliers lived, had plumes of smoke coming out of theirs.

After lunch he resumed work, and when his dad passed to go into his office, he glanced at the painting and pulled a face saying, "So far there are four deliveries for you tonight."

"Thanks," replied Gordon while carried on.

At ten past five, Gordon set off on the first delivery. Ten minutes later, he pulled up outside the house, got out, and knocked on the door. "Oh hello, please come in," asked a woman, was aged mid thirties. She had her blonde hair set like Dusty Springfield and also wore a flimsy see through dressing gown, loosely tied.

She smiled while held the door handle then eyed him up and down. "I'll just get these set of draws first," replied Gordon, turned and returned to the van thought, *she's got a nice pair of tits*.

After he struggled inside the hallway with them, the woman closed the door. Gordon leant on the draws while wrote out the receipt and she did the same displayed most of her chest. "Err, are they alright here?" he asked while eyed her.

While flashing her long black eyelashes, "Oh, I would be ever so grateful if you manage them upstairs. I live here on my own you see and haven't anyone to help me."

"No problem," he replied then pulled out the draws to make it lighter.

When Gordon returned from upstairs, she passed him carrying two draws saying, "I'll give you a hand in a minute," then turned to enter a bedroom.

Eventually, with everything in the bedroom, while about to replace the draws, "I won't be a minute, I'll give you something for your trouble," she said while walked out.

"No problem love," he replied, but after replaced the last draw, about to walk out, she walked past the door stark naked.

"Hang on I can't find my purse," she shouted while opened another door to walk inside.

"Don't put yourself out," he shouted then smiled raised his eyebrows.

She returned, smiled at him saying, "Tell you what then, because I don't know where the hell it is. I'll just give you a quickie for your trouble," and turned off the light.

Now running an hour behind schedule, when Gordon returned home to park the van at the rear of the shop, his dad stood at the back door watching and asked, "You're late?"

"I've just been talking to a few old schoolmates," replied Gordon, checked the right key, and smirked while locked the van doors before continued inside.

"Your dinners ruined," moaned his mum.

"It'll be alright," he replied while sat at the table.

"I thought you'd had a puncture?" asked his dad after closed the door then sat with him.

"No, I've just been chatting that's all," he replied then smiled when his mum put his plate on the table.

Later that evening, after a couple of hours painting in his studio, Gordon called it a night and decided to go to bed. Downstairs, after made himself some Horlicks, he said goodnight to his parents, were sat in the front room watching TV then went upstairs.

After undressed he sat on his bed, had a drink, recalled what the woman did to him, and couldn't believe his luck. Gordon smirked then moaned; "All these years, if I'd have known," suddenly thought, *bloody hell. I wonder if dad has ever received the same.*

Over the next twelve months, Gordon was more selective with who pleased him. Having many offers he didn't push his luck purposely so none became a regular girlfriend. His parents finally decided to buy one of the new houses, and sat in the kitchen on his own eating lunch his mum had prepared, deliberated his future.

They had been informed the houses were nearly ready and gone to view one. Unfortunately Gordon was feeling downhearted, when suddenly thought of Caroline, had not seen her for ages.

Gordon decided to call at her shop when made the evening deliveries and this idea perked him up. Fifteen minutes later after opened the shop, his parents walked in, and now with someone to serve, he continued upstairs to commence work on his painting.

Just after five o'clock with the van loaded, Gordon set off, purposely rushed and quickly made the deliveries. When pulled up outside Caroline's shop, he noticed her sweeping up, pipped the horn and got out. Eyeing her when he walked inside, he didn't like the look of her body language and knew something was wrong. "So what can we do for you?" she snapped then looked away.

Gordon shrugged his shoulders replied, "What a greeting? I was going to ask if you wanted to call for a drink. I was just trying to be sociable that's all."

"On your bike Gordon, surely you'll call at Mrs Thurston's later on your way home, you usually do," she snapped.

Staring at her he gasped, "Pardon?"

"Come off it Gordon, everyone's talking about you. What's up is it her wrong week?" she asked while swept clippings into a dust pan then dropped them in a bin.

"Caroline. What the hell are you on about?" he asked, and stared at her bemused.

"She happens to be one of my customers and can't keep a secret, so bugger off Gordon and close the door behind you," she shouted then stared at him.

"Who the hell's Mrs. Thurston?" he asked, and shrugged his shoulders.

"Go away Gordon," she snapped, now glared at him.

Looking totally perplexed Gordon turned and set of moaning, "Oh bloody hellfire, what have I done?"

Sat in the van, Gordon watched Caroline tidy round before turned off the lights. When she locked the door, he started the engine and set off, but had to smile thought, *I always thought that woman was too good with her mouth.*

On his way, he glanced in the mirror, noticed Caroline marching up the street and sighed saying, "Bloody hell, it seems sodding hard work to get round you."

From that night on Gordon decided to clean up his act. Fancying Caroline something rotten, he stared at her painting, and would love to get his hands on her body. Unfortunately his present painting was put on hold, couldn't grasp the scene, and in a somber mood, carried on renovating others. Gordon, glanced out of the window moaning, "Well, if she wants me I'm here. I haven't met anyone better, mind you; I wonder whatever happened to Andrea Hastings?"

Two days later, his dad returned from a sale had bought a dozen paintings, mainly for the frames, and after Gordon had inspected them, he seemed impressed. "Did I do right then?" asked Colin looking surprised.

"Depends how much you paid for them."

"I gave one hundred and fifty pounds for the lot," said Colin, then winced didn't know if he had done right or not.

"Did you indeed? Well that one there is worth that alone. I'll clean them all up and hang them in the shop. When that chap calls for the others, I'll ask if he wants to buy them," he replied, picked up two, and took them upstairs.

With no formal training other than experience, plenty of talent, a steady hand and a keen eye, word of Gordon renovating paintings was now spreading fast, mainly due to the auction house. They had to divulge the source of renovations to a painting entered for sale, although not all. Many private collectors had him earmarked for future work and of course, he didn't know this yet.

With a steady income from his restorations, and not having anything to spend his money on, Gordon's savings grew. Eventually he decided to buy a car, and after studied about it, really didn't need one at the moment so put it on hold.

With Tracy now resident at Sheffield University which pleased Gordon, even more so when Barbara had been accepted at Durham. David still repaired second hand furniture in the workshop and between him and Colin they served in the shop. Doreen and Jessie were getting restless wanted something to occupy their spare time, and could not wait to move into their new houses.

Gordon didn't know both were moving, and was speechless when found out moaning, "So what are you doing with your house?"

"We've decided to rent it out," replied Doreen.

"Bloody hell, I am on my own then," he moaned, and sat down seemed bewildered.

"I don't know why the hell you are moaning. When we've gone it's all yours anyway," said Colin, while filled the kettle.

"That's not the point. We've all been one family here and now you act as if you couldn't care less," replied Gordon staring at him.

"I've told you once lad, it's time to sow your seeds. All you can do is bloody paint," he replied, and switched it on.

Quietly, Gordon, replied, "That's what you think."

"And what's that supposed to mean?" he asked staring at him.

"It means when I find the right woman, I would sow them big style."

"That's my boy," said Colin, and laughed.

"You can wipe that smile off you face now, don't forget we have to alter all the prices in the shop soon for when decimalization starts," said Gordon shaking his head thought he might ending up having to learn all about it.

"Oh hell, mind you there will be less change to hump around," he replied, and smirked while poured out the tea.

Jessie walked in from the front room saying, "Go on love I'll have one."

"And talking about the Chancellor of the Exchequer, will you keep your spending down?" asked Colin while passed her a cup.

"If you want to sleep on the floorboards again my love, we could do," she replied, took it from him and winked.

Business at the shop remained stable; however, families in the locality became restless. As wages increased, many chanced their arm, and when new private dwellings appeared, were obviously in better surroundings and mainly on the outskirts of town, they risked buying one.

Of course this meant new tenant's for the council houses, and many were young married couples, with not a lot of spare cash. Again, this meant the second hand part of the business picked up, so kept David busy.

Maintaining his experience through practice, and occasionally using reference books, Gordon kept himself busy renovating paintings for the auction house. Really not taking much notice of comings and goings at home, so when it was time for his parents to move into their new house, it hit him hard, especially when it dawned on him, he would be on his own and had to fend for himself.

What took the sting out of the situation was, and gave them all a shock, when it was announced VAT was to be introduced. Colin sat in his office reading his mail moaned, "Well chuff me, all we are going to be is bloody tax collectors."

"When's it start?" asked David, while trying to read over his shoulder.

"Next year, seventy two, so we have ten months to get clued up."

"So long as we can still make something on the side," said David, and nudged him smiled.

"It says here they are sending out a bloke to teach us all about it. I think we had better have words with the accountant first, don't you?" he asked, turned and looked at him.

"I do that, I hate not being in the know. The trouble is will it push up prices? It did when they altered our money. Crafty buggers are the government; it's all paying tax now-a-days."

The early seventies went haywire. First VAT was introduced and did put up all the prices, and then to upset the country even more, the colliers came out on strike. Meanwhile Gordon had amassed a small fortune with his painting, had never paid tax on his earnings, or disclosed anything to the VAT man.

Now with customers to renovate their private collections, Gordon was often asked to work away on them, but always declined giving the excuse of having to look after the shop. Eventually resigned to the fact he would have to, Gordon made up his mind when inspected a dinted frame of an oversized painting he had damaged while taking it upstairs.

Another problem was he now lived on his own. Colin and David worked in the shop during opening hours, and his mum brought his lunch then went home with them. Gordon made the deliveries later, and in most cases, now tried to make the customers take their purchases with them, often making the excuse, he didn't want to come home to an empty house.

It was work-work-work, and time began to fly. One night while eating his dinner, it suddenly dawned on Gordon that it was over three years since he was last with a woman. Caroline was constantly on his mind, and studying she was in a rented flat, and seeing as no one had yet rented David's house, and it looked doubtful under the present economic climate, he wondered if she might be interested in it.

That night after made deliveries, Gordon drove slowly by her shop saw the lights on, and noticed her doing a woman's hair. Deciding to stop, he got out, and chanced she would not get onto him when there was a witness present. When he opened the door to walk inside, "Oh hello," said Caroline lightly but stared at him.

Quietly, he asked, "Do you mind. I thought I'd ask if you would cut my hair please."

"Ten minutes, please sit down," she replied while carried on.

Gordon did, and watched, admired her figure and the way she gave attention to the woman, always politely asked if her hair was alright. "That is perfect my love, there is only you that can do it properly," she replied, while checked through the mirror.

After brushed it out and lacquered her hair, the woman stood up, smiled then took out her purse to pay her. "Thanks very much," said Caroline, smiled then helped her on with her coat. Soon as she left the shop, "Right, come on?" she snapped, and gestured to the chair. Gordon took off his coat, left it on the seats, walked over, and sat down. "Square neck?" she asked.

"Please," he replied while raised his chin when she placed a cape round him.

"I suppose you've called to gloat then?" she asked, while trimmed his hair.

"Over what?" he asked, and stared at her through the mirror.

"I've decided to close at the end on the month," she replied looking disappointed.

"Never," he gasped, and turned his head.

Caroline pushed his head round snapped, "Keep still…it was either move out of the flat, risk staying in here or close down. Something had to go."

"I thought you were doing well?" he asked, and bowed his head when she trimmed his neckline.

"I was until this bloody VAT started. I can't afford the accountant's fees," she replied.

"Listen Caroline and I aren't being funny in any way. Please let's have a drink after you close to discuss the future? My situation has altered as well and who knows we might be able to help each other out," said Gordon, trying not to smile knowing she watched him through the mirror.

Caroline sighed before replied, "Go on then. I'm just fed up to the back teeth with it all now."

Insisting he paid for his hair cut when she refused to take anything, Gordon left the money on his chair, picked up his coat, walked out, and sat in the van. After Caroline locked up she approached the van door. Gordon reached over, opened it and smiled when she got inside. Waiting until she closed it, he started the engine and set off to a nearby local pub.

Not a word was spoke between them until fifteen minutes later, after parking and locking up the van, while walking inside, "After you," said Caroline, and both had to look round as it was a rare occasion to go out.

Gordon was relieved when noticed not many customers inside, approached the counter asked, "Right then, what do you want to drink?"

"Err, vodka and lime please," replied Caroline, but seemed unsure.

"Make it two," said Gordon, and smiled at the barmaid.

After paying for them, Gordon carried their drinks, and settling in the corner of the lounge next to each other, "Right then, what did you say earlier?" asked Caroline, sat up and had a sip of her drink.

Smiling he replied, "First and please excuse me because I don't really know your business. Maybe I could help you now my uncle's house next door to us is empty. You could live there rent free, and it might help you out."

Caroline instantly thought there would be complications with the word free. She snapped, "Bugger off Gordon," placed her drink on the table and rest back.

"Why? What's the matter now? Then you will be able to keep your business going," he replied but not understanding her attitude.

Caroline stared at him, and nearly shouted, "What? So I can be at your beck and call? No way, you have your regulars."

Gordon sat up and defiantly stared back decided to raise his voice snapped, "I don't know who the hell has told you all that but its bloody rubbish. Listen Caroline, I've always liked you and yes I did that painting to remind me, silly I know, but I want us to go out, in fact you're the only one that's kept me in the area, otherwise I'd have been gone long ago."

His appealing eyes gave away his emotion and it made her study. Caroline had a drink to break his stare then asked, "Would you help me with my business? That bloody VAT is getting me down."

"Whenever you are ready my love," he replied now smiling.

They continued to chat about old times at school, and for the first time Caroline noticed how cozy they seemed together. When both drank up, while walking out, she admired his manners when held the door open for her, but looked away and smirked.

Later inside the van, they travelled in silence and Gordon knew she studied his suggestion. When he parked outside her flat, "How much rent do you pay here?" he asked while glanced out of the windscreen.

"Twelve pounds a week."

"Bloody hellfire that's high."

"What else can I do?" she asked while stared at him.

Smiling he asked, "Right then, tomorrow night when I've finished the deliveries, I'll call and pick you up. I'll take you home and then you can look round the house. It's all furnished, because when they moved to the other house they bought knew. Sorry, and I'm not bragging, they earned it so good luck to them, anyway will six o'clock be alright?"

Looking unsure she replied, "I should think so," suddenly was taken aback when he quickly kissed her. "Right then, err, see you later," said Caroline, and half smiled before opened the door.

Gordon waved when he set off, and ten minutes later, at the back of his house, parked the van. After unlocked and opened the back door, he walked inside and locked it behind him. Feeling peckish he made a sandwich and after sauntered into the shop as usual checked the door. Continuing upstairs into his studio, Gordon stared at the painting of Caroline and smiled saying, "It won't be long my love then I will paint you properly."

Throughout the rest of next day, Gordon worked like hell, and finished three paintings. Two he really liked, took his time and cleaned them properly before touched them up. Because of their age, were roughly one hundred and fifty years old, he admired his work, and proudly said, "Just like new again."

His dad was suspicious knew something was going on because of his pleasant mood, and after lunch began to run out of patience asking, "So what the hell is up with you today?"

"Right then, sit down and I'll tell you," replied Gordon, then began to inform him about Caroline renting the house, and also there might be a relationship in the offing.

"Why didn't you say earlier, I always thought you were gay," said his dad, laughed and slapped him on the back.

"If only you knew it all," said Gordon quietly, but looked away while pulled a face.

"Well, go on enlighten me then, on the other hand better not. God knows what the younger generation of today gets up to. I'll tell you what, I'll ring David and see what he says about it, he should be home now he went to the dentist this morning," said Colin while continued into his office.

Gordon smirked before saying, "Very wise dad."

Chapter 5

In between serving in the shop, Colin and Gordon conversed about their new house. When a young couple left without buying anything, "That's that bloody VAT that's put them off," moaned Colin staring at the door.

"The best thing we could do at the moment is start selling more second hand," said Gordon, had though he was right.

"And where the hell am I going to buy it from?" asked his dad, quickly turned and continued into the workshop.

Gordon watched him shouted, "Start going to the sales with David again."

That night, Gordon dashed round made the deliveries and was surprised when there was more than normal, thought his dad must have had a good afternoon, however, when reached Caroline's shop he smiled when she was waiting for him. She turned off the lights, locked the door and got inside the van. Gordon smiled saying, "Right then madam, here we go," and set off.

Caroline pulled a face thought he seemed too chirpy, and listened intently when he informed her David had approved her moving in. Parking the van at the rear of the shop, Gordon locked it and both approached his back door. Gordon politely allowed her to walk inside first, closed and locked it behind him. Gesturing he said, "Please go through into the front room and sit down," had previously made them a sandwich, picked up a bottle of wine off the worktop and hurriedly began to open it.

"Gordon, I've called to see the house that's all," said Caroline while continued into the front room and sat on the sofa looking round.

"And I've invited you here to view it, have a drink with me and have something to eat. More to the point, I hope to hell I can get round you to go out with me." Gordon smiled with relief now he had got it of his chest, walked into the front room, passed her a plate, and feeling slight embarrassed with his statement, quickly returned into the kitchen.

Picking up two wine glasses he returned, put them on the coffee table then sat with her. While they ate, "I'm sorry but is has to be on a business footing. Yes I do need help with my business, and I've been thinking, no, I can't go out with you. Sorry," said Caroline, was really putting him under pressure on purpose.

"Oh," said Gordon bowing his head and really looked put out.

Looking straight ahead, "Sorry," she said while finished her sandwich.

"Well, I am too. I wouldn't have done it for anyone else, so, never mind," he said then had a drink.

Really to tease him she asked, "So, I can't rent the house then now?"

Staring straight ahead, mainly to hide the disappointment on his face he replied, "No. Sorry."

"And why not?" she asked but smirked.

"I told you yesterday, I really like you I have done for years. I don't mind helping you out but, well, you know," he replied while stood up. Gordon shrugged his shoulders walked over and stared out of the window on purpose to hide his disappointment.

"I don't know what the hell that means Gordon so. Well… it looks like it's time for me to go then?" asked Caroline and leaning back seemed perplexed.

"Yes, if you don't mind," he replied, tried not to show it, but was really gutted.

"You bugger Gordon Mathews. Yes I do fancy you; it's just your motive. Why are you doing all this?" she asked, and stared at him when he walked over and sat with her.

Gordon turned, stared into her eyes and saw mischief. When she smiled, he knew she had been teasing him. Sitting up straight he snapped, "I'm a bugger? You got me on a knife edge there then kicked me off."

Caroline leant forward and kissed him. "Sorry mate it's got to be better than that. I've waited years for this," said Gordon, wrapped his arms around her and kissed her passionately.

Coming up for breath, "You sod," she gasped, kissed him again, and both suddenly sat up straight when heard a key in the kitchen door lock

Colin and Jessie walked inside, and continued into the front room. "Oh hello mum and dad, fancy seeing you here tonight," said Gordon sarcastically then stood up.

"Shut up and just put the kettle on," said his mum while sat opposite Caroline asking, "Hello my love, and how are you keeping?"

"Fine thanks," she replied, but seemed uncomfortable shuffled in her seat.

"It's a bit nippy out tonight," said Colin then rubbed his hands together before sat down.

"Milk and sugar dad?" asked Gordon then stared at him while continued into the kitchen.

"You know what I have, and sorry are we in the way?" he asked.

"No, not at all," replied Gordon, sarcastically, and cocked his eyes in the air.

Throughout the following two hours, much to the disgust of Gordon while his parents reminisced about the past. They discussed Caroline's mum and dad, how they all helped each other out years ago, and then Jessie recalled other families in the area and where some of their offspring are living now. When Colin asked about her hairdressing business, Caroline informed them how she started, with money from an insurance policy from when her mum died. "And how are you doing at present?" Jessie asked.

While frowning she replied, "Not too good I'm afraid," and suddenly looked up when Gordon passed her another cup of tea.

"Oh dear, well never mind he will help you out from now on," replied Jessie, and nodded toward Gordon when took her cup.

"I've told her that already," replied Gordon, stared at her and nodded to the door as if meant, it's time for you to go, before passed his dad a cup.

"I've been thinking it might be better if I sell up and move in with my aunt in Sheffield. She asked me before when things weren't going right and then they picked up," said Caroline before had a drink.

"You'll do nothing of the sort," said Gordon, and frowned at her.

"Looks like it's time for us to go," said Colin, and after drank up, stood up.

"Right then, nice to have met you and you are very like your mum," said Jessie, leant down and kissed Caroline on the cheek. She turned, looked at Gordon, and smirked asking, "Do you want one as well?"

"No thanks," he replied, knew his night was buggered and to further his relationship with Caroline fruitless.

"Goodnight all," said Colin, waited for Jessie, followed her into the kitchen and closed the door after them.

A frowning Gordon said, "Sorry Caroline, I shouldn't have told them I'd asked you to call."

Seeming surprised she asked, "Oh, you told them I was calling tonight?"

"Of course I did otherwise they wouldn't have called. They were only being nosey," he replied while pulled a face of impatience.

"Well then," she said, smiled and while finished her tea thought Gordon was more compassionate than he looked.

"Come on then, if you're ready, I'll run you home now," said Gordon, stood up, took her cup, walked into the kitchen and put it with his in the sink.

"You have nice parents Gordon," said Caroline, stood up, and followed him.

"Everyone has nice parents, it all depends on how you treat them," he replied.

"Very true, that's if you get chance to know them," said Caroline, and frowned.

"Sorry, I didn't mean it that way, I meant it like," paused, and suddenly lost his temper shouted, "Oh this is bloody ridicules."

Smiling she asked, "And why?"

"You know why? I respect you, I like you and I don't want to offend you but sometimes it's just like treading on bloody glass," he replied staring at her.

With a serious expression, Caroline stared into his eyes asking, "Gordon. Please take me to your bedroom?"

"What? Your... err... are you joking?" he asked, now looked really put out.

"Listen, you asked me here for a reason and I don't think it was for me to sleep with you. It's nice and warm in here and my place isn't so come on before I change my mind," she replied, then suddenly thought of Mrs Thurston and what she said they used to get up to.

Gordon quickly sat down and seemed in a quandary. Caroline began to think all the tales about him were false, when he sheepishly looked up at her saying, "Honest, I didn't bring you here to get you into my bed."

"Well, I'm tired now, and don't fancy going home so I might as well stay," she replied.

"No, it's just not right," he snapped, had thought she made the suggestion to trap him.

When he quickly stood up, and picked up the van keys. "What are you doing?" she snapped staring at him.

"Taking you home," he replied, and spun round set off towards the back door.

Caroline stared defiantly at him asking, "At least let me view the house first?"

"Oh hellfire, come on then," he moaned, threw them down, and picked up David's house keys.

Locking the door after them they continued next door. Caroline followed him inside and when he turned on the light, she looked round saying, "It's very similar to your mums."

"It is. David said it's a tenner a week, but I thought it should be more," he replied.

Caroline smiled recalled him saying she could live there rent free. She smiled saying, "At least it saves me five pounds a week, the rent on my flat has just gone up again."

"Shall we go back round now? I don't like leaving our house empty too long," he asked looking impatient.

"Did you do those paintings as well?" she asked, while walked towards the back door.

"I did indeed," he replied, turned off the light, locked the door behind them and thought Caroline wasn't interested because she didn't have a good look round.

When they returned inside his kitchen, Gordon swapped keys, and turned saying, "Right then."

Caroline sat down, leant on the table, and looked up at him asking, "When can I move in?"

"What? You mean you still want the house?" he asked looking shocked.

Smiling she replied, "Why not, it's far better than my flat and beside I can keep an eye on you."

"You awkward bugger," he moaned while sat opposite her. About to ask when she would move in, Gordon suddenly looked up when the telephone rang. Standing up he picked up the receiver, and impatiently asked, "Hello, who is it?"

"Is Caroline still there?" asked his mum.

"Oh hellfire, go bugger off mum," he replied, and replaced the receiver.

Having got the gist of their conversation, Caroline stood up saying, "Right then, you can run me home now please."

"Bloody women," he moaned while opened the door.

Caroline smirked, followed him to the van and when he unlocked it, opened the door to get inside. Trying not to smirk when he set off, she waited while he joined the main road then asked, "Well, can I move in or what?"

"How much notice have you to give on the flat?" he asked.

"A week," she replied, but had to smile.

When he pulled up outside her flat, Gordon snapped, "Well, just do it then and when I make the deliveries whatever you have to bring round I'll pick up on the way."

"Thank you Gordon, and there is one more favour please. Sometime this week will you help me with my books? It's all going over my head and I don't want to get into more trouble, they keep sending them back," she asked looking soulful at him.

"I suppose so," he moaned, as if didn't want to.

Staring at him she asked, "What's the matter now?"

"Nothing, well, oh just nothing," he replied while purposely leant on the steering wheel and stared out of the window.

Smirking she asked, "One minute you're wining and dining me and seemingly over the moon, and now you look as if you have lost a fiver?"

"Because I don't know which way to take you that's why, one minute you look serious and the next your teasing me. It's so bloody confusing," he replied, and shook his head seemed bewildered.

"Point taken, and see you later," said Caroline, leant over and kissed his cheek.

As he suggested throughout the following week, Gordon made repeated calls to Caroline's flat and took her belongings to the house. Unfortunately their relationship didn't progress the way he had hoped and he was beginning to lose heart.

Two weeks later, Caroline had settled in the house and worked as normal at the hairdressers the same hours as the shop so she didn't see Colin or David. Jessie occasionally called with Gordon's dinner, and now with Doreen, had their hair done every week at Caroline's. Of course their conversation was always about Gordon and how they were going on together, which had progressed no further than a kiss and a cuddle as Caroline always returned home to sleep.

Gordon was still confused, when one minute it seemed Caroline was his girlfriend and the next she kept a distance, not understanding why, he stuck to his guns, didn't put pressure on her, just continued as normal, worked in the shop and painted whenever he could.

Thursday evening, Gordon craftily smiled, recalled her teasing him the previous night had decided to reverse the role and tease her. After a very busy day when he returned from the making deliveries, he sat in the kitchen eating his dinner. Hearing a knock on the back door, he stood up, walked over unlocked and opened the door. Gordon smiled asking, "Come on in?" returned, sat down and picked up his knife and fork.

"You're eating late tonight?" asked Caroline while closed the door.

"I had two extra deliveries on the far side of town, and unfortunately had to hump it all up two flights of stairs," he replied before carried on eating.

"Oh, hellfire, I bet you're buggered. Shall I make us a cup of tea?" she asked, and winced on purpose to make it seem as if she was concerned.

Gordon decided to make light her reply and purposely said, "No, it doesn't matter because when I've finished this I might go to the pub for a drink."

"Oh. That's not like you. Is anything wrong?" she asked, while studied his face.

"No, not really, I just fancy a change that's all, according to form it's supposed to do you good," he replied, and nonchalantly carried on eating.

"Oh, right then, anyway I'd better go wash up. I had my tea earlier," said Caroline while walked towards the door.

"See you and goodnight love," said Gordon, and placed his knife and folk on his plate.

Gordon didn't go for a drink; however, for the rest of the week he kept up the pretence until Saturday afternoon. Caroline was in his studio watching him paint and was mesmerized thought he had a great talent. Suddenly when her stomach rumbled Caroline grimaced knew she hadn't had a proper meal for weeks, was living on toast with either beans or eggs. She glanced over his shoulder and suggested she made them a Sunday lunch but only if he would go through and correct her books.

Gordon agreed, and when she went down to make them a cup of tea, thinking she might stay with him, however, he was disappointed when after the shop closed and his parents went home, Caroline walked towards the foot of the stairs shouting, "See you tomorrow love I've some washing to do."

"Right love," he replied then sighed when heard the back door close. Because there was no sign of improvement with their relationship, Gordon thought, *I think I've dropped a bollock letting her stay there. It's a good job we didn't sign any contracts. Anyway on Monday I might drop a hint David might want his house back. I could always say he needs it for relations.*

Sunday at noon, while Caroline prepared their meal, in between watching her, especially when she bent down to use the oven, Gordon studied her books saying, "You need a minimum of seventeen customers per week. Over that you are in profit."

"That's what the accountant said. I've been averaging twenty seven now your mum calls," she said, walked over, and glanced over his shoulder.

"Anyway I'll pay all the bills for your house, you're hardly ever in it," he said while closed the ledger.

"No you won't I can manage now," she replied, and returned to the cooker.

"We'll see then," he said, and rest back in his chair.

Over the last couple of weeks, Gordon noticed it was like having Tracy at home. Caroline seemed very independent and their relationship hadn't improved much other than she acted more like his sister. Occasionally calling in his house during the week and this was the first time Caroline had stayed for any length of time.

Usually after he made the deliveries and parked the van, he would stare at the light in her kitchen and reluctantly enter his own home. His fear was being refused entry made him think he was the maker of his own dilemma. Gordon didn't want to force the situation, would have his dinner, then go upstairs and paint.

With her books finished and after cleared the table, Caroline laid it and served their meal, during which there was little conversation. Gordon enjoyed it, thought it tasty, and smiled saying, "That was very nice, and thanks," carefully placing his knife and fork on his plate.

"Thank you," said Caroline, but smirked.

Gordon noticed, stood up, and continued into the front room. Sitting on the sofa, he was about to use the remote to turn on the TV, when Caroline walked in. She sat with him asking, "Are you going to wash up then?"

"Bloody hell, it's like being married," he moaned, and quickly stood up.

After Caroline watched him continue into the kitchen, she picked up the remote, turned on and watched the TV. Five minutes later, hearing the rattle of pots and pans, she smirked, settled back and studied various rumours about him. Thinking he was too shy and reserved to have done what was said, Caroline thought most were just out of jealousy, then suddenly smiled when heard him whistling.

When Gordon finished, he dried, and put the crockery away. Thinking the meal was good and enjoyed it, he decided to compliment her more. With everything done he returned to the front room, and sitting down said, "Dinner was very nice love."

A smiling Caroline replied, "Thank you."

"Well, if you don't mind, it's time to go up and do a bit of painting," he said standing.

"Can I watch?" she asked.

Setting off he replied, "Well, yes but it'll be boring."

Inside his studio while Gordon prepared brushes, Caroline walked inside, noticed the same paintings leaning against the wall as they were last time she visited asked, "Have you these to do yet?"

"Yes he's calling on Wednesday for them," he replied while studied a painting on the easel.

She eyed her painting on the wall asking, "Would you like to do a proper nude painting of me?"

"Sure love, just get your clothes off and sit on that settee," he replied, and laughed at the suggestion. Gordon's jaw suddenly dropped then he stared when Caroline began to undress. Now looking embarrassed he gasped, "I was only kidding."

"I wasn't, but it's for me. I want it for in the house and when it's finished you will have to sign it as well," she said, had her back to him while put her clothes on a chair. Caroline sat on the settee, looked up, and smiling cheekily asked, "So how do you want me?"

"Err... well...I well... err, just rest back and relax," he stammered, while eyed her top to bottom.

Caroline brought up her knees, leant her arms on them, mainly to cover her breasts. She turned, and looking at him asked, "Like this?"

"Sort of," he replied, and now thought the other painting, didn't do her figure any justice at all.

Placing a blank canvas on the easel he began to prepare it, and occasionally eyed her while drew a sketch. Gordon did his best to imagine a back drop, turned asking, "Are you cold? Would you like a cup of tea?"

"I'm fine thanks, but one thing bothers me. I read the other week about that new painter in London. He always does his work in the nude. So why don't you?" she asked then smirked.

"If you want me to I sure can," he replied, and cheekily grinned.

"It's just that it's so unfair when you are ogling me. I should be able to do the same," she said, and rest back when her legs ached.

"I'll go make a drink first," he replied, turned and quickly continued out of his studio, mainly to gather his senses and calm down.

When Gordon returned, Caroline was inspecting some paintings, noticed some damaged, and some like new. She turned, and took a cup from him saying, "Thanks love."

Staring at her chest, Gordon quickly turned, put his cup on a small table used for his oils then took a packet of biscuits out of his pocket. Opening them he handed it to her, and smiling said, "I'll finish the sketch first."

Caroline took the biscuits then watched him use a pencil to lightly sketch on the canvas for a few moments. When she turned, walked over and sat down, Gordon noticed her slender back and long legs. Nodding with assurance as now knowing his first painting wasn't like her at all.

A silence prevailed while he drew. Caroline finished her tea, put her cup on the floor and resumed her position sat on the settee.

Thirty minutes later, and because of cramp in her arm, Caroline, shook it asking, "Are you going to get undressed then or what?" Gordon smirked, used a waste rag, and after rubbed a light blue paint all over the canvas, put it on the table. He began to take off his shirt and Caroline watched, eyed his chest, and smiling said, "That's better."

"Oh, is it?" he asked while removed his trousers then underpants as at the same time concentrating to control his emotions.

"You were always drawing or painting at school," said Caroline while rest back eyeing him.

"I always tried my best to learn," he replied while continued painting. For obvious reasons, Gordon tried to keep his back to her suddenly decided to add a window to her left side to add more light to his subject, then changed his mind and drew it bigger mainly to add more light on his subject.

Caroline smiled, stood up and walked over. She stood behind him, glanced at the canvas, and smirked while slid her arms around his waist. When leant against his back, she smiled when he shivered with the warmth from her body and gently squeezed him. Gordon slowly placed his brush on the table, turned, wrapped his arms around her and stared into her eyes before kissed her. Taking hold of her hand, and in silence, they walked into his bedroom. With the house empty, and now with the girl of his dreams, he quickly turned the situation into fun.

They romped all over the house, although daren't go in the shop because the windows had no curtains. Caroline laughed, screamed, and giggled while Gordon chased her all over the place. Eventually, when they returned to his bedroom, she threw her arms around his neck, and pulled him back on the bed. Gordon stared into her eyes whispered, "Good God do I love you," and kissed her passionately.

Thinking it strange when she didn't respond, however, he smiled knowing he hadn't given her chance, and they remained in each other's arms until the flowing morning.

"Hellfire, is that the time?" gasped Caroline, quickly jumped out of bed and sat on the edge. She glanced round, suddenly realized her clothes were in the other room, stood up and walked out.

"No rush is there?" asked Gordon, while rest on his elbow watching her.

"Maybe not for you but there is for me. I have to travel to the shop yet," she replied while returned with her clothes then began to dress.

In the kitchen, after a quick slice of toast, Gordon drove Caroline to the shop in the van, kissed her before she set off inside, waved then in haste set off back home.

At the rear of the shop, Gordon parked the van locked it, and dashed inside the kitchen quickly he locked the back door, trying to beat his dad and David, knowing they would ask where he had been.

Gordon just managed to unlock the shop door then casually walked round began dusting furniture. Two minutes later when his dad and David entered the workshop, his dad glanced through into the shop, and eyeing him moaned, "You scruffy bugger, go get a shave," had always insisted whoever served were smart.

"Oh, I forgot," replied Gordon, rubbed his chin, threw down the duster before dashed upstairs.

After a quick wash and brush up, Gordon changed then returned downstairs saying, "There's a sale tomorrow at Otley dad," while watched David varnish a table top.

"I've seen it, and on Thursday its time to swap the van. The others seven years old now and it's time we had a new one," he replied but purposely eyed him, thought he seemed in a good mood and wondered why?

"That looks better now," said David admiring his work.

"It sure does," said Colin before turned then continued into the shop.

Gordon remained in the shop to serve while his dad with David worked in the workshop. At twelve o'clock, his mum and Doreen called, began to prepare lunch and noticed dirty trays in the oven, When Gordon came in to make a drink of tea, she asked, "Did you make yourself a Sunday lunch?"

"No, Caroline made it," he replied.

"Oh, it's alright then," she said, and smiled put them in the sink.

Smirking he asked, "So if I'd had made it, you would have played hell up with me?"

"Yes," she snapped.

Gordon decided to torment her saying, "Well it was me that washed up and I forgot," then poured out the tea.

Turning to face him she asked, "Are you two going out now or what?"

"More or less," he replied, but had to smile when picked up three cups and winked while carefully walked out.

Chapter 6

The following Tuesday afternoon, David and Colin returned late from a house clearance and quickly began to unload furniture into the storeroom. Straight away Gordon began to load it with furniture to deliver that evening. Fifteen minutes later, after he set off, Caroline returned, unlocked her door, went inside and first prepared something to eat.

When Gordon returned, he parked the van and stared at the light in Caroline's house. Undecided whether to knock or not, he smiled in devilment while continued into his house. Opening the oven door he frowned when found his mum hadn't made him anything to eat, cursed and decided to make some beans on toast.

Later, after washed up, as instructed, Gordon sorted out the documents for the van, and left them for his dad on the sideboard. Deciding to go upstairs to paint, Gordon suddenly spun round when heard a knock on the back door.

Opening it he smiled when Caroline walked inside saying, "Hello love," and kissed him.

"I was just going up to paint," said Gordon, closing the door after her and locked it.

"Not tonight love I'm tired. I've had a hell of a busy day," she replied smirking.

Wearing a faint smile he asked, "Just time for a cup of tea then."

"Go on then," she replied while continued into the front room.

Caroline slipped off her shoes, and rest back on the sofa. Gordon walked in, passed her a cup and had a sip of his. Sitting down he asked, "You know the other week when you mentioned you might have had to move into the shop. Is there any room in there for living quarters?"

"The reason I got that shop cheap was there used to be two either side of an alleyway, one up and one down. The owner halved the upstairs of my shop to make two bedrooms for the other next-door and knocked a door through. That increased its value, and then he sold it as with living accommodation," she replied before had a drink.

"Have you a toilet then?" he asked frowning.

"That's in the back of the shop, behind that partition near the emergency exit," she replied while held the cup in her hands.

"So what is there upstairs then?" he asked before had a drink.

"It like a big box room, similar to your studio," she replied.

"And it's all yours then?" he asked.

While studying she replied, "Yes, and if trade keeps up like today, mind you I might have to set someone on to help me soon."

"How many can you do at once?" he asked smiling.

Laughing she replied, "There are four chairs and four dryers, so the answer is four isn't it?"

"Sorry. I had noticed but I am not into hairdressing," he replied, and smiled thought she seemed content.

"Well, if you are going up to paint, I'm off to bed," she said, and drank up before passed him her cup.

Taking it he smirked saying, "If that's the case then, we both will,"

"Better go wash up first in case you're mum calls, you always leaving a sink full," said Caroline, and smirked while followed him into the kitchen.

Placing the crockery into the sink he asked, "How is it women always have to have the last word?"

"Because you men are no good without us," she replied then craftily nipped his backside.

Rubbing himself he moaned, "You bugger."

"Shall I do that, because that's something else we are good at?" she asked then heartily laughed.

With the colliers back at work, the railways were now on strike. Unfortunately this had a knock on effect, seemed everyone wanted more money and better working conditions. Then to top it all, the council proposed to make the area a smokeless zone and in the locality, people were in uproar about it, eventually knew it would cost them extra money.

When officially given a date of April nineteen seventy five, the council was going to enforce the clean air act. This allowed tenants plenty of time to make up their minds what heating they wanted to change to. Now with the option of not cleaning out a dusty grate out on a morning and making a fire, it saved collecting newspapers and chopping firewood. Many chose gas, when it was just a matter of turning it on and off and the Gas Board regularly toured the area to promote sales.

Late Thursday morning, Colin dropped Jessie and Doreen off at Caroline's for their hair appointment before carried on to a local garage to part exchange the van. Receiving a good deal he bought the same model again only new. Arriving back at the shop, he began to explain the controls to Gordon, who went out on a quick run to try it out before the evening deliveries. Of course driving round to Caroline's he noticed his mum and Doreen sat having their hair done, knew they would only natter on, so he didn't bother calling.

The rest of the week went well for Caroline, and also Gordon in the shop until Saturday morning. With few customers that morning, Caroline worked a half-day then returned home at one o'clock. Going straight into her house she had a good soak in the bath was looking forward to a weekend of relaxation. Having had a busy week and with takings high, she was in an exceptional mood so began to consider advertising for part-time help.

Gordon was in the shop serving while his dad and David were in the workshop choosing furniture to renovate. Caroline entered the kitchen, decided to treat them and make everyone a cup of tea.

Suddenly the shop door flew open. A young chap aged late twenties, stared round before shouting, "Are you that fucking Gordon?"

"Why what's up mate?" he asked.

Caroline walked into the workshop carried three cups of tea. Suddenly she stared when the chap shouted, "I'll knock your fucking head off you bastard, you've been shagging my wife," and ran towards him.

Colin heard, dashed into the shop but was too late when the chap grabbed hold of Gordon's arm. Pulling him off, Colin held him tight round the neck before dragged him towards the door. "I'll fucking get you later mark my words" shouted the chap was waving a fist at Gordon who stared seemed in shock.

"Bloody hell, he's mad," said David, and smiled patted Gordon on the shoulder.

After bundled him through the door, Colin waited until the chap set off down the street hearing him shouting abuse. When it seemed safe he turned, walked towards Gordon, and caught his breath before saying, "That's Christine Pritchard's husband, you want to be careful with him, anyway to put it blunt, have you been there?" he asked then raised his eyebrows.

Caroline stared while waited for the reply; she heard Gordon mumble and when they all laughed out loud, assumed he said yes. She turned put the cups on an old table and quickly walked out returning into her house. Shaking with emotion, she instantly began to pack stuffing her clothes into two old battered cases.

With tears streaming from her eyes, as an afterthought, she quickly locked the back door in case Gordon called, then flopped on the sofa cried her eyes out. Caroline was devastated, had always liked Gordon and getting to know him better over the last few weeks had fallen in love with him.

Next door, Colin noticed cups of tea on the table, put two-and-two together, and turned noticed Gordon going upstairs to his studio had a smirk on his face. "Very kind of you," said David while picked up a cup.

"Not me pal, I just hope it wasn't Caroline. She might have heard everything and if she has, oh boy will he be in trouble," he replied and grimaced nodded upstairs.

That evening, with her house in darkness, and not answering any knocks on the door. After waiting until Gordon set off to make the deliveries, Caroline rang for a taxi. When it arrived, she walked out and quickly stuffed her cases inside including four carrier bags. Quickly sitting inside, Caroline slammed the door, turned and gave him the address of the shop. "Will do my love," said the driver, and studied thought she looked distressed.

Travelling in silence, arriving there and after paid him, Caroline opened the door, began to carry everything inside. She locked it, took everything upstairs and with nothing to sleep on, began to make room on the floor.

After laid her cases down, she sat on them and bowed her head was heartbroken. Again she cried her eyes out, knew she loved Gordon now knew some of his exploits mentioned by customers were right then decided that was the end of their relationship. Her mind spun with torment, had looked forward to a future with him, but glanced round the room sobbed, "Well, at least I have a roof over my head."

When Gordon returned from the deliveries he noticed no light on in her house, got out and banged on her door. When there was no answer, he began to study what had happened and with mixed emotions, reluctantly turned to his house.

Inside, after closed the door he rang his mum asking if she knew anything, but when she explained Colin said she might have been in the workshop and overheard the melee, he winced while put two-and-two together.

Gordon drove round to her shop, noticed it in darkness and banged on the door, knew she would be inside had nowhere else to go. Gordon banged again and when people walking by stared at him he eventually gave up. Sat inside the van he moaned, "Chuff me to cock it all up," started the engine, and drove home.

Throughout the following week, and doing his best to concentrate, Gordon returned to his painting while his dad tended the shop. On a night when made the deliveries, he always drove by Caroline's shop and it was always in darkness.

On Sunday his mum called round had made his dinner, and asked if he had seen or been in touch with Caroline. "No. When I got up this morning the house keys had been put though the shop letter box and it looks like that's it."

"Have you been in it yet?" she asked, while studied his face.

"No," he replied while shrugged his shoulders.

"I'll call in and have a look round when I've finished made this," she said and sighed knew he was upset.

On Tuesday, the chap from Leeds called and carried two paintings inside. He noticed Gordon stared at the door behind him was watching a tall woman aged mid thirties and dressed up to the nines. When she followed him inside, he smiled saying, "This is Mrs Bartholomew Smyth, she is a private collector and has some paintings for you to clean and restore."

"Pleased to meet you," said Gordon while held out his hand.

She shook it daintily, and smiling replied, "And you, and I must say this, isn't this a quaint little shop."

"It is indeed, and how large is your collection?" he asked then cheekily raised his eyebrows.

"Sufficient, but I must say this. I have seen some of your restoration work, and my collection as you put it is rather valuable. First I want to know if you are up to it?" she asked while glanced round.

"If you wish to come up to my studio I will show you other paintings I am on with at the moment," replied Gordon then gestured the way.

She glanced at her watch before saying, "Please lead the way then?"

Following him upstairs, when inside his studio Mrs Bartholomew Smyth glanced round, didn't know Gordon did the same. Suddenly he pulled a face hoped the chap didn't recognize the frame and painting with Caroline's face on it. "Oh, you do nudes as well?" she asked, had noticed the half finished painting of Caroline on the easel.

"Occasionally, but really only for special clients," he replied while positioned himself between the chap and the painting.

"Rather tasteful," she said before daintily leant forward to inspect three more paintings propped against the wall.

"First, I must ask what size are your paintings, and hopefully not too big to travel here?" he asked, but eyeing her thought, *I bet you can be a right clever bugger.*

"I'm afraid they are. One is six feet by nine feet. It is of my husband's great grandfather, and he his rather proud of it. Obviously and for that reason alone it must be done on site," she replied half smiling.

Gordon pulled a face of displeasure saying, "Oh, so that means travelling."

Facing him and raising her eyebrows she asked, "Is that a problem?"

"Until you inform me where you live it might be," he replied, suddenly turned when the chap sauntered towards the door thought, *where the hell are you going mate?*

"Harrogate, and do not fret I will pay all expenses," she replied while staring at the nude painting.

"That is not the point, it's travelling that it takes time. It also becomes a bore and you quickly lose concentration," said Gordon frowning.

"You may live in then," she said, while leant forward to inspect the painting of Caroline more closely.

"I think it would be best if I called and inspected your paintings first. I will then ascertain the time needed for restoration then give you a price accordingly," said Gordon while keeping an eye on the chap.

"As you wish and would Sunday evening be convenient for you?" she asked, while glanced out of the window.

"It is indeed, shall we say about seven pm?"

"Very good, I must be on my way, bye for now." Gordon followed them thought *she looks as if they are rolling in money.*

Continuing towards the shop door, the chap opened it turned, and waited until Mrs Bartholomew Smyth walked out. Handing Gordon a card he winked before quickly followed her to a car. Gordon closed the door and sauntered over towards the window. As if not wanting to be seen, he cautiously glanced out, noticed the woman drive off in a maroon Rolls Royce and whistled. His dad walked in from the workshop asking, "What's up with you?"

"Just thinking of sowing a few more seeds dad," he replied, smirked, turned and walked upstairs.

All that week, when Gordon finished his deliveries, he always drove by Caroline's shop and each time was disappointed. On Saturday night, deciding he wouldn't go by again, he arranged with his dad to borrow the van to go to Harrogate on Sunday. "If you must, so is this a big job?" he asked frowning.

"That I don't know until I get there," he replied, and falsely smiled at him.

"Put it this way lad, it had better be and well paid. Anyway you can fill it up with petrol this buggers not as economical as the last one," he moaned, waved and closed the van door.

"Will do dad," he replied, smiled, and waved, before closed the back door.

Later that evening, sat watching TV and drinking tea, now feeling rather foolish that his past had caught up with him again, Gordon moaned, "That's the last time I have anything to do with women round here, they are all jealous to death." Feeling downhearted again, and with only work to look forward to he moaned, "What a bloody life this is, anyway I think a drink of wine wouldn't go amiss right now."

On the last Sunday in September, at teatime Gordon set off to Harrogate. An hour and a half later and now dark, he eventually found the house, was a big detached stone mansion on the outskirts of town. In the darkness Gordon carefully drove slowly up the driveway, continued round the back and smiled seeing the back door. Getting out of the van and listening to absolute silence he glanced round before knocked. Five minutes later, and hearing it unlock, when it slightly opened a small thin grey haired elderly woman dressed in black had glasses perched on the end of her nose eyed him asking, "Yes, may I help you?"

"I'm Gordon Mathews the painter," he replied then quickly checked the van keys were in his pocket.

"Oh yes, madam is expecting you," she said turned and gestured for him to enter.

Looking round, Gordon waited for instructions then suddenly smiled when she asked, "Follow me please?" He did and again looked round when she continued into a large wooden paneled reception room, opened a very large door she turning asking, "Please wait here."

While she disappeared inside, leaving the door ajar, Gordon tried to peer inside then jumped when she returned saying, "Madam will be here in a moment," then continued past him.

Mrs Bartholomew Smyth walked in saying, "Oh hello there, Mr.....Mathews, isn't it?"

"It is," replied Gordon, but purposely didn't say any more when it seemed she couldn't be bothered to remember him.

"Right then, follow me please?" she asked, quickly turned towards another large door, opened it, set off and gestured towards a large staircase.

Gordon discretely followed couldn't help admiring her trim figure, however, thinking she watched him out of her eye corners he looked up eyeing a very large portrait of an elderly gentleman and guessed by the way he was dressed thought it Victorian.

It was surrounded by others of varying sizes and he cringed at some of the damage, including large cobwebs hanging from them. When they neared the top of the stairs, "Right then Mr. Mathews, all hanging here we want doing," she said, smiled while gestured to them.

Looking at her Gordon moaned, "They will have to be removed from the walls, it would be impossible to work on them where they are."

"And that's what I said, so if you will follow me please?" she asked, turned and continued towards a door.

Gordon followed her into a room, and glanced round. Mrs Bartholomew Smyth turned and smiled saying, "In here has all the basics, I was also thinking you could stay in here to do your work. I will have my man take the paintings down one by one, and you can have them in here to work on."

Gordon glanced round thought, *to keep us workmen out of your way more like.* However, politely said, "It seems suitable and looks comfortable."

While walking towards the door she asked, "Right then, there are eight paintings of varying sizes and ages, so what will be the cost?" suddenly turned and stared at him.

Gordon had not really assessed them only noted their size and certain damage. Feeling put out when it seemed she put him on the spot on purpose, he glanced over her shoulder at the large painting behind while replied, "At this moment I wouldn't like to say."

"I will tell you this Mr. Mathews. We had a chap come up from London and he gave a quote of six thousand pounds. Of course my husband dismissed the amount and informed him that was far too much," she said while eyeing him.

"Did he indeed?" asked Gordon, thought she was lying and refrained from smiling at her poor business standard.

Looking impatient she said, "However, I must say this, that was three years ago."

"Was it indeed?" he asked, purposely looked away then walked towards the window and looked out. Staring into darkness, however, quickly assessing while feeling her eyes on him, Gordon turned saying, "I know you have already assessed my work and I think about five and a half thousand is nearer the proper cost."

Smiling as if bartered him into a good deal she asked, "Very good Mr. Mathews so when can you begin?"

"A week tomorrow," he replied, but thought, *that smile is so false.*

"Very good and I shall make all the necessary arrangements. The room and the paintings will be ready for when you arrive. So I will show you out now," she said then spun round.

Gordon allowed her to walk down the staircase first and again glanced at the paintings on the way down ending up eyeing her backside. At the main door she opened it, bid him goodnight and walked off. "And a good night to you two," he replied while closed the door behind him.

Walking round the rear of the house towards his van, Gordon thought she had an ignorant attitude then began to fumble in the darkness for his keys moaning, "It's always so bloody dark in the countryside."

On his way home, Gordon was over the moon to have this large private commission for restoration and especially on site. Knowing he must do a good job, hoped there would be others on the horizon and had to smile at the price, was way over the odds.

When he arrived home, his parents had waited for him and after Gordon explained the work involved. "How much?" gasped his dad.

"Well, she tested me for a price, but at five and a half grand, it's still way over the top."

"Well chuff me, and how long will it take you?"

A smiling Gordon replied, "I'll have to make it spin out else she'll think I'm on the make so maybe three weeks."

"Bloody Nora," moaned Colin, and stared at Jessie.

The following Monday morning, Colin drove Gordon to the Smyth's house. Arriving there he was very impressed with their house and its location. After made sure Gordon had both his cases, one with his equipment, and the other contained clothes, he waved before set off home.

Gordon watched his dad go down the drive continued up the few steps to the front door and when he was out of site, turned to ring the door bell. Two minutes later, the same small grey haired old lady opened it and welcomed him inside. Carrying his cases, Gordon waited while she closed the door, followed her up the staircase and smiled when she ushered him into the room.

Gordon noticed a painting on an easel ready, and when he approached it, "Lunch is at twelve thirty," said the maid, and faintly smiled.

Smiling at her he asked, "Thank you, and what may I call you please?"

Without batting an eyelid, "Ann," she replied then closed the door behind her.

During the rest of the day, with the only interruption for meals, Gordon had nearly finished the first painting and when Ann collected his dishes. "Will you ask if they could bring in the largest painting in the morning?"

"I will indeed sir," she replied, turned and closed the door behind her.

While sat watching a portable TV, Gordon winced while ate a light tea didn't like the bread thought it tasted funny then suddenly looked up when there was a knock on his door. "Come in?" he shouted.

A tall chap well dressed walked inside, and beamed a smile saying, "Good evening, and sorry to bother you, I'm Thomas Bartholomew Smyth," and held his hand out towards him. Gordon stood up and shook it, noticed him staring at a restored painting. Suddenly he gasped, "My good Lord, oh very good very good indeed."

"Are you pleased with the result?" asked Gordon now stood at his side.

"Oh very, I had heard you were one of the best in the country, and it shows," he replied, looked well pleased.

"Is that so?" asked Gordon, and studied.

"When you begin the last one we must arrange a party to celebrate, and I must say this, I never thought they would look that good," he replied now smiling at him.

"Maybe a week on Friday," said Gordon.

"That's a date then," he replied then slapped him on the back before set off to the door.

The largest painting was in the worst condition so Gordon knew it would take the most time, and for that reason was undecided to leave it while last. Eventually it was propped up against the wall in his room, so he intermittently worked on it while did others. When the smaller ones were finished and hanging, he spent the remaining four days cleaning the largest, during which, he studied the artiste's work and style. Most impressed and not recognizing his name, Gordon completed his work but had learned a lot, however, and more to the point, he was rather proud of his effort.

Chapter 7

While everyone in Harrogate was singing his praises, what Gordon didn't know was that while Jessie and Doreen still visited Caroline's to have their hair done; they discussed him with her, in great detail.

The second Thursday before the party at the Smyth's house, and with Jessie and Doreen being her last two customers, Caroline suddenly burst into tears and dashed into the back room. Jessie thought she was the problem, followed her, slipped her arm around her shoulder and quietly apologized, "Sorry for going on love," really knew it was her nattering that had upset her.

"It's alright," she replied while wiping her eyes.

"Come on then spit it out, what's he been up to now?" asked Jessie, really thought it was Gordon at fault.

"Well, for a start I'd heard a lot of rumours about him from customers. I always dismissed them thought they were just bragging but obviously they weren't, anyway it's all over now. I'm in a mess with my books again, so I'm packing this in, trouble is I'll have nowhere to live yet. God knows how I'm going to carry on," she sighed before wiped her eyes again.

"Don't be so silly my love, I'll send Colin to do your books so don't you worry about them. I'll get him to call first thing in the morning and get you straightened out," said Jessie while patted her back.

Caroline tried to smile saying, "No, I've made my mind up."

"Listen to her, and when he gets back we'll set about Gordon as well," snapped Doreen looking serious.

"Why? Where is Gordon?" she asked staring at her.

"As usual painting, he's working in Harrogate for a private collector," replied Jessie then frowned thought, *well, I hope he is.*

"I suppose it'll be for a woman," said Caroline while wiped her cheeks.

Jessie bit her lip, stared at Doreen but purposely replied, "No it's for a chap called Bartholomew Smyth and he's paying him a lot of money."

With the paintings all done and hanging in their usual places, Gordon wore slacks and an open neck shirt, was in attendance when the guests began to turn up for the Bartholomew Smyth party. Suddenly he smiled seeing a petite short black haired girl, aged middle twenties, walk inside the dining room with what seemed her parents, but looked thoroughly bored to tears.

The host began to introduce them, and gestured saying, "This is Gordon Mathews the painter, and this is Michaela Chisholm," then walked off arm-in-arm with her parents.

Gordon watched and thought it rude saying, "It seems we must have to chat together."

Michaela sighed while pulling a face of disgust snapped, "That's all Melanie ever does. She's noted for her ignorance."

"Oh sorry, could I get you a drink?" asked Gordon was smiling at her bluntness.

Again Michaela sighed and looking round as if wishing she was somewhere else moaned, "Please and anything will do."

Gordon noticed, and looked round before walked off. Two minutes later, he returned carried two large glasses, contained Brandy and lemonade. When he passed her one, "Well, I must say this, those paintings do look a lot better," she said before had a sip.

"Thanks," he replied, did the same, and instantly pulled a face thought the drink over strong.

"Dad has been thinking about having our paintings done. We have about twenty in the dining room, and some are really naff," she said while glanced up the staircase.

"And what does that mean?"

"Tatty."

"Oh, well, one can only do so much with restoration," said Gordon before had another sip. Gordon began watching other guests, especially when seeing Thomas point towards his paintings, seemed especially pleased with the one of his great granddad. Turning to Michaela, Gordon asked, "Is it me or is it generally accepted that the more money you have the more boring life becomes?"

"Believe you me, the more you have the more boring it does become," she replied and pulled a face of displeasure.

Liking her personality Gordon tested his luck asking, "Shall we have a walk anywhere?"

Smugly she replied, "Don't be silly, their house isn't that big," had a sip, then craftily smiled saying, "Mind you, their garage has lovely central heating.

"Well then, shall we go check their plumbing?" he asked while held out his arm.

"Why not," she replied, smirked and gave him her glass.

Thirty minutes later, Michaela was laid on the back seat of the Smyth's maroon Rolls Royce with her legs in air and laid in between them was Gordon, with his trousers round his ankles. His arse was going fifteen to the dozen but the only trouble was Michaela screamed out with pleasure. Placing his hand over her mouth, as didn't want them to be heard this made her giggle, and eventually, both ended their pleasure in muffled peace.

One hour later they sauntered back into the house arm-in-arm. Melanie eyed them and also noticed they looked flushed. She put two-and-two together and with the evening drawing to a close, after bid goodnight to two guests, wondered over to them asking, "You two seem to have got on well together?"

Gordon smiled while replied, "We have indeed."

When Michaela's parents wondered over, were about to leave, her father, most impressed with the paintings, suggested to Gordon, he should ring him later to organize a viewing of his paintings. After explained he wanted the same type restoration work done, however, he stressed, "Some of mine are very old and priceless."

Gordon took the opportunity to meet Michaela again, had taken to her, and courteously replied, "Please ring me the end of next week."

"Will do my lad, so right then, let's hit the road."

"Bye," said Michaela while sexily winked at Gordon.

"Bye and have a pleasant journey home," he replied while watched them walk out.

Next morning, after breakfast, Gordon rang his dad and asked him to come over and pick him up. Carrying his case and with a cheque in his pocket, an hour and a half later, he shook hands with Thomas then continued down the steps towards the van. After waving he got inside, and soon as his dad set off, he asked, "Well then, how did you get on?"

"Superb, and paid," replied Gordon while patted his pocket.

While they travelled, Colin began to inform him about Caroline moaning, "The poor bugger was in a right mess."

Gordon stared at him asking, "And in what way?"

Waiting at a junction to turn right, when he had Colin said, "Well, the room she lived in upstairs was really cramped, anyway, David went round and made her a bunk bed with storage underneath and above."

Gordon suddenly frowned said, "I didn't think it was that bad."

"She looks a lot happier now. She's had a shower fitted next to the toilet downstairs. Before that she was having a strip wash in the sink the poor bugger. Anyway I've done her books and changed her to our accountants," he replied looking both ways before turned off the main road.

When he pulled up behind the shop, Jessie noticed them out of the window and opened the back door. She instantly bombarded Gordon with questions about his work, and still did the same while made them a cup of tea. David walked in saying, "Oh your home, I've just closed for lunch."

"And according to form their might be a spin off from this job. They had a party last night and by hell were there some right snobs there. One or two were very impressed," said Gordon before drank up.

"So to get back to Caroline, she has a woman work with her on a Friday and Saturday now. She is a trained beautician, does nails and eyebrows, anyway they seem to be doing fine," said his mum while stared at him for a reaction.

"She knows you have been working away, I told her," said his dad.

"Good for you," said Gordon, stood up, picked up his case then continued upstairs.

In his studio, Gordon unpacked his case and laid everything out on his table. Having just placed a painting on the easel for repair when his mum walked inside and eyeing him she smiled saying, "I told Caroline you might call at the shop tonight to see her."

"Did you indeed, anyway what's for dinner? I'm starving," he replied.

"There are plenty of beans in the cupboard," she replied then laughed.

Staring at her he moaned, "Thanks very much."

"Anyway, we are going home now, me and your dad are going to a show in Leeds tonight, and by the way, something else you won't know, Caroline's had a phone put in, here's her number," she replied, put a card on his table, craftily smiled, turned and walked out.

Five minutes later, hearing the back door close and the shop door open, Gordon knew David had stopped behind to serve. Studying before began work on a painting, when he did and not allowing his mind to drift elsewhere, after an hour, Gordon decided to make a cup of tea. Admiring the work he had done so far, he put down his brush, picked up the business card and went downstairs.

After made a sandwich and a drink of tea, Gordon sat at the kitchen table, suddenly made up his mind to ring Caroline and ask if she wanted to go out for dinner to a local pub. Finishing his sandwich, Gordon reached over, picked up the receiver and dialed the number on the card. Recognizing her voice and fully expecting her to put the receiver down when she heard him. Quietly he said, "Hello, it's me Gordon."

In that flat business tone, "Oh hello there, just a minute please," she replied, and he didn't know if she was talking to him or a customer.

"Are you busy? Can you chat?" he asked, and for some reason felt nervous.

"At the moment," she replied, in the same tone.

Gordon could hear chatter as if the shop was full, but dreading another scolding asked, "I'm calling to see if you fancied going out for dinner tonight?"

"Hang on a moment please?" she asked, and Gordon strained to hear when as if she had her hand over the receiver asked someone, "Do you mind if I go out for dinner tonight? It's an old flame."

"You go ahead, it's alright love," replied a woman.

"Yes, and what time?" asked Caroline, which made him jump.

"Is seven alright?"

"Superb, will you pick me up at the shop? Just a minute, yes use that tint. Excuse me, will that be alright," she asked sounding impatient.

"It's a date then," said Gordon, but smiled with relief.

"Thanks and by for now," said Caroline, and quickly replaced the receiver on purpose.

The rest of that afternoon, Gordon helped David in the shop, who after closing quickly made the deliveries. Gordon prepared for the evening, and when David returned, was all ready to drive him home before continuing to pick up Caroline.

Pulling up outside the shop Gordon noticed the light on and watched a woman sweeping up. She looked in her mid-forties, was tall, well dressed, had dark brown hair and wore plenty of gold Jewellery. Gordon pipped the horn, and smiled when Caroline walked in from the back room. She placed her hand on the woman's shoulder, smiled and said something to her before carried on towards the door.

Caroline opened the van door and Gordon couldn't help but notice she looked radiant. She smiled saying, "Hello Gordon," before got inside and sat down.

Gordon nodded towards the shop asking, "Hello to you, and who's that in there?"

Caroline looked away from him, and smirked while closed the door replied, "Tell you all about it later."

Fifteen minutes later, in the same pub they called before, after ordering their drinks they sat in the lounge. Gordon had a drink before asked, "I hear my dad has been helping you out?"

"Yes and thank God. I was at my wits end and three weeks ago when Janice started, well, put it this way, last week I did a bomb and next week we are booked up solid," she replied, and for once seemed very enthusiastic.

After the waiter served their meal, he returned put a bottle of wine on the table. "So how was your commission?" she asked before picked up her knife and fork.

"Very good, they were really satisfied, and paid," he replied while picked up his.

Smirking she asked, "Did you ever finish that one of me?"

"Yes all about, although I must say this, oh never mind," he replied then carried on eating.

"Go on?" asked Caroline, and purposely stared at him.

Noticing Caroline looked radiant and relaxed. Quietly Gordon smiled before saying, "It was just that the first day you stayed with me was so beautiful and I will never forget it."

Frowning as if didn't understand she asked "And in what way?"

"In the way it was exciting and sexy. Not just making love, all about that afternoon, and night there was a great love between us, it was just so beautiful," he replied was now looking impatient.

In devilment, Caroline lightly asked, "Was it that good with Christine?"

"Oh come on, so you are telling me I was your first? Give over Caroline," he replied, quickly put down his knife and fork, picked up the bottle of wine and poured out their drinks.

"That is something you should never ask a lady," she replied while continued her meal.

"I don't know about that, women soon get the rat on when they find out their man hasn't been good, and it's bloody different the other way round. If only everyone in this world was innocent, by hell what a dull place it would be," he moaned, but had to smile.

Caroline quickly decided to change the subject asking, "Have you any more commissions in the pipeline?"

"Maybe, and next week I'll have to buy a car. Dad looked really put out running me up and down," he replied had nearly finished his meal.

"So you will be working away again soon?" she asked, placed her knife and fork on the plate, and picked up her glass.

Leaning on the table to purposely stare at her he replied, "Oh yes, I have to anyway because some of those paintings are huge, they would get damaged in transit, anyway, about us, is it possible to continue our relationship or is it all over and finished with?"

"Well now, a lot as gone off for me over these last few weeks especially since meeting Janice. Well, I'm cozy and secure now," she replied while put her glass down.

"And what is that supposed to mean?" he asked not understanding.

"She only lives three streets away from the shop, so I've moved in with her. It's far better than my old room, a lot less cramped," she replied, reached over and poured out some wine.

Gordon noticed she seemed a little flushed asked, "That won't stop us going out, or will it?"

Tongue in cheek Caroline replied, "In a way yes, she might get jealous."

Staring at her, Gordon didn't understand asked, "In what way?"

Trying not to smile, "Put it this way Gordon, living with a woman is less stressful than living with a man. We are lovers."

"What?" he gasped, stared at her and noticed she was now red faced. Caroline had only said it to torment him as it was not the truth. She picked up her glass, had a drink of wine, noticed Gordon stared in shock.

Suddenly he picked up his glass then drank his wine in one go. Gordon had taken her statement as an insult when had told her he loved her, and seeing as he had made love to her, suddenly asked, "But, why?"

"I've just told you," she replied doing her best to keep a straight face.

A silence prevailed because Gordon was at a loss for conversation. Not only had been rejected again by the woman he loved, now knew he could never have her. Suddenly he looked up when Caroline lightly asked, "Have I insulted you in any way?"

"Oh yes, and if you are ready I'll drop you off home now," he replied, couldn't eat a sweet, pushed his plate away, quickly wiped his mouth on a serviette and stood up.

On the way out, Gordon paid for their meal. Caroline followed him out of the dining room, and had to smirk was teaching him a lesson. In the van while he drove her to Janice's house, where she did now live but had her own room, noticing he was driving faster than normal she asked, "Please don't take it to heart Gordon?"

"Take it to what? Bloody hell, I've never been so humiliated," he replied, was that upset he stared out of the windscreen and shook his head bewildered.

Outside the house, Caroline opened the van door, and smiled quietly said, "See you later Gordon," leant over and kissed his cheek.

"Maybe," he replied, watched her get out but just half waved when set off.

Gordon carried on to his house and once inside let rip, cursed himself, thought he had caused her to turn shouting, "And now she's gay, Good God above."

Sunday morning at eleven o'clock his dad knocked loud on the back door. Gordon groggily dressed, sauntered downstairs, unlocked and opened it. Squinting he sighed asking, "Oh, come on in."

Colin walked inside and Jessie followed carried a large dish wrapped in a tea towel and placed it on the worktop saying, "This is a casserole, you can warm it up later."

"Thanks mum," he said while sat at the table.

While his dad made them a cup of tea, Jessie pulled out a chair and sat opposite him asking, "Well, did you take Caroline out for dinner?"

"Oh yes, I sure did," he replied then took a deep breath.

While nodding upstairs she asked, "Did she stay over?"

"Did she hell, and why didn't you tell me she was gay?" he asked staring at her.

Jessie sat upright, suddenly frowned not believing him asking, "What? Never, and who told you that?"

"She told me herself. She said she was living with that Janice," he replied now looked angry.

"Here you all are," said Colin before put their cups on the table.

When he sat down, Gordon looked at his mum saying, "She told me you had been helping her out, and when I picked her up there was another woman in the shop sweeping up. Caroline got in the van and we went to the White Horse pub for a meal."

"It's nice in there we've been in," said his mum, and smiled while folded her arms.

"Well, with everything going smooth, I asked her to go out permanent, and she refused. She said she was living with that woman. I think she said Janice was her name."

"Oh, well, I would never have guessed that for one moment," said Colin then studied.

"And neither would I." said Jessie staring at him.

"Anyway, that's that now," said Gordon before drank his tea.

"I think there more to this than meets the eye," said Colin then frowned.

Jessie stared at him asking, "And what does that supposed to mean?"

"Tell you later," he replied before drank his tea.

Chapter 8

Soon as they left, Gordon went upstairs to begin work on his paintings, knew the chap from Leeds was calling on Wednesday. Deciding to get stuck in, and with everything going smooth, he did finish them on time.

After the chap called and didn't leave anymore, only informed him a Mr. Chisholm was ringing him later that evening about a commission and it would probably take him three to four weeks to complete. "And how do you know that?" asked Gordon, seemed bewildered.

"Because you spoke with him at the Bartholomew Smyth's," he replied.

"Oh yes I remember now," said Gordon, and smiled recalled it was Michaela's father.

When Mr. Chisholm did ring, Gordon arranged to commence work the following weekend. Upon arriving there, "Do you wish to view them first, I have been told you might?" asked Mr. Chisholm.

"I have a rough Idea, just give me your address, and then I can start straight away. I have a busy schedule coming up," replied Gordon craftily smiling.

"Very well," he replied but though his reply abrupt.

The following afternoon, Colin took Gordon in the van then toured round Leeds to find a BMW agent, had made his mind up on the make and model. "There a bit pricey you know," said his dad, when pulled onto the forecourt.

"I can afford it," replied Gordon before got out.

An hour later, after paid for the car, and arranged it to be delivered on Friday morning. "Right then and here's my address," said Gordon while wrote it down.

On their way home, his dad studied asking, "I am not being nosey but can you afford all that?"

Gordon turned, and looking at him asked, "Yes and why?"

"Have you any money left then?"

"Why? Do you want to borrow something?" asked Gordon then laughed.

"That'll be the day, so how much will you get paid for this other painting job then?"

"A lot more than I paid for that car," replied Gordon, and laughed again.

"Good grief," gasped his dad while stared at him.

Friday afternoon with the car parked at the back of the house, Gordon was upstairs staring at the painting of Caroline. It was now finished and with the frame cleaned he was undecided to call at her shop and give it to her. Standing up he moaned, "What a waste of a good body," took it off, and put the first one on the easel, where he had put on her face.

Gordon was undecided to change it, sell it on or instead with a week spare, decided to finish the urban scene. Knowing that had to be finished because he was learning a different aspect of his trade, although it wasn't his forte, knew he had to diverse to improve.

The rest of the week flew by; however, nearing the end Gordon became fidgety. Friday morning, he sat with his mum in the kitchen while Colin and David served in the shop. "Have you run that car in yet?" she asked.

Gordon looked up at her asking, "No, and do you still have your hair done at Caroline's?"

"Yes, but she hasn't said anything to me, and I'm sorry but I can't see any body language between them, I think she is telling tales," she replied.

"It's a big thing to lie over, it's your reputation and I can't see her doing that," he replied then waved his hand as if dismissed her.

"Anyway, what time are you setting off there?" she asked, and noticed thought *that is nerves*.

"In an hour, my cases are in the boot already," he replied then sighed.

Raising her eyebrows she asked, "Disappointed aren't you?"

"Yes, you know I am."

"I'll have a quiet word then."

"You'll do nothing of the sort; I am not sharing, especially with a woman."

His mum pulled a face of impatience snapped, "Don't be so bloody silly."

"I should have got her pregnant in the first place; mind you she might have turned gay after. I'll never know now so maybe it's a Godsend really," moaned Gordon while stood up.

Looking gob smacked his mum asked, "You mean you did try to get her pregnant?"

"Of course," he snapped and continued out to his car.

Watching him his mum thought, *he's in love with her*, turned, and began to fill the kettle. When she heard Colin shout for a drink, she shouted back, "Two minutes."

It was bitterly cold on the way to the Chisholm's house, which was in between Harrogate and Wetherby. After finding it, Gordon drove slowly up the drive had large lawns either side and it looked very bleak. Staring at leafless trees, he smiled moaning, "It looks a bit like Transylvania."

When eventually reached the front door, walking up to it, it suddenly opened and Michaela came out to greet him. She kissed him on the cheek, took hold of his arm and ushered him inside.

After the introductions with her parents, Gordon was asked to inspect the paintings in the dining room and was amazed when an over inflated price was accepted. Knowing he would have to live in again as some of the paintings was very large with one having a gigantic gold effect frame and must weigh half a ton.

Escorting him upstairs and shown into a room, Mr. Chisholm asked if it was comfortable enough. Looking round, Gordon agreed but tried to contain a smile when Michaela winked at him. Turning to Mr. Chisholm, Gordon arranged to start work immediately and while the first painting was being taken down, he returned to his car for his cases.

Michaela followed him everywhere and Gordon smiled knew this commission would have its advantages, however, he also knew he must concentrate fully, make no mistakes else wouldn't get paid.

At dinner that night, after close inspection of all paintings and weighing up the work involved, Gordon informed Mr. Chisholm it would take about a month. "And please inform me Gordon, how do you arrange a costing for your services?" asked Mr.

Chisholm while picked up an expensive looking wine glass.

Gordon looked sheepish when quietly replied, "The price I gave you of fifteen thousand pounds, is not only for restoration and cleaning of your paintings it's the cleaning of the frames as well. Obviously there is the cost of materials, and the rest is the cost of my experience."

"That's my boy and I thought the same. If you make as good a job same as you did at the Smyth's I shall not be disappointed in the least," he said and smiling had a drink.

Good God, and he didn't even bat an eyelid, thought Gordon before drank his wine but noticed Mrs Chisholm didn't say much. With not more conversation, after gave his thanks for the meal Gordon asked to be excused. Returning to his room and after a wash and brush up, later that night Gordon continued work on the first painting, knew exactly what would happen when at eleven o'clock, Michaela joined him then they ended up in bed.

Over the weeks Gordon worked there, her parents noticed Gordon and Michaela had become close so Friday night at dinner, with only two paintings left to do, her mum pushed the situation and smiling said, "Why don't you take Gordon to Paris on holiday with you?"

Looking very sheepish Michaela replied, "I was going to ask him mum."

While looking at Gordon her dad grinned saying, "To be honest the way they have been acting, you might as well bring it into the open and just get engaged."

Michaela smiled saying, "We might later on."

Gordon was gob smacked, did like Michaela but knew he didn't love her and also didn't want any commitments. Quickly gathering his wits he stressed, "The thing is, I have more commissions coming up and will have to work away again, and obviously that's a poor way to start any relationship."

"Well said my boy, and there is nothing stopping you working and travelling together," said her dad while raising his glass before had a drink.

Oh boy, get out of this then, thought Gordon who half-smiled at Michaela saying, "We might work something out later on. I have always put my career first; after all it is my only income."

"Well now, I can assure you my boy, with your looks and talent, you will never be out of work. You are very fortunate as yours is a specialist job, and there aren't many that can do it," said Mr. Chisholm staring at him.

Gordon smiled saying, "Thank you for that assurance."

At the end of the month with his work completed and cheque in his inside pocket, Mr. Chisholm began to persuade Gordon to stay on another few days while he arranged a party for friends who he would like to assess their paintings. Knowing this meant more work Gordon agreed, rang his mum and informed her he would be a few days late.

Unfortunately, Gordon had noticed over the last week, Michaela seemed over friendly with one of the female cleaners, She was a tall blonde haired girl aged early twenties, had a nice figure and wouldn't mind having a go at her.

Unfortunately when he returned with her dad on Wednesday afternoon, had arranged another commission at one of his business friends, Gordon went straight up to her room, opened the door and stared in shock.

 The girl cleaner was laid in bed with Michaela knelt over her kissing her breasts and both were naked. She sat up, looked round and grinning asked, "Oh hello love, come on get your kit off and join us this is bloody great."

Gordon spun round, marched out, continued into his room and quickly began to fill his case with clothes. Ordinarily he might have been tempted, but now angry, having just completed business through her father he took the opportunity to end their relationship closed his case moaning, "It would have been a disaster anyway."

Having previously packed his paints and brushes away, after checked he had everything, he picked up his cases and set off downstairs. Continuing through the kitchen area, the cook stopped him asking, "Excuse me sir, Michaela has been looking for you."

"Has she?" he asked then sat down as if in shock.

Michaela walked in and nodded to the cook to leave. Waiting while she had, then walked up behind Gordon and slid her arms around his neck then kissed his cheek asked, "What's the matter love? Are you feeling off it?"

Gordon quickly stood up, walked over, turned on the tap, leant down and washed his face in the sink. Turning off the tap he picked up a towel growling, "You disgust me."

Staring at him she asked, "What's the matter?"

"You've been sleeping with me then her. What's up aren't I good enough?" he replied while dried his face.

"You know you are, but variation is the spice of life."

"And how long have you been in this variation?"

"Since she's worked here, oh come on love, you can have us both together, it's very nice," she replied, and smiled as if it was of no concern.

"Get stuffed," he replied but quickly thought, *and how does she know that?* Picked up his cases then stormed out.

"Oh Gordon, please, have I offended you?" she shouted.

"Too bloody true mate," he moaned while continued towards the front door.

On his way home, the more Gordon thought about Michaela, the more incensed with anger he became and it interfered with his driving. "That's two. Bloody hell what is it being gay," he moaned, and decided to stop at a roadside café.

Gordon bought a carton of tea and returned to his car. Now calming down, he took a deep breath before sat inside and had a drink. Deliberating events of the previous month, he shook his head with disgust moaning, "Everybody will think I'm no good at it, what a chuffing insult."

Arriving home, after a thin explanation for arriving early to his mum and dad mainly to keep out of the way, Gordon went up into his studio and emptied his cases. Staying there for the rest of the evening, he couldn't concentrate and in the end, mainly through hunger, risked it then sauntered downstairs.

His mum was waiting in the kitchen until Colin had finished receipts, looked up and asked what was wrong. "Nothing," snapped Gordon. Not liking the tone of his voice, his mum quickly stood up when Colin walked in. She gave Gordon, that I am angry scowl, then informed him he would have to make his own dinner. "Thanks very much, I won't forget this," he moaned while watched them leave.

The following Wednesday the chap from the auction house called and brought more paintings. Walking inside the shop he smiled saying, "I didn't think you would be here, I only called on the off chance."

"And what made you think that?" asked Gordon while took two paintings from him.

"You've another commission on the way haven't you?" he asked then dusted his hands.

Gordon picked up each painting in turn to inspect them then set off towards the stairs snapped, "It hasn't been confirmed yet."

"It will be, I can assure you of that" he replied while followed.

In his studio, Gordon propped the paintings against the wall asking, "What's in the pipeline then?"

"I'm saying nothing until it's all confirmed. Just let's say you're in the big time now lad," he replied had a big satisfied smile on his face.

Not having said anything to his parents about the events with Michaela, when Colin and Jessie called on Sunday with his lunch, they dropped a bombshell, informing him Tracy was getting married soon and with her future husband, who she met at university, intended to move back home.

Gordon quickly sat down asking, "When will that be?" was really thankful to live on his own.

Raising his voice, and as if stating the decision was final, his dad looking serious said, "Look lad, your mum and I have given this great thought. With

David and Doreen, we had a meeting last week and have decided to stop selling furniture."

"What the hell for? You are still making a profit?" asked Gordon looking dumfound.

"Yes, but a slender one," he replied staring at him.

"So you are going to sell the shop?" asked Gordon then slumped back in his chair.

His dad sighed as if wanted they to do it, replied lightly, "No, Tracy and Peter are turning it into offices and with Barbara, she's courting as well now, they are going to develop it into a design studio, it's all the rage now,"

"I say no, besides I've nowhere to live," said Gordon, and sighed had always thought Tracy came first.

Smiling his mum said, "You can always live with us."

"You can bugger off, you've only asked me twice to visit and the second time you were out," he replied staring at her.

Thinking they were getting nowhere, Colin looked impatient asked, "Can you afford you own place yet?"

"Yes, but that's not the point," replied Gordon thought, *why the hell should I?*

Jessie nodded knew he would be awkward asked, "So you are against it then?"

"Mum, while this business makes a profit I don't know why you should end it and start something else that's iffy. If our Tracy wants to starts a business she should set up on her own, that's the only way," he replied, sounding adamant and folded his arms to make the point.

"It's like that is it?" she asked, really knew he would say no.

"Yes it is, bloody women. The countries going haywire, what with Northern Ireland and bombs going off everywhere, even the colliers are on about coming out on strike again. I'll be glad to see the end of the bloody seventies," he moaned, stood up, and switched on the kettle.

Jessie looked at Colin and smiled when he frowned. "And don't pull faces behind my back. I know I'm thirty and should be married and away from this lot, but I aren't," snapped Gordon while made the tea. Jessie raised her eyebrows and nodded to Colin to go. When they stood up, Gordon moaned, "Oh I'm sorry."

"Listen love, you have done well and we are both proud of you, by the way did you see that article in the evening paper about you?" asked his mum while sat back down.

"No, when was that?" asked Gordon, put their cups on the table, and sat down opposite them.

"A week last Wednesday, anyway, Caroline did and she was very pleased," said his mum.

"Oh leave off with her, them days have gone," he moaned.

Smiling she asked, "You think so?"

His dad sat up asking, "You are getting off the subject lad; there is more than you in this family. So what are we going to do then?"

"Let me think about it," asked Gordon, then Colin jumped felt Jessie nudge him with her knee and knew that meant keep quiet.

Monday afternoon while Gordon was in his studio painting, David shouted upstairs "You have a visitor Gordon."

"Send him up," he shouted, thought it might be the chap from the auction house.

Gordon froze and stared at the door when Caroline walked inside. She smiled saying, "Hello."

"Err, hello," he replied, and being disturbed, put down his brush and palette before wiped his hands.

"I've just call to see how you are going on?" she asked while slowly walked round as if inspected the paintings.

"Fine thanks, and how are all the clit-lickers?" he asked, purposely to insult her.

"Pack it in Gordon?" she snapped staring at him.

"Don't forget madam, we made love in here. You're the one that turned, now if you don't mind I'm busy," he replied staring at her.

"Sometimes things might not be as they seem," she said, while walked over and glanced out of the window.

"Caroline, don't gloat, you are in a different league now. If you had married me, mind you if I couldn't satisfy you, you would have walked out on me by now so what's the difference," he moaned then picked up his brush.

"You never asked me to marry you?" she gasped staring at him.

"And would you? I think not," he replied while picked up his palette then began to paint as if ignoring her.

"Anyway, I've called to make you a proposition?" she asked while watched.

"Is that so? Well go on then and be quick about it?" he replied while carried on painting.

"Would you paint me and my partner in the nude?" she asked while smirked behind his back.

"Go get stuffed Caroline," he snarled.

"Then would you just paint one of us in the nude then?" she asked while placed her hand on his shoulder.

Gordon quickly turned, and staring at her snapped, "Sorry, I don't do queers," spun round and carried on.

"Oh are you? Sorry," she asked and laughed.

"You know what I mean," he replied then shrugged his shoulders.

"Gordon, I was winding you up."

"There's no smoke without fire," he replied, tried to carry on painting and couldn't when his hand shook with temper.

"Oh my good God, you are so bloody impossible at times," she moaned.

"Listen Caroline, you told me you were gay, well so be it. If you have had a fall out with her and think you can come round here and make it up with me, you are one off, I am not interested. I told you long ago I love you, and if you are going to be so silly and fuck me around making silly damming statements like that, just go piss off and in future keep away from here," he shouted while gestured to the door with the brush.

Now looking soulful, as if had made a great mistake, Caroline, as if knowing she had overstepped the mark, turned to the door and quietly said, "I do love you."

"It fucking sounds like it as well," he snapped while carried on painting.

Caroline knew he was angry when he swore, hadn't heard him before. She slowly continued but was so upset couldn't say anything. Outside the room she flopped down on the stairs and cried her eyes out.

Two minutes later and still angry, Gordon couldn't concentrate, slammed down his brush and pallet then sat on the settee. Staring out of the window he thought Caroline had left when noticed smoke still coming out of some of the colliers houses were now supposed to be completely smokeless. Sighing he moaned, "Oh my good God. The only girl I have ever loved and she ends up bent."

Caroline heard him and with tears in her eyes sobbed. She slowly stood up, turned and walked back inside then slowly continued up to him. Reaching out, she tentatively placed a hand on Gordon's shoulder making him jump, spun round and stared at her. Noticing the state of her face, he quickly stood up and quietly asked; "I thought you had gone?"

"How could I? And please let me say this before I do. I said all that about being gay just to get my own back on you and it is not true. You were right, how could I go with anyone else when we made love in here. Yes it was beautiful Gordon, exciting and loving, and I am not gay. Your only problem is will you ever be true to me? I don't think so," she asked, took out a hanky, wiped her eyes, and after sighing to regain her composure, spun round then walked out continued downstairs.

Hearing her walk down the stairs, Gordon wanted to go to her but instead bowed his head. Unfortunately recalling what had happened to him over the last few months, and himself feeling rock bottom he moaned, "She says she's gay then say's she isn't. Well that bloody thing at Wetherby definitely was, and then there are my parents who want to kick me out just to favour my money grabbing sister. Oh hellfire, what a fucking great life this is."

Picking up his brush and pallet then staring at the female portrait he was trying to repair a crack in her Edwardian bonnet, Gordon asked, "What would you do my dear?" began to laugh, and moaned, "Chuff me, I'm going round the twist now."

Unfortunately not doing a very good job, he stopped working and stood back eyeing the painting. "That's shit" he moaned and threw down his pallet, then flopping back down on the chair he moaned, "Shall I go after her or what?" Staring out of the window again Gordon quickly stood up saying, "No. I declared my intentions and she fucked me off. Admitted she came here to apologize but that was a shameful thing to do. No there must be better than that somewhere."

Chapter 9

Gordon decided that because of all the rumours he had to move away from the area, and for the rest of that week deliberated where to go before finally made up his mind what to do. Just for a break, he relieved David of his duties that night and made the deliveries for him. After the last drop off, Gordon called at a pub, and while sat in the bar leaning on the counter while having a drink, knew he could only have one with the new drink driving law. Gordon eyed the customers, noticed how many of the men looked effeminate, and was astound.

There were girls had their arms around each other snogging away and blokes pawing each other while chatting and laughing. Feeling really out of it and disgusted he drank up. Leaving there, Gordon called to an off-license; bought two bottles of wine to drink for when he arrived home, had decided to get pissed on his own.

When he did arrive home, noticed a letter on the mat without a stamp picked it up, opened it and read it. Mr. Barras asked him to call at his house near Ripon to assess his collection of paintings for restoration, and would he phone him soon as possible.

"You can go fuck off," he moaned, threw it on the worktop, picked up the corkscrew and began to open a bottle.

Sat in the front room in darkness drinking wine, Gordon contemplated the offer from his parents. It seemed nothing was going right at the moment, and after finished one bottle he began the other.

Half way down it, he suddenly looked round when heard a loud knock on the back door. Gordon stood up moaning, "If that's mum calling to get round me she can go piss off as well." Walking unsteadily into the kitchen, Gordon unlocked and opening the back door stared at Caroline asking, "What the hell do you want now?"

She entered, forced him back, closed the door behind her and watched Gordon lean on the wall for support when followed him into the front room. Caroline switched on the light asking, "Have you been drinking?"

"What's it look like?" he replied while flopped on the sofa.

"I've called to apologize," she snapped then stared when noticed he hadn't had a shave and didn't seem his normal self.

"So what," he replied then loudly belched.

She leant forward took the glass out of his hand, and put it on the coffee table snapped, "What the hell's the matter with you?"

"Caroline, get back to your lover whatever she is. Just fuck off will you and leave me in peace," he moaned.

"Stop swearing, you sound common?" she snapped.

"Would it be common if I slept with a man?" he asked staring at her.

"Forget all that," she said looking away.

"How the hell can I? You know I love you. We made love all over this house and it was beautiful and do you know what? It spoilt my life. No one I ever meet can better it, the rest are just a waste of fucking time," he moaned while rest his head back.

"It was that good?" she asked when sat at his side.

"Not really, I've have had better, but there is big difference in having a one off shag and making love. I could kiss every part of your body and make you come, I did it twice remember?" he asked staring at her.

"I can," she replied, and smiled knew he was drunk.

Reaching out he picked up his glass and drank the contents. Gordon carefully stood up, went to refill it, and turned asked; "Do you want one?"

"Please," she replied.

After passing her a glass, he sat down asking, "What's up has mum being having words with you?"

"No, although she still calls in with your auntie Doreen every Thursday," she replied.

Gordon laughed asking, "So what have you called for, not another nude painting?"

"No just you," she replied, leant forward and kissed him.

"Sorry love I'm pissed. Pissed off and according to form have to move away. My parents are selling up, because my ungrateful sister is moving in here and God knows what sort of shambles they will make of the place. Oh God, what a fucking world," he moaned, and rest his head back.

"By hell you are in a bad mood," said Caroline and laughed.

Smiling through blurry eyes he moaned, "Do you know something love, we should be married now, have at least two kids, and everything would be rosy in here."

Raising her eyebrows she asked, "Oh, should we?"

"Oh yes, anyway go fuck off now and get back to your partner, that's the new term isn't it?" he asked then purposely stared at her while drank up.

"I wouldn't know."

While replacing his glass on the coffee table he slurred, "Come off it."

"You just won't listen will you?"

"Unless of course you fancy a quick-shag on the side without her knowing?" he asked and smirking tried to stand. When he did about to finish the rest of the wine, Caroline stood up and stopped him.

"Give over?" he asked while knocked her hand away.

"Come on you, it's time for bed," she snapped, grabbed his arm then pulled him towards the stairs.

"I am tired," he moaned while carefully tried not to knock over the glass before headed for the stairs.

Tired, miserable, downhearted and absolutely fed up, Gordon entered his bedroom and flopped on his bed. Caroline smiled began to undress him. "Lock the back door after you go?" he moaned then laid back closed his eyes.

When he was naked, Caroline pulled the quilt over him, turned and set off downstairs. She locked the back door and turned off all the lights before returned upstairs. Inside his bedroom, she stared at Gordon, seemingly asleep, quickly undressed and got in with him. In his stupor, Gordon instantly smiled, wrapped his arms around her, and snuggled up to her back moaning, "That feels good."

Next morning when he woke, Gordon looked round and stared at Caroline next to him. Quickly throwing back the quilt he dashed into the toilet. When he returned Caroline sat up asking, "Go make some breakfast please."

"Oh hell, I don't know," he moaned, looked completely bewildered and got back in with her.

Wrapping his arms around her Gordon asked, "We didn't? Did we?"

"What in your condition, you were drunk."

"Oh hell, what did I say?" he asked, then quickly buried his face in her neck while slid his hand over her belly.

"Get off," she snapped, took hold of his hand, and smiling said, "Just let us say this you were downhearted."

"You must be joking, what with what's gone off. Bloody hell Caroline," he moaned then sat up. Gordon slowly looked down was admiring her chest. Caroline noticed then quickly covered herself with her arms. "Who's opening your shop?" he asked before leant down kissed her.

"My partner," she replied then smiled while slipped her arms around his neck.

Gordon forced his leg in between hers and Caroline smiled, pulled him down on her to kiss him. Gordon was just about to move over her when she snapped, "Oh no, we have to talk first," sat up, making him do the same resting back on his ankles.

"What's up now?"

"What I just said," she replied while rolled off the bed.

"Oh, my good God," he moaned, did the same and continued out into the bathroom.

When Gordon came out, he pulled up his trousers, continued downstairs and heard a noise in the kitchen. Carrying on inside he watched Caroline stood at the cooker carefully placing two eggs in a pan of boiling water. Scratching his head Gordon asked, "What time is it?"

"Eight," she replied, and leant past him to check the time.

"Dad and David call about quarter to nine," he said while sat at the table and smiled heard the toaster.

"Don't get comfy, these are nearly ready so butter that toast first?" she asked, while took out the eggs.

Sat at the table, while they ate, "So when are we going to have this chat then?" he asked while spread some butter.

"Tonight, fancy going out for dinner and this time I'll pay," she replied then drank her tea.

"No thanks, I have to ring a client this morning about a commission, so I might be away for another month or so," he replied before picked up his cup.

"Where will you be working?" she asked before took the top off her egg.

"Ripon, it's very near the castle. They've a nice house, I called last week and viewed their paintings," he replied before had a drink of tea.

"Does it pay good money?"

"Not bad and when I've been paid for this job I might buy my own house with the proceeds," he replied, stood up, picked up and returned with the teapot, began to pour out some fresh tea.

Raising her eyebrows she asked, "Earn that much do you?"

"It won't last forever though," he replied then looking at her frowned.

"Why don't you have a sale with your own paintings?" she asked while poured in the milk.

Laughing he gasped, "What, all four of them?"

"Get some more done then," said Caroline before picked up her cup.

"It takes time to paint, you need inspiration," he moaned while doing the same.

"Like having sex all over the house?" she asked then laughed.

Gordon stared but admired her smile. "It does help, but not for landscapes."

"So, put this commission back a couple of months and get some paintings done. When you have finished them, why not continue and try to organize a sale before next Christmas, that's the best time," she said, finished her tea then suddenly looked round when there was a knock on the back door.

"Do me a favour please go and open it," he asked smiling at her.

Caroline knew why, stood up, walked over unlocked and opened the door. Colin stared at her asking, "Oh hello love is he in for a change?"

Caroline smiled replied, "Of course," and when Colin and David walked inside, she closed the door behind them, continued to the sink and filled the kettle.

All sat round the table. Colin noticed egg cups and guessed Caroline had stayed overnight asked, "Right then, about the shop, have you given anymore thought to our suggestion?"

"We've just been discussing it," replied Gordon smiling watched Caroline put their cups on the table. Waiting until she sat down he said, "I think its best not to do anything until the end of the financial year in April."

"That's what I suggested," said David, seemed satisfied.

"By the way, your aunt Janice did make a big difference to your takings. Those two days she works as a beautician has really worked," said Colin then drank his tea.

Gordon stared at Caroline, and noticed her face went bright red. She suddenly smiled saying, "I thought it might, no one offers facilities like that around here."

When David went into the workshop, Colin continued into the shop to open it. Gordon stared at Caroline then snapped, "You bugger she's your aunt."

"I told you," said Caroline, while began to clear the table.

"You get on about me. You've lied, connived behind my back, tormented me, ridiculed me, put me down, and now I suppose, you want me to forgive you?" he snapped.

"You can please yourself," she replied while walked round then leant down kissed him. When she walked away he nipped her arse made her squeal out. Caroline rubbed her backside and smirked before moaned, "Give over, I bruise easily."

"You will tonight when I've finished with you," said Gordon then stood up.

"Oh and why?" she asked, and grinned while washed up.

"You'll see later," he replied and purposely grinned back.

"I don't know what time it'll be, I'm very busy today," said Caroline while rinsed out then put cups on the drainer.

"Right then, come round here from the shop tonight and let's get some painting done. I'll do as you suggested, and from the proceeds of the sale let's buy a house together."

"That's very good of you my love," she said, turned slipped her arms around his neck, and kissed him before smeared soap suds on his face.

"You are tempting providence," he moaned while wiped them off.

"Good," she replied smirking at him.

After run Caroline to her shop, Gordon returned to inform his dad what he intended to do. Gordon continued up to his studio, stared at the painting of

Caroline on the wall, and smiled before commenced work.

Finishing the paintings for the auction house first, Gordon began to copy the painting of Caroline, and the only interruption he had was when his mum brought his dinner. Smiling when she said it was a casserole for two and had left it in the oven to keep warm until they were ready. Gordon said, "Thanks mum," but noticed a smirk on her face.

That evening, David made the deliveries, and then to continue home in the van saying he was going to a sale with Colin first thing in the morning. Gordon decided to ring Mr. Barras at Ripon that evening; however, first had a quick shower then changed before dinner.

Thirty minutes later when he did ring then explained his reason for the delay, Gordon quickly turned when the back door opened. Smiling at Caroline he noticed she carried a large green bag gestured to lock the door and stood upright saying, "Right then Mr. Barras, that would be better all round, I will ring you a week before the date."

When Gordon replaced the receiver, Caroline noticed the oven on, opened the door and looked inside asking, "Have you made this?"

"No mum. She brought it round earlier," he replied while washing his hands.

"Do you mind if I go up and shower first?" she asked then swapped hands with the bag.

"No, go on love I'll finish it off, and I've just put back the date of that commission," he replied while drying his hands.

"Very good, and I don't think you'll regret it," said Caroline before set off upstairs. Caroline craftily had a peek inside his studio and smiled noticed a canvas on his easel, carried on to the bathroom saying, "Well, it looks like he's trying."

Fifteen minutes later when she returned, dressed in jeans, fluffy pink slippers wore a grey tea shirt and no bra. Gordon noticed when she brushed her hair straight back. Smiling he bent down took the casserole out of the oven and when placed it on top. "It smells nice," said Caroline while sat at the table.

"Typical women, as usual watching us men do all the work," he moaned before passed some plates.

Caroline served and while they ate, discussed her shop informing him it hadn't been busy as she expected, having had three cancellations. "Mondays are always slack anyway, so in between I had a good clean round."

"When I've finished this I'm going up to paint for a couple of hours. I'm on with a copy of that painting of you at the moment," said Gordon smiling.

Staring at him she snapped, "I'm warning you now Gordon, you had better not sell that original painting."

"Don't be silly, anyway you can take it home with you tonight for safe keeping," he replied, stood up, put his plate in the sink but had a sly grin on his face.

That's what you think, she thought, recalled when his mum rung that afternoon and informed her they would not be disturbed until in the morning when his dad would turn up to open the shop.

Since reading about Gordon in the evening paper, Caroline had taken notice of paintings or prints on people's walls and their different styles. She came to the old conclusion; beauty was in the eye of the beholder when didn't like most of them. "What about doing a more modern type painting, you know such as me, only this time with my clothes on?"

"Actually the way you are dressed now is just perfect, casual and especially barefoot you can't beat it. You might not believe this, but that light grey tea shirt suits your complexion," replied Gordon faintly smiling.

"Ready when you are then," she said while stood up.

"You'll have to wait while I've washed up. If mum calls and sees a sink full of mucky pots she will go balmy," he moaned then turned on the tap.

"Oh, come on then, just to stop you wittering," said Caroline then began to give him a hand.

After helped him wash up, with all crockery away, Gordon turned off the lights as they went upstairs.

Inside his studio, he changed the canvas on the easel as Caroline took a magazine out of her bag then sat on the settee began to read, occasionally watching Gordon as he prepared it.

Suddenly she became engrossed in an article, didn't know he was sketching her but undecided the best angle, Gordon asked, "Just turn this way a little?" Smiling he altered the scene, finished the drawing which had her sat on a tall stool with one foot on a rung, while reading a book.

When Gordon began to apply the foundation for the backdrop, again he used light from the window; giving her a paler complexion then made her hair wispier, satisfactorily smiled then began to paint.

An hour later, Caroline put the magazine down moaning, "That's it I'm bored."

"Get undressed then?" he asked then smirked.

"Only if you do?" she replied stood up and quickly pulled off her tea shirt.

Gordon smiled while undressing but moaned, "Why is it women have to have the last word?"

"Because for," she said while watched him.

The last time Caroline stayed over, only to later storm home, she was thankful not to be pregnant. It caused her concern for three weeks, however, this time; while they romped all over the house again it was the last thing in her mind as now couldn't care less.

It was nearly midnight when they slipped into his bed, and laid snuggled up to each other. Chuckling he moaned, "You've buggered me up."

Caroline rolled over and turning her back to him sighed, "Just like a man to give up first, they always have an excuse."

Reaching down he suddenly slapped her arse asking, "And how would you know that?"

"I've just read it in that magazine," she replied then giggled.

Next morning because the weather was bad, blowing a gale and raining heavily, Gordon took Caroline to her shop in his car. Winking before kissed her he said he would pick her up that night. "About six love. I have two late customers," she said smirking.

"Right love," he replied, waited while she closed the door, waved then set off home.

Arriving there, noticed his dad and David unloading the van, Gordon locked the car then gave them a hand. "Well then, did everything go off alright?" asked Colin, while carried in the last table.

"So so," replied Gordon, closed the van doors, locked them, and followed them inside began to make them a cup of tea while they assessed furniture from the sale.

Unfortunately the economic climate was changing again. Colin and David discussed the night before, had decided to keep the shop open and weren't going to inform Gordon just yet.

While drinking their tea, Gordon informed his dad about the commission in Ripon, was also was going to paint a collection of his own and arrange a sale at the end of next year. "It's about bloody time," moaned Colin, and smiled had only said it to spur him on.

"Give over dad it takes a lot of doing, anyway I'm going to try and do one painting a week, if I can do more all the better," he replied.

"Well just don't look at me, go get started then," moaned his dad then drank up.

Chapter 10

Over the festive season trade had increased at the shop and unusually continued over the following three months. Gordon now had nine paintings ready, was very pleased with them all, as in three he had used Caroline as a subject, her aunt Janice in another, also his grandparents and his parents. To broaden his range more as he wanted to do more industrial landscapes Gordon was over the moon when Janice leant him photos kept from her childhood in Sheffield.

Throughout the winter months due to the bad weather, visits from the chap from the auction house dwindled. Gordon didn't despair just continued with his own work, however, began swapping canvases more when boredom crept in.

When the weather did change for the better and visits became more frequent from the auction house, Gordon informed the chap his intentions and from then used him to deliver new brushes, canvases and oils.

From the amount earned Gordon was adamant he deducted the cost. With everything finalized the chap smiled, put away his wallet saying, "Uncannily, due to a sudden turnaround, we now have a backlog at the auction rooms."

"Right then next week, bring four and I'll try to get them done before I go to Ripon," said Gordon, picked up his brush then sighed while eyed his work.

"I can see you're busy and by the way, where are you having your show? My boss said you can use our action room. If you do he'll look after you with advertising and what have you," he asked, and watched when Gordon began to paint.

"Tell him thanks and I might," replied Gordon then smiled when thought it would be appropriate.

With their relationship perfect, now seemingly working for each other, two weeks before going to Ripon, Gordon sat cozily on the sofa in the front room with Caroline discussing his commission, and how long it would take. With paintings finished for the auction room and eleven done for his show, she was over the moon when he asked her opinion. However, being inexperienced, Caroline decided to remain candid, rest her head on his shoulder to explain, "The best one is that of those two men working in an iron foundry, the colours are superb."

"I thought I had done well with that one," said Gordon, and relaxed back while held a cup of tea in his hands.

"It's so imaginative and striking. Those flames are so very real," she said, then sat up to drink her tea.

"I am not being funny my love, but what are you going to do while I'm away?" he asked.

"Work," she replied smiling.

"Dad told me about the shop next door to your might come available soon and he's looking into it for you," said Gordon, and finished his tea.

"If I can afford to buy it I will, if not I'll have to let it go," said Caroline then stood up.

Lovingly smiling at her Gordon said, "I'll help if I can."

Pursing her lips and winking at him Caroline said, "I knew you would."

The following Tuesday, the chap from the auction house called for the restored paintings, inspected them and again looked well pleased. After paid Gordon, he slapped him on the back saying, "I've had a word with my boss about your sale and he said just say the word and he will help you in any way he can."

"Right then mate, I should be done in Ripon at the end of August. Give me another two months to prepare more, so could I arrange a sale say about the second week in December?" asked Gordon, then smiled, recalled that advice was given to him by Caroline.

"I shouldn't see why not, that's a bad time for us anyway and it'll also financially help us."

"And then I want a rest, so don't call until the end of January. Oh bloody hell its nineteen eighty then, God how time flies," moaned Gordon then suddenly recalled his dad saying they were going to assess the shop at the end of April, and studying what it might be about thought, *it must be because the takings are up again, or has he something else up his sleeve.*

With his commission to start on Saturday afternoon, Friday night, while sat in the front room with Caroline drinking tea after dinner. "Bloody hell, I'm thirty three next," moaned Gordon and frowned.

"And I'm thirty two," said Caroline then squeezed his arm.

"Do you mind putting your career before having a family?" he asked, always thought Caroline was on the pill.

"I can work round it, anyway it's a matter of having to now," she replied then stood up, took his cup before continued into the kitchen.

Gordon quickly stood up, when suddenly he frowned then followed her asking, "How do you mean having to?"

"Because I think I am pregnant that's why," she replied while washed up.

"But, oh hell never," he moaned, and quickly sat down.

Frowning at him she asked, "Don't you want kids?"

"Oh yes, but, well, it's just the shock," he replied then leant on the table.

"It wasn't a shock to me."

Staring at her he asked, "And why not?"

While trying not to laugh, "Give over Gordon, we've been at it hammer and tong these least four months."

Trying not to laugh he asked, "Is that what you think of me?"

"No, I think the world of you, and next time you ever let me down; I'll make sure you'll never perform again, now come on and dry these?"

That night in bed, Caroline half-laid on him, and staring into his eyes asked, "Please don't mess around Gordon?"

Stroking her hair he asked, "And when will I have time to?"

Quickly sitting up she snapped, "Oh, so you would if given the chance?"

"Don't be so stupid, those days are over now," he replied, gently ran his hand down her chest then lightly patted her belly.

"And they had better be," she said while laid with her head on his chest.

Next morning, his mum and dad, with David and Doreen arrived at the house at eight thirty. Fortunately Gordon and Caroline were dressed ready, usually had their breakfast scantily dressed. "Right then are you ready for the off?" asked his mum.

"I'm dropping Caroline off at the shop on the way," replied Gordon before picked up his cases continuing out to his car.

Jessie turned to Caroline saying, "Don't take this wrong Caroline, but our Tracy and Peter are arriving at ten, I've asked them to stay and look after the shop, mainly for security."

"It's alright, I'll stay at the shop, we've already arranged it because I've been putting on Janice lately," she replied, and half smiled didn't want to offend her.

Gordon walked into the kitchen asking, "Right then if you are ready?"

"Watch what you are doing lad," said Colin frowning at him.

"Good grief dad, I'm only off to work," he replied shaking his head at his moaning.

"I know that, I meant with the roads. They are a bit tricky this morning," replied Colin staring at him.

Gordon raised his eyebrows asking, "Did you just say our Tracy was staying in here?"

"Yes but only temporary. They are going into Leeds on Monday morning looking for premises," said

Jessie walking in between them to glance out of the window.

Studying her face for a reaction he asked, "I thought sometime this year they were moving in here permanent?"

Quickly turning his mum, looking straight at Caroline replied, "We haven't made up our minds yet. There is a lot to take into consideration, isn't there?"

Taking hold of Caroline's arm when she stood up, Gordon moaned, "Such as keeping Tracy happy."

Five minutes later, Gordon and Caroline sat in the car and waved when he set off. As Gordon drove down the street, he moaned, "I wonder what they are going to do now? They are getting more secretive than you."

"Watch it," said Caroline then playfully hit him on the shoulder.

Outside her shop when they kissed goodbye, "Watch what you are doing and look after yourself my love," said Gordon before quickly kissed her again.

"And you do your best," she said, and smiled before opened the door.

Waiting until Caroline was inside the shop, Gordon waved when set off. Carrying on he continued towards Garforth then on towards the A1, had planned to go north through Wetherby then on towards Ripon.

In good spirits, the traffic lights and his directions correct, Gordon arrived there just before noon. When he pulled up outside the house Gordon noticed the main door slowly opened. Mr. Barras came out to greet him, seemed over the moon he had turned up and vigorously shook his hand. "I'll just get my cases," said Gordon then turned opened the car boot.

Visiting there house before, Gordon partially remembered the layout, especially where the paintings hung and knew the amount of work to be done to them. Gordon smiled when asked if it was possible for him to start straight away. Mr. Barras agreed, escorted him up to his room, and inside Gordon suddenly smiled when noticed a painting on an easel ready.

Suddenly as if an afterthought Mr. Barras asked, "Right then, I'll leave you in peace. Oh please forgive me, shall I have you dinner brought up her or do you wish to eat with us?"

"If you don't mind please, could I eat up here? I have my first public sale just before Christmas and it is paramount I meet the deadline," replied Gordon smiling, but craftily thinking, *I wonder if he would be interested in buying any.*

"Very well, and if that's the case, I shall inform our friends of the event. However, could I be the first, so do you know the date of your sale yet?" he asked raising his eyebrows.

"Not really, probably the second or third week in December, I'll give you a ring when I find out the date," replied Gordon while opened a case.

Soon as Mr. Barras closed the door behind him, Gordon began inspecting the painting and smiled at his enthusiasm at being in the know. But back to business, having viewed his paintings before knew this was the worst one and nodded saying, "This is the tester. He'll want to inspect this when it's finished, so I'd better make a good job."

Using a spirit based cleaner his dad used on furniture, Gordon first cleaned the frame, checked for woodworm, and smiling found none.

Two hours later, while having a rest, a tall very well dressed woman, aged late fifties entered the room was carrying his dinner on a large silver tray. Gordon stood up saying, "Thanks," took it from her and carefully placed it on a small table. Assuming it was Mrs Barras with all the jewellery on her fingers and around her neck when she began to inspect the painting he said, "It might be finished tonight."

Smiling she said, "I'm very impressed."

"And I'm pleased as well. It is a great painting and very valuable," said Gordon, was starving and eyeing his dinner thought, *hurry up and bugger off.*

"I must be off now. I believe my husband said he will call with another painting later this evening saying your time was of the essence," she while turned continued towards the door.

"Unfortunately that is quite right and thank you again," said Gordon, politely waited until the door closed before sat down.

One hour later, after enjoyed his meal and used their toilet, Gordon flushed it, glanced round and was impressed when the bathroom looked brand new. It was tiled in white with highly polished brass piping and fittings had a large separate bath and separate shower cubicle. Studying he said, "I would like something similar fitted at home."

After a quick wash to refresh his mind before returned to his work, while dried off, Gordon decided to first check his notes about the artiste and his painting. Continuing to renovate until finishing at nine o'clock he spun round when there was a knock on the door. Gordon was cleaning his brushes and sat admiring his work turned shouted, "Please come in?"

Mr. Barras walked inside, and smiled while continued straight to the painting. Now finished it was looking remarkable when suddenly he turned, held out his hand and beaming a smile said, "That is excellent work my boy."

"Thank you," replied Gordon but had to smile when he vigorously shook his hand.

"If it is possible and you don't mind, I'll have them hang this straight away, it looks magnificent. I'll have them bring another one in soon," said Mr. Barras while unscrewed the wooden lock, and took the painting off the easel, carefully carrying it out of the room as if it was an unexploded bomb.

When he returned, while placed another painting on the easel and securing it, his wife followed shortly carrying a tray had on it tea and biscuits pleasantly smiled before carefully placed it on the table. "Thank you very much," said Gordon, had noticed both looked exceptionally pleased, desperately didn't want to offend them so tried not to smile.

"This one is not as old as the last. I bought it at Sotheby's twenty years ago for fifteen hundred pounds," said Mr. Barras was stood admiring it.

Gordon instantly recognized the artistes work, leant forward and smiled saying, "Its worth a lot more now," when the artiste signature at the bottom confirmed it.

"You think so?" he asked seemed surprised.

Without batting an eyelid, "Oh yes, his work is very acceptable now. It's probably worth around ten thousand today," replied Gordon.

Mrs Barras sauntered to the side of her husband asking, "You seem to know a lot about the old painters Mr. Mathews?"

"I had to study them so I could restore their work to individual perfection. All have differing styles and of course, detail differs from one to another."

"And rightly so," she said, as if knew.

Mr. Barras smiled saying, "Right, we won't keep you any longer. Thank you very much Mr. Mathews and breakfast will be brought up to you at eight thirty."

"You are very kind," said Gordon really thought they were a genuine loving couple.

"Think nothing of it," said Mrs Barras, and smiled slipped her arm in her husband's before they walked out.

Throughout the rest of the week, Gordon worked like hell and on Saturday night, with a third of the work complete, he accepted an invitation to have dinner with them, didn't know they had guests, and one of them was Michaela with her parents.

Gordon was sat in the dining room chatting to Mr. Barras when heard the door open. Turning he stared when Mr. and Mrs Chisholm entered. They continued inside, followed by another middle aged couple and then Michaela with head sheepishly bowed behind them.

While they walked to their places round the table, Gordon stood up then was shocked when Michaela, as if meant it to be a surprise, went straight to him. She threw her arms around his neck, kissed him on the cheek then smiled saying, "Hello my darling."

"Hello to you two," he replied, but eyeing her dad he had a great big smile on his face.

Mr. Barras smiled while watching said, "Please, may I introduce Mr. Crowther and his wife Bridget."

"Please to meet you," said Gordon, and smiled while shook their hands.

"I know you have met Mr. and Mrs. Chisholm," he said, and watched with pride when Michaela slipped her hand in Gordon's arm.

Gordon now wished he hadn't accepted their dinner invitation replied, "I have indeed," then shook their hands but felt uncertain, because if they knew what he knew about their daughter, they should know why he left.

"Shall we all be seated?" asked Mr. Barras while gestured to his wife.

This seemed the start to a jovial dinner party when they all chatted and laughed. When a maid served their starter, with Michaela at his side, Gordon became restless and felt uncomfortable, especially when she always leant on him while conversed with the others.

Enjoying the fact that Mr. Barras included him in his conversation with Mr. Crowther, then found out why he had invited himself that evening, when stating he also had work for him to do. Living near Stamford, he had accumulated a small but valuable collection, and when asked if he could call to assess them, Gordon replied, "It would have to be sometime early next year now; I have a sale of my own coming up very soon."

"If that's the case then, we will also have to attend it," he replied while beamed a smile at his wife as if relished the prospect.

Earlier that morning, with her first customer due at nine thirty, Janice was in attendance in the shop while Caroline attended an appointment at the doctors. After a pregnancy test, he confirmed she was expecting but quickly leaving there, had to dash back, with many customers booked in for the rest of the day.

It was when they finished at seven that night Caroline purposely waited until the last customer left to save rumours. While cleaning up she informed her aunt the news. After kissed her on the cheek Janice asked, "Oh my love that is great, does Gordon know?"

"He has an idea, but wasn't sure."

"Better ring his parents and inform them, they will be over the moon," said her aunt while slipped on her coat.

Wearing a pleasing smile, Caroline said, "I'll wait until Gordon gets back, he'll want us to tell them together."

That night in her little room upstairs, Caroline began to make plans and wrote most down. The tenants next door had put in their notice were due to leave at the end of next month and the way her business was going, she might be able to afford an extended mortgage, buy it and live in there. She had rung the owner and asked if he would sell the property, and he replied that he would consider it, however, if he did she was first on the list.

Caroline remembered Gordon said he would financially help her, knew it would take a lot of money and work to knock both accommodations into one to make a livable house. After undressed, she laid on her bed, thought to ring Jessie in the morning and ask them advice about one or two mortgage matters. Suddenly she smiled, had decided to inform them she was pregnant as with not many relations of her own to celebrate with, knew they would and it would all seem worthwhile.

In Ripon, having a drink after dinner, Gordon carried a large glass of wine, and excused himself before stood up. About to go up to his room he heard Michaela excuse herself under the pretext she wanted to inspect the renovated paintings.

Gordon knew she wasn't interested in them, just wanted to get him on his own, however, when she joined him at the foot of the staircase, to save an argument he chatted about the weather. While they walked upstairs, Gordon winced wished she was somewhere else especially when he opened his door.

Soon as he closed it after them, Michaela flung her arms around his neck and kissed him making Gordon spill his drink. When he held her back,

"What's the matter my love?" she asked staring at him.

"You know damn well," he replied turned and placed his glass on a small side table. Gordon continued over to the easel and stood in front of a painting. Beginning to inspect it mainly to get away he also studied the best way to get rid of her.

Stood behind him Michaela slipped her arms around his waist moaning, "Oh come on Gordon, you know I love you."

"Sorry, I don't like sharing, especially with the opposite sex," he snapped turned and quickly walked away. Michaela let go of him but watched with interest when he picked up his glass and sipped his drink.

"Don't be silly now Gordon. When you are young you have to try everything else you miss out and will never know other pleasures," she moaned, slipped her arm round his waist and squeezed him.

Sarcastically smiling at her he replied, "Normally that pleasure is between a man and a woman."

"What like this," she said, turned him round then quickly knelt down in front of him.

Gordon looked down and tried to walk away when she grabbed his legs. With one hand wrapped round his knee, Michaela reached up and began to undo his trousers. Looking for somewhere to place his drink, Gordon suddenly frowned when they dropped down. Looking up at him Michaela smiled saying,

"Try running away now," then slid her hands up his legs.

Stood rigid enjoying the experience he thought, *you keep on going that my love and you'll get the lot*, watched her head bobbing up and down. Fortunately when Michaela stopped for breath and ran her hands down the inside of his legs. Gordon took the opportunity, reached out and carefully placed his glass on the table before grabbed hold either side of her head.

Ten minutes later, with Gordon staring up at ceiling was rigid with ecstasy, Michaela smiled while wiped her mouth with the back of her hand. She looked up asking, "Was that worth waiting for my darling?"

"You could say that," he replied, coming to his senses then quickly bent down pulled up his trousers.

Standing up Michaela adjusted her dress saying, "I'll just go say goodnight to mum and dad, I'll be back soon," spun round and set off to the door.

"What do you mean?" he gasped while rushed to fasten buttons.

"Well, I might as well stay the night with you now," she replied smiled at him.

Gordon set off towards her snapped, "You'll do nothing of the sort, what will the owner think? I'll come with you and insist you go home with them."

"Spoilsport," she moaned, opened the door but Gordon, quickly checked his attire before followed her.

Mr. Barras smiled saying, "Ah, she's here," while watched them walking down the staircase.

"You're here just in time, it's time to leave for home sweetheart," said Michaela's mum smiled at them.

Thank God for that, thought Gordon then respectfully smiled when Michaela kissed him on the cheek.

Mr. Crowther walked up to him and shaking his hand said, "When you get organized we'll arrange a meeting lad."

"My pleasure," replied Gordon.

"By lad," said Mr. Chisholm waving.

"Goodnight all," replied Gordon, watched them leave but with relief smiled thinking, *thank God Michaela didn't stay she could have ruined everything.*

Hearing the main door close, "Right lad, another glass of wine?" asked Mr. Barras.

Gordon respectfully declined saying, "Oh no thanks, I must keep a clear head for in the morning."

"Very wise," he replied frowning.

Next morning, after a quick spruce up, while eating breakfast, Gordon continued his work, however, after an hour, through lack of concentration had a break. Regretting what had happened the previous night even though enjoyed it, however, the only problem was he knew Michaela could return before finished his work then would possibly insist on picking up on their relationship and that was the furthest thing in his mind.

At home, Caroline had informed Gordon's parents of her condition and both were delighted. Colin was especially over the moon and informed her they were calling at the shop that evening for a chat. Later, while discussing Caroline's pregnancy with Jessie, who had a big smile on her face, "I suppose that's made your day?" he asked while sat down.

Raising her eyebrows she replied, "It has, so I think we had better alter our plans now."

"Yes I think we had. I've noticed our Gordon is doing more than he should be and he wants to ease up a bit," said Colin while studied.

"You've soon changed your mind," said Jessie while purposely frowned at him.

"Oh I know, but you know me I've always hated hangers on," he moaned.

When Colin and Jessie did call at Caroline's, they sat in the shop and waited patiently until she finished off her last customer. When she paid, said goodnight and left, Jessie began to sweep up for her asking, "So our Gordon doesn't know yet?"

"Not officially. Obviously I had an idea, called at the doctors and he's confirmed it, but I've found out next door have handed in their notice," Then

Caroline looked at Colin while he put away brushes, scissors and spays asked, "If the owner sells, I wondered if it was possible to buy it. Do you think I could?"

"I don't really know love, I'll ring the account tomorrow morning and let him get on with it, besides our Gordon should have some spare cash to help," he replied seemingly perplexed at all the different scissors.

Grinning Caroline said, "He said he would, but he's such an independent bugger, mind you I am as well."

"And we all know who he gets that from," said Jessie, and laughed while nodding towards Colin.

With half the paintings done, Gordon was pleased and going great guns. The owner was delighted, gave praise every time one was restored and replaced back on the wall. Often staring at them with a great big smile on his face Mt Barras also daily informed his business colleagues of Gordon's progress.

Of course he also informed close friends, and three weeks later, on the Friday evening when Gordon finished the last painting, he felt relieved then suddenly frowned when Mr. Barras informed him he had arranged a big party for Saturday night and most of his friends would attend.

"I must apologize but I cannot stay. Unfortunately I have prior arrangements and it is impossible," replied Gordon purposely lied to save his reputation.

"Oh my boy that is a great shame. There is one particular friend of mine from Norfolk who is especially coming up to appraise your work. He is in the know with the upper echelon, know what I mean son?" he said frowning.

"I do, but it is a matter of urgency, you have my phone number," replied Gordon while washed out brushes and dare not stay in case Michaela turned up with her parents.

"And I will do you justice. Will you be leaving immediately or in the morning?" he asked.

"When I am ready, I shouldn't be long now," replied Gordon, while wrapped brushes in a cloth.

Smiling Mr. Barras asked, "Right then, can I take this one and hang it before you leave, I wish to take a photo of you with them?"

With relief Gordon smiled saying, "Of course, I'll be down in about half an hour."

Chapter 11

Mrs Barras took photos of her husband with Gordon stood in front of three paintings, and with the cheque in his pocket, Gordon heartily shook hands with them both before going out to his car, moaning, "I hope the bugger starts," then beamed a smile when it did.

Waving to Mr. Barras when he set off but feeling relieved as he drove down towards the A1, Gordon craftily smiled knowing he would now avoid Michaela, who wasn't all that bad really; it was her personal habits such as sleeping around with the opposite sex that put him off.

Laughing he said, "She isn't a patch on my girl," and put his foot down to overtake a lorry moaned, "Oh hell, there won't be anything to eat at home and I'm bloody starving."

Arriving there an hour and a half later, Gordon pulled up at the back of the shop and noticed a light on in the kitchen. After locked the car he continued to the back door, tried the handle and found it locked. About to unlock it, Tracy beat him, and opening the door smiled saying, "You've just missed mum and dad."

"Have I? Did she leave me anything to eat?" he asked while glanced over her shoulder, didn't see Peter but noticed a light on in the front room.

While filled the kettle she replied, "No, but I think the fish shops open yet."

"Don't make me one, I'll call at Caroline's first," replied Gordon, turned and walked out.

"Thanks very much," moaned Tracy, watched him for a moment then pulled face of impatience before closed the door after him.

When Gordon pulled up outside Caroline's shop, noticed it all in darkness, he got out of the car and knocked on the door. Staring disappointedly when there was no answer he knocked again. Gordon began to feel apprehensive, then suddenly smiled with relief when the light came on. Caroline stared at the door noticed who it was, and quickly walked to unlock it. Opening it she dived into his arms then kissed him asked, "Have you seen your mum and dad?"

"No, and why?" he asked.

Smiling she replied, "Oh nothing love, have you eaten I'm starving?"

Grinning he replied, "I haven't and I'm the same, get your coat."

Half an hour later, while sat cozy in dining room of a local pub, Caroline asked about his work. Gordon began to inform her then suddenly leant back when interrupted by the waiter. Waiting until he had served them, when he walked away, Gordon carried on, then craftily took the cheque out of his pocket and handed it to her.

When Caroline read it then gasped, "Bloody hell Gordon," but reluctantly passed it back.

"So tomorrow, first thing, it's back to work and get more of my own work churned out, oh hell, I forget our Tracy's at home," he moaned and winced when put the cheque in his pocket.

"She's going home tomorrow afternoon sometime," replied Caroline, picked up her knife and fork began to eat.

Picking up his knife and fork he asked, "How do you know that then?"

"Your mum told me the other day," she replied, and smiled watched him tuck in.

Smirking he asked, "Anything else she told you?"

"No, but I told her plenty," she replied then laughed.

When they finished eating and carefully placed her knife and fork on her plate, while having a drink Caroline asked, "Are you staying at the shop with me tonight?"

"I might as well; I don't fancy listening to our Tracy moaning about what she has and hasn't got all night long. Typical women, it's like listening to a record player," he replied frowning.

"Oh, thanks very much," said Caroline staring at him.

"Sorry I didn't mean it like that, of course I will, it's just that she gets on my nerves. She's never done a day's work in her life and all she does is order you around, always trying to be something she isn't."

Caroline picked up her glass saying, "Right then, let's drink up and go get sorted out."

Frowning he asked, "Will there be enough room in there for two?"

Standing up she smiled saying, "Just about," and winked.

Leaving the car, parked half on the road and kerb outside the shop Caroline unlocked and opened the door. After walked inside and locked it behind them, purposely leaving the light off continued upstairs. Gordon had never been in her room, felt for the light switch, found it, turned it on, and looking round asked, "Is that the bed what David made?"

"Yes, and don't you think he made a very good job," she replied, took off her coat, hung it up behind the door then turned holding out her hand for his.

Gordon took it off, handed it to her and half-smiling sat on the bed looking round moaned, "You were right about there not being a lot of room in here."

"The beds big enough that's all that matters," she replied while undressed.

After Gordon undressed when he got in with her Caroline snuggled up saying, "By the way, I am pregnant."

"You are?" he gasped then quickly sat up banging his head on the cupboards above. Gordon rubbed it groaned, "Bloody hell fire."

Caroline laughed, pulled him down then stared into his eyes asking, "Are you pleased though?"

"Very," he replied, leant over then softly kissed her on the lips.

Next morning, and because it was downstairs, both quickly showered before Janice arrived. Caroline explained they had twelve customers that day and maybe more with odd caller taking a chance in between appointments. "I thought you worked a half day on a Saturday?" he asked.

Smiling she replied, "I need the money, tell you all about it later love."

"Give me a ring when you're done then I'll call and pick you up." Suddenly Gordon looked round when the door opened, then glanced at his watch saying, "Hellfire, I'd better go get cracking myself."

After saying a quick hello to Janice, Gordon kissed Caroline before set off to the car. Waving when he drove off, and ten minutes later, soon as he pulled up round the back of the shop, noticed the van parked so Gordon knew his parents were already there.

Taking his cases out of the boot, Gordon continued inside then left them near the table. Suddenly he spun round when Tracy walked in saying, "I've just made us all a cup of tea."

"Have you?" he asked but stared at her thought she seemed unusually happy. Gordon picked up his cases then cheekily pulled a face at his mum when she walked into the kitchen. Quickly saying, "Hello all," he continued upstairs.

"That's gratitude for you," snapped Tracy while stared at her mum.

"I'll take it up for him when it's ready," said his mum then smiled waited while she passed her a cup. Jessie continued up the stairs continued into his Gordon's studio, but eyed him while placed his cup on his table. Trying to judge his mood she said, "Here you are."

"Thanks mum," he replied, while sorted out brushes.

Jessie walked over and sat on his settee, but watching him thought he seems content enough, decided to test the water saying, "Caroline has told me the good news."

"Caroline told me last night and how long are they staying for downstairs?"

Jessie purposely snapped, "If you mean your sister and Peter, they are coming home with us and staying at our house tonight. They are travelling home to his parent's early tomorrow morning."

"Haven't they anything else better to do?"

"They have because it looks like they have acquired premises in Leeds now, well that's subject to confirmation," she replied, and watched when Gordon began to secure a painting on the easel.

"Good for them," he said while stood back, picked up his pallet then began to select tubes of oils.

While sighing Jessie asked, "Why do you never have a good word for our Tracy?"

"Because she's bone idle that's why. She's all take and no give," snapped Gordon while hurriedly began to apply colours out of tubes onto his palette.

Knowing he was right his mum didn't argue, stood up and watched when he began to paint. Smiling she asked, "I know Caroline is staying here tonight, so when are you going to make an honest woman of her then?"

"We discussed it last night so first, and if possible, we are going to buy the shop next door to hers so she can continue her business. If everything goes well and maybe after my sale, we could start the alterations and what have you," he replied while staring at the frame as if trying to recall his intentions, then began to paint.

Jessie watched him asking, "So does that mean you will live at the side of her shop? I just thought if that's the case why not buy a newer property? It will save a lot of messing about after all time wasted with alterations is money lost."

Staring at her Gordon snapped, "Mum. You know that costs money and I haven't got that much to spare. You are after packing up in here and selling this place means I will be homeless. Anyway go ahead if you want to, really it's nothing to do with me."

"Oh yes it is, you know very well me and your dad aren't getting any younger. And let me tell you this my lad, I want you to help him more often when he's humping furniture about, he's been all moans and groans of late. Let's be fair love he does needs help, he's sixty plus now you know," she replied frowning.

"I will don't worry, now bugger off and let me earn some money," said Gordon then when had changed the subject.

"I've done some braising steak for your dinners, it's in the oven," said Jessie while walked towards the door.

"Is there nothing for afters?" he asked trying not to grin.

"I could say something to that but I won't," she replied, and smirked set off.

Although Gordon had an excellent eye for detail, he wouldn't finish a painting unless was completely satisfied with it. Working to attain a reasonable amount of paintings for his show and although still worked for the auction house to maintain a regular income, his collection was building. His relationship with Caroline was also building and everyone had noticed how very much in love they were.

Every morning Gordon would run Caroline to her shop and every evening he picked her up. After dinner, they would relax together in the front room and make plans for their future before attending to their individual business matters.

While their relationship grew, Jessie did her best to help, knowing they worked hard, so always returned with Colin when he relieved David in the shop. She regularly brought their dinner, would leave it in the oven and then walk round. It wasn't to inspect the house; it was to suit her mood. Jessie would lovingly reminisce, recalled memories in the house and with a grandchild on the way, knew that would make the house complete.

When it was time for home she would leave with Colin, however, Jessie knew they were getting older and regretfully always wished there had been more love between Gordon and Tracy. She could understand the saying, he's more like his dad, or she's more like her mum. However the difference between Gordon and Tracy's attitude, not only towards life in general but other people in the way of respect was vast.

Plans to close the furniture business were forgotten when Tracy, out of the blue, announced they were getting married later that the year. Instantly Gordon was annoyed and although they hadn't officially got engaged, in the back of his mind, if his work and savings allowed, if she accepted, he had planned to marry Caroline about that time.

Not long after, Barbara also announced she was getting engaged, and sat in the front room Saturday night while watching TV, Gordon and Caroline discussed her. "She's just like our Tracy, what one does the other has to," moaned Gordon.

"Gordon, it is up to them," said Caroline, and smiled at his moaning but he seemed content.

"It isn't that love, I know what will happen. They will start that business together and rely on mum and dad for money. I never did, I have never asked them once not even for a penny," he replied while shook his head with disgust.

Caroline asked, "So what?" as if tried to dismiss them, knew he didn't get on with his sister.

Sighing he replied, "Oh sorry love, I know I am moaning on, but she just gets to me, she's all take."

Mainly to change the subject Caroline asked, "So how many paintings have you done now?"

Staring up at the ceiling he replied, "Twenty two."

"And how much are you selling them for? The costing of such art work has always intrigued me," she asked, really was unconcerned, however, tried to keep their conversation going.

"I'm leaving that to the auction house. I have an idea but I want them to compare my work with other artistes first," he replied then stood up.

"Yes I'm tired as well love," said Caroline, stood up then turned off the TV.

Next morning after breakfast, Caroline was in Gordon's studio inspecting the paintings and was impressed, especially with the time he had to do them in. Watching Gordon painting, she pointed said, "I really like that one love," had thought it was a scene from the river near his mums.

"The only problem with round here is bloody pylons, they are everywhere and spoil the scene," he replied while stood back.

Raising her eyebrows she asked, "Do you have to put then in?"

"Not really," he replied while mixed some paint on his pallet.

Walking over to sit on the settee Caroline said, "Well don't and then you won't spoil it."

Gordon studied for a moment, decided to take her advice, and began to adjust saying, "You are supposed to paint factually."

Caroline smiled, stood up and glanced over his shoulder. She watched for a moment saying, "Even photographer's now mask out the worst bits."

Frowning he asked, "I know what you mean love. By the way, when that chap calls on Wednesday I'll arrange a date of the sale. What do you think about Saturday the tenth of December?"

"I think that is spot on," replied Caroline, walked over to the settee and picked up a magazine. She instantly smiled when it was months old, still sat down and began to read.

"Right then, will do," he said, stood back and began studied his work.

While turned a page she asked, "Will you be ready though?"

Gordon studied saying, "Should be, well, near enough."

The following Wednesday, when the chap from the auction room arrived, and even now in later summer he wore the same raincoat and trilby. Glancing round when entered the shop carrying two paintings for him to restore. Gordon welcomed him and eyed them when he leant them against the wall. Not knowing anything about the organization of the sale rooms, Gordon began to arrange the date and time of his sale, asked, "Does that give you enough time to get everything ready in time?"

"Consider it done. Two days before, you will have to bring them all over and get set up over so we can arrange a public viewing on Friday for a sale on Saturday. Meanwhile I'll make sure the place is empty, clean and all ready for you," he replied, while eyeing three paintings Gordon had ready for him.

Assuring him the advertisements would go out immediately, after paid him, the chap arranged to call next week, picked up the paintings and set off to his car. Seeing Gordon was apprehensive about his sale, so before set off, he waved shouting, "Don't worry Gordon, it's all in hand lad."

"I hope so," he replied but did look worried.

Over the next couple of months and to Gordon's surprise, trade at the shop increased twenty five percent. Even Colin was surprised so they reverted back to using a rota for delivering on an evening.

Caroline began showing her pregnancy; however, embarrassment was beginning to wear off now most customers knew. Unfortunately later in the week, she heard the threat that another hairdresser was going to open in the vicinity. It did give her cause for concern and during a slack period discussed it with her aunt.

They didn't come up with an answer, decided their clientele was honest, however, always knew prices mattered most so would cost accordingly and not bother Gordon who was working flat out, so Caroline kept it all to herself.

With a week to go before delivering his paintings, now had twenty six, Gordon called it a day. Feeling apprehensive and running out of inspiration, so over the next two days, he did some painting for the auction house and then decided it was time for a rest.

Although Caroline had contacted the owner next door to her shop, and Colin had arranged a mortgage for her, at this moment it time everything was in limbo as she hadn't heard a thing.

Constantly being informed by his mum, who had seen adverts of his sale in the national evening papers and local press, Gordon was more concerned about Caroline, who visited the doctors that morning. Taking her there he waited room sat nervous quickly looked up when she walked out, noticed a big smile on her face, and then knew everything was alright.

In the car going back to her shop, she informed him, "He said everything was just perfect."

Grinning he asked, "Very good, so does that mean we can have a-bonk tonight?"

"I'll think about it. So are you picking me up later?" she asked, when he pulled up outside her shop.

Pursing his lips he replied, "Of course my love."

"Get out you daft bugger," she said then kissed him.

On Thursday morning before his sale, after dropping Caroline off at the shop and when she kissed him for good luck. "I'm only delivering them and setting up there," he moaned.

"Oh I know, and Saturday is all arranged with Janice, she is looking after the shop so I can go with you," said Caroline while got out then held the car door open.

"You only want to come with me to see how much I make," he said then laughed.

"Too true mate," she replied while closed the door.

Gordon waved when set off, and ten minutes later, arrived at the shop, noticed his dad and David waiting for him. "Come on let's get them loaded up, I haven't seen any of them yet," said Colin before entered the kitchen.

Following him he replied, "You won't until they hang them, they are all covered up."

Half an hour later, with all the paintings in the van and secure, Colin set off to drive them to the auction house. Discussing the sale on the way he asked, "Is it a big place?"

Smiling Gordon replied, "I don't know, I've never been in it."

An hour later, Colin pulled up round the back of the sale room watched Gordon set off inside. The he was met by a tall well dressed chap who wore a light brown dust coat. While shaking his hand he beamed a grin saying, "My name is Mick Simmons and this is going to be a great pleasure my lad."

Looking unsure Gordon asked, "In what way."

"Because it will be the first time we have ever had an artiste in attendance with his paintings, usually all the buggers are dead," replied Mick then heartily laughed.

Two hours later, with his paintings hung all round the auction room; Gordon, now accompanied with his dad, walked round the outside of a restraining rope to inspect them. Mick walked up to them asking, "I think they look well, not too high or low. What do you think mate?"

"They look fine to me mate," said Colin looking rather proud.

"Right then, we have to catalogue a price list, it's just a run off but we must give them out when they enter. Is anyone of them special you want to put into auction, or will it be on a first come first serve basis?" asked Mick then grinned as if knew the reply.

"No auction please, they can do that after I am dead," replied Gordon laughing.

"Right then, we'll start here with this nude. What do you value it at?" he asked, and wrote down a price.

Gordon noticed, and as it was the copy of Caroline's painting, said, "Really it's priceless, however, let's say about fifty pounds."

"I've already put seventy five, so we'll leave it at that," he replied, then smiled when moved onto the next.

Colin was all ears was very impressed and followed when they ambled from one painting to another discussing its value. When they reached the one of the men working in a furnace, "Now then, I class this as most sellable, shall we say two hundred?" asked Mick raising he eyebrows while waiting for a reply.

Frowning Gordon replied, "I think that's too much."

"I certainly don't, it's a very powerful painting and depicts a heavy industrious scene. That was painted from the heart, blood sweat and toil. Very well done lad," he replied, made a note, didn't wait for a reply and carried on to the next.

Colin raised his eyebrows, had mentally totted up the amount while they walked round. Now really appreciated his son's work, at the end, when they all stood near the auctioneer's box, he was amazed when the chap shook Gordon's hand, saying, "Right then tomorrow if you could be here, say just after lunchtime, your presence will keep the punters in and a lot will wait just to meet you."

"I will, so see you tomorrow," replied Gordon, and with his dad, they walked out to the van.

Chapter 12

All the way home, Colin chatted enthusiastically, was none stop about the chap and some of the estimates of Gordon's paintings. "All in a day's work," said Gordon grinning.

"Just let's hope the public turn up and buy something that's the main thing," said his dad studying.

"It's just luck dad. Some will turn up to view, sort of assess me and some will buy as investment," said Gordon glancing out of the window but had to smile, had never known his dad take as much interest.

Jessie was waiting for them when they arrived home, and while Colin informed her about the sale, to keep out of their way, Gordon went into the shop to David. "Hello lad, all done and set up?" he asked while dusting furniture.

Gordon smiled could hear his parents chatting however, replied, "Yes, and it's been very interesting."

"Very good lad, oh and are you making the deliveries with your dad tonight? Mind you I could go with him then he can drop me off home after," asked David, and smiled walked towards him.

"As you wish, and what's Barbara doing with our Tracy, have they all sorted it out now?" asked Gordon before glanced at his watch.

"More or less, they've bought a place in Leeds, going to refurbish it and plan to open about February. I don't think our Barbara is getting married though. We've all been to see the place, its three stories and massive. Tracy and Peter are having the top floor and they are welcome to it there's no lift," he replied, and smiled while wrote out receipts.

"I thought she would have had more sense seeing as she's pregnant, anyway I might as well go pick up Caroline now, see you later," said Gordon then waved when walked out.

"Dinner is in the oven for later," shouted his mum, watched him continue to the back door.

"Right mum, see you later," said Gordon before closed the door after him.

When he pulled up outside the shop, Gordon noticed two women had curlers in their hair, and were sat in chairs reading magazines. Continuing inside he said, "Hello love."

"Hello and at the top of the stairs are two bags, I'll take them home with us," said Caroline, smiled and kissed him when he walked by.

At the top on the stairs Gordon noticed the bags, and a magazine. Picking it up he sat on the top step began to read it while waited. Hearing a noise, he looked down, smiled at Caroline, and quietly said, "I'll wait up here love."

Half an hour later, Caroline walked up the stairs saying, "All done love," passed him and continued inside for her coat. She put it on asking, "Will you drop Janice off on the way love?"

Standing he replied, "Of course."

On the way to Janice's house, Caroline explained they were really busy tomorrow with loads of customers. Gordon raised his eyebrows saying, "Don't forget Saturday."

"That's why we are doing extra tomorrow, and then I can cope on my own," said Janice frowning.

Caroline smiled saying, "Sorry."

"Not to worry it's only a one off," said Janice, and when he stopped outside her house, opened the car door.

After waving to her, on their way home Caroline chatted about some of her customers. When they reached home, Gordon took the bags inside while Caroline unlocked and opened the door, waited then locked it after them saying, "Mum said there's some dinner in the oven love," before carried on into the front room.

"Thank goodness I'm starving," she moaned before opened the oven door.

Fifteen minutes later, after checked messages, orders, and instructions from his mum, while they ate, Gordon explained the layout of the gallery then how his paintings had been hung. Explaining, "We priced them together and it was marvelous. The only one we were miles apart on was that scene in the foundry the appraiser said it was worth a lot more."

"That is a very good painting though," said Caroline smiling at his enthusiasm.

"Anyway about tomorrow lunchtime he said I have to be there only for an hour or so, it keeps their interest. God knows why?" said Gordon while finished his meal.

"What time have we to be there on Saturday?" she asked before placed her knife and fork on the plate.

"It opens at nine and we have to be there half an hour before," he replied.

"Very good, come on let's wash up love and I must say I am really looking forward to tomorrow," said Caroline then stood up began to clear the table.

"That makes a change you helping," he moaned while carried their plates to the sink.

"Watch it pal, else you'll do them all yourself," she replied then laughed.

That night while laid in bed, Caroline felt proud of Gordon, when he had worked his guts out knowing it was for them. Although feeling slightly disappointed when it would be ideal, she had not yet heard anything about the property next door to her shop.

Being an only child, Caroline couldn't understand why Gordon nattered on about Tracy and put it down to brother and sister jealousy. She had only met Tracy a few times and though she had never said anything wrong in front of her, Caroline changed her opinion about her, especially when in company, noticed she hung onto her boyfriends arm and falsely smiled turning any conversation towards their future exploits.

Next morning, they rose early and had a quick breakfast. Later, Gordon dropped Caroline off at the shop and both waved when he set off to Leeds. Feeling chirpy, he looked forwards to the day and was in for a big surprise when arrived early for the viewing of his paintings.

After parking the car, Gordon walked inside the auction house and suddenly stopped dead when instantly inundated for his autograph. Looking embarrassed and overwhelmed, while signed as many as he could, Gordon grimaced when noticed a queue of people extending round the gallery then occasionally smiled when asked to pose for a photograph.

Two hours later, when the amount of people in the queue had reduced but still with the sale room half full of people noisily chatting away, Mick saved the day by politely explaining that Gordon had other work to do, slipped his arm around his shoulder and escorted him away.

When the crowd seemed to settle down and brows his paintings, half an hour later, after finishing a cup of tea, Gordon decided to join them. Watching an elderly chap staring at one painting, he sauntered over and stood by his side. When he asked for criticism, Gordon was taken by surprise when the chap turned then suddenly snapped, "And why do you ask me?"

Noticing his spectacles slide down and were now perched on the end of his nose. Trying to refrain from smiling, Gordon maintained a serious expression replied, "It is essential for my future work."

"Well my boy, who am I to criticize? If I like someone's work I buy it as an investment, if I don't I walk out and I'm still here aren't I?" he replied then heartily laughed.

Gordon raised his eyebrows asking, "Ah but have you bought anything yet?"

"Good lord, chance would be a fine thing," he replied while turned away repositioning his spectacles.

Gordon pulled a face didn't understand his reply then politely asked to be excused and sauntered away. Walking over he stood at the back of one elderly couple who admired the copy of Caroline's painting. When heard the woman say, "That is created with taste, what excellent brush work." Gordon again raised his eyebrows, sidled away but quickly stopped when asked by a well dressed middle aged woman for his autograph.

Fifteen minutes later, while chatting to Mick, Gordon noticed around thirty people left who were just ambling round. Deciding to return home, he politely informed Mick who heartily shook his hand then slapped him on the back. Gordon smiled while carried on outside to his car. Sitting inside and feeling really pleased with the reception he had received, very much looked forward to the following day.

On his way home, Gordon recalled some of the compliments and really couldn't wait to inform Caroline. First, he called home and of course his mum and dad had waited for him. After informed them the news, "Me and your dad are going, we'll be there about two in the afternoon though we can't leave David with too much to do," said his mum while made him a cup of tea.

His dad grinned when asked, "Do we get any discount if we buy anything?"

"Bugger off," replied Gordon while sat down then smirked.

Frowning at him he snapped, "And you can bugger off as well lad. I'll remember that when you want to borrow the van again."

Gordon set off to pick up Caroline at the shop for six thirty, and when he did she looked buggered. After helped in the shop clearing away, when reached home he began to prepare their tea while she had a quick shower. Putting their plates on the table when she returned downstairs, he sat down saying, "Here you are love."

Smiling at him she replied, "Thanks love."

Although while eating and looking a picture of health, Gordon put Caroline's lack of conversation down to overwork then decided to ask her if possible to reduce her hours.

After they ate, Gordon washed up while Caroline sat in the front room watching TV. When he finished, made her a drink of tea and carried two cups returned and sat with her. "Thanks," said Caroline taking one.

"Are we having an early night love? We have to be there early in the morning," he asked before had a drink.

Smiling at him she replied "Might as well love and I must say I'm really looking forward to it."

Laughing he said, "So am I. I just hope the punters fetch their check-books with them," then suddenly looked round when the phone rang. Gordon stood up, walked over, picked up the receiver and leaning on the sideboard said, "Hello."

"Oh hello there, it's Mr. Hammond from the auction house and sorry to disturb you at this time of night," he said sounding very chirpy.

Gordon wondered why he had rung asking, "What can we do for you?"

"I want to know if you have any more paintings for your sale, all these you have here have been sold," he replied then heartily laughed.

"What?" Gordon shouted.

Caroline wondered what the matter was. She quickly stood up, went to him, and placing her hand on his chest mouthed, "What's wrong?"

Gordon seemed shocked and shook his head as if meant nothing. "Sorry no, all that are complete are there, and what do you mean they are all sold, the sale isn't until tomorrow?"

"We have been having offers all day long lad and shortly after you left five chaps came in. They looked real toffs so I watched them while they walked round. Well, about an hour later, they came up to me making offers. Some I couldn't refuse were way above the odds. It's all on record for you lad and with other offers I've had, well, if I'd have known I would have put them in an auction now, we would have made a bomb," he replied then heartily laughed again.

Caroline, with her head near the receiver strained to hear. She suddenly smiled when Gordon said, "That means a guaranteed sell out then?"

Laughing he replied, "It sure does lad, so get some more knocked out quick."

"I'll try, maybe later next year, so we'll see you tomorrow then," said Gordon, now had a big smile on his face.

"Right lad will do," he replied then replaced the receiver.

Caroline walked towards the sofa had grasped their conversation saying, "That is great news."

"I never thought that would happen in a million years," said Gordon as they both sat down.

"Does that mean I will have to pose in the nude again?" she asked lightly.

"It looks very much like it," he replied then laughed.

"I dare you to do when of me when I'm showing more, even especially when I'm nearly due?" she asked while sticking out her belly.

"I'll do it know if you want? I have a vivid imagination," he replied, raised his eyebrows and grinned.

"We know you have, so come on up to bed, now" she said pulling his arm.

Next morning at seven o'clock, Colin and Jessie knocked on the back door. Gordon was barefoot and with just his trousers on, opened the door asking, "What's up?"

Jessie smirked before pushed him aside then continued inside saying, "We don't want you sleeping in on such a special day like today do we?"

"Get the kettle on," said Colin while followed.

"You can put it on yourself, while I get showered," replied Gordon, closed the door then walked past them continued upstairs.

Caroline was already in the shower so Gordon sat on the bed and waited before decided to prepare his clothes. When she came out he went in, and thirty minutes later, both dressed and ready for the occasion walked downstairs.

When Gordon and Caroline entered the kitchen, Jessie smiled with pride while she poured out the tea. Not only did she think they seemed the perfect couple, both looked fit and well. She could see a love between them, gestured to the cups saying, "Here you are."

"Toast won't be a minute," said Colin waiting for it to pop up.

While sat down Gordon joked, "Its nice having your own servants."

"Don't push your luck lad, you're washing up," snapped his mum staring at him.

Eventually all sat round the table, Caroline was intrigued and pleased by the way his parents fussed them, was not used to it. She had to smile when Jessie asked, "And if there any photographers there, wait while we turn up, I want my picture in the paper as well."

"Give over mum," moaned Gordon before finished his toast.

Colin had a drink of tea before said, "Anyway we have decided which one we want."

"Your too late mate they are all sold," replied Gordon then grinned.

"Never," gasped his mum.

"They have. Mr. Hammond rang last night from the auction house last night and told him," said Caroline was smiling with pride.

Colin looked gob smacked saying, "Well bugger me."

Jessie folded her arms, and frowned said, "Well now, that throws a different light on the matter."

"In what way mum?" asked Gordon then smirked was going to pinch a slice of toast from Caroline, but she playfully smacked his hand.

"I mean with the shop," replied Jessie while inspected a piece of toast before picked it up.

Colin noticed moaning, "What's up now isn't it to your usual satisfaction?"

Gordon stared at his mum asking, "Never mind that, so why? What are you doing with the shop now?"

Staring back at him she replied, "We can't sell it now can we? When they find out where you live they'll be calling in here to see your work."

"But I haven't any more to see," he moaned.

"Better get cracking with some then," said his dad looking pleased.

"And wait for us while we get there, we'll have to come in a taxi because the bus doesn't stop near there," said Jessie then ate her toast.

"What's up with walking from the bus station?" asked Gordon then laughed.

"It's a long way and besides we have to leave the van for David haven't we," replied his dad staring at him.

"I never thought of that," he replied.

Colin chuckled saying, "Mind you, you won't need it to bring paintings back if they are all gone."

Ten minutes later, Jessie washed up while Gordon and Caroline put on their coats. When they walked into the kitchen; she turned, smiled and kissed them both. Colin kissed Caroline but nodded to Gordon saying, "Look after him."

"I will," she replied, and smiled when they went out to the car.

All waving as they set off, once on the main road, Gordon smiled asking, "You're looking forward to this aren't you?"

"I am especially with you taking me out to lunch as well. Its ages since I had a Saturday off," replied Caroline before glanced out of the window.

Gordon smiled, looked forward to the day even more so when he didn't have to worry if his work had sold. His main problem was providing more, knew he had the time to do it and was going to restrict himself with commissions, especially with a child on the way.

Fifty minutes later, Gordon pulled up round the back of the auction house and parked the car. After locked it, when they walked inside the auction room were greeted by a different chap. wearing a fawn flat cap, dark brown kipper tie, light brown smock and dark brown trousers. Looking very jovial he held out his hand saying, "I'm Albert Speight the auctioneer."

"Pleased to meet you," said Gordon shaking his hand then introduced Caroline.

"Pleased to meet you my dear, and if you'll come this way we'll have a drink of tea first, it's all prepared," he said gesturing the way.

Chatting about some of the sales, in-between drinking tea, when Albert mentioned some of the individuals who purchased his paintings he stated a Mr. Chisholm had bought the copy of Caroline. Gordon suddenly frowned, noticed Caroline watched him but half heartedly smiled when Albert said, "He rang and when I informed him half were already sold, he said, hold the fort I'll be over in two hours," then laughed.

"I have done some work for him," said Gordon, now looking serious had instantly thought of complications, such as his daughter.

Caroline studied before asked, "Didn't you work for him last?"

"No, err, the one before, they are a really nice family," replied Gordon, purposely drank up and began to gather their cups.

"Leave them lad. Anyway, by hell, you should have seen his face when I said he couldn't take the painting with him. Really mad he was, I think he's calling for it at four," replied Albert and smiled while took Caroline's empty cup.

Gordon tried to smile at Caroline thought, *I hope to hell he comes on his own.* Unfortunately she recognized the half heartedness in it and began to study.

When the doors opened to the general public, half an hour later, with more than a forty folk walking slowly round, they seemed to diligently inspect every painting. About eleven o'clock and now nearly half full, Gordon stood near the auctioneer's box, noticed Caroline looking slightly bored as she looked around. Albert walked up to them saying, "If I was you, I'd go have lunch about twelve. Round here people tend to do their shopping first and brows later, it should get really busy about one o'clock."

"It's a lot quieter then yesterday," said Gordon pulling a face was unsure.

"That's usually the case. About two o'clock, I'll have one of my men go round and put sold signs on them all that will look good for the press. They should be here about half past to make the evening papers so we might as well make hay while the sun shines," he replied looking round.

Caroline winked Gordon saying, "We might as well go now love, I'm hungry."

Gordon knew she was bored said, "Come on then love," and smiled helped her stand up.

Outside the auction house, on foot, they continued up the main street and found a little café. Both glanced inside through the window, noticed an empty table near, continued inside and sat down. A waitress came over, politely waited until they read the menu, and smiled when took their order. When she walked away, once again they discussed their day, "It been really boring so far," moaned Gordon while looking round.

"What difference does it make, you've sold out," said Caroline smiling at him.

Gordon began to rabbit on about what have might have been, what he should have done or could have then moaned he should have been better prepared. Knowing he was wittering on Gordon then suddenly went quiet saying, "Well, it's true," while sat back when the waitress served them.

Caroline picked up her knife and fork, began to eat then stopped saying, "Thank you for today love."

Gordon picked up his knife and fork, and waiting until the waitress walked away said, "One thing that bothers me is if that Mr. Speight wants commission on the sales. I never thought to ask him."

Caroline laughed now knew he was nervous then staring into his eyes said, "Don't be so tight Gordon."

"It's alright saying that but sometimes it can be as much as thirty percent," he gasped frowning at her.

"Never," she gasped.

"Oh yes, that's why I've never bothered in the past. Some of these buggers can rip you off big-time," he moaned then looked round, thought someone might have heard him.

An hour later, when Gordon and Caroline returned to the auction room they were surprised when it was nearly full. Mr. Speight waved them over and when they walked up to him, he smiled saying, "The press will be here in ten minutes, I've had sold signs put on three quarters of the paintings already to make it look good."

"Very good," said Gordon before looked round for a chair so Caroline could sit down.

"It is lad and listen to me I wouldn't make it too long before you have another sale. Always try and make money while the sun shines," he replied rubbing his hands together before walked off.

Gordon noticed a chair near the auctioneer's box, reached over and turned it for Caroline to sit down. Then instantly watched with pride while he began to sign autographs and shake hands with passers-by.

Caroline suddenly frowned, when noticed Gordon stared at the entrance. Wearing a tight red mini skirt, and low cut black top, a young flashy brunette walked inside with what looked like her parents. Michaela's face suddenly lit up. She dashed over to Gordon, threw her arms round her neck and gave him a smacker of a kiss.

"Hello my boy," said her dad, grabbed hold of his hand and shook it while Michaela still hung onto him.

Michaela was gazing into Gordon's eyes when her mum leant round her, reached out and shook his hand saying, "Hello Gordon, we hoped you would be here."

Caroline was annoyed and stared at them, especially when they blocked her view to Gordon as if ignoring her. Gordon tried to introduce her, thought it might put them off but unfortunately Michaela began to drag away shouting, "Come on darling show me round?"

When Gordon stood his ground, "Go on my lad she's been waiting for this for weeks, and watch her she's still after a ring on her finger," said her dad then heartily laughed slapped him on the back.

Caroline stared at them and then looked at Gordon when Michaela's mum moved in between and blocked her view. Suddenly she stared and was incensed with anger, when Michaela kissed him and laughed heartily shouting, "Come on lover boy," began to drag him away, reached down and nipped his arse.

"She's a bugger is that," said her dad and heartily laughed again while linked her arm in her mums, and then both watched when they disappeared into the crowd.

Caroline was gutted; slowly she stood up then set off towards the exit of the auction room. It was obvious Gordon and that woman knew each other very well by the way they behaved. Fuming with anger she and marched up the main road, suddenly noticed a taxi and flagged it down. When it stopped, she got inside and trying very hard to restrain tears informed him where to go.

"Right love," he replied then set off. Caroline stared out of the window began to shake with emotion. For the second time with Gordon, her world had fell apart and with her lips trembling with emotion she glanced down at her belly, rubbed it but suddenly wanted to scream out with anger.

Through the crowd, Gordon tried to see Caroline, and every time he set off, Michaela pulled him the opposite way. Being constantly asked for autographs he duly obliged then suddenly stared at the door, when a TV crew walked inside.

While signing more catalogues, Gordon noticed they spoke with Mr. Chisholm who pointed in his direction. They walked over, began to introduce themselves and very orderly, quickly arranged an interview in the centre of the room.

People around them, including Michaela, who eventually shuffled forward, managed to get her arm on his, had a permanent smile on their faces. Unfortunately Gordon noticed, and thought it all false.

Chapter 13

Soon as Caroline reached home, she paid her fare before continued into the house. David was there and informed her Colin and Jessie had set off to the auction rooms. Suddenly he grimaced knowing she was upset by the state of her face and asked what the matter was. "I was not feeling well and had to return," she replied, turned and quickly set off upstairs.

"How's it going on for Gordon, has he sold up?" he asked watching her.

"Oh yes Gordon's fine," she replied while continued into the bedroom.

In their bedroom Caroline packed what clothes she had and suddenly cringed had let the taxi go knew she couldn't manage to carry all her bags. After taking some downstairs into the kitchen she returned for others then glanced into the shop noticed it was empty. Quietly she approached David asking if he would run her to her shop. "Of course my love, and are you sure there's nothing wrong?" he asked, had noticed her face looked strained.

Picking up two bags she asked, "I'm sure, but could we go now?"

David carried the rest, put them in the van then drove to her shop. Noticing Caroline was quiet while stared out of the window; obviously he thought she didn't want to talk, so kept quiet.

When David pulled up outside the shop, they got out, waited until Caroline unlocked and opened the shop door carried her bags inside. Leaving them on the floor David said, "I'll go get the rest for you love," turned and walked out.

Caroline was on the phone when he returned. She looked at him saying, "Thank you very much David."

Frowning again he asked, "It's my pleasure love, but are you sure you're alright?"

"I'm okay thanks," she replied trying to smile.

"See you later then love," he said while continued outside, got in the van and sighed because knew she wasn't.

Caroline waited until he drove off, began to explain to Janice what had gone off. Unfortunately Janice didn't believe her snapped, "I'm calling round."

"Don't bother, I want to be on my own," replied Caroline then sobbed out loud.

Sounding annoyed Janice snapped, "You can't stay there in your condition."

"I have nowhere else, have I?" shouted Caroline then slammed the receiver down. Picking up two bags, she carried them upstairs, dropped them on the floor, turned, flopped on her bed and cried her eyes out.

In the auction house, after the TV interview, Gordon was pestered by the press. Constantly he glanced to where Caroline was sat, and when the crowd dispersed, noticed her chair empty, he stared thought, *oh hell, am I in trouble now.*

Michaela tugged his arm, and smiled asked, "Are we going to our hotel now my darling?"

"No, I have to go home," he replied, while still scanned the room for Caroline.

Staring at him she shouted, "What's the matter with you now?"

Staring into her eyes he asked, "Did you notice that girl that was sat near me?"

"No, and besides what difference does it make?" she asked while slightly backed off thought he was angry.

"Well, that girl is my fiancée," he replied then turned and walked off.

Michaela stared as he approached the auctioneer's box. "Gordon?" shouted Albert.

"Did you see where Caroline went?" he asked.

"No lad, and by the way, a Mr. Chisholm has informed me that at the Griffin hotel he's organized a party for you tonight," he replied looking well pleased.

Gordon spun round and while walking towards the exit shouted, "Tell him to go get fucked. I'm off now; see you later in the week."

"Pardon," gasped Albert looking gob smacked.

When Gordon walked outside, his mum and dad were walking in. "Is everything going alright?" asked Colin grinning at him.

"Is it hell, Caroline's buggered off," he replied while continued past them.

Jessie followed him to his car asking, "Hang on a minute. What do you mean buggered off?"

"I mean just that, one of the blokes I painted for, his daughter came here mouthing and she's cocked it all up," he replied while unlocked the door then got inside.

"Oh Gordon," moaned his mum.

"I'm off to try and find her, see you later," he said starting the engine then drove off in haste.

Colin partially heard, continued up to her asking, "What's he say love?"

"Come on, I'll tell you inside," she replied before slipped her arm in his.

When Gordon pulled up at the back of the shop, David pulled alongside of him. Waved for him to wait he got out to inform him Caroline had called earlier. When he explained that had taken her to her shop and she had bags with her. "Thanks," said Gordon then reversed out.

Ten minutes later, pulling up outside her shop, Gordon got out and knocked on the door. Impatiently waiting he knocked again and again. With his heart pounding fifty to the dozen, when no one answered, he was about to go when Caroline walked inside, continued to the door and unlocked it. Staring at him she asked, "Yes? What do you want?"

"Please let me explain my love?" he asked then grimaced at the state of her face.

"No, not anymore, I said it before, that was your last chance Gordon," she replied.

Quietly, he asked, "Can I come inside please? I think at least I'm allowed an explanation?"

"You bloody well can't. That's it Gordon, it's all over and done with. I know it will be like this all the time now, so please go and never call here again," she replied, closed the door then locked it.

Gordon watched her walk towards the back room. Slowly he turned, went to his car, and sat inside moaning, "And what a great day this has turned out to be," then stared the engine, and carefully drove off because wanted to burst into tears.

An hour later, inside his kitchen eating beans on toast, Gordon looked up when his mum and dad returned. Jessie stared at him asking, "Did you find Caroline?"

Quietly, he replied, "Yes, she's at her shop."

Colin pulled a face asking, "Is she alright?"

"Upset but fine," replied Gordon, sounded impatient.

His mum was running out of patience with his coolness snapped, "Well at least sound bothered."

"I bloody well am, she's having my kid isn't she?" he asked staring at her.

"Do you know? All your life you have never shown any emotion towards anyone and what for I just don't know why. Sometimes you're too bloody cold for my liking," she moaned then quickly stood up.

Looking up at her he asked, "And what's that supposed to mean?"

"Come on Colin lets go," replied Jessie, and set off to the door.

"That's your answer for everything, isn't it?" shouted Gordon, now seemed angry.

"If you are after an argument lad you can have one," growled Jessie then purposely glared before walked out. Colin gestured to Gordon to keep quiet, followed her and closed the door after them.

When they left for home, Gordon, now used to Caroline being with him was again on his own and instantly he felt uneasy. Looking lonely and lost he day-dreamed stared into space. Bewildered at the quietness in the house this unnerved him so he went upstairs into his studio. Gordon stared at Caroline's painting and sat on the settee. With the elations and excitement of the day now gone, he was bitterly disappointed. When his emotions took over, he bowed his head in his hands and cried his eyes out. Knowing for sure he had now lost Caroline, what made it worse was that getting to know her better over these last couple of months he adored her.

Wiping his eyes on his sleeve, he stood up, and stared at her painting whispered, "I know I've blown it and I know you won't return. I'm just so very sorry my love."

At eight o'clock, and now feeling distraught, Gordon decided to drive round to Caroline's shop again. Making up his mind that if he could talk to her and explain his side of the story she might understand. However, when he did, there was no answer and after fifteen minutes of banging on her door, eventually gave up.

On his way home, Gordon suddenly made his mind up and diverted to the off-license. Very much hoping that getting drunk would ease the pain, really knew it wouldn't but it least it would make him sleep.

Sunday morning, his mum and dad called at eleven, had brought him some lunch. When Gordon opened the door, staring at his state Jessie tutted moaning, "Good grief have you been drinking?"

"What else have I to do," he snarled, turned and walked upstairs.

Jessie followed and watched him before put his dinner in the oven. She began to make them a drink of tea then sat at the table with Colin discussing him. "I'll ring Caroline in the morning on the pretext about the shop next door to her and see what she has to say," said Colin then had a drink.

"Don't you go putting any pressure on her," snapped Jessie stared at him.

"I won't bloody hell, but I will him when he comes down," he replied while nodding upstairs.

Five minutes later, Gordon walked into the kitchen, and while poured a cup of tea Colin watched him said, "Right then lad, come on sit down and tell us all about it."

"What the hell for?" he moaned.

Colin purposely stressed the severity of the situation shouting, "Because if I am going to be a granddad I want to be able to see the child."

"And the same here," said Jessie in agreement.

Reluctantly Gordon sat with them then reluctantly informed them what had happened with Michaela. Jessie stared at him snapped, "You should have had more bloody sense."

"Give over mum," he said then stood up.

"I haven't done with you yet," said Colin staring at him.

"Why?" asked Gordon while poured out another cup of tea.

"Because you have upset all our bloody plans again that's why lad," he snapped.

"Oh have I? So go on then, for what it's worth you might as well unravel them now," moaned Gordon before sat down.

Colin and Jessie between them explained they had helped Tracy to buy their apartment same as David and Doreen had done with Barbara. "I thought you might have," said Gordon and smirked while held a cup in his hands.

"The point was we didn't want you all falling out over money when anything happens to us. So we agreed to help them and said she could have our house. You could have the shop and stay here, and as we thought with Caroline," said Jessie staring at him.

Raising his eyebrows he asked, "So you gave her money and your house?"

"Yes, so you have the business, the shop with this house and David's house. It's all equally valued," said Colin while read his face because knew he wasn't his usual self.

Quietly, Gordon replied, "Mind you, it's a good job really."

Jessie smiled saying, "And we are off to sunny Spain again."

"Thanks," said Gordon then finished his tea.

"So is that all acceptable to you?" asked Colin while rest back in his chair.

"On one condition, the workshop wants repairs to the roof and the shop front wants painting. So do all that, and the answer is yes," replied Gordon, watched his dad but thought he seemed over relaxed and couldn't understand why.

Colin stood up, and wondering why he hadn't barted said, "Right then, let's be off, we'll call at David's and let him know the news."

"You could rent his house out and make a bit of profit there," said Jessie smiling.

Gordon leant on the table snapped, "Leave off mum I'm not in the mood at the moment."

Jessie raised her eyebrows because knew the reason why, and soon after they left Gordon washed up. Studying because knew he could ring Caroline, or even call at her shop during the day; however, fearing her wrath in front of witnesses didn't relish it.

Now the nights were drawing in, he decided to chance seeing her on an evening while passing the shop. In other words taking the coward's way out, if there was no one in, he would call, however, more often than not, there was.

The following Monday afternoon, Colin rang Caroline. Janice answered and said she said she was upstairs resting. "It is very important," he stressed, did want to speak with her.

"Honest Mr. Mathews she told me not to disturb her under any circumstances," she replied.

"Really I wanted to have a word about that place next door to her, I'm calling at the accountants in the morning and may need a signature," he replied, hoping to tempt her to the phone.

"We had a word about that last night and she said she wasn't going to bother now. Caroline's moving back in with me this afternoon," she replied.

"Oh, well, tell her I rang won't you?" he asked while frowned knowing he had more phone calls to make, but with explanations.

"I will," she replied then replaced the receiver.

Tuesday morning, Gordon walked into the shop began dusting furniture. His parents had gone to help Tracy and Barbara and he deliberated about their intentions. Sarcastically smiling he moaned, "I suppose I can't complain really."

Later while rearranged furniture, he thought about painting had again put it on hold. Knowing he could do some on a night, this would make a long day for him. Gordon suddenly looked up when a middle aged couple walked in looked round. Smiling he asked, "Hello there and what can I do for you?"

That night it felt strange to Gordon when he loaded the van to make the deliveries hadn't done it for ages. Sales wise he had a decent day, unfortunately he now had all the work to do on his own.

Setting off, Gordon decided to drive by Caroline's shop after made the last drop just to see if she was in. Unfortunately she wasn't so again carried on to the off-license, only this time didn't buy two bottles, bought two cases.

From that day on Gordon's drinking habit increased and his mum regularly frowned, noticed empty bottles in the bin when called at lunchtime. She made sure his dad noticed before they carried on into the kitchen to leave his dinner in the oven. Colin's first job was to check the books. Unfortunately the only trouble was, second-hand furniture sales were dwindling fast, and knowing Gordon couldn't repair any, he began to worry.

Over the next two weeks, done in his spare time, with three industrial scenes paintings finished, Gordon hung them in the shop to sell and was pleasantly surprised when did sell two. Suddenly he thought about another sale, had received a cheque from the auction house and banked it. Unfortunately the spin off, expecting people calling at the shop to enquire about more paintings, had never materialized, however, he often moaned, "At least I've a roof over my head."

Having saved press cuttings his mum gave him and kept them in a scrap book, however, Gordon never saw himself on TV. After adjusted the level of a hanging painting he moaned, "It looks like I will always be a second hand man."

Jessie became more concerned about Gordon's drinking habit and often moaned him about it. In the end she gave up, knew he might retaliate and drink more. Instead she encouraged Colin to begin the renovations, so she could spend more time at the shop, just to keep an eye on him.

The trouble was, Colin's health was deteriorating fast and although he had never mentioned retiring, she was going to make him the following year.

The same could be said of Gordon, because over the next three months and even though he occasionally wandered off and intermittently painted in his studio, Colin had noticed Gordon began to look more than his age while helped him with the renovations to the shop.

Gordon had purposely reduced his drinking because his mum was regular in attendance and he would often lapse into silence when thought of Caroline. However, when they nearly finished painting the outside of the shop and houses, including renovating the shop sign, Gordon decided not to pass Caroline's shop again, had decided that if she wanted him she knew where he lived.

They had worked hard including Gordon, and his mum thought it was a blessing, regularly made them all dinner, so knew he was being fed properly.

Friday night while making the last delivery, Gordon changed his mind, drove slowly past Caroline's shop noticed it empty and suddenly stopped dead. Getting out of the van he stared through the shop window then stepped back to glance up at a for sale notice above the door. His heart felt like a lead weight while slowly got back in the van, turned round and drove straight round to Janice's house. On his way Gordon moaned, "I know I should have called here ages ago. Oh bloody hell, I hope she's alright."

Reaching there, again he stopped dead and stared at her house. With no lights on or curtains in the windows, Gordon got out, walked up the path and banged on the door. When there was no answer, he went to the room window, stared inside and noticed it was empty. With his heart beating like hell with disappointment, Gordon spun round and stared at next door, noticed a light on, and set off towards it.

After knocked, the door opened slightly, had a chain on to restrict it. An elderly woman peeped through the crack asking, "Yes?"

Gordon tried to smile not wanting to scare her asked, "Could you tell me where Janice has gone to? She lived next door to you."

"I don't know love, I didn't know her all that well," she replied then closed the door and locked it.

"Oh my good God," he moaned while set off to the van. Gordon was gutted and now knew that was the end. In the back of his mind, he always hoped they would get back together, especially with her expecting his child.

Sitting inside the van, he closed the door and with tears in his eyes stared down the street. Gordon started the engine, slowly set off moaning, "I bet the only time I see her now is if she wants some money for the kid."

What he didn't know was his mum felt really guilty when fount out Caroline was selling up but was under orders from her not to inform Gordon under any circumstances. Jessie agreed but pleaded with her to stay but she wouldn't, however, when in secret, Caroline moved back to Sheffield, it hit Jessie hard now knew she would never see her grandchild.

Chapter 14

Over the next twelve months, Gordon carried on painting and unfortunately to his disgust the economic climate was changing again. In every newspaper or while watching the local news on the TV someone somewhere was threatening to come out on strike.

Gordon couldn't care less, decided to advertise and rent out David's old house because takings were dwindling fast. He was also loosing concentration quickly when painting, decided to give it a rest and instead tried to renovate an old table, but made it worse so gave up.

David occasionally called to help, but it was a full-time job renovating furniture and he didn't have the spare time with helping Barbara in Leeds. He also didn't have the inclination, was now past retirement age, so reluctantly Gordon decided to paint again and with the intention of having another sale, cracked on and so far had done another five.

The following week, same as before, Gordon brought his easel downstairs into the shop and painted until customers came in. This did help increase his production but by Wednesday lunchtime, made up his mind phoned in an advert to the local press to rent out David's old house stipulating it was for a professional single person, didn't want a family living there because of the noise.

Gordon suddenly stared out of the window when a van reversed and stopped knowing it was his dad and David returned from a sale, but when Colin walked inside the kitchen he looked terrible and had to sit down. "Have a rest dad, I'll get them," said Gordon then helped David.

With all the furniture in the workshop, David began to examine a table saying, "I've decided to call up one day a week from now on and prepare some furniture for you Gordon, it's only fair my lad."

"Thanks and what's been up with dad?"

David smiled when replied, "Same as me lad, its called old age."

With no application's to rent the house and with the business just ticking over, two weeks later, Gordon received a phone call from his mum. She was upset and he tried to calm her, was suddenly stunned to silence when she said his dad had collapsed while in Leeds. Calling to the bank he outside fell on the causeway and had been rushed into hospital.

"I'll be over in two minutes to pick you up," he said then slammed down the receiver. Gordon dashed into the shop, locked the door. Dashed upstairs and closed the windows. Putting on his coat while ran downstairs, he grabbed his keys off the sideboard, quickly locked the back door after him and ran to his car.

Setting off in haste, however seeing a police car on the way, impatiently Gordon slowed down. Outside his mums she was waiting for him then they set off to the hospital. On arrival both were quickly ushered into a side room to be informed, Colin had passed away. Jessie fell into Gordon's arms, and he hugged her while she sobbed her heart out. With tears streaming from his eyes, Gordon asked the nurse if they could see him.

Doreen and David arrived and after been informed the news, all together, and heartbroken they followed the nurse into a side ward where Colin lay. "Oh my God, he looks so peaceful," said Jessie, walked up to Colin and took hold of his hand.

With tears in his eyes Gordon was bewildered and slipped his arm around his mums shoulder. Hugging her he said, "At least he didn't suffer mum."

"Since we have been fourteen we have never been apart, did you know that?" she asked then sobbed out loud.

"I do mum, and he's been a great dad in fact a great man providing for us all," he replied while wiped his eyes.

"There isn't many in this world that has done that," she said, leant down and kissed Colin on the lips. Jessie stood up and smiled sobbed, "Thanks for everything my love; I will always be proud of you."

With one arm around Doreen who was sobbing her heart out, quietly, David said, "And my thanks as well pal," reached out and patted Colin on the arm.

That night, Jessie refused Gordon to stay with her, stated she wanted to be on her own. After kissed her goodnight, she waved to him when he set off. Gordon didn't pester her, knew she was still upset and also knew David and Doreen was going round later to keep an eye on her.

When Gordon returned home, he sat in his car outside the workshop recalled his dad joking with David while carrying furniture inside. Again he was rock bottom, feeling bewildered, lonely and in many ways now scared when suddenly he burst into tears. After wiped his eyes, Gordon got out and opened the back door continued inside the kitchen. Turning on the light he glanced round and tried to smile. Wiping his eyes he sobbed, "Well dad, if you are here now, I need looking after so do your best for me pal."

On the day of the funeral, Gordon didn't open the shop. Local folk knew why as many had called in to pay their respects. About to lock the back door when the phone rang and thinking it was his mum, returned to answer it. Gordon picked up the receiver and glanced out of the window said, "Hello, Mathew's furnishings."

"Oh hello, this is Moira Duding, I'm making enquiries about the house you have to rent," she said, and listening to silence asked, "Hello is there anyone there?"

"Oh sorry, would you mind ringing back please, I'm just on my way to a funeral," he replied while glanced at his watch.

"Oh I'm very sorry and what time would be convenient?" she asked.

"Say about seven tonight and if you don't mind, I must go now," he replied impatiently.

"Very well and bye," she said then replaced the receiver. Gordon did the same, and thought no more about the call was more concerned about his mum, quickly locked up before set off.

At Jessie's side throughout the service and at the burial, Gordon occasionally glanced at Tracy who never came near her mother, just leant on Peter, while he consoled her.

Tea and biscuits had been provided in the church hall nearby and in the end Jessie's patience snapped when Gordon followed her everywhere moaning, "For God's sake, will you please leave me alone."

"Good grief you are my mother. I am supposed to look after you," he growled.

"Oh sorry love," said Jessie, looked ready to burst into tears.

"It's alright mum, however, I would have thought your daughter might have shown a bit more concern," he replied, while glanced at Tracy, stood with Peter and now happily chatting to relations.

Again he thought it ignorant when Tracy and Peter left early, had to attend a party that night, and when they shouted goodnight to him, he just smiled and waved. "When you are ready you can run me home," said Jessie, and sat with him.

"Oh, I come in useful sometimes then?" asked Gordon, and smiled.

Looking slightly bewildered and tired, "Sorry for going on love, it's just the pressure of the day. For over forty five years I've have your dad at my side. Oh yes sometimes it's been hard, but he knew a kiss and a cuddle would always put things right."

"Come on then mum," he asked, stood up and gestured to David they were going.

"Can we have a lift with you?" he asked, and pointed to the door.

"Of course," replied Gordon, and smiled when his mum slipped her arm in his.

While escorting her to the exit, there was hugs and kissed from relations and Gordon raised his eyebrows, noticed they weren't many left. He was going to comment, thought it unwise and decided to keep quiet.

With not much conversation between them while they travelled home, inside his mum and dad's house, Gordon looked round at all the photos, ornaments and nick-knacks. His mum brought him a cup of tea, and smiling said, "You can open the shop tomorrow as normal. Today has been the first time it has ever been closed midweek."

"I will and just a quick question mum. Please don't take this wrong but are all the funeral expenses covered?" asked Gordon before drank up.

"No problem, me and your dad sorted all that years ago but have you?" asked Jessie raising her eyebrows and smiled.

"No, it's never entered my head to. I'd better call at the solicitors and make a will just to be on the safe side," said Gordon, winced and drank up.

Jessie began to gather the cups. She said, "You had indeed, especially with property prices rising as they are."

"Oh hell, and that reminds me, a woman rung about David's house, she was ringing back at seven," he said then glanced at his watch.

Smiling at his dilemma she said, "You've twenty minutes to get home then."

Chapter 15

After Gordon kissed his mum, he asked if she would be alright on her own. Jessie constantly reassured him before he set off, however, Gordon felt unsure and tentatively waved.

When Gordon arrived home, after parked the car, although it was cold, he got out and stared up at the clear sky. Seeing all the stars he smiled continued to unlock then opened the back door.

Walking inside, he turned on the light, closed and locked the door behind him before continued into the shop. Gordon made sure everything was safe before returned and checked the front room. In the kitchen he filled the kettle when the phone rang, quickly turned pulled round a chair and picked up the receiver saying, "Hello."

"Is that Mathews Furnishings?" asked a woman.

"Yes it is," he replied, sat down and smiled recognized the voice.

"This is Moira Duding, I rang this morning about renting your house," she said sounding rather stuffy.

"Oh sorry, right then, do you want any details over the phone?" he asked while leant on the table.

"Yes please, and namely the amount of the rent?" she replied.

Gordon was still undecided about the amount to charge and had priced it same as adverts in the local paper. Deciding to elaborate he replied, "Its eighteen pounds per week, but it's partially furnished and of course the utilities are extra."

"When may it be possible, to view?" she asked then her voice trailed off as if looked for something to write on or with.

"Whenever, I live next door, its part of our shopping complex," replied Gordon, just to make it sound nice.

After a brief pause, lightly she asked, "Oh, well, would tomorrow night about six be possible?"

"That's fine, shall I give you directions?" he asked before smiled knowing the extra money would come in handy.

"Please," she replied.

After informed Moira the way to get there, Gordon replaced the receiver, recalled when informed Caroline it was ten pounds saying, "How times change," but while made his tea thought, *I wonder how she is going on.*

Ten minutes later, staring at a pan of baked beans while waiting for them to heat up; suddenly Gordon turned and glanced at a calendar. Frowning he moaned, "I wonder what Caroline had. I would have thought at least she might have informed me."

Early next morning, Gordon was surprised when he sold a sideboard and a double bed. Just before lunch after sold a large hall mirror to a young woman and thought he knew her. David called asked him to sign some documents and broke his thoughts. After gave him some more paperwork saying he had been holding them on his dad's behalf. Gordon took them asking, "What are they for?"

"You'll find out when you read them, anyway I'm off now, Doreen's not too good today," he replied while continued to the door.

"Look after her and see you later," said Gordon then threw the documents on the sideboard.

After a sandwich for lunch, Gordon continued to paint while the shop was empty, had decided to do a portrait of his mum and dad for a keepsake. Enjoying the quiet as it helped his concentration; he suddenly jumped and looked round when the door opened. Gordon smiled when Christine Pritchard walked inside held the hands of two young lads aged about ten or twelve. Frowning she said, "Please, from all of us, except our condolences Gordon."

"Thanks Christine," he replied trying not to smile. However, Gordon stared at the oldest lad, had thick curly black hair and the other had blonde.

"I know how you must be feeling, I lost my dad last year," said Christine, and impatiently smiled while ushered the lads outside.

"It makes you grow up quick doesn't it?" asked Gordon, and watched as she smiled when closed the door. Beginning to study when he had a fling with her, and when it dawned on him, suddenly laughed saying, "If you've been listening dad, now you know," and with a big grin on his face carried on painting.

That night with one later sale to add to the deliveries, after Gordon locked the shop, he set off. At the first drop, he knocked on the door and had to smile when a little girl aged about four or five, opened it shouting, "It's the second hand man mum."

"Right love," she replied while walked up to her. The woman smiled at Gordon asking, "Oh hello, err could you leave the mirror in the hallway, that's where I intend to hang it?"

"Of course," replied Gordon then set off to the van.

When he returned and after propped it up against the wall, while making out a receipt, the woman stared at him asking, "It is Gordon isn't it?"

Suddenly smiling when it dawned on him, "It is and you're Andrea from school."

"The name was familiar and I thought it was you when I called in the shop but I didn't like to say," she said while taking the receipt from him.

Frowning he replied, "Sorry I didn't recognize you either but, err, well, my dad has suddenly died and it been chaos for us all. I'm not thinking straight yet."

"Oh sorry, I know how you must feel because my husband was killed in the mines two years ago. At first you can't think straight and when you do wake up by hell is it a struggle," said Andrea while slipped her arm around the little girl's shoulder who was taking in their conversation.

"I know what you mean love," replied Gordon, and smiled at the little girl when she leant her head on her.

Gordon thought her cute and when she smiled, slipped his hand into his pocket taking out some change and gave her fifty pence. "Say thanks," said her mum.

"Thank you very much," shouted the little girl while ran off.

Andrea smiled saying, "Thanks Gordon that was very kind."

"My pleasure love," he replied, opened the door and waved before set off to the van.

After made the last delivery, returning home took him by Caroline's shop and again Gordon stopped dead when they had started to knock it down. While staring in shock, "Bloody hell," he gasped at the rubble, recalled when they had made love in there.

Slowly he set off moaning, "I suppose that's what they call bloody progress," then carried on home. Unfortunately Gordon had forgot about the time, so when he pulled round the back, turned off the ignition he stared at a tall ginger haired woman, was waiting at the back door.

"Oh sorry, I do beg your pardon, I've been making deliveries and been delayed," said Gordon before closed the van door then locked it.

"That's quiet alright, I've only just knocked," she said, turned and waited until he unlocked the back door. Gordon walked inside, turned on the light, gestured her to come inside then closed the door after her.

"Please sit down, I'll just make some tea," said Gordon then gestured before spun round to switch on the kettle.

"Thank you, and is this the house?" she asked looking round while unfastened her coat.

While preparing their cups Gordon replied, "No its next door, it's very similar though."

"This area is very suitable for me. I'm a primary teacher and started the beginning of last term. It's only a mile away so the location is just right," said Moira watching him.

"A teacher you say, and what do you teach?" he asked taking milk out of the fridge.

"Art and music," she replied, then began to eye a painting on the wall.

"Art is my subject," said Gordon while poured out the tea.

"I thought it was you when I applied for the house. I know you're an artiste, I have read about you," she said and smiled reached out to take a cup from him.

Gordon put his cup on the table, and sat opposite her saying, "I must confess I haven't done much of late."

Smiling she asked, "And why not?" then had a drink.

"Well, that funeral I was going to was my dad's. He died sudden and, well let's say I'm suffering a lack of inspiration at the moment," he replied before had a drink.

"That's life, cruel as it is," she said, and pondered while held the cup in her hands.

"Sorry, would you like to view the house now?" he asked standing up.

"Go on then while this cools," she replied, put down her cup and stood up.

Watching while following him next door, inside David's house, Moira had a good look round upstairs and down. Entering the front room, she turned and smiled saying, "What more could I ask for, I'll take it."

"Very good, shall we return now?" asked Gordon while gestured the way.

"Why not," she replied smiling, and waited at the doorway while he turned off the lights. Moira waited until Gordon locked the door and curiously eyed him while followed him to his house. Inside she sat at the table picked up her cup and drank her tea then suddenly pulled a face when it was cold. When Gordon replaced her cup with fresh tea she asked, "Will there be a contract to sign?"

Not relishing the extra work "Well at the moment no. When I see our accountant next I'll ask him for one and also a rent book. The trouble is I now have to learn how to adjust the books as well," he replied but winced as if didn't relish it.

Moira guessed Gordon didn't want to do the paperwork involved with renting smiled saying, "We all have to occasionally learn something new sometime. So then, when is your next show? I missed the last and I understand it was a sell out?" but mainly changed the subject to get better acquainted.

"That I don't know yet, maybe next year," replied Gordon, stood up, walked over and filled the kettle before switched it on.

Moira leant on the table asking, "I'd like to paint more but I lack technique. Please tell me, who did you study under?"

"Completely self taught," he replied then waited until the kettle boiled before switched it off.

Moira eyed him while he made the tea, and when he turned towards the table said, "I wouldn't have guessed that in a million years. I've seen photos of your work and was very impressed."

Gordon put their cup on the table then sat down asking, "So how long are you staying in the area?"

"Well now, maybe until next summer. I'm part of the new breed of supply teachers that have to move round for work. I started at the school last month and at the moment living with a colleague.

Unfortunately it is very cramped, so as soon as I can move out the better?"

"Whenever, the only thing I ask is please leave the house as you found it. I know it needs decorating and everybody's tastes are different. I've also been thinking about doing in here."

Moira smiled knowing he was in a somber mood, was nothing like other landlords she had rented from, were normally all questions about her background and finance. Leaning on the table she asked, "Do you require a deposit? You know a bond."

"Pardon, oh sorry, oh no. You can pay one week in advance if you like," he replied then drank his tea.

"Right then, I'll be off now and get prepared. Tomorrow if possible could I bring a few things round after work, and I'll move in at the weekend?" she asked before drank her tea.

"Of course, I'll just get you the keys," said Gordon, stood up, and picked them up off the sideboard.

Moira took the keys from him, and eyed them saying, "I should be here about six."

"I might be out making deliveries, so I'll see you later on," he replied, opened the door then suddenly stopped moaning, "Oh hell, please forgive me. I can't let you walk home in the dark I'll run you home," turned and picked his keys up off the sideboard.

"That's quite alright, it's not far," she said quickly fastening her coat then continued outside.

"Are you sure?" he asked then shivered felt the cold.

Waving she replied, "Positive," and carried on.

After locking up, Gordon sat in the front room was having a drink of wine while watching TV. Beginning to deliberate his future, he still felt lonely and bewildered often wondered if Caroline and his child were both alright but it upset him when she hadn't let him know. Gordon replenished his glass moaning, "I think it's time to move on now, only what the hell that saying means I'll never know."

Deep down Gordon knew he should have tried to find Caroline and could have obtained an address from the agent that sold her shop. On the other hand she could have contacted him, and at least to let him know if both were alright. Taking the blame for not being adamant to see his child or indeed to stop her moving away, Gordon flopped down on the sofa, sighed at his inadequacies, and shaking his head moaned, "I will never learn."

The next day with no sales or deliveries, after locking the shop, now back upstairs in his studio, Gordon began to paint. However, after an hour, heard a noise outside, went to the back window and looked out. Noticing a van parked at the side of his and Moira with a young chap helping carry boxes and bags inside. *It must be her boyfriend because she could have asked me to do it,* he thought while watched them.

Gordon continued his work, and ten minutes later, heard the phone ring. Going into his dad's old office, he picked up the receiver saying, "Hello, Mathews Furnishings."

"Hello lad it's Albert Speight from the auction house here, just to let you know if you're interested you might have a commission on the way. Mr. Broughton from near Kings Lynn rang me this afternoon and asked for your telephone number," said Albert sounding very enthusiastic.

"To be honest Albert I haven't the time or the inclination at this moment in time," replied Gordon, sounding far from interested.

Instantly Albert began to stress, "Listen to me lad, this is the big stuff. We are talking money here and there might be another as well, near Stamford. Cash wise these jobs are too big to throw away."

"Albert, my dad has just died and my life is in turmoil at the moment," moaned Gordon while sat on the corner of the desk.

"Oh hellfire lad, I'm very sorry I didn't know that so may I offer you my condolences. Anyway if that's the case then, I'll leave it another two weeks and ring back." said Albert and not waiting for a reply replaced the receiver.

Gordon did the same, returned to his painting and when the phone rang again moaned, "Oh bloody hell," before picked up the receiver.

"It's me love, are you alright?" asked his mum.

"Yes and you," he replied then cocked his eyes thought she was just nattering.

Very quietly she asked, "Listen love, Doreen is very poorly and David said he can't get over to the shop tomorrow so will you be alright on your own?"

Pulling a face because she knew he had been on his own often enough, "Of course I will, anyway I haven't sold a thing today."

"Right then and listen I've been thinking. Its bloody boring being on my own here so I'm going to work at the shop during the day. It'll take my mind off a few things," said Jessie then waited for a reaction.

"You don't have to mum, I'm managing alright really," he replied then suddenly smiled knew the quality of his meals would improve.

"That's not the point love, it's bloody lonely over here," she moaned.

"I know how you feel mum," he replied, had begun to feel the same.

"Anyway at least you will get fed better," she said then laughed.

"There is nothing wrong with bread and jam."

"There certainly isn't," she replied, now sounded serious

In the middle of the eighties the country went haywire. The colliers came out on strike again and seemingly the rest of the workers were behind them even though it caused great hardship. Money became scarce, and after Gordon pawned Jewellery and rings for a young woman aged mid thirties, who was in tears and begged him to do so, before put them in the safe, he examined the contents of a large leather pouch and could not believe it.

His dad had never sold anything he had pawned for goods and kept everything. Gordon retained the woman's jewellery in case she returned, although thought it unlikely before informed his mum that sometime in the near future he would arrange to go into Leeds to get rid of them.

Although his money was now subsidizing the shop, Gordon still did repairs for the auction house and now with Moira's rent, plus the odd sale, it collectively paid the rates and utilities.

Doreen recovered but was still frail however, now at home this gave David more spare time, but because of the present day economic climate two days a week he now helped renovating second hand furniture taken in part exchange.

Unfortunately under government pressure the striker's money soon dried up so their customers began to dwindle more. It was now a matter of surviving trying to keep a fair amount of stock for when the area recovered. Gordon was well aware of this, had gone through it all before but always hoped the outcome would be in the shops favour.

The next day while visiting a pawn shop in Leeds, after Gordon introduced himself the owner who immediately asked how his dad was going on Gordon explained that his father had died. Noticing he never batted an eyelid when suddenly he looked up saying, "I'm very sorry lad I didn't know."

"That's alright," said Gordon and didn't haggle with his offer. After called at the bank to deposit the money, on his way home, decided if his mum could look after the shop he had decided it was time to do a commission for the extra money.

That afternoon, when he asked Jessie, at first she disagreed, however, later in his studio while Gordon painted, his mum began to inspect nine finished paintings, and knowing it was his only joy, and as it was helping the business, in the end agreed.

Two days later Jessie was glad she did agree while read a letter Gordon had received from their insurance company. They were insisting the whole building had to be alarmed and the workshop would require a sprinkler system fitted or else their policies would dramatically have to rise. Gordon walked into the kitchen, and while switched on the kettle asked, "What do you think mum?"

Looking worried she replied, "It looks like it's time to close down."

"I've been thinking that way as well. However, since my dad went without for us and fought to have his name on the shop front, I've decided to pay for it all. It's just that I don't want our Tracy coming here in years to come and claiming half, because I know if given the chance she would."

"She won't do that love, the solicitor's got it all in writing," she replied looking very near to tears.

"Then I'll get some estimates straight away. Do you want a cup of tea?" he asked standing up.

"Go on then love," she replied forcing a smile.

A month later, and accepting the second estimate because Gordon went to school with the boss, he arranged with them to commence work to their insurer's wishes. The only trouble was it took nearly two months to complete with the noise and dust interfering with his painting.

Once completed and after slight decorations Gordon was relieved it was back to normal. Moira had now been in the house four months and not seeing her much other than calling in on a Friday night to pay her rent; she would have a cup of tea with Gordon and discuss her week. She was an attractive woman but he always thought she was courting so left well alone. She wasn't and appeared to be doing well at the school so applied for a permanent position, would know the result in a month's time.

Moira had met Jessie on several occasions and got on well with her, especially now she had tastefully decorated the house throughout and occasionally asked her advice. Jessie knew she was interested in

Gordon who at this moment in time was thinking more about his intended commission at Norfolk in two weeks time, and when he returned from having his car serviced, they sat in the kitchen eating a sandwich discussing her.

"Give over mum she not interested in me, she's too educated," he replied then pulled a face.

"So what, so why do you think she's stayed here? She could have got a council flat nearer the school there's plenty empty now and cheaper," she snapped staring at him.

"Let's wait and see," he said before drank his tea.

Gordon was more interested in Andrea Hastings. She had called in the shop two days before was undecided to buy a single bed for her daughter. They had got on well at school, and Gordon recalled her travelling on the bus had also taken to her daughter who was very well mannered for her age.

Jessie eyed them talking, read their body language, began to put two and two together, decided to make a cup of tea before entered the kitchen. Gordon waved when Andrea left, knew she was calling again that afternoon, and was undecided whether or not to ask her out. His mum walked in the shop, and passed him a cup of tea moaning, "Why didn't you ask her out then? Good grief lad, you were always slow on the uptake."

Gordon smirked saying, "That's what you think."

When Andrea did call in, she bought the bed then paid for it asking, "How much do you charge for delivery?"

"Nothing to you, only on one condition, we go out for dinner on Friday night," he replied then grimaced while waiting for an answer.

Suddenly staring at him Andrea blushed saying, "That's the first time anyone has asked me out in years."

"I mean properly, I don't mean, oh you know," sighed Gordon lost for words and also blushed.

Andrea browsed round the shop to compose herself saying, "I'll have to let you know, I'll have to get a babysitter first."

"Your little girl can come as well. What do they call her?"

"That's very kind of you, and she called Tracy," replied Andrea now looking flushed.

"Another Tracy," said Gordon then laughed.

"Yes, and if I recall correctly they called your sister that, didn't they?" she asked but frowned wasn't sure.

"They do indeed. Shall I pick you about seven?"

"I'll see, could I tell you tonight then when you drop the bed off," replied Andrea while walked to the door.

"Of course and bye for now," shouted Gordon.

Soon as the door closed, "What a chat up line," moaned David, had overheard their conversation.

"Thanks, and if we have time are we going to that sale tomorrow afternoon," asked Gordon, now looking flushed.

"Why not, you're a bloody slave driver just like your dad," replied David, craftily smiled and winked. Replacing his mask he waved before walked into the workshop to continue spraying a table top with varnish.

Now in a better mood, Gordon went about his painting for the auction house and smiled had never known the name of their delivery man. However, when he last called informed him these had to be the last because of his commission and was surprised when he knew.

Not socializing for ages, Gordon looked forward to Friday night when it suddenly dawned on him about Moira, because if she was interested in him as his mum said, why she hadn't called in when it was the school holidays. Always assuming she stayed at her boyfriends, although he had never seen or heard anyone at the house with her. Gordon thought she was playing it safe such as didn't want to get kicked out, and craftily smiled saying, "There's one way to find out because when I get back I'll ask her to pose for me."

That evening, after Gordon delivered the bed to Andrea's he carried it upstairs and assembled it for her. Half-smiling and looking unsure quietly she said, "Thanks very much and Friday is alright."

"Right then it's a date. I must be off now more to do as they say," replied Gordon then quickly set off downstairs didn't want Andrea to think he was nosey. Of course he had a good look round and even though the house only contained the basics, it was clean.

"Bye second hand man," shouted Tracy waving.

Grinning he waved saying, "its Gordon to you."

The rest of that week Gordon continued his painting, and on Friday night, all dressed up, he drove round to Andrea's house. Soon as he stopped outside, the door opened and Andrea walked out wore a light two piece suit. Gordon reached over, opened the door asking, "Where's Tracy?"

"She's a bit off it and very disappointed. My mum is babysitting," she replied while sat inside then closed the door.

"Where do you fancy going then?" he asked while slowly drove down the street.

"Wherever," she replied looking uncomfortable but managed to smile.

Half an hour later, sat in a little pub on the outskirts of the next town, "I'm famished," said Gordon while passed Andrea a menu.

Andrea smiled, and reading the menu asked, "Are you sure all this with good intentions Gordon?"

"Sure love and why not?" he asked then stared at her thought it was hard to believe she was a widow with a young daughter.

"It's just that, why me? There are plenty of fish in the sea."

"Andrea, I think you knew I always liked you. You were the good looking one with style. Nothing ever ruffled you, even on the bus going home. You were the one that was always reading when others were fighting," replied Gordon but thought, *good grief you are lovely, and what a beautiful profile.*

Andrea blushed slightly and smiled saying, "Gordon, that was years ago."

The waiter returned and they gave him their order. When he walked away, "So how come you have never married?" she asked.

"Now that is a long story," he replied raising his eyebrows.

"I remember you going out with Caroline," then purposely stared at him for a reaction.

Clasping his hands together after leant on the table, "So do I the only trouble was she had a warped sense of humor. She teased me something rotten and I never knew where I stood with her."

Frowning she asked, "Whatever happened to her?"

Shrugging his shoulders because really wanted to change the subject, "I think Caroline returned to Sheffield. She just picked up sticks and left."

"What? Never even said goodbye to you," she asked then sat back staring when didn't believe him.

"No. We had a fall out of course but that was that, and I must mention this she was also pregnant," he replied then sat back when the waiter arrived began to serve their meal.

"Has she never contacted you?" asked Andrea then smiled at the waiter said, "Thanks."

Waiting until he walked away, "No, I don't even know if they are alright," replied Gordon while eyed his meal.

While they ate, Andrea mentioned her husband and Gordon could tell it still hurt her when she said he was crushed to death on the coal face. Quietly she said, "The trouble was it left me penniless. I was rock bottom with only my parents to help and went months without any money."

Gordon frowned asking, "Didn't the council help you?"

"In the end yes. They lowered my rent, and when I received compensation from the coal board they said I had to repay it. Anyway I did, and since then, I don't owe anybody anything."

"That's a good state to be in," said Gordon while continued eating.

"The compensation wasn't that much and it didn't last long. When Tracy started at nursery school I got a part-time job at the bakery and that helped us out. Unfortunately trade has dropped off that much it seems my employment there will be coming to an end soon," she said looking slightly worried.

Gordon studied saying, "We've all had it hard in the past and that makes me more determined to look after my future."

"That's true, but the money I received was small recompense for a life."

"That is so very true, life is very precious. It's worth a lot more than any amount of money."

The waiter broke their conversation had brought a bottle of wine. Gordon gave thanks picked it up and began to pour it out asking, "How did Tracy take it?"

"Like any youngster, she didn't know any difference," replied Andrea staring at her plate.

Gordon bowed his head knew he had put his foot in it and went quiet. At this moment in time Andrea was a sparkle in his life, and he wished to make it permanent. Unfortunately taking Caroline's departure as a failure, so with Andrea he had decided to play safe and stick with compliments and good manners.

Chapter 16

Ready for home, after Gordon paid for their meal, as they walked out to the car said, "You know it often makes me wonder; when someone dies can they still influence us down here?"

"I've always thought the same. My husband Jack used to say if I go first, I'll send you the winning pools numbers and although I do them now and again, I've won nothing yet," said Andrea and laughed.

Gordon smiled, opened the car door for her and when Andrea sat inside, closed it before walked round to his. Sat inside, he started the engine saying, "Thanks Andrea, it's made a very good change to go out and be in good company."

Chatting about Tracy on the way home, when Gordon stopped outside Andrea's house, they noticed an upstairs light on. "Well Gordon, thanks for the meal it has been great," said Andrea then leant towards him kissed his cheek.

When she opened her door, "Thank you and it's been my pleasure," he replied smiling at her.

While holding the door open, "I'll repay the compliment someday," said Andrea smiling.

"I'm away for three weeks on a commission soon, so may I call when I return and we'll arrange another date?"

"Of course," replied Andrea, didn't know what he meant, decided not to ask before closed the door, smiled and waved when he set off.

Parking outside his back door, Gordon studied about Andrea, had noticed she was dressed well for their evening out. Knowing she had a placid temperament was well mannered and he really liked her, Gordon opened the car door moaned, "I wish I could have got to know her daughter better."

After locked the car door, he turned and was about to unlock the kitchen door when Moira's back door opened. Looking out she smiled saying, "Oh, I wondered who it was."

Deciding to delve wearing a smile he asked, "Did you think it was your boyfriend?"

Opening the door wider she asked, "That'll be the day, I've just made a cup of tea do you want one?"

"Go on then," he replied, and slipped his keys in his pocket while walked towards her. Inside the house Gordon closed the door, and looking round commented, "You've done it up nice."

"I'll pay my rent now, I came round earlier but you were out," said Moira, while poured out the tea.

While watching her, "I had a dinner date and just milk please."

While pouring in the milk she asked, "Been anywhere nice?"

"The hope and anchor, it wasn't bad a bad meal really," he replied while eyeing a thick gold charm bracelet on her wrist and numerous gold rings on her fingers.

"Please sit down," she asked before put two cups on the table. Waiting until he did, Moira said, "I've been talking to your mum this afternoon, and seeing as my grant has come through, I informed her I would like to buy this house."

"Sorry, it's not for sale," said Gordon before picked up his cup and had a sip.

Sitting opposite, "That's a shame; but your mum did say it was up to you."

"You could buy a lot better than this," said Gordon looking round before placed his cup on the table.

"It's just the location and style, there aren't many left like this anymore," said Moira and picked up her cup had noticed he seemed more relaxed than normal.

"It won't be long before you are moving off anyway, you said you might," said Gordon while admired her complexion which suited the colour of her hair

"I'm here permanent now. Luckily I really like the area and the local folk. The school I'm at has achieved good grades so I've decided to stay," replied Moira then finished her tea.

"So what has your boyfriend had to say about it all?" he asked, was really testing her for information.

Smiling she replied, "That's twice you've mentioned that and I haven't one. I have had of course but not at the moment."

Leaning on the table Gordon asked, "You're not telling me a good looking woman like you is single?"

While smiling she replied, "I am, but not fancy free. I set my stall out to go teaching and when I found a permanent position, I'll take it from there."

Gordon stared, and began to admire her thought with the colour of her hair she would look well on canvas asked, "Have you ever been painted?"

Laughing she replied, "Only when I did in here, I was covered in it."

Gordon had to laugh with her before asked, "If you are free this weekend you can sit for me. I've only a week left then I'm on a commission."

"Thank you for that compliment and I'll consider it," said Moira then stood up picked up their cups.

"I'll take that as a hint to leave then, and don't forget my offer," said Gordon standing up then continued to the door.

"I won't, oh and here's your money," she said holding out the rent book.

Saturday morning, Gordon served in the shop until his mum arrived. David dropped her off, and when she brought him a cup of tea Jessie asked, "Good morning love, and what are you on with today?"

"Good morning mum, and if it's not busy in here I'm off up to my studio to paint. I'm trying to get another collection together for a sale."

"Get on up then. I'll have a dust round seeing as you haven't done it yet," said Jessie, and looked round as if where to start before picked up a cloth.

In his studio and again painting an urban scene, Gordon was engrossed, suddenly jumped when Moira said, "Good morning."

"You dizzy bugger," he gasped while held his chest.

"Oh my," she gasped, and went straight to the painting of Caroline.

"You like it?" he asked while stared into her eyes as if assessed her looking at it properly.

"I certainly do. Now that is class," she replied standing back to allow more light on the painting.

"I've done my best with it," he said smiling while mixed a colour on his palette.

"Was it done from a photo?" she asked.

"No a live model, she sat on there," he replied pointing to the settee with his brush.

Moira stood back, glanced round the room saying, "Yes, I can gather the scene, and that is excellent as well, same model?" she asked then raised her eyebrows.

"Yes and the only trouble is good models are few and far between," he replied while carried on painting.

"Right then, if you want to paint me you can," said Moira looking slightly flushed.

"First I must explain this. She was my ex girlfriend, and it was easy for her to model, so obviously being naked didn't bother her," he replied.

"I understand that," said Moira, while studied another painting.

Gordon smirked when saying, "And of course when you are intimate with someone with no inhibitions, you paint with love and affection. It guarantees it to come together much better."

Moira folded her arms asking, "So how long did it take you?"

Sounding nonchalant, "I suppose just a few days."

Moira sauntered over and stood at his side saying, "I want roughly the same pose with me."

"Sorry, that would be unwise and also it's the time factor, anyway I'm working away in a few days time," he replied but had to smile while mixed a colour.

Staring at him she asked, "Can't you start now?"

"Oh I, and if mum walked up here and saw you naked sat on my settee, what would she think?" turned to face her and raised his eyebrows.

Smiling she raised her eyebrows, "So go tell her not to come up then or lock the door."

"I've a better idea, go tell her yourself," replied Gordon, and laughed, however, suddenly went quiet when she walked out.

Gordon continued to paint, didn't think Moira would return began to smile now taking it all as a joke. Ten minutes later, hearing a noise on the landing, he looked round when Moira returned saying, "Right then get a canvas ready," continued over towards the window looking out.

Staring at her thinking she was kidding he asked, "Are you sure, Moira?"

Scanning the housing estate including fields and trees beyond, Moira knew no one could see her, turned began to undo her blouse saying, "This is always something I've always wanted doing, but it's always been a problem to find the right artiste to do it," took it off, threw it on the settee, reached behind her to undo her bra.

Gordon began to change the canvas but eyed her when she took off her skirt, then when she turned he turned noticed her tits stuck out thought, *chuffing hell; this is another that looks better with no clothes on.*

Using a different background to Caroline's painting because Moira had red hair, he glanced round and noticed her laid on the settee watching him. To save embarrassment, he said, "How come women always have a different colour hair in-between their legs than on their head."

"Have I?" she asked, and brought a leg up looked down.

Gordon looked away could see in between them turned and began to lightly sketch. Occasionally he glanced at her, noticed she had her eyes closed, then suddenly jumped when his mum knocked on the door shouting, "I'm bringing you up some lunch in ten minutes."

"Right mum," he replied but carried on.

Ten minutes later Gordon put down his brush saying, "I think you had better get dressed now."

Standing by his side she asked, "Can I have a look yet?"

When the odor of her perfume wafted by him, Gordon turned to Moira saying, "I hope you don't mind me saying this, but your breasts are beautiful to paint, I mean the right shape," then blushed slightly.

She looked down at them asking, "Are they?"

Staring at the painting he replied, "I'll try to keep them prominent in the painting, they are an asset to you," then decided because of her skin colour to use more of her body close up.

Smiling she said, "Thanks for that compliment," then looked round when his mum knocked on the door.

Moira walked over, and slipped on her blouse while sat on the settee with her legs together. Gordon waited, walked over, opened the door, and took a tray off his mum saying, "Thanks."

"You'll get thanks," she replied, and winked before set off down stairs.

Holding the tray in one hand a smiling Gordon closed the door, turned then tidied the table to make room looked round saying, "There's a sandwich here."

"Thanks love," replied Moira, stood up, took one and returned sat down.

Gordon remained standing and ate his while studied his work saying, "No, I've changed my mind."

Moira looked at him asking, "What over?"

"Tell you when we've eaten," he replied, and smiled carried on eating his sandwich.

Moira stood up leaving her plate on the settee arm asked, "No tell me now?"

Gordon stood back, and eyeing her arse replied, "Sorry and again I aren't being forward."

Standing with him she laughed then said, "And you had better not be."

While studying he replied, "No listen… this pose is all wrong; you have long legs and a cute bum. When you have finished eating, kneel on the settee, turn, and look at me. The point is we have to show off your body at the right angle. This is not quite right."

Staring at him she gasped, "Gordon, what do you think I am you're not looking up my arse?"

"Don't be silly, with your breasts hanging down it will be just perfect," he replied but couldn't help smiling.

"For what?" she gasped.

"To paint,"

"Give over this is just a turn on," said Moira before picked up her plate and began to finish her sandwich.

After she put her plate on the table off came her blouse. "Excuse me madam, you turned me on when you undressed and now I'm supposed to paint you, so just do as you are told," he asked, and smiled put his plate on hers.

Moira knelt on the settee, turned, and looking at him asked, "Like this?"

"Perfect, now hold that pose a minute," he replied, began to sketch over the backdrop.

Knowing what he had in mind, Gordon finished the sketch asking, "Come and look at this?"

Moira rolled off and stood up stretched, continued over and studied it before replied, "Oh, I see what you mean now, but it is very provocative."

"That's the idea, you have a nice body so show it off, the only trouble is having ginger hair you have freckles. I suppose I could put a few in here and there," he said while studied.

Moira looked down asking, "I've always had these on my chest. Have I many more?"

When she looked up at him, "There's some on your back, but I don't have to paint them on," he replied then picked up his palette.

"Anyway my Gran always used to say they were beauty spots," said Moira then laughed.

Smirking he said, "I have some too, so I'll agree with her there."

When Gordon continued to paint, Moira regained her pose, however, when it began to get dark, neither had noticed. Moira sat up asking, "My back is killing me can I have a rest now?"

"Sorry, oh hell," he replied, glanced at the window, walked over, began to close the curtains. Moira stood up and stretched while walked over, waited until he had then turned on the light having a quick glance at the painting.

While dressing, Moira stood back still stared at the painting. She smiled saying, "You're not fooling me. You are going to do more paintings of me in different positions aren't you?"

Smiling he asked, "How did you guess?"

While glancing at her watch she replied, "Because over these least few hours when I began to get cramp and moved to get comfortable you have seen my body in nearly every position."

"Let's wait and see then," he said, walked over and opened the door.

Going downstairs, and noticed the shop lights off, when they continued into the kitchen, "Looks like David has run mum home," said Gordon while filled the kettle.

"Don't make me one I'll have to go now, and will you want me to sit for you again?" she asked, continued to the door and looked at him before opening it.

"I shouldn't think so, the rest I can do from memory," he replied, and smiled.

"I thought you might," said Moira, and smiled continued out closing the door after her.

After made his tea, Gordon sat at the table studying. With his commission about to start, he hoped to take Andrea out more really liked her but knew he had to get round her daughter to like him as well. Not really minding the fact she had a child, but with Moira, now she was different, then he suddenly laughed saying, "There must be something special about that room, every time a woman goes in it they want to strip off."

Two days later, Gordon arranged with his mum and David to look after the shop while he was away. As usual after checked the post he left it in a pile on the sideboard. Still with an inkling Caroline would try to get some maintenance money out of him Gordon frowned when hot heard anything, however, one evening it dawned on him she could have lost the baby and the thought unnerved him.

When he was due to depart for his commission, with his cases in the car ready, Gordon sat at the table was checking the directions. Jessie sat with him asking, "How far is it?"

Pulling a face at being interrupted, he replied, "About a hundred and forty odd miles."

"Watch what you are doing and have you seen Moira of late?" she asked then smiled sarcastically.

"I saw her yesterday," he replied, folded up some papers, and slipped them in his inside pocket.

"She seems a nice girl," she said, then looked up at him when he stood up.

"So so," he replied, and again seemed impatient while checked his pockets.

"I hear you took Andrea Hastings out," she said eyeing him.

"You hear a lot of things mum, and yes I did and will again when I return home. Anyway I'm off now, just make sure you sign her rent book she pays on a Friday evening," said Gordon, leant down and kissed her on the cheek.

"It's she and her, is it now?" said Jessie, and smirked thought they hadn't hit it off.

"That's right," he replied while continued out to the car.

Waving to her when he drove off, once on the main road, Gordon decided to drive straight there without a break, hoped to arrive in time for dinner. As to his directions, turning off the A1, one hour later, when he approached Kings Lynn, he eyed the road signs and noticed one for Norwich.

Gordon thought he had done well not only for time but only having had to ask once for directions. In town he turned off and nearly three hours from leaving home, pulled up a long driveway.

Parking outside a very large red bricked house was nearly overgrown with ivy; the owner came out to greet him, heartily shook his hand and welcomed Gordon inside. In a large wooden paneled reception room, again it was all handshakes when he introduced his wife and the butler, who carried his cases while escorted him up to his room.

Purposely leaving his room door open while he unpacked his clothes, ten minutes later, Mr. Broughton knocked on it asking, "Please excuse me, have you a moment free?"

"Yes of course, please come in," replied Gordon while closed his case.

"Dinner is in thirty minutes, Raymond will call and escort you down and later I will show you to my study. All my art work is in there. Right then, so we'll see you later," said Mr. Broughton, smiled then nodded before closed the door behind him.

After Gordon hung up his clothes, he took his case containing his painting utensils now knew he would be working elsewhere and placed it near the door. Eyeing his room he was impressed by its contents. It had a very large double bed with huge carved headboard when a knock on the door made him spin round. Staring at it he asked, "Come on in?"

The butler opened it and smiled saying, "Excuse me sir, this way for dinner please."

"Thanks," said Gordon then followed him downstairs and into a reception room.

Walking inside the dining room, Gordon smiled at Mr. Broughton was sat at the head of the table with his wife at his right side. When he turned to two young gentlemen on his left, about Gordon's age, "These are my two sons, this is Adam," said Mr. Broughton, and gestured to the first one.

Adam stood up, reached over the table, and shook his hand. Beaming a smile he said, "I'm very pleased to meet you pal."

"Likewise," replied Gordon, and faintly smiled.

"And this one is our tear away of the family, Gregory," said Mr. Broughton, and laughed.

"A pleasure pal," said Gregory, stood up and held out his hand.

"Pleased to meet you," said Gordon while shook his hand.

Mrs Broughton gestured saying, "Please, will you all be seated?"

Gordon sat down opposite her sons, smiled at Gregory, and to make conversation asked, "And in what way are you a tear away?"

"I professionally race cars. Yours is a good model, though I prefer the two point five sports version."

While laughing Gordon said, "Mine has never been over sixty."

"Where we race a hundred and sixty is nearer the mark," replied Gregory then suddenly sat up straight.

A young chubby faced girl aged about seventeen, and slightly overweight walked inside carried a large silver tray. Starting with Mr. Broughton she began serving the soup. After served everyone, while eating his, "Do you intend to begin the renovations in the morning?" asked Mr. Broughton before wiped his mouth with a napkin.

"Yes, first thing," replied Gordon, glanced across and noticed his sons heartily tucked into their meal.

Mrs Broughton said, "No talking shop at the table Edwin," then suddenly scowled when Gregory belched.

"Very good my dear, we'll retire to my study later then I'll explain all," said Mr. Broughton while carefully placed his spoon in his dish.

While eating, Gordon had enjoyed the main course, however, noticed all their conversation was directed towards Gregory. It seemed Adam didn't mind when he didn't take any notice, just carried on eating while his brother bragged and boasted about his exploits on the race track. Mr. Broughton looking rather proud, always encouraged him, and would grin before comment, "Well done son."

Gregory beamed a smiled saying, "You know me dad I always do my best."

I wonder how true that is, thought Gordon while placed his knife and fork on his plate. Having eaten a superb dinner Gordon gave compliment for it and smiled at Mrs Broughton when asked to be excused. In silence with his sons following, Mr. Broughton escorted Gordon to his study.

On the way, he informed him with relish about their family history. Mr. Broughton entered his study, smiled and gestured round a Tudor oak paneled room. It was lit by a very large chandelier and underneath was situated what seemed an antique solid oak table surrounded by chairs from the same period. Gordon was amazed when with the rest of the furniture and atmosphere, made it appear he was back in the late fifteen hundreds. Ambling round he stared in wonderment at original paintings mumbling; "Now I know why you keep them in here."

Mr. Broughton proudly stuck out his chest saying, "This one is especially my favorite. It's Oliver Cromwell in all his finery and I might add is a distant relation."

"Excellent," said Gordon while inspected it from every angle before moved on to the next.

After inspected all the paintings, Mr. Broughton eyed his sons while they gazed out of the window and chatted without interest. Quickly turning he asked, "I think it would be best if you worked in here Gordon. I have an easel ready and even that is older than me," then heartily laughed.

"It would, however taking them off the wall I will not do. Two are fixed solid and if I might suggest at a later date those three there, after restoration in future would be better kept under glass," replied Gordon pointing to them then suddenly turned when his sons laughed out loud.

"Indeed," replied Mr. Broughton frowning.

"With restoration one can only do so much and if you intend them to stay in the family please keep them under glass. From then on they will need no more and it is best kept that way," replied Gordon, had eyed four large radiators in the room and knew if they weren't regulated properly were a potential danger.

"You are the expert, and so be it," he replied.

When they returned to the dining room Mrs Broughton had replenished their glasses. Gordon politely waited until they all sat down then did the same. Mrs Broughton looked at him while gestured to the cheese and biscuits saying, "So when did you start this illustrious career of yours Mr. Mathews?"

"Please, it's Gordon, and I was about seven years old when I took particular notice the varying styles of the masters. I became intrigued and copied them. In time I began to read everything about them then it sort of took off from there," he replied lightly.

"Are you not married?" she asked before picked up a large crystal wine glass.

Thinking they must have cost a fortune he replied, "Not yet, although I do have a regular girlfriend."

"And what does she think about you flying all over the country?"

"Not very much I'm afraid. Obviously when I do eventually settle down I will have to make our shop my base and in the future work from there."

"A business colleague of mine has you in mind. He's at Stamford and boy what a collection he has. It's insured for a few million, but I think he's waiting for to judge your work with ours before making a decision to employ you," said Mr. Broughton then had a drink.

"I always do my best, I can assure you," said Gordon, had a drink then thought, *like the meal, this wine is delicious*.

While they carried on drinking, as if with nothing else to do, Gordon had decided on an early night and asked to be excused. After saying goodnight, he went up to his room, but couldn't resist a glance round on the way.

Later in his bed, looking round the room he studied but feeling content said, "This is the life," and although not yet arranged a fee for his services, decided to do so first thing in the morning before starting the first painting.

Chapter 17

Two weeks into his work, Gordon was getting fed up and it showed. First he was sick to death of Gregory, who was repeatedly boasting about his achievements; having raced twice while he was there and won. Adam was the moody one and always seemed to have the huff on over something. Constantly moaning over something he would drift from one room to another while pretending to read a book.

Mrs Broughton always kept the peace and insisted on respect at the dinner table. Even though Gordon had requested his dinner served in his room, mainly for peace and quiet, she always refused stuffily snapped, "In this house we all dine together. My grandmother always stated that eating together generates conversation and she is right."

Breakfast and lunch he had in Mr. Broughton's study while continued to work, and was thankful when it kept him out of his son's way. Gordon couldn't take to them at all when all they did was constantly inform everyone they had money.

Other than them, the job he liked, was working on paintings done by the masters giving them respect when cleaned them, or restored partial damage caused by old age and neglect.

During this time Gordon also pondered his future had decided to ask Andrea if she wanted a relationship. On the plus side he knew Andrea was well mannered, polite and educated. She had a pleasing personality and good figure. On the minus side, he knew he didn't love her, however, Gordon liked her very much and in time, who knows? Working on that assumption unfortunately it was Tracy he was more bothered about, when there was every possibility she might not take to him.

When Gordon worked on the last painting, Mr. Broughton walked into his study, went straight to his desk, picked up the telephone receiver and sat down. Gordon eyed him when in conversation he mentioned his name, noticed he glanced at him and smiled. Mr. Broughton gestured to him to stay calm saying, "He's working here now and I must say this Terrence, what an artiste. The guy is phenomenal, a master in his own right."

Gordon raised his eyebrows thought, *he can't be talking about me*, and carried on painting when Mr. Broughton said, "I will, I think he finishes today, so I will inform him."

Mr. Broughton replaced the receiver then waited a few minutes as if studied. Standing up he paused for a moment before from a distance glanced over Gordon's shoulder. "Two hours and I will be about finished," said Gordon knew he was being watched.

"Will you be staying for dinner?" asked Mr. Broughton.

"If you don't mind, and thank you very much for your hospitality it has been fantastic, but I must refuse. It is time to hit the road," replied Gordon looking apologetic.

"As you wish, I'll just go get my cheque book," said Mr. Broughton then spun round.

Gordon frowned then became worried as this was the first job he had undertaken without arranging a price first. Not doing so because when he was about to his silly sons interfered in their conversation. "Here you are my boy, and I hope this is to your satisfaction," said Mr. Broughton while passed him a cheque.

Gordon read the amount of twenty five thousand pounds, and tried not to smile saying, "You are extremely generous Mr. Broughton."

Laughing he replied, "Wouldn't you be? You must have doubled the value of those paintings."

"That's true," said Gordon then studied thought, *yes, and the next commission will pay even more.*

Four hours later, with his cases packed, in the reception room, Gordon shook hands with everybody and again gave thanks for their hospitality. After bid them good day, he smiled at the butler when he opened the door for him then picked up his cases when he continued out to his car.

About to set off, Gordon noticed everyone was at the door, so he smiled and waved when it seemed they were waving off a family member. Going down the driveway, Gordon stopped at the main road, checked the road was clear and set off for home, and with a satisfactory smile on his face thought, *that has made my day, just a little more security for my simple way of life.*

Driving on the A57, Gordon thought about the payment saying, "To me it was over the odds but he said it's increased the value of his collection so by Jove the next one is definitely going to pay very handsome for my services."

When Gordon arrived home, his mum was in the shop dusting while David prepared the evening deliveries. After the hello's and how have you got on then. "I won't be ten minutes," said Gordon when returned to his car then drove round to Andrea's.

Fifteen minutes later, Gordon drove up her street, and parked outside her house felt nervous when locked the car. Approaching her front door he took a deep breath before tentatively knocked on it. When it suddenly opened; Andrea looked at him surprised asked, "Oh, hello Gordon, please will you come in?"

Tracy popped her head round the door before ran into the front room shouting, "It's the second-hand man."

"Sorry," said Andrea, and apologetically smiled.

"No problem and sorry but there is something on my mind. Can you mange to go out to dinner tonight?" he asked then pulled a face when thought he didn't use the right words.

"Well, it's a bit short notice for a babysitter," she replied before studied.

Smiling Gordon said, "I mean all three of us."

"Well now, if you can put up with her, how can I refuse," said Andrea then smiled noticed Tracy listening through a gap in the door.

"Can I pick you up at half past six?"

Smiling Andrea replied, "We'll do our best to be ready."

"Must dash then, see you later," said Gordon, nervously leant forward and gave her a kiss her on the cheek, smiled turned and walked out. At the front door, Andrea watched him get in his car, and waved when he set off. She noticed Gordon wave, and waved again having always liked him but somehow Gordon always seemed troubled, was in a rush and wondered why.

When Gordon returned home, after parked and locked the car he said a quick hello then goodbye to his mum and David when they were about to set off for home. "And a goodnight to you too," said his mum, watching him disappear upstairs, turned and continued out to the van.

"I'll lock up in case he forgets," said David before closed the back door.

Gordon had a quick shower and after changed ready suddenly smiled because he looked forward to some decent company for a change. Also looking forward to a night out, he was all ready, glanced at his watch, and locked the door after him before went to his car.

When he drove round to Andrea's he noticed her waiting at the door for him. She walked towards him holding Tracy's hand, and when she got in the back of the car, Andrea got in the front. "So why the rush to go out Gordon," she asked smiling when he set off.

Tracy interrupted her asking, "Mum, are you going out with the second-hand man now?"

Gordon looked at her through the interior mirror asking, "Please, will you call me Gordon?" then turned to Andrea saying, "If we are it doesn't like we can have any secrets?"

"Sorry, and can we discuss it later?" she asked before laughed.

Smiling he replied, "I should think so."

In the pub, Gordon gave attention to Tracy, tucking a serviette in her top saying, "Try not to spill anything on that dress it's too nice?"

"Is it?" she asked looking down.

"Yes it is. Your mum bought that so look after it."

Andrea watched, had a permanent smile on her face, and appreciated his concern quickly turned when he asked, "What do you want to order?"

She replied, "Well now," and leant on the table staring at him.

"What's the matter?" he asked.

"Can I have some fish mum please?" asked Tracy, and grinned knew she interrupted.

"Of course," replied Gordon, but appreciated the word please.

Andrea frowned at him saying, "Don't spoil her."

"I'm not, fish is good for you," he replied.

"Gordon, please, you are treating her like your own," said Andrea.

Smiling he looked straight into her eyes saying, "That's both of you, so what do you want to eat?"

"Well now, if that's the case, I'll have fish as well, and when we get home I think we have some serious talking to do?"

Smiling he replied, "I'm ready for it."

Later that evening, when they returned to Andrea's house, Tracy was fast asleep on the back seat. Gordon carried her, waited while Andrea unlocked and opened the front door before followed her into the house.

Continuing into the front room, when Gordon laid her gently on the sofa, "She'll be alright there for now. Do you want a drink of tea?" asked Andrea, turned and continued into the kitchen.

"Please love," he replied, followed her, and waited patiently behind her while she filled the kettle. After Andrea switched it on, when she turned round, Gordon leant forwards and kissed her. Andrea stared into his eyes saying, "You can't stay."

"I don't want to, honest. Well, I tell a lie there, but all I want to know is this. I have been away for three weeks and missed you. If you have missed me that will make my day and also, I do want us to go out, permanent."

Andrea sighed asking, "And what about Tracy?"

"What about her?" he replied pulling a face as if didn't understand.

"She isn't yours," she replied, stared into his eyes and waited for a reaction.

"Don't be daft Andrea. I'm not that callous to take your past out of a child. She's a great little girl."

"She can be a handful, and hurtful. She can also remember her dad," she said then grimaced.

"I should bloody well think so, and you should encourage her to as well. Never take that memory away from here," he replied then placed his hands on her shoulders.

Frowning she said, "And I'm the same."

"Andrea, we all have memories that are precious and most should never be forgotten. I really like you a lot and at this moment in time that's all I am saying. You have a gorgeous daughter and, anyway, I am going now. When you are ready, give me a call, I'll be waiting," said Gordon then spun round, and walked out.

"Gordon?" shouted Andrea.

Gordon stopped, turned to face her, heard Tracy moan, and then the room door open. She walked out rubbing her eyes asking, "Can I have a kiss night night?"

"Of course you can my love," he replied, picked her up, and kissed her cheek. Gordon was taken aback when she wrapped her arms round his neck and hugged him. "Come on now, straight upstairs and straight into bed," he said while lowered her to the floor then smiled when watched her hanging onto the handrail while walking upstairs. Watching through glassy eyes Gordon said, "Goodnight love," turned, and opened the front door.

"Gordon?" shouted Andrea.

Gordon slowly turned, and Andrea noticed his eyes were glassy, quickly walked towards him she threw her arms around his neck then kissed him. Gordon held her at arm's length saying, "Sorry, but kids have a way, don't they?"

"Well she's got to you; mind you she's a crafty little bugger at times."

"Look. I am not being forward Andrea, but can we make this a regular habit?" asked Gordon then glanced upstairs.

Smiling she replied, "I should think so."

Frowning he asked, "Right then, next Wednesday at six thirty. We'll all go out again, that's if it's alright with you?"

"We'll be waiting," replied Andrea, and smiling placed her hand on his chest before kissed him. The kiss lingered, and Gordon wrapped his arms tight around her. Andrea turned it into a passionate embrace, didn't know, Tracy sat on the top step watching them.

Gordon waved when he set of for home but on the way, made up his mind that all future commissions had to be done in the shop. Suddenly he smiled, decided when finished the painting of his mum and dad, he was going to paint one of little Tracy, really liked her facial features.

Arriving home after parked the car and locked it, when Gordon walked towards the back door, Moira opened hers shouted, "Oh Gordon, could I have a minute please."

"Sure," he replied, and walked towards her.

"Come in a moment please?" she asked, turned and walked inside.

"What can we do for you?" he asked before closed the door behind him.

Seeing very nervous she asked, "I feel slightly embarrassed about this. Is it possible to loan me fifty pounds."

"I thought you had your grant approved?"

"I have, but seeing as you wouldn't sell the house, I invested it with the bank. This morning I've received the gas and electric bill and now I'm short of cash," she replied frowning at him.

"I'll have to see you tomorrow. I haven't that amount on me now," he said, but purposely lied, didn't want to flash his wallet in front of her.

"Oh thank you and I feel such a fool, I just forgot all about them," she said, looking relieved.

"No problem, see you tomorrow," he replied before opened the door.

"Good night Gordon," she shouted.

Gordon didn't reply, but inside his house, after locking the door, opened a bottle of wine. After poured himself a drink he walked into the front room, and turned on the TV. Sat in darkness, he smiled was satisfied with his progressing relationship with Andrea and Tracy, but couldn't recall her husband Jack then studied how he had died thought, *what a bloody awful way to get killed, working underground.*

After two glasses Gordon decided to go bed, and after turned everything off, when walking upstairs thought he heard a knock on the back door. Stopping he smiled then moaned, "Go bugger off Moira."

Early Sunday morning, Gordon was in a chirpy mood so commenced painting. After finished the one of his parents, he hung it in his studio, stood back, admired it and was very pleased with the result. Later, he continued the one of Moira, and after two hours, took the canvas off the easel, replaced it with another. Gordon began to sketch, and had to smile when started one of her in another pose.

Just before lunch, David called with his mum, had brought his dinner and left it in the oven. She made them all a cup of tea, passed David his, placed a few biscuits on a plate and with his cup continued upstairs. When she walked inside his studio, "Hello mum," said Gordon.

"Here you are," she replied when passed him a cup.

"Thanks, I was just going to make one, and is David in the workshop?" he asked.

"Yes, he's cleaning up a sideboard, someone's calling in the morning to view it so don't sleep in," she replied then noticed the painting of her and Colin, and walked over to it saying, "That is very nice of your dad."

"Thanks, it is for you if you want to take it with you," said Gordon and smiled while dunked a biscuit.

"No love, leave it here, I'm still sorting out your dads clothes and it hurts like hell having to get rid of stuff he liked most," she replied while walked to the door.

Just to change the subject and put his mum in a better mood, he asked, "Heard anything from our Tracy of late?"

"Not a thing, anyway see you later love," she replied before carried on downstairs.

After his mum left with David, Gordon continued painting until he was hungry. When his belly rumbled he moaned, "That's it," put down his brush and set off downstairs.

In the kitchen, after made a drink of tea while the oven warmed his dinner, Gordon sat at the table and wished he hadn't made it so long before he saw Andrea again. Suddenly he sighed when noticed Moira walk by the window and then heard her knock on the door.

Standing up Gordon walked over, unlocked and opened it asked, "Come on in?"

"What a greeting," she replied when closed the door after her.

"Sorry but I'm starving and waiting for my dinner to warm up," he replied, noticed she wore a cream colored blouse, and tight black slacks. When she sat down, he suddenly stood up saying, "Oh, that money," before continued into the front room.

Gordon quickly counted it, returned, and noticed her sat at the table. Handing it to her he said, "Here you are."

"Thanks and it will be at the end of the month before I can return it, is that alright?" she asked while slipped it into her blouse pocket.

"No problem," he replied while bent down to glance through the glass oven door.

Smirking she asked, "Right then, and I don't suppose you want me to pose for you later tonight?"

"When my memory fails me, I'll ask," he replied before turned to face her.

Standing up and while continued to the door asked, "Have you nearly finished it?"

"I'm about halfway there," he replied, picked up a tea towel before opened the oven door, bent down, and took out a dish.

"I'd better go then, see you later Gordon," said Moira then closed the door behind her.

While eating Gordon began to suss out Moira and didn't like what he thought. Although he lent her the money, and even though the length of time she had lived here, for some unknown reason he just couldn't take to her.

After his dinner he relaxed in the front room, and dozed while watched the TV. Dreaming of Caroline and his child he wondered why she hadn't let him know and as usual it began to bug him.

Later, upstairs in his studio, while tried to finish the painting of Moira, Gordon smiled saying, "I wonder if she fancies a jump tonight?" However, unbeknown to him, Moira was having difficulties at the school she worked and had been reprimanded for poor results of the children she taught.

The headmaster had informed her to pull her socks up else she would be moved on. Moira suddenly frowned before turned on a sob story inform him it was through lack of concentration because her long standing boyfriend had dumped her.

The headmaster reluctantly accepted her explanation, began to stress that standards must improve and quickly. Moira accepted his ruling and returned to her class however, she cursed when used to having her own way. In the past and in decent employment she began to fiddle the books giving her a better standard of living.

Of course she was eventually caught and dismissed, however, when applied for unemployment money was offered to train as a teacher. She accepted and when passed out, eventually given a post. Unlike her past position, a teachers wage was not enough for Moira to expand her wardrobe, in fact after paying her way renting Gordon's house this didn't leave her with much left over.

To Moira the only way forward was to get round Gordon and really thought he was easy meat. Her objective was to try to get as much cash out of him as possible while paying the minimal rent before getting into arrears with the utilities because as they weren't in her name she could then take off.

Monday morning, David, Jessie and Gordon had a meeting in the kitchen before the shop opened. They discussed suitable times for serving, and arranged it between them. "Last month's accounts I have read and turnover has picked up slightly," said Gordon, while made them a cup of tea.

"I can only manage three days a week now and I think we should reduce stock. We can't buy in second hand furniture like we used to, those days have gone now because most sellers class them as antique," said David, and smiled while took his cup.

"Your right there, anyway it's too much like hard work," said Jessie while took hers.

"Prices from our manufacturer have gone up again. If we can get a better supplier or argue a reduction, better still," said Gordon before put his cup on the table then sat down.

"It's funny how we can always sell mirrors," said Jessie, and shook her head was bewildered by it.

"It's because folk don't want to break them while travelling home from Leeds," said Gordon then laughed.

"That could be true, so right then, are we all agreed to carry on regardless," said David before drank up.

"Of course," said Jessie then did the same.

With paintings again regularly delivered from the auction house, which provided Gordon with a steady income, one of the agreements he arranged with his mum was he had Wednesday night off. This was so he could take Andrea and Tracy out, and she smirked when he was adamant about it.

Gordon also began to hang finished paintings in the shop again. This made a better display and with that in mind, he decided to advertise in the local press. The advert stated his work was available for viewing with small map underneath explaining how to get to the shop. When asking for to run it for a month, when paid for it, he gasped, "Good grief I'm in the wrong business."

Wednesday evening, Gordon drove round to Andrea's, picked them up and continued to a pub on the outskirts of town. Glancing at Tracy through the rear view mirror he asked, "You look nice are you going courting?"

Wearing a big smile she replied, "I told my Nan you were kissing mum."

"Oh, did you indeed," he said then pulled a face.

"And I bet you can guess what she asked, can't you?" said Andrea, and smirked before glanced out of the window to hide her embarrassment.

"I should think so," he replied tongue in cheek.

Andrea turned to look at him said, "I didn't fob her off I told her the truth."

"I wouldn't have expected anything else," he replied, and winked when turned into the car park.

Just looking like a normal family out for the night, relaxed and eating, Tracy loved being the centre of attraction when both fussed her and helped with her meal. Gordon cut up her meat and had to smile, when she said, "Thanks Gordon."

Picking up his own knife and fork, he glanced at Andrea and noticed her smirking. However, when Gordon allowed her to have a sip of his wine Andrea intervened saying, "That's enough, you will be getting drunk."

Grinning she asked, "Will I?"

"Yes so pack it in, else you will get us all locked up," replied her mum but had to laugh.

Later that evening, parked outside her house, with Tracy asleep on the back seat. Andrea leant towards Gordon, slipped her arm around his shoulders and kissed him. While gazing into her eyes he said, "You look lovely tonight."

"Thank you, and are you busy Saturday night?"

"No not really, well, only painting," he replied then shrugged his shoulders.

"Right then, do you want to call for your dinner? I will make it for a change."

"Of course but will it be right with madam in the back," he replied then laughed.

"I think she will approve," replied Andrea smiling at him.

Chapter 18

Over the following month, and with both always being open in front of Tracy, Gordon increased his friendship with Andrea. They would go out on a Wednesday night, and on a Saturday he would call at her house for dinner. Leading up to Christmas, bought both him presents but as normal they were going to spend the festivities at Andrea's mums.

Gordon knew this, turned up two days before, and handed them round. "You had no need to bother buying her anything, she gets enough," said Andrea while smiled watching Tracy open her present

"It's only fair," he replied, slipped his hand into his pocket, pulled out a small packet and handed it to her.

When she opened it, noticed a wrist watch, Gordon had bought it because he had never seen her wear one. "Thank you very much," said Andrea, lovingly smiled and kissed him.

"Mum look at this," gasped Tracy, sounded excited, had opened hers and took out a Barbie doll.

"Gordon, those are expensive," said Andrea staring at him.

"So what?" he replied then kissed her.

Feeling pleased with himself, when Gordon reached home, he wasn't bothered they hadn't bought him anything knew their income was limited. Having a drink of wine he sat in the front room watching TV when suddenly it dawned on him Moira hadn't yet returned the money she borrowed or as of yet hadn't paid this week's rent. Frowning he thought, *I must confess she isn't my cup of tea; mind you she has a nice body though.*

Gordon very much hoped his relationship with Andrea continued, even though he hadn't pushed sleeping with her, knew there was plenty of time. A card or present he didn't care about, thought of the cost and knew money was tight for them. Gordon stood up to replenish his glass moaning, "Although it will be to me if I don't get some more paintings done."

Obviously that was far from the case, and on Christmas day Gordon had lunch with his mum at her house. As in years gone by, Doreen and David joined them later and handed round presents. "It seems strange not having to traipse round Leeds to buy Colin something," said Jessie while opened hers.

"What have you bought your mum?" asked Doreen, before sat down looking at Gordon.

"It hanging on the wall," he replied, and nodded the direction.

"I told him not to bring it but he has," said Jessie then half smiled.

"Oh Gordon, that looks magnificent," said David, stood up, and walked over to inspect the painting more.

Doreen walked up to him, and stood at his side saying, "It is beautiful Gordon."

"Thanks," he replied.

"Has Barbara called to see you lately?" asked Jessie, while inspected their present of a large silver photo frame.

"No, she said they might call after the holidays. They are too busy decorating at the moment," replied Doreen, walked over and sat down.

"Tracy said the same, mind you it is a fair way to travel when you've no transport," said Jessie before reached over to place the frame on a side table.

Gordon decided to change the subject, and standing up asked if anyone wanted a cup of tea. "I thought you'd never ask," said David smiling at him.

At eleven o'clock, Gordon kissed his mum and said goodnight to Doreen and David, who had stayed late to keep his mum company. Waving when he set off, unfortunately while on the way Gordon sighed because knew his mum was lonely. However, because he maintained good health and seeing her house was too big for her to manage, Gordon was going to suggest she gave it up to Tracy then move back in with him.

Knowing she would refuse, at the next opportunity he would offer because it had also crossed his mind, if everything went well with Andrea, she could also move in with him. However, when he pulled up at the back of the shop, Gordon noticed Moira open her back door then looked out waving to him.

Gordon got out, locked the car door, and smiling said, "You'll catch you death of cold dressed like that," noticed the outline of her figure through a flimsy see through nightie.

Wearing a big grin she asked, "Fancy a drink for Christmas?"

"Why not," he replied, walked towards her and waited while she turned inside. Gordon followed, and closing the door joked; "I hope you haven't been posing for somebody else?"

Moira shivered, rubbed her bare arms, and smirked pursed her lips saying, "Cheeky, and by the way, there's your money on the table. It's the first time I've seen you to give you it." Turning she opened the fridge door then purposely bent down before took out a bottle of wine.

Gordon eyed her arse thought, *nice one,* but knew she did it on purpose. After opened the bottle, when she poured out their drinks, Moira turned, passed him a glass and raising hers said, "Compliments of the season to you."

"And the same to you," replied Gordon before had a drink.

"Right then," said Moira while sat opposite him.

"Right then what?" asked Gordon staring at her.

"For a start you never told me you were courting?" she asked then had a drink before held the glass in her hand.

"Do I have to?" he replied before had another drink.

"Oh no, it's just that I've been trying to get you into bed and didn't know why you wouldn't take on. Now I know why," she replied before had a drink.

"Why go to bed? I go there to sleep. Making love anywhere else makes it more exciting and dangerous," said Gordon but had to smile thought, *bloody hellfire, you look full of it.*

"Does your girlfriend agree with that? Or is that an impertinent question," she asked then cheekily raised her eyebrows.

Staring into her eyes he replied, "Of course," knew full well she was fishing about Andrea but he couldn't understand why.

"Right then, so if we were to make love in here, where would you start?" she asked, put down her glass, and leant on the table smirking at him.

"One has to make sure the curtains are closed properly then I'd make a start with you laid on this table, although my uncle David made it," replied Gordon while rubbed the palm of his hand across it. After finished his wine he said, "Once fully undressed, possibly later end up in the front room with you bent over the sofa while watching TV. Then we will end up on the stair steps, it is more comfy than what you think you know, carry on into the bathroom and finish off the proceedings before ending up in the bedroom. Bobs your uncle, pull the quilt over you and go to sleep," he replied before placed his glass on the table.

Moira looked flushed, reached out for the wine bottle then filled up their glasses. She looked up saying, "I must say that sounds far too energetic for me; there's no romance with it."

"That comes first with the preparation. One must be at boiling point first, simmer for an hour and then explode. It's a guaranteed remedy for insomniacs," he replied before had a drink.

"Right then, let's get the preparation over with," she said then reached down and pulled off her nightie over her head.

"Sorry, I exploded yesterday," he said, drank up but eyed her tits.

"Spoilsport, that's the trouble with men, one go and it's all over with," she moaned before picked up her glass.

Smirking he replied, "You think so? Well, first of all I have nothing to wear. We can't be spreading stuff can we? And secondly you never locked the back door."

Moira studied before shared out the rest of the wine. She put the bottle on the table, stood up, walked over and locked the door. Gordon eyed her arse, when she spun round continued into the front room. Moira returned two minutes later, and threw a packet of condoms on the table asked, "Will three, be enough?"

"Could well be," he replied standing up noticed Moira approach him with head bowed as if embarrassed then reached up placed her hands on his shoulders. Gordon couldn't understand her little miss lost look, when she looked up then kissed him.

Gliding his hands down over her back made her gasp and really in two minds to proceed, he eventually continued them over her arse. Breathing heavily through her nose, Moira greedily kissed him, forced her tongue in his mouth while at the same time undid his trousers, and then the action began.

After romping all over the house, it was two o'clock in the morning when they reached her bedroom. While using the last condom, sitting on him Moira looked down at Gordon saying, "I take it back, all men aren't the same."

"Too true mate," he replied while slid his hands up her belly.

Next morning when Gordon woke, he glanced round then suddenly realized where he was. Moira had her back to him and she woke when he got out then quickly set off to use the toilet. "Hurry up love I want to go as well," she said, watched him go inside the bathroom.

Closing the door he replied, "Two minutes."

After both dressed, five minutes later downstairs in the kitchen, Moira began to make a cup of tea. She poured it out, turned, placed two cups on the table, and sat down asking, "What are you doing today?"

"Painting," replied Gordon.

Raising her eyebrows she asked, "Even on a boxing day?"

"Certainly, the show must go on," he replied before finished his tea.

Smiling she asked, "Could I watch?"

Standing up he replied, "Not today. I have to do the books later and hopefully mum will bring my dinner."

"Right then, I'd better get cleaned up," said Moira, did the same, fully expected him to kiss her but Gordon didn't, continued to the door and unlocked it.

Waking out, "See you later," he said, continued to his house and suddenly smiled noticed his car covered in frost.

Inside his house, Gordon filled and switched on the kettle, then went straight upstairs and undressed. While in the shower, he had enjoyed his romp with Moira, but there was something about her he couldn't take to and didn't know what it was.

When recalled her saying she had been courting then hoped she didn't know Andrea, because Gordon thought she was the type that if she did, might start to tell tales. The consequences began to worry him and when the word greed came to mind, it suddenly dawned on him what she reminded him about.

Two weeks later, after a good night out with Andrea and Tracy, Gordon was in a relaxed mood had paintings finished for the auction house and two more completed for his collection. Thursday morning, while making a drink of tea, he received a phone call from a Terrance Carpenter. Gordon recalled the name saying, "Oh, yes I remember now, you are a business colleague of Mr. Broughton's."

Sounding sympathetic he asked, "That's right from Stamford. He gave me your number and I hope you don't mind me ringing at this hour."

Gordon had to smile when asked, "Not at all and how can I help?"

"I have seen your restoration work and wish to commission you to restore my artwork. I have ten paintings, and if possible could you call to my house and give me your valuable opinion," he replied.

"Unfortunately, I cannot. I have recently lost my father and my mother's health is not too great. Circumstances now dictate I have to confine all future work in my shop," replied Gordon, had decided there was no more travelling.

"Oh, that is a great pity. Please tell me, is it secure there?" he asked sounding unsure.

"It has to be because of my profession. I have had some extremely valuable works of art to restore here," replied Gordon, had purposely sounded serious because he could do with the work and grimaced hoped he didn't turn him down.

"If you inform me of your address, may I call there sometime in the near future? I would very much like to peruse your work," he asked but sounded excited by the prospect.

Gordon smiled now knew he had the work asked, "Of course, and what date would suite you best?"

"Will the last Monday in January be alright for you?" he asked, while flipped through his diary.

Gordon heard, and smiling said, "Of course, I will be about somewhere. If you have you a pen handy I'll give you my address."

After informed him and replaced the receiver, Gordon studied. Although his finances were sound and for the last month had not subsidized the shop he knew it was because David and his mum were in it more often. It made the difference with them having a better sales technique; however, he had another problem now and she lived next door. Unable to weigh Moira up even though she was a very sexy lady, had the looks and figure to go with it, but Gordon didn't really fancy her and put it down to her personality.

That afternoon, Andrea called in the shop after taken Tracy to the local infant school for the first time on a trial run. When it suddenly dawned on Gordon that Moira worked at the same school, smiling he asked, "How long is Tracy stopping there for?"

"Two hours. I thought she might not want to stop and cry to come home but she hasn't," replied Andrea while glanced round.

While gesturing the way, "Cup of tea time then, come on through love?" asked Gordon taking her into the kitchen.

Andrea meekly followed, sat at the table and watched him make the tea. When Gordon poured it out, "How's your mum going on?" she asked before sat up straight.

"So far so good, its knocked hell out of her losing my dad but what else can she do," he replied while put their cups on the table.

"It does indeed," she said, picking up her cup to have a sip.

"When does Tracy start school permanent then?" he asked while pulled out a chair and sat down.

Staring at her cup Andrea asked, "A week on Monday, and Gordon, why have you never asked to stay over at my house?"

"When the time is right I will," he replied was trying not to smile.

"Playing it safe are you?" she asked, looked up and stared into his eyes.

"No, I just didn't want to offend you. I happen to like you a lot, well, I think you know that. It's that just over one silly mistake I might lose you and I don't want that to happen," he replied before had a drink.

"Thank you Gordon, and I know what you mean," she said before finished her tea.

Still smiling he asked, "Well then, seeing as you are now a lady of leisure what are your plans now?"

Laughing she replied, "Housework, that little bugger makes more mess than a bulldozer."

"I can imagine," he said then listened. Gordon stood up and after listened more said, I won't be a moment there's someone come into the shop."

Waiting while he served a young couple, eventually sold a matching set, chest of draws and a book case, Andrea stood in the doorway watched him. Gordon wrote out a receipt saying, "Delivery will be about six tonight," watched them walk out of the shop then turned, noticed her and smiled.

"I must be off now. Will you be calling for dinner on Saturday?" she asked.

"My pleasure love," he replied and leaning forwards kissed her.

Andrea smiled then patted his chest saying, "See you later love."

While waving to her, for the first time, Gordon didn't want Andrea to go. About to go after her suddenly the door opened and in walked a young chap, who after looked round asked, "Got any good second hand kitchen tables mate?"

A smiling Gordon replied, "I should think so."

David and his mum arrived at half past four and brought Gordon his dinner. Jessie placed it in the oven, carried on into the shop and noticed him moving furniture round asked, "What the hell are you doing now?"

Looking round at her Gordon replied, "Making more room, I'm going to have this corner for a display."

Frowning at him she asked, "What, just for your paintings?"

"That right mum. I might have a commission coming up, and the chap that's hiring me is calling to view the place so I might as well make it look like a gallery," he replied before picked up a duster then wiped a table.

"Does that chap from Leeds still call with paintings for you to do?" she asked while watched him.

"Once a fortnight now, I thought it would drop off eventually," he replied before looked round.

David walked in asking, "What the hell are you doing now?"

"Mind your own business so come on let's load the van, there's four deliveries tonight," replied Gordon smiling at him.

With the deliveries done, and suggested they were easy and could have been done on his own, when David was ready to leave for home, he agreed to call in the morning to make Gordon four easels out of scrap wood. Gordon stared at him asked, "Are you sure?"

"Positive lad," said David, seemed confident.

"Anyway my thanks, however, those easels I do badly need," said Gordon before kissed his mum then waved when they were about to set off.

"Stop moaning else you'll do them yourself," said David laughing before closed the door behind him.

Gordon locked up, rubbed his hands together then craftily smiled saying, "I wonder what mum has made."

It was corned beef hash and he thoroughly enjoyed every bit. After washed up; Gordon went upstairs into his studio to paint. Two hours later, he had finished off the second painting of Moira and began another of her in a different pose. At this moment in time he decided not to display them but would the one of Caroline.

Gordon sat down on the settee and stared out of the window. Seeing frost on cars parked in the street, he suddenly smiled could see smoke coming out of the collier's houses. In a melancholy mood he moaned, "I wonder what this bloody year has in store for us."

Although the colliers had returned to work the government set about to decimate the industry. There weren't as many colliers living on the estate now when many had left the pits. Retraining and re-education was the in-words now, however, during this process, again it had left the local economy totally buggered.

Gordon turned on the light, began to paint then recalled what Andrea said about the death of her husband and the way she was treated by the council. Deliberating he made up his mind to give Moira three months notice to leave the house and would make the excuse his mum was moving back in. Grinning Gordon said, "I'd better tell her first, else she'll drop me right in it."

Saturday night Gordon drove round to Andrea's and was welcomed inside. Instantly Tracy began to inform him she had been to school and liked it. "Did you have your dinner there?" he asked smiling at her enthusiasm.

"No I didn't stay that long," she replied looking disappointed.

Andrea while finished prepared their meal in the kitchen, listened and smiled. After laying out the table she shouted, "When you two are ready."

"Right love," shouted Gordon.

Tracy ran into the kitchen and Gordon followed then lifted her up placing her on a chair. "Thanks," said Tracy, picked up her knife and fork watched her mum and waited.

Gordon sat down and smiled when Andrea put her plate on the table saying, "Don't make a mess else I'll tell your teacher."

"You won't tell mine will you?" asked Gordon smirking when Andrea passed him a plate.

"I might," she replied, and smirked put hers on the table before sat with them.

While they ate, Tracy asked questions about their schools, and if they liked it. "I sure did," replied Gordon while placed his knife and fork on his plate.

She noticed, and did the same with hers asking, "Is that good manners?"

"It is, it means thank you very much, I have enjoyed my meal," he replied then winked at her.

"Going to play mum," said Tracy, and held onto the table while slid off the chair.

"Come on then let's wash up," said Gordon while stood up.

Later when they walked into the front room, Tracy was asleep on the sofa, "I'll take her up she looks buggered," said Andrea while gently picked her up.

Gordon looked round at her toys, knelt down, began to tidy them and put them in a toy box she had in the corner near the TV. When Andrea returned, she smiled saying, "You had no need to do that they'll be out again in the morning."

"It's alright," he replied while sat on the sofa.

Andrea sat with him and rested back moaned, "Glorious peace and quiet for a change."

"It is nice to relax," said Gordon and did the same. Andrea leant towards him and he slipped his arm around her shoulder and hugged her saying, "Thanks for my dinner love, it was very nice."

"You are welcome, but it was only pork steak," she replied, looked up and then kissed him.

Feeling cozy, relaxed and now in an atmosphere he longed for. Gordon began to drowse; suddenly he opened his eyes wide when Andrea asked, "Will you stay with me tonight please?"

"Are you sure about it?" he asked frowning at her.

"Positive," she replied, sat up then slowly leant forward and kissed him.

Gordon wrapped his arms around her, and hugged her. Suddenly he gently held her at arm's length saying, "Honest there is no pressure. You know, there is plenty of time."

"I know," she replied before stood up.

Turning the lights off after them, Andrea walked upstairs first and entered her bedroom. Gordon followed and this time with no romping all over the house or with the fear of waking Tracy, after he undressed her, she undressed him. They lay in bed, and for the first time, Gordon, feeling totally relaxed, didn't need excitement for him to make love to a woman, it all seemed so natural.

Later, laid with his head on Andrea's chest, she had her arms tight around him whispered, "What shall we do about Tracy in the morning?"

Looking into her eyes he giggled saying, "We'll all have breakfast together."

Chapter 19

Next morning, all sat round the table it was blushes all round when Tracy began to ask questions. "Don't be so nosey, I'll be glad when you start school full-time," said her mum slightly red faced.

Tracy turned, and looking at Gordon asked, "Will you take me there."

Gordon looked straight at Andrea while had to work out a respectably reply before said, "Not just yet, maybe I might later on."

When Tracy went in the front room to play, Gordon stood up began to clear the table. "What did you mean by that?" asked Andrea while watched him.

"When I've washed up, I'll have to go to go open shop. I have various alterations to do and on Wednesday night when we go out can we have a serious talk please?" he asked placing the dishes in the sink.

Andrea was sat with her elbows on the table and her head bowed. Without looking up she asked, "Gordon, last night was wonderful, please don't use me? I think you know what I mean."

"I have no intentions of doing that my love. All I have done is waited for you. I know it must be hard when you loved Jack then lost him so who am I to force my way into your life. I'll take a back seat and wait until you are ready," he replied before turned on the tap.

Hearing Andrea put away cereal boxes and milk, Gordon began to wash up. Placing the dishes in a rack he glanced out of the back window, noticed a swing in the garden and smiled. Andrea stood behind him asked, "So you have good intentions then?"

Gordon turned, and smiled replied, "Andrea, I am falling in love with you. Sorry I can't help it, that's why I am here and under no other pretext."

"Thank you for saying that and you do know the neighbors will start talking seeing your car parked outside all night."

"So what love? I'm hoping it will be there more often," he replied then kissed her.

When Gordon arrived home, first he had a quick shower and dressed before going downstairs to make a cup of tea. Returning into his studio he began to paint and at eleven o'clock heard the van pull up. David with his mum entered the kitchen and Jessie placed a dish in the oven, watched David continue into the workshop had to sort out some wood for the morning. She decided to go upstairs to

Gordon, entered his studio and eyeing him said "Good morning and your dinners in the oven."

Smiling he replied, "Thanks mum," and watched her sit on the settee.

"Have you done the books this week yet?" she asked while glanced round.

"No, later today and don't worry the shops ticking over nicely. It does better when you've been in serving though," he replied, then began to mix some paint.

"I'm not worried about that, it's your future. Anyway Tracy called last night with your invitation to her wedding. She told me she had called here first and said there was no one in," said Jessie watching him for a reaction.

"Is that so," he replied while studied his work.

"So where were you?"

"I stayed at Andrea's," he replied then carried on painting.

Smirking she asked, "What all night long? Hellfire it must be serious then."

"It is, and why did our Tracy bring me an invitation? She knows very well I don't want to go," said Gordon mainly to change the subject.

"Don't be so silly you're her brother, she expects you being there."

"Well she can keep on expecting because I am not going," he snapped, then rest his brush on his palette rubbed his nose.

Jessie stood up and purposely raised her voice stressed, "Don't let us argue over it Gordon."

"I am not arguing with you and I am not arguing with her. She knows what I think about her, besides I might be on holiday with Andrea and Tracy about then," said Gordon then stood back eyed his painting just to aggravate her. Knowing she watched him he asked, "What do you think about this then?"

"Not bad really," she replied then stormed out.

Gordon knew she was angry, took the painting off the easel and leant it against the wall. Picking up a new canvas he began to fit it had decided to paint Andrea, knew what he had in mind, however, couldn't grasp a pose.

Ten minutes later, when Gordon went downstairs, his mum had made them a cup of tea. David walked in from the workshop, asking, "I've enough spare wood to make you six easels will that do you?"

"Just superb," replied Gordon then took his cup from his mum sat down at the table.

"So where are you taking Andrea?" asked his mum while sat with him.

"Maybe to the coast," he replied before had a sip.

"I must confess I told our Tracy you wouldn't go," said his mum then had a drink.

"Mum, you have had this business since I was born, people round here have had it hard with stupid stoppages and wild cat strikes, many lasting for months. Dad always kept our business affairs quiet, had a van for the deliveries but never owned a car, and do you know why? Because he thought it was showing off," said Gordon staring at her.

Bowing her head Jessie said, "I know what you're going to say my love."

"I've seen dad pawn worthless trinkets so people round here could buy food. Even after years had passed they still respected him for it, and when they had a bit of spare money came here to buy their furniture. Now our Tracy was always the one that had to spoil that image and brag about what she had. She was always dolled up to the nines while some of her mates didn't have the bus fare and had to walk to school, did you know that?" Then Gordon suddenly decided to keep quiet when it sounded like jealousy and picked up his cup.

David leant on the worktop sipping his tea, knew what Gordon meant, had argued with Barbara not to go into business with Tracy, and failed. He also had leant them money to start with and was the same as his dad, to give respect to their customers had never owned a car.

"So you are not going then?" asked his mum.

"No, I'll open the shop as normal," replied Gordon now sat with the cup in his hands.

"You just said you were going on holiday?" she asked then stared at him thought he was lying.

"I'll put it back to keep the shop open and go on honeymoon later," he replied before drank his tea.

"So you are getting married then?"

"Maybe, but I'll work for my money first,"

"Hang on a minute, you do mean to Andrea?"

"If she'll have me, yes," he replied then walked out.

"That's telling you," said David, and smirked.

"Don't you start, if only I knew it was the truth," replied Jessie then studied.

While smiling David said, "It will be, because one thing Gordon has never been it's a liar."

"He doesn't lie, he just bends the truth and usually to suit himself," said Jessie then studied.

While painting in his studio, Gordon heard them leave, smiled and continued to sketch Andrea. Finally making up his mind he positioned her laid naked on a bed and smirked saying, "You ought to be here now my love I didn't see much of you in the dark."

At two o'clock, because his belly rumbled, Gordon had a rest, decided to have dinner and set off downstairs. After turning on the oven on, he poured out a glass of wine, continued into the front room and switched on the TV. Uncannily he grimaced when now really missed Andrea's and Tracy's company, however, was still annoyed over the invitation to his sister's wedding. Sighing Gordon moaned, "She's been nowhere near here to help out and I bet she's never helped mum once in her house the bone idle sod," then stood up walked into the kitchen.

After checked his meal, Gordon turned off the oven, used a tea towel to take out the dish. It was hot and he quickly turned, was about to put it on the table when there was a knock on the back door. Gordon unlocked then opened it, and seemed impatient asked, "Oh hello, please come on in and shut the door? I'm just having my dinner."

"Sorry to interrupt you," said Moira, continued inside and closed the door after her.

"What can we do for you?" he asked, sat down and took the lid off the dish.

"I thought you might have called for a drink last night?" she asked, sidled over towards the table, and eyed the casserole before pulled out a chair to sit down.

"No, I was out on business," he replied, served his meal and replaced the lid before picked up his knife and fork.

"And all night?" she asked, raising her eyebrows then sarcastically smiled.

"I was at my girlfriends," he replied while began to cut up large pork sausage thinking; *she is getting too nosey, it's time to nip this conversation in the bud.*

Smirking she asked, "That serious is it?"

"Very serious," he replied before started to eat.

"I want a favour doing again. I know its short notice but if possible could you lend me a hundred pounds please, I have to go on a school trip and all the deposits have to be in a week on Monday?" asked Moira sounding confidant.

Gordon studied, and quickly decided to take the opportunity saying, "I don't have that amount with me, but while you are here, it is unfortunate that I shall have to give you three months notice on the house."

Staring at him she gasped, "Never."

"Mum has decided to move back here with her house far too big to manage now," he replied, didn't look at her, but could feel her eyes on him.

Quickly standing up she snapped, "You can't do that."

"I can do what I like it's my property. And when anything happens to mum, the lot is being knocked down and a new house built on it for me," he replied.

"Oh my God," she moaned, spun round, walked out and slammed the door after her.

Gordon heard her door slam and craftily smiled while carried on finished his meal. Later, after washed up, he confidently strolled into the shop and browsed the area he had cleared. Deciding where to arrange his display he thought, *the only trouble is Andrea knew Caroline and knows about Moira next door. I'll have to be careful what I display now,* turned and continued upstairs.

Working until ten o'clock that night but satisfied with the progress of Andrea's painting, Gordon called it a day then went to bed. Laid in darkness, he thought about the previous night with Andrea and wished she was with him now. Obviously he would very much like her to move in with him, and also knew it would not be wise at the moment as wanted Moira out of the way first.

Knowing he gave her three months notice and really knew he could not kick her out at all, could get into trouble for it if he did. Gordon suddenly moaned when realized he hadn't done the books for that week and would have to do them first thing in the morning. Rolling over he moaned, "Never mind, David will be here to help me."

Next morning, David arrived and knocked on the back door. Gordon opened it asking, "You have just timed it right, and where's mum?"

"She's a bit off it, she said I have to pick her up after lunch so you'll have to make your own dinner," he replied, and smiled while continued inside.

"That's nothing new," said Gordon before closed the door.

"I'll make a start, so go make some tea first if you want those easels finishing," said David, and smiled before continued into the workshop.

Ten minutes later, after passed David a cup, Gordon walked into the shop and unlocked the door. Beginning to dust furniture he knew Andrea was taking Tracy to school and waved when they walked by. While sorting out receipts and invoices, Gordon looked up when Andrea returned and smiling she entered the shop saying, "Hello love."

"Hello and has she gone in alright?" he asked, while walked towards her then kissed her.

"Straight in and no messing," she replied pulling a face of approval.

"That's good, don't worry she'll soon settle in. Come on though and I'll make a cup of tea," said Gordon while slipped his arm around her waist.

David walked in carried an easel and opened it saying, "Oh hello love and here you are this is the first one."

"Very nice, two minutes and tea's up," said Gordon as they continued into the kitchen.

After made some tea and took David one, Gordon returned, sat at the table with Andrea. Looking sheepish at her he said, "First I have a confession to make."

"Oh, and what's that?" she asked while had a drink.

Staring at her he replied, "Yesterday I started a painting of you and unfortunately you're in the nude."

Frowning she asked, "Oh, and why for?"

"Because you have a beautiful body and it wants showing off," he replied but looked relieved when it seemed she wasn't offended.

Smiling she asked, "When it's finished, will it go on display anywhere?"

"That is entirely up to you," he replied purposely sounding serious.

"I'll wait while it's done then give you my opinion," she said then finished her tea.

"I worked like hell on it yesterday, you can have a look later if you want," he said before finished his.

"Alright then, but it had better be tasteful else you are in a lot bother," she said then laughed.

"My work is always tasteful madam," he replied but couldn't help smirking.

David had completed another easel and eyed them as they walked upstairs. Remaining in the shop, he suddenly looked up when the door opened then smiled at elderly couple walking towards him asking, "Can I help you?"

Inside Gordon's studio, "Have you completed many more paintings," said Andrea while glanced round, noticed the one of Moira and thought she had seen her face before.

"What do you think?" asked Gordon, purposely stood in front of her and gestured to a painting on an easel.

"You have my face to do yet," she replied before inspected it closely.

"That bit is easy because you have short hair."

"Oh is it? And it's so kind of you to use a different bed, they might have recognized mine," she said then laughed.

Smirking he asked, "Why? How many more people have been in it?"

"Just you and. Well, yes it seems tasteful enough, it should look better when you've done my face though," she replied then kissed him.

Gordon smiled while eyed her profile asking, "Do you pluck your eyebrows?"

Suddenly pointing to the painting she asked, "Yes I do, and that one there, is that the woman that lives next door to you?"

"Yes, she's a teacher," he replied while slipped his arm around her waist.

"Do you know her well?" she asked while frowning at the provocative position.

"Only when she calls to pay her rent and not as well as you," he replied before kissed her cheek.

Andrea looked in a devilish mood turned, slipped her arms around his neck and kissed him. "By hell, that was a smacker," said Gordon, then kissed her softly on her lips then her cheek, continued down and kissed her neck.

"To be really honest I really missed you last night," she said while craftily smiled before slowly bowed her head rest it on his chest.

"And so did I," he said then kissed her forehead.

Andrea suddenly looked up, and looking flushed smiled saying, "I think it's time to go."

Gordon smirked before said, "By the look in your eyes madam, I think its bedtime."

"I know," she said and grinned before quickly kissed him.

"What about now?"

Trying to pull away from him she gasped, "Give over, your uncle is downstairs."

"So what," he replied, grabbed her arm and dragged her towards his bedroom.

"Gordon, we can't," she whispered loudly and stifled a yell when he pulled her onto his bed.

"Listen a moment, can I call round to your house tonight? Something as just dawned on me," said Gordon then quickly kissed her.

Andrea pulled away, and smirking replied, "Only if you lock your door first."

"Why is it women always have to have the last word?" he moaned then rolled out of bed.

An hour later when they casually walked downstairs, David was in the kitchen making a cup of tea. He turned saying, "You're just in time."

Knowing full well the bakery Andrea worked at had closed, Gordon pulled out a chair saying, "Good and when you pick up mum later we'll have a mini meeting because I've just had a good idea," and when Andrea sat down he pulled out a chair and did the same.

"Go on then inform us before hand," said David while and poured out the tea.

Gordon looked at Andrea asking, "I haven't asked her yet but I will now. What about Andrea working part-time in the shop dusting. You know, doing a bit of cleaning for us. Is that alright my love?"

Andrea shrugged her shoulders before replied, "Well, I don't know."

David interrupted asking, "Can we afford it?"

"Just about but that doesn't matter, with Tracy at school now you have some free time and we'll be together more," he replied smiling at her.

"I should ask your mum first," said David but still smiled knew he had made up his mind.

"The extra money would be nice," said Andrea then studied.

David passed the cups round and smiled knew Gordon thought a lot about her said, "I have no objections because you're a scruffy bugger anyway and you need looking after."

When David laughed, "Oh thanks very much," said Gordon staring at him.

"If you don't mind, I finish this and set off home. I have to clean up and get Tracy's dinner ready," said Andrea before had a drink.

"Is she full time now?" asked David before did the same.

"Yes, this is her proper first day, nine while three," she replied while put her cup on the table.

"Tell you what then love, I'll call tonight about half six after I've made the deliveries," said Gordon then patted her hand.

"That reminds me, you've only have one so far a couple have bought a dining room table and six chairs," said David, drank up and put his cup on the worktop.

"See you tonight then love," said Gordon then winked.

Later, Gordon adjusted a painting on his easel when David was about to set off for his mum. At the foot of the stairs, he shouted, "I'm off Gordon and there's three drops now."

"Right, just coming," he shouted while cleaned his brush, put it on the table and stood admired his work.

After a fleeting visit from his mum, who dropped his dinner off, while he ate they discussed the shops finances. Not reaching any conclusion, however, when she left with David using Gordon's car,

Gordon dashed upstairs, quickly showered and changed.

Before he left, checked the shop and locked the kitchen door after him. Gordon noticed a light on in Moira's, smiled and got in the van then set off knowing there were now three deliveries to make.

With the deliveries completed Gordon arrived at Andrea's fifteen minutes late and knocked on her door. Tracy opened it saying, "Oh hello."

"Come in Gordon," shouted Andrea.

Closing the door after him, Gordon continued into the kitchen. Tracy grinned at him saying, "I've been to school today," then dashed into the front room.

Gordon popped his head round the door, fully expected her to say no when he asked, "I know, but did you enjoy it though?"

"It wasn't too bad really I suppose," replied Tracy, now sat on the sofa and opened a picture book.

"Very good, see you in a minute love," he said, and pulled the door to before entering the kitchen.

Andrea turned saying, "Hello love," then kissed him.

"You look in a good mood?" he asked before patted her shoulders. When she smiled, he pulled out a chair, sat down and rest on the table looking at her.

"You had better be as well because this morning you did. Well, you know and you didn't wear anything," she replied looking flushed.

Smiling he asked, "Oh, err, well, I know what you mean, but so what?"

"I wouldn't be wise just yet, would it?" she asked, while made some tea.

"And why not?" he asked, then frowned couldn't understand her change of mood. One minute seemingly cheeky yet lovable, and then next, looking perplexed and unsure.

Gordon didn't know how accurate he was when suddenly Andrea snapped, "Because I'm still unsure about us yet that's why, and don't take this wrong Gordon, but why me? You could have who you want if you wished; you have the looks, the money and have all the trappings."

When she stared at him Gordon decided there and then to put her mind at ease. Staring into her eyes he quietly said, "I've told you once Andrea and I'll say this confidently now, I love you, and while Tracy is quiet, can we work something out more on a permanent please, because I think it's about time we did," and smiled as if to assure her.

"I think I'll make a drink of tea then first," she replied, turned, and quickly began to fill the kettle mainly to regain her composure.

Chapter 20

During the following week, Gordon made enquiries at the local dole office to enquire if Andrea could work in the shop for fifteen hours without it affecting her rent or benefits. What did surprise him was on Saturday night when he called for dinner, after informed her about the councils conditions, when he asked if she could start on Monday morning and also consider moving in with him sometime in the near future. Suddenly he was stunned to silence when Andrea half smiling said, "Sorry, but at this moment in time I must have to say no."

"Why not?" he gasped then rest back frowning with disappointment.

"Gordon, yes I do like you a hell of a lot and another important fact is Tracy has taken to you. It's just that I am frightened about our future together," she replied then rest back on the sofa seemed dejected.

Knowing the chap from Stamford was calling Monday morning and he would have liked her there, seemingly dumfound, Gordon asked, "And may I ask why you are frightened?"

Now seeming nervous she replied, "Because I've lost one husband and after found out he had a fling while we were engaged, although I think he stayed true after we were married."

Raising his eyebrows he asked, "So you think I won't?"

Bowing her head Caroline asked, "I'm not saying anything Gordon. It's just that at this moment in time we have a love and it's good. Can we leave it like that for now, please?"

"Will you still work for us in the shop?"

"Yes of course, the money will come in handy. But please don't put pressure on me for us to live together just yet, and that's why I don't want another child, it would complicate things further," she replied then leant on him.

Gordon slipped his arm around her and smiling said, "I understand love," then squeezed her.

Sunday morning when he returned home, Gordon went straight upstairs, showered and changed. Obviously he was disappointed with what Andrea had said but understood her feelings. Returning downstairs, first he did the books and made out an order for new furniture required. When Gordon sealed the envelope ready to post, he suddenly looked up when there was a knock on the door.

Gordon opened it saying, "Oh hello," and then stood back when Moira walked inside and closed it behind her.

Not looking in a good mood, "Here's your rent, I didn't see you on Friday," she snapped while held out the book.

"I was busy, and thanks," he said, took it from her, put the money in his pocket, signed the book then gave her it back.

"Is the notice to quit still on?" she asked while watched him filled the kettle.

Lightly he asked, "Yes it is, do you want a cup before you go?"

"Please," she replied, walked over to the table and sat down. "I have to say this, when you gave me three months notice it knocked the stuffing out of me. I thought we had a future together," she said while watched him.

"Pardon and I think not. I had told you I was engaged," he replied while poured milk in the cups.

"You're just playing the field aren't you?" she asked then slyly smiled.

"What field? Anyway from today, David will call on a Friday for your rent. I shall be very busy from now on," he replied while poured out the tea.

"Are you going away?" she asked, seemed taken aback.

"No, but I have a commission to do, and my fiancé will be running the shop for me," he replied, turned and put their cups on the table.

"So you want me to keep out of the way then?" she asked before picked up her cup and had a sip.

"Not at all, it's always business before pleasure and at the moment its all systems go," he replied, had a sip, had noticed she never mentioned the money she wanted to borrow.

"I haven't found anywhere else to go yet," she said, and frowned before had a drink.

"I've told you once, you have three months and that's plenty of time," said Gordon then did the same.

"Very well then," said Moira, stood up, glared at him, spun round and set off to the door.

Gordon watched, sat down and finished his tea. After studying his forthcoming commission, knew he had to finish the books so set about them. Nearly completed and up to the previous week when David and his mum called. "Feeling any better," he asked, watched her put a dish in the oven.

"Just about," she replied before closed the door.

"Have you set all up yet," asked David, swapped the car keys, for the vans, picked up the kettle began to fill it.

"Not yet, maybe this afternoon, I think that chaps calling about lunchtime tomorrow," replied Gordon before closed the ledger.

Sitting opposite his mum smiled asking, "Are you sure about setting a cleaner on?"

"Andrea's not a cleaner; she's just helping me out. I can't do everything, besides I want her to move in with me later, well, soon as she can," he replied.

"What about Moira next door?" she asked, and stared into his eyes.

Looking away he replied, "I've gave her notice to quit."

Turning to take David's cup she smiled asked, "I thought you two had hit it off."

"No, she's too, well, pushy and very underhand," replied Gordon, took his cup and held it in his hands.

"And Andrea isn't?" she asked before had a sip.

"No she isn't, she's refused to move in when I asked her and gave good reason as well," he replied before had a drink.

Smirking she asked, "So is that why you've asked Moira to go then?"

"No, because eventually I want to knock all these houses into one, and in time, that's if it's possible, knock them all down and have a new one built on top," he replied then smiled.

"Oh," gasped his mum, stared and then suddenly turned looking at David.

"You can't blame him for thinking that Jessie, building land is getting scarce and expensive now," he said before sat with them.

"So have you changed your mind about coming to the wedding yet?" asked Jessie then smirked.

While laughing Gordon replied, "No, I'm not mingling with bloody yuppies, in time their bubble will burst and they'll all be crying in their pink gins."

"That's no way to talk about your sister," snapped Jessie staring at him.

"It isn't mum and you should be grateful because I could call her a lot worse," he replied before stood up.

Glaring at him she snapped, "I had better not hear you."

"You won't, I'll say it all when you've left."

"So it looks like me giving her away then," said David raising his eyebrows.

"You can do what you like, that's all she's worth in my eyes," replied Gordon then laughed.

When they left, Gordon went upstairs to paint, and was pleased about his progress with the one of Andrea. When it became dark and because he didn't like working under artificial light, he took some paintings downstairs and arranged them in the shop.

After hanging five paintings on the walls, including the one of Caroline, he decided not to display the one of Moira. With six more on easels arranged in a half circle, Gordon looked round saying, "That looks better, besides it gives me more room upstairs."

Turning off the lights he continued into the kitchen, and began to make a sandwich. After poured out a glass of wine, Gordon noticed it was the last bottle, picked up the tray, went into the front room and put it on the coffee table before switched on the TV.

While watched the news, Gordon was undecided to finish the painting of Andrea, would liked to have it displayed when she began work tomorrow, however, wanting it to look exceptionally good, he knew it would take at least two more days.

Later in bed, and struggling to sleep, Gordon hoped the following day the chap calling about a commission would accept his offer and could work on his paintings in the shop. The money would come in handy, and seeing as the shop was again ticking over nicely, Gordon could manage without Moira's rent so could afford to pay Andrea a wage. Suddenly he sighed when remembered he hadn't yet worked out a rate of pay for her moaning, "I'll have to that first thing."

Next morning, after a shave, Gordon cleaned his teeth, showered, and all spruced up went downstairs to make breakfast. Having just sat down he was about to eat when his mum and David arrived. Gordon stood up, switched on the kettle, turned and unlocked the door. "You're on the ball this morning," said his mum continuing inside.

"I have a busy day," he replied when sat down.

When the kettle boiled, "I'll make this," said David, and switched it off.

While smiling Jessie asked, "What time will Andrea be here?"

"After she's taken Tracy to school," replied Gordon before carried on eating his toast.

"Very good, so where will she start and have you worked out a routine for her yet?" she asked while pulled out a chair then sat down.

Looking round he replied, "The shop is most important part. So after polished in there, she can carry on in my living quarters."

David in devilment, put their cups on the table asking, "Have you tidied up already?"

"Just a little, I've done my display in the shop so if you want to go through and give me your opinion," replied Gordon, and gestured, had purposely changed the subject to save embarrassment.

"Will do lad," said David, and set off.

"How many hours is Andrea working? I hope you have worked it all out properly?" asked Jessie before picked up her cup.

"Three hours on Monday, Wednesday and Friday and with less tax and what have you, that will keep her just under her allowance so it won't affect her rent."

"Oh, and did you work all that out for her as well?" asked Jessie smiling.

"Give over fishing mum, you know very well I have," he replied, stood up and continued into the shop.

Standing with David, both were looking round when Jessie entered saying, "They look good."

"I bloody hope so they are meant to impress," replied Gordon, set off to the shop door, unlocked and opened it.

When he glanced down the street, "Right then, I'll just go tidy up in the workshop," said David, and smiling he winked at Jessie before set off.

"Yes and I'll go wash up to keep out of your way," said Jessie and smirked when continued into the kitchen.

Gordon turned, closed the door, picked up a cloth and began to dust a table occasionally glanced out of the window. Suddenly he smiled when Andrea came into view opening the door. When she closed it after her, "Hello love, did she go in alright?" he asked before kissed her.

"No messing, straight in, shouted bye mum and ran off," replied Andrea then grinned with relief.

"Come on let's have a drink of tea first," said Gordon while slipped his arm around her shoulder.

Andrea noticed the paintings when they walked by them continued into the kitchen. Jessie was washing up, turned and smiled asking, "Hello love and how are you keeping?"

"Fine thanks, better now Tracy has started school, sometimes she's hard work."

"Sit down love," said Gordon before picked up the kettle.

Jessie wiped her hands, passed Gordon the tea towel saying, "Here you are," the sat opposite Andrea noticing she seemed a little nervous.

Knowing Gordon's mum and dad originally owned the shop, quietly, Andrea asked, "You don't mind me working here do you?"

"He's paying your wages I am not," replied Jessie, rather cold.

"Mum, say that again only better," snapped Gordon, not liking her tone of voice.

"Sorry love and I didn't mean that as it sounded Andrea, but it is Gordon's business and he can do whatever he likes," said Jessie the smiled patted her hand.

"I know what you meant," said Andrea, but thought different and noticed Gordon was shaking his head as if in disgust.

David walked in saying, "There that all done, just waiting for customers now, oh thanks lad," and took a cup from Gordon.

When he turned passed his mum one and then Andrea's, Gordon asked, "Will you be calling back later with my dinner mum?"

Smiling she replied, "There's one thing about you, you know how to make a hint, and the answer is yes."

When David and his mum set off home, in the shop, Gordon began to explain that the furniture on display was dusted daily. Smiling he said, "It doesn't look good if customers come in and there's dust all over the place."

"That's very true, so do you want me to make a start in here now?" asked Andrea smiling but felt unsure.

"If you want love, and just give me a shout if anyone comes in, I'm trying to finish off your painting," he replied then gave her a quick kiss before set off upstairs.

"Will do," she said, and watched him.

Constantly checking his watch while painting, an hour later, Andrea shouted he was wanted. Gordon put down his brush and quickly wiped his hands before dashed down stairs. A customer wanted a large mirror for over her fireplace and while he served, Andrea went into the kitchen, filled and switched on the kettle. To keep busy and while it boiled she went into the front room, dusted and began to tidy round.

After making a sale and giving the woman a receipt, when Gordon walked into the kitchen, Andrea passed him a cup asking, "Have you a vacuum?"

"It's in that cupboard there, and why what are you doing now?" he asked while gestured.

Smiling she replied, "Cleaning up, it's as your mum said, you are a mucky bugger."

Spot on lunchtime Mr. Carpenter arrived, heartily shook hands with Gordon and immediately began to inspect his paintings on display. After studying them, he turned asking, "Which one could I buy lad?"

"All these are for sale. I have others upstairs in my studio and as you will be aware I am trying to build up another collection for a sale," replied Gordon while eyeing him.

Andrea realized they were talking business and courteously continued into the kitchen. Gordon noticed, thought her polite and now decided to sell the one of Caroline. Not being surprised when Mr. Carpenter chose it, but when he asked to buy another, the river scene near his mums, Gordon explained, "It is just a local scene of the Aire-and-Calder navigation."

"Right then and now down to business, I've brought my paintings they are in the car boot," said Mr. Carpenter while reached into his coat pocket then took out his cheque book.

"You never have? Let's go bring them in first," asked Gordon while set off.

Twenty minutes later, with his paintings upstairs in his studio, and the ones he bought safely in the car boot, an impressed Mr. Carpenter arranged a date to pick them up. However, when he wanted to pay him in advance, "I would much prefer you to wait until they are ready which will be at a rough guess, in about two weeks," said Gordon while walked with him to the door.

"Right lad, then I will wait for your phone call," he replied before shook his hand.

Gordon waved to him when he set off and closed the shop door. Andrea walked in saying, "Here you are love," and passed him a cup of tea.

Gordon glanced at his watch moaning, "Oh hell is that the time? Sorry for neglecting you love."

Andrea laughed, and continued into the kitchen saying, "I'm on overtime now." Gordon was about to follow when the shop door opened and in walked a tall well dressed middle aged chap continued inside and casually looked round.

After sold two sets of small chest of draws for a bedroom, Gordon passed him a receipt and informed the chap he would deliver them about six o'clock that evening. Soon as he left, Gordon dashed into the kitchen and noticed Andrea sat at the table, had patiently waited for him. Frowning he moaned, "Sorry again my love."

"That's alright, I might as well wait until it's time to pick Tracy up from school then go straight home," she replied before finished her tea.

Gordon glanced round then asked, "Have you cleaned up in here as well?"

"That's what I'm here for isn't it?" she replied.

"Well, yes but don't go mad, there's always another day," he replied while sat opposite her.

Gordon heard the van pull up outside and looked round. Two minutes later, his mum walked in carrying a dish, and looked at them before carried on to the oven. After placed it inside, she closed the door saying, "Don't let him put on you else he'll keep you here all day."

Andrea smiled saying, "I'm only passing time while it's time to pick up Tracy from school."

"If there are only these two to drop off, I'll take them and drop after dropped your mum off first," said David, while read the receipts.

"Very kind of you, then I can get some painting done," said Gordon while stood up.

Jessie looked at Andrea asking, "Are you calling on Wednesday as well?"

"Yes, at the same time I believe," she replied then looked at Gordon.

Gordon smiled saying, "It's been a bit hectic with Mr. Carpenter calling today it'll be better the rest of the week now."

"If you let me know, I'll make enough dinner for you all then you can bring Tracy straight here, it'll save you time," said Jessie before checked her pocket for her keys.

"Oh no it's quite alright," said Andrea, and stood up quickly looked at her watch saying, "I might as well set off now."

Gordon walked with her into the shop and kissed her. Andrea smiled, waved and set off. Closing the door after him he rubbed his hands together saying, "Yes," was looking well pleased with the day, continued into the kitchen, then kissed his mum on the cheek before said, "Don't be late tomorrow, I've a lot of painting to do."

Andrea was embarrassed with the status of Jessie and David, who thought she might not have the conversation to mix with business people. Of course this was a typical working class upbringing, keep your nose out of my business and do as you are told.

Being fifteen minutes early to pick up Tracy, Andrea waited outside the school gates chatting with two other mums who were also passing time until the bell rang. When it did they all turned towards the school doors, however, Tracy was the last out. She held her teachers hand and was crying. "What's the matter my love?" asked Andrea before picked her up.

Moira smiled before said, "She's had a little accident, unfortunately spilled a little paint on her dress."

"Not to worry love it'll wash out," said Andrea then hugged her.

Smiling at them Moira asked, "There I told you, and I believe you are Gordon Mathew's fiancé?"

Andrea smiled at Tracy saying, "Pardon young lady, have you been telling tales again?"

"That is a possibility because Gordon usually spins a few. I live next door to him and that reminds me, I must call in and see him tonight, I believe we are going into Leeds on Wednesday night, only for a bit of socializing," said Moira smiling while glanced at her watch.

"Oh are you? Well, see you tomorrow" said Andrea, and quickly turned towards the school gates. On her way home, Andrea couldn't understand why Moira had said that. She put two-and-two together, thought it was jealousy and knowing Gordon picked them up and took them out on a Wednesday evening; however, as she was a good looking woman, Andrea began to get jealous.

Tuesday with David in the workshop and his mum making dinner, in between serving in the shop, Gordon began work on Mr. Carpenter's paintings. Being in an exceptional mood Gordon worked like mad had begun with the worse one. Luckily David did the deliveries for him that night, and now with a purpose in life, Gordon looked forward to the next day, when Andrea and Tracy would be with him again.

Wednesday, after shaved, cleaned his teeth, showered, and changed ready, Gordon waited in the kitchen while ate his breakfast. Just before nine he unlocked the shop door, and when Andrea walked in, he smiled, kissed her then asked, "Good morning my love and is Tracy alright?"

"Superb," she replied, seemed rather cold.

"Come on in the teas made," he said then nearly dragged her into the kitchen.

While he poured it out, Andrea sat at the table watching him then asked, "How well do you know that Moira next door?"

"And why?" he asked then frowned smelled a rat.

"Because she teaches Tracy and of course Tracy has been talking about us. On Monday Moira informed me she was calling in to see you because you were taking her into Leeds tonight."

"I don't think so my love," he replied while put their cups on the table.

Andrea purposely stared at him saying, "She looks a bit shifty to me and little girl's minds can be filled with all sorts of useless information."

Gordon sat down saying, "She has never said anything to me, but I will see her and put her right straight away."

Andrea now sat prim and proper asked, "It doesn't seem right her living next door, so how often do you see her?"

"Only on a Friday when she pays her rent, and from this week she will pay David," he replied before had a drink.

"I am not playing the jealous girlfriend Gordon, it's just that I don't trust her," said Andrea now staring at her cup.

After put his cup down he said, "She's on notice to quit anyway."

Not looking up Andrea asked, "How long as she to go?"

"She's about ten weeks left and listen my love, do you think that for one moment I would have brought you in here if there was anything going on with her." he replied then stood up.

Andrea quickly stood up saying, "No, but I don't need all this Gordon. With what I have gone through and if you don't mind, let's have a cooling off period until she's gone. I'm very sorry Gordon but I don't want to take any chances."

Staring at her he asked, "You mean…not go out or even work here?"

"I think its best," she replied, stood up and set off into the shop.

"What about tonight? Tracy will wonder what the matter is," he asked, now looked upset and followed her.

"Don't try to use Tracy, because I bet a pound to a penny her next door will," she snapped, and opened the door walked out.

"Oh my God, not again," moaned Gordon was looking bewildered.

Chapter 21

Gordon watched Andrea marching down the street and grimaced because he did understand how she must feel. When it seemed he had lost another girlfriend, his heart sank, slowly returned into the kitchen and sat down. With his mind spinning, Gordon suddenly looked up when the back door opened and when his mum walked inside. Noticing his face she asked, "And what's up with you?"

"Nothing," he replied, stood up, and continued upstairs.

In his studio, Gordon was painting when fifteen minutes later; Jessie entered had brought him a cup of tea asking, "Is Andrea not working today?"

"No, something's cropped up," he replied while mixed some paint.

Jessie put his cup on the table. She eyed him asking, "Have you fallen out?"

"Thanks and no," he snapped.

Smiling his mum said, "She did make a difference to your house; it did look a lot tidier."

"Mum, just leave me in peace will you, please?" he asked while continued to paint.

"Sorry I spoke," she replied, turned and set off downstairs mumbling away.

Gordon was very upset, had not only fallen for Andrea but had taken to Tracy like his own. It upset him more when thought he might not see her again then heard his mum shout they were going. Suddenly Gordon dashed downstairs and asked David if he would call back. After explained he wanted more time to finish a painting, and when Gordon agreed returned upstairs.

While painting, it had dawned on Gordon he owed Andrea a day's pay and decided as an excuse he would call that night to pay her. After helped David load the deliveries, soon after he set off, Gordon dashed upstairs, quickly changed then dashed downstairs set off in his car.

Arriving at their house and noticed it all darkness, he felt bitterly disappointed. Feeling stunned, he stared at a ten pound note in an envelope, got out of the car, walked up the path and pushed it through the letterbox.

"Gordon," shouted Tracy. Gordon spun round watched them walking up the street. Smiling when Tracy dived into his arms, he scooped her up and hugged her.

Andrea walked up to them, and smiled said, "Hello."

Quietly, Gordon asked, "I thought you had gone out so you purposely wouldn't see me?" then smiled when Tracy slipped her arm around his neck.

"Nonsense, I'm not that cruel," replied Andrea while set off to unlock the door.

Gordon carried Tracy and followed Caroline but when she opened it, noticed the envelope on the floor. Picking it up she asked, "What is this?"

"To be honest I thought you might be out tonight and seeing as you might not come to the shop anymore it's your wage," he replied while lowered Tracy to the floor.

Tracy looked up at him asking, "Can I have a kiss night night?"

"Of course," he replied, leant down and kissed her.

Tracy ran upstairs shouting, "Going to bed mum."

"Goodnight love," said Andrea while opened the envelope.

Smiling at him she said, "You had no need to do this."

"You earned it, anyway I must be off now," he replied, really thought she didn't want him there.

Raising her eyebrows she asked, "Going to Leeds are we?"

Quietly, Gordon replied, "No, I'm not going anywhere; I would much rather be here with you."

"You can stay Gordon, I'll just put the kettle on," she replied then turned continued to the sink.

"Andrea, we have been going out on a Wednesday night for months and I look forward to it. Being with you is fantastic and you know what I think of

Tracy. Please don't spoil it love?" he asked while watched her.

"We had to go out tonight anyway, my mum is poorly and sorry I didn't ring and tell you. I was in two minds to, I just didn't know if you told me the truth or not," she said before switched on the kettle.

"In other words you believed her instead of me?" he asked then frowned.

Andrea spun round, and stared at him looking very near to tears slowly bowed her head sobbed, "I don't know what to believe anymore."

"I'm very sorry my love," said Gordon, spun round, slowly walked out, closed the door after him, and continued to his car.

As usual, again at rock bottom, Gordon called at the off license and bought a case of wine. Arriving home, he carried it in the house, and when returned to lock the car door, Moira's back door opened. Watching him she asked, "You are in early tonight?"

"I've been very busy. I had to call at the solicitors to arrange the sale of my mum's house. Have you arranged to move out yet?" he asked while continued to the back door.

"Not yet," she replied before quickly closed hers.

"Big mistake was that Gordon," he moaned before locked the door after him.

After opened a bottle of wine, Gordon poured some in a glass and went into the front room. He flopped down on the sofa moaned, "Well, the bloody seventies weren't all that good, and I couldn't wait for the eighties. Now all I can say is stroll on the bloody nineties," then had a drink.

Eventually finishing the paintings for Mr. Carpenter, who was very pleased with the result, later that afternoon after he left, the chap called from the auction house. Informing Gordon that at this moment in time there were no more paintings for him to restore, but would contact him when there was. Gordon didn't mind, continued with his own work, took some downstairs, displayed them in the shop and over the following six weeks sold two.

As quick as she appeared, Moira moved out, and as Gordon expected owed two weeks rent including the quarterly gas and electricity bills. He didn't know where she had gone to and didn't care, was just thankful she had. Gordon could now implement his plans for the house and Sunday morning was in for a shock when Tracy and her husband called. "And what do we owe this unexpected pleasure?" he asked, while filled the kettle.

"I haven't seen you for years and we just wondered how you were going on," she replied, and with Peter sat at the table.

"I'm still the same," he said, while prepared the cups.

"We've just called at your mums and thought we would call here before we go home," said Peter while rest his elbows on the table.

"Is she alright?" he asked, while made the tea.

Tracy smiled while replied, "As well as could be expected."

Gordon poured out the tea, passed their cups, picked his up, and suddenly smiled asked, "How's your business going on?"

"Fine thanks," replied Peter, but looked taken aback when Gordon conversed normally with him.

"And you're a designer aren't you?" asked Gordon before had a drink.

"That's right, but doing more on the architectural side," he replied, sounding smug.

"Very good, and after this drink I want a job doing. It shouldn't take you long," said Gordon before craftily smiled.

After they drank their tea, Gordon took them next door into David's old house then asked about the possibility of knocking both houses into one. Peter took the opportunity to make friends, and replied it was possible. "Right then seeing as you are designers get it measured up, do the plans for the council and I'll pay you," said Gordon rubbing his hands together seemed pleased.

"The interior is nothing to do with them unless you are making serious structural alterations," said Peter looking round.

"Well I am aren't I? Come on upstairs a moment?" asked Gordon setting off.

In the front bedroom Gordon gestured round saying, "I want that wall knocked out and with my old bedroom next door, it will make one big one and the same with mums old room," said Gordon then looked at Tracy.

"And the same downstairs?" she asked.

"Yes, want a tape measure?" he asked then laughed.

"No, I'll have to call tomorrow evening with a colleague and do it properly," replied Peter still looking round.

"We'll see you tomorrow then," said Gordon, smiled, and when they set off downstairs, craftily smirked whispered, "Don't worry mate, I'm only using you."

Next day, late afternoon, Peter called with another chap, began to take measurements and sketched rough plans. When they left, Gordon spoke with David about the alterations and hoped he didn't mind. "It's your house and I must say it will make the place a lot bigger, the only trouble is its age, only certain things are allowed now," he replied frowning.

"That's what Peter said, and that's why he is calling to the council to seek permission first," said Gordon, heard the door open and set off into the shop.

Gordon's only trouble was money and a week later when the accountant called thought he might land up in trouble. After deliberating he had to explain a ten thousand pound load made to the shop two years ago. After going through the books, the accountant sighed then advised him to get rid of some money, began to stress he had far too much in the bank and the amount might be queried. "And why is that?" asked Gordon, didn't understand.

"Because you have never disclosed any earning's to them that is why. You say renovations to the house might cost about thirty thousand so where has it come from?" he asked staring at him.

"You know where," he replied while stood up.

"Of course I know, but the tax man doesn't. You've even got bloody paintings on display in the shop now," he snapped, and shook his head in disgust.

"Yes, and all unsigned, I do that when they buy them," he replied, while filled the kettle.

The accountant tutted while put papers in his briefcase moaned, "You should have more sense, I was surprised when your dad let you carry on."

"All I am bothered about is the shop, are we making a profit?" he asked while made the tea.

"Yes, but get rid of a bit more cash out of the bank, buy another car or something," he replied while leant on the table.

"Will do then," said Gordon but had to smile while poured out the tea.

With Gordon's bed inside the spare room next to his dad's old office, and most of his furniture cleaned, polished and put on display in the shop for sale. Three months later, with the plans approved, work began on his house.

David called regularly, but now with severe arthritis in his hands, had ceased renovating furniture so it was decided to knock down the workshop. In its place, Gordon wanted a garage built for his car and when it was done would part exchange it for a new one.

During the renovations, turnover at the shop never dwindled and Gordon thought it was because of an exceptional easy going economic climate. He would often stare out of the window trying to see Andrea taking Tracy to school, but never saw her and thought she had moved away or was deliberately taking another route.

Occasionally, if his mum was up to it, she would look after the shop, while Gordon took David to a sale and with his advice bought second hand furniture. It cost them more when had to purchase the best that only required a good polish however, there was still a niche for the second hand market, when most was better made than new.

When the builders were nearly finished, Gordon asked the foreman for an estimate, wanted a perimeter wall six foot high built round the back of the shop and also wrought iron gates giving access to the garage. They never had one before, didn't need one, but he was thinking on the lines of insurance. The builder agreed, would commence when completed the house and also stated no plans were needed for that because it was at the rear of the property.

When he explained to his mum, "Don't you think it will make it look like Fort Knox," she said then laughed.

"I don't care what it looks like, it's all adding value," he replied while craftily smiled rubbing his hands together. Jessie noticed thought he looked more like scrooge with his actions, then recalled Andrea with him, hadn't seen her for ages but always thought she brought the best out of him.

It was a busy time for Gordon, had to serve in the shop and would paint on a night. Luckily his mum, with David called regular, brought his dinner and always inspected the alterations.

Soon as the house was finished, the builders began to knock down the workshop. Jessie and David watched when Gordon walked up to them quietly saying, "The end of an era."

"It is my love, there's been a lot of work done in there," said Jessie, was very near to tears.

David tried to ease a solemn occasion, slipped his arm around her shoulder saying, "To be honest Gordon, it wanted knocking down, a lot of it is rotten now."

Gordon was amazed with the amount of timber used in its construction, realized his dad and David made a good job then suddenly laughed saying, "In two weeks time you'll have to ring a bell to get in."

"And if that's the case you'll find your dinner on the causeway," said his mum smirking.

When inside the house was finished the builders were now on with the boundary wall. Using trade contacts, Gordon began to have each room decorated then carpeted. Furniture was no problem, however, his taste was. "Oh Gordon, that doesn't look right over there," moaned his mum.

"Tell you what then, you tell me where to put it," he snapped, walked over and glanced out of the window.

"I will in a minute," she replied, and smirked while walked towards him. When Jessie noticed he watched some schoolchildren going home she asked, "Do you ever see Andrea?"

"Occasionally," he replied.

Smiling she said, "I thought you would have ended up with her."

"I thought the same but never mind, so right come on what do you want me to do now?" he asked then rubbed his hands together.

"Bloody hell Gordon, will you stop doing that. You look like that Scrooge bloke in Oliver twist," she moaned.

"Good grief, I'm off to put the kettle on then," he snapped then walked out.

Having taken over two months, with the house now finished and garage erected, it was now surrounded by a boundary wall with two huge wrought iron gates. Gordon decided to part-exchange his car and bought a new BMW. His finances were badly dented, but knew his property had increased dramatically in value.

Trade at the shop was just ticking over, but unfortunately his painting had suffered, had only completed two while the alterations were going on. On the back wall he hung one of Moira and Andrea, with the one he had altered of Caroline, and one day while dusting, stared at them, had always thought the one of Andrea was best.

Sunday afternoon a week before Christmas, Gordon was going through the books, obviously had kept all the receipts from the alterations and had to smile when read the one from Tracy for eighty pounds. Having paid it though the post thought he might receive a discount from his sister hadn't seen her since last time she called. "Never mind it was worth it," he said looked round, now had a large kitchen cum living area, and the front room had an extended lounge with a large central coal effect gas fire.

Gordon was going to have a drink when it dawned on him he had run out of wine. Thirty minutes later, he set off to the pub to have a swift drink before call at the off license on the way back. Locking the back door after him, he opened the gates then the garage. After reversed out his car, he got out, locked it all up after him then moaned, "It might look nice but it takes more time and effort to set off," suddenly laughed saying, "And I paid for it like that as well."

Inside the pub Gordon ordered a pint of lager, and when paid, suddenly turned when someone laughed loud. Sat on a bar stool leaning on the counter but while drank listened to conversations of who had what and how much they paid for it. It seemed everyone was bragging and were pleased about the amount they spent, and he just couldn't believe it.

The worlds gone crazy, he thought then suddenly stared, when heard a chap say, "And if the government passes the bill all the council tenants will be buying their houses as well." Then two young lads walked in and when stood by his side threw their mobile phones on the bar with their car keys. One said, "Two halves of lager please mate," and while the barman served them their conversation began about whose car cost the most and whose was the fastest.

Bugger this, thought Gordon, drank up, said goodnight to the barman and walked out. In his car he set off moaning, "That must be the new breed of yuppies, good God am I glad I didn't end up like that."

Leading up to Christmas, Gordon's uncertain mood continued spending a miserable time on his own. Unfortunately two weeks into the New Year, Doreen was rushed into hospital. She had never been a well woman, had suffered every ailment under the sun. Unfortunately she had contracted a serious chest infection, and then it turned into pneumonia. The following day after he visited with his mum, was glad they had when the day after she died.

At the funeral, David was heartbroken and again it was Jessie and Gordon that consoled him. But a month later, there was no one to console Gordon when his mum suddenly died.

Jessie had fallen down the stairs and broke her hip. David found her unconscious and rushed her to hospital. When Gordon arrived there, the doctor informed him she just gave up, and had died peacefully. Again, in a way he was glad that she didn't suffer and always knew she desperately missed his dad.

With all the arrangements he had to make, Gordon had to put his grief to one side. With David still mourning his loss and Tracy, supposedly too upset to visit, again he shook his head with disgust at her attitude, but as usual just got on with it.

Returning home after the funeral, in the front room, Gordon decided to drown his sorrows, got drunk and fell asleep on the sofa. It had now hit him hard that he was on his own and now knew all the arguing would start with Tracy. Really thankful David was still here to keep the peace, but what had taken him by surprise was the amount of condolence cards posted through the shop letterbox.

One was from Andrea and Tracy, and Gordon placed them all on the shop window sills for them to see. This was to display their respect, so in return he gave his thanks by pinning a notice on the shop door.

Gordon refrained from painting, began to give more attention to the shop. It did reap benefits; however, six months later nearing the end of summer found out Tracy had put his mum and dad's house up for sale. Knowing it was just for the money, he had taken out what he wanted; especially the painting of his parents, and hung it in the shop.

The one of Moira he had sold for fifty pounds and two more, but not in the mood for painting was suddenly taken aback when the chap from the action house called. Wanting him to restore five paintings for them but not really in the mood, it took a bit of persuasion before eventually Gordon agreed.

In a way Gordon was glad, knew he needed some incentive, and that night refrained from drinking. In his studio, after dusted round and after a bit of organization he began to work on them.

David occasionally called to see him, now had the van permanent, and when he informed him it was on its last legs, Gordon informed him he had no use for one now, instead would offer discount if customers if took their goods with them or arranged their own transport.

"That's a good idea is that, so when the road tax runs out at the end of the month, I'll leave it in your back yard," said David, while inspected the painting of Colin and Jessie.

"Might as well it's nearly scrap, mind you it's been a good purchase," replied Gordon, while made out a receipt.

"Well, see you later lad I must be off now," said David before walked out.

"See you David," said Gordon, but watched him thought, *the poor bugger looks lost.*

The nineteen nineties rolled on, and for a change badly needing the exercise, twice a week on an evening, Gordon would walk to the pub. Having only two drinks he would then walk home, and inside would watch TV while had a drink of wine then later go to bed. It was all getting very repetitious and boring, and he had to smile when he had a car in the garage with less than a thousand miles on the clock.

"The only thing I'll ever be known for is being a second hand man," moaned Gordon while undressed. Looking very much his age and now more portly, he sat on his bed and staring at a full moon shining through the curtains moaned, "We'll, let's be fair, I deserve what I've got because I've fucked everything else up," then fell back pulled the quilt over him.

Friday morning Gordon was in the shop dusting when a girl aged about ten or twelve walked inside. Looking nervous as she approached then half smiled at him, he asked, "And what can I do for you my love?" then suddenly stared, when she burst into tears and ran towards him.

She hung onto his neck sobbing out, "My mum's ill."

"Oh my love, it's Tracy," he gasped then hugged her.

Sobbing she asked, "Gordon you must help us, please you must?"

Holding her at arm's length he asked, "What the matter with your mum?" then smiled when noticed tears streaming down her cheeks.

Repeatedly blinking with the tears in her eyes she said, "She's in bed poorly and won't get up."

"And what does the doctor say?" he asked, while pulled a hanky out of his pocket and held it to her.

Tracy let go of him, took it, and while wiped her eyes replied, "She has pneumonia and my Gran died with that," then sobbed before wiped her eyes again.

"Right then, just a minute," he said, walked over and locked the shop door. Gordon turned and after looked round as if checking the shop, smiling he asked, "Come on then, let's go see her."

In the car on the way, Gordon asked how long her mum had been Ill and smiled when Tracy wiped her eyes again. "Three weeks ago she caught a cold, and it went to a chest infection. The Doctor's been to see her, but a few days after soon after she went delirious. She's been talking rubbish ever since," she replied then sobbed out loud.

"Right then here we are," he said when stopped outside their house. Gordon watching her open the door asked, "Why haven't you asked the Doctor to call again."

"Because the woman in the office said she'd make her an appointment for next Wednesday at three in the afternoon. I just shouted that's too late and ran out."

Chapter 22

Gordon slowly followed Tracy into the house closing the door after him, glanced into the front room and noticed it had been decorated. "She's upstairs," said Tracy, while undid her coat.

Smiling Gordon said, "Tell you what then, you go make us all a nice cup of tea and bring them up to us, I'll go surprise her."

"Does that mean take your time?" she asked then smirked.

"Yes it does," he replied then reached out patted her shoulder.

When Tracy set off into the kitchen, Gordon set off upstairs. Andrea's bedroom door was open and it felt uncomfortably chilly on the landing. Looking round he approached the door then slowly continued inside, noticed Andrea asleep but looking very pale and had lost weight.

Noticing boxes of tablets and a glass of water on a bedside cabinet, Gordon continued sat on the bed and stared at her. Slowly Andrea opened her eyes, stared at him, and then suddenly burst into tears.

"Hey come on there's no need for that," said Gordon took hold of her hand and patted it.

Andrea grabbed his hand, and squeezed it sobbed, "If anything happens to me please look after Tracy."

"You know I will love, but nothing is going to happen apart from you getting better," he said, glanced round the room then grimaced seeing condensation running down the windows even though it was cold in the room.

"God I'm so weak," she moaned then looked away.

"I'm here now, so what do you want doing?" he asked, raised her hand and kissed it.

Andrea tried to smile saying, "I was wrong wasn't I?"

"We all make mistakes my love, that's life," he replied then squeezed her hand.

Faintly smiling she whispered, "You don't look any older."

"And you still look lovely," he replied, and smiled.

Andrea sighed, "Give over and sorry to hear about your mum, I did send a card."

"I read it and thanks. I still have it but as they say nothing lasts forever," he replied then suddenly looked round when Tracy brought them a cup of tea.

Andrea moaned, "I can't manage one love," then closed her eyes.

"Yes you can, and if I'd had known I would have brought some brandy to put in it," said Gordon smiling while put her cup on the cabinet.

Tracy walked out saying, "I'll leave you alone."

"Thanks love," said Gordon, turned, looked at Andrea and with her eyes closed seemed peaceful. Thinking his accommodation was better than her house, knew she would have a better chance of recovery. Gordon studied before asked, "Could you manage to get in my car?"

Andre opened her eyes saying, "Don't be silly."

Gordon smiled saying, "I'll have to carry you then."

"You can't carry me downstairs," she gasped stared at him.

"Don't be silly I'm used to humping heavy furniture about," said Gordon then laughed.

"You bugger," gasped Andrea then started to cough.

Gordon watched, then stared before asked, "Come on sit up, and have a drink of tea?" Reaching down he helped Andrea sit up, passed her cup, and she took it had a sip.

"Oh good God," she moaned then settled down but seemed lifeless.

"I won't be long love, I'm just going having a word with Tracy," said Gordon before set off downstairs.

Sat in the kitchen Tracy was reading, and again, Gordon noticed condensation running down the windows. Shivering with the cold damp air he asked, "Have you any suitcases love?"

Tracy looked at him and not understanding asked, "No and why?"

"Right then, I want you to fill some carrier bags with clothes for yourself and your mum, and go put them on the back seat of the car," he replied looking round for essentials.

Standing up she asked, "What for?"

"Because you are coming to live with me, we can call round later on for the rest," replied Gordon then smiled when she quickly set off.

Returning upstairs, Gordon sat on the bed heard Tracy rummaging in her bedroom. "What's she up to?" asked Andrea.

"I've told her to pack, you are coming to live with me," he replied.

"How can we Gordon? I can't travel, it takes me all the time to get to go to the toilet," she snapped, then set of repeatedly coughing.

"You'd better go now before we set off then," said Gordon, and laughed.

Tracy entered the room and smiled at Gordon while stuffed her mum's clothes in carrier bags. Andrea raised her head, wheezed then snapped, "Stop that," and suddenly flopped back looked exhausted.

"You are in no condition to argue, sorry pal. Tracy, don't forget your school things and your dirty clothes. You can wash them when we arrive home," said Gordon, and had to smile when she winked at him, but looking much happier than she did an hour ago.

Turning away from him Andrea moaned, "Oh Gordon I can't."

"Oh yes you are," he replied then took two full bags from Tracy while she filled more.

Half an hour later, with the bags in the car, Gordon helped Andrea out of bed, and then helped on with her coat and shoes. She had difficulty standing upright, and waiting until she regained her breath then wheezed, "I can't do it."

With Tracy at the door ready, Gordon bent down, and when Andrea wrapped her arms round his neck, he scooped her up but paused when heard her moan.

"Alright love?" he asked then suddenly smiled when Andrea nodded a yes before dropped her head on his shoulder. "Lead the way Tracy and close all the doors behind us turn off all the lights, and don't forget to lock the front door?" asked Gordon, while carefully walked down the stairs.

"Yes Gordon," she shouted, while sorted through keys.

"Run past us love and open the car door quick?" he asked but while waited in the hallway, Andrea suddenly flinched with the cold. "Can you manage a little longer? Do you want another coat?" asked Gordon while watched Tracy open the car door.

"I haven't got one," replied Andrea then hung on when Gordon dashed out to the car. After gently placed her inside, Gordon quickly closed the door, turned and shouted, "Is everything locked Tracy?"

"Yes, just coming," she shouted, and after locked the front door, ran towards the car.

Gordon started the engine, put the heaters on, and smiling said, "Ten minutes my love," waited while Tracy closed the door then set off.

Fifteen minutes later, inside his house and settling Andrea on the sofa in the front room, "Won't be long love," said Gordon, and smiled went out to give Tracy a hand with the bags.

After a further five minutes, "Tracy, in that cupboard there, take out two tins of soup, the opener is in that draw and a pan is in that cupboard, put it on love while I phone the doctor," said Gordon before continued into the room.

"Right boss," she shouted, which made him smile.

Gordon picked up the receiver, looked for the surgery number, and dialed. "Oh hello, this is Gordon Mathews speaking, I wish a doctor to make a house call so can you advise please?"

"If it's an emergency you will be better going straight to the hospital," replied the receptionist.

"It's for Andrea Hastings, she is now resident at my house," he replied.

"Oh hello Gordon this is Mrs Tempest, and my condolences for your mum, I knew her well you know," she said, rather chirpily.

"If you don't get a doctor out here quick you will have to send more condolences soon," he snapped.

"Right then... err I'll try and get one out straight away," she replied, and Gordon smiled when heard a rustle of papers.

"Thanks," he said, replaced the receiver, turned and stared at Andrea on the sofa. She looked very poorly and he wondered if he had done right moving her. Gordon walked over, carefully sat at her side disturbing Andrea who opened her eyes. Trying to smile she said, "Thanks love."

While they waited, Tracy walked in carried their soup on a tray, "Thanks very much sweetheart," said Gordon was admiring her initiative and took it from her.

When he placed it on his knee, Tracy returned to the kitchen saying, "I'll have mine in here after set the washer off."

"Do you know how to use it?" shouted Gordon who hoped she did when he only knew two settings.

"Of course," she replied, sounded confident.

Gordon turned to Andrea, and held a bowl of soup in front of her asked, "Come on love have some of this?"

"I have to take my tablets first," said Andrea then winced when tried to sit up.

After taking them and eating what she could, thirty minutes later, Gordon was washing up and had to smile noticed Tracy sat at the kitchen table doing her homework. Hearing a knock on the back door he quickly looked round, dried his hands before opened it and smiled at the doctor asked, "Please come on in?"

After the Doctor examined Andrea and changed her tablets, he gave her an injection and noticed Gordon look away. Rubbing her arm he said, "In the morning you should perk up a bit. Try to keep in a stable temperature and eat something, medicine is no good without food."

When Andrea nodded a yes, he smiled, stood up began to close his case while nodded to Gordon to go outside. Closing the kitchen door after them, in the back yard, Gordon asked, "Is she going to be alright?"

"Oh yes, she'll be a lot better here than where she lived. Her parents were patients of mine but Andrea was with another practice," he replied, then slapped him on the arm said, "Don't worry; you did the best thing bringing her here."

"Thanks and is there anything else I can do for her?" he asked.

"TLC my boy, so see you a few days," said the doctor before got into his car.

When he set off, Gordon waved, closed the gates then locked them. Closing the back door after him, he locked it while watched Tracy writing, and smiling asked, "Want to see your bedroom now?"

"Oh yes please," she replied, and instantly put down her pen.

Tracy followed him upstairs carried two bags, and in his old bedroom, Gordon asked, "Will this do for you?"

"Superb," she replied, and smiled while looked round.

"Right then, get it comfy, I'm going down to your mum now," said Gordon before set off downstairs.

At the foot of the landing, Gordon glanced into the room, before walked over and sat next to Andrea. It disturbed her and she opened her eyes. "Feeling any better?" he asked, and suddenly tears flowed from her eyes. Gordon smiled leant forwards and kissed her. Andrea slowly raised a hand, tried to push him off, and when sat back he asked, "What's wrong now?"

Andrea pulled a face of disgust, and looked away from him moaning, "I stink."

Gordon took his hanky out of his pocket, and dabbed her cheeks. Smiling he said, "It's a fact of life my love; we all do when we are poorly."

Looking very soulful, Andrea faced him asked, "Why have you done this Gordon?"

"The answer to that is very simple, because I love you," he replied, and when tears flowed down her cheeks again he said, "If you carry on like this I'll need a tea towel."

Andrea tried to smile while took hold of his hand. Gordon rest back and slipped his arm around her. Both began to drowse and were unaware that when Tracy had finished her homework and the washer stopped, she filled it with more clothes.

Later, Tracy sauntered into the shop and checked the doors. Gordon heard her, however, when she returned noticed the painting of her mum hanging on the wall. She stared at it and thought it beautiful even though she was naked. Carrying on into the kitchen, after checked the back door was locked she continued into the room. Tracy kissed her mum, kissed Gordon on the cheek, knew he was awake, and whispered, "Everything is locked up, I'm going up to bed now so night-night."

"Good night love," he replied but had to smile.

Next morning Gordon suddenly moaned, "Oh hell my arm," and gently eased it from round Andrea's neck and then shook it. Smiling at him she asked, "Has it gone to sleep?"

While staring at her, "Bloody hell, you look a lot better this morning."

"I feel it, but I still feel a bit queasy though," she said, and gasped while rubbed her stomach.

Gordon glanced at his watch, then quickly sat up moaned, "Hellfire, its eight o'clock already."

"Breakfasts coming up," shouted Tracy. She walked inside, carried a tray then carefully placed it on her mum's knee.

"Have you had a bath?" asked, Andrea noticed her hair was damp.

Tracy looked straight at Gordon asking, "No a shower, you didn't mind did you?"

"Not at all," he replied, and smiled when she returned into the kitchen noticed she was dressed ready for school.

"Watch it she'll take over," said Andrea before picked up a slice of toast.

"If she can sell furniture she can do," he replied then laughed.

After Tracy set off for school, Gordon went upstairs and showered. Later he changed, returned into the kitchen and shouted he was going to open the shop, quickly dust round and then make them a cup of tea.

Andrea settled still had her coat round her knees, began to look round and noticed the house was different. The rooms seemed bigger, suddenly turned and smiled when Gordon passed her a cup. She gave her thanks when he set off into the shop, when had a drink nearly spilled it. Andrea looked down to check, and noticed new carpets thought, *I wonder why he's had all this done.*

Half an hour later, and wanting to use the toilet, luckily Gordon returned and asked if she was alright.

Looking embarrassed, Andrea informed him. "Tell you what then, I'll carry you upstairs then after you can lay on my bed and rest," said Gordon, took the cup from her and noticed it was empty.

"Please love, I'm so weak I don't think I can manage the stairs regularly," she replied. Gordon pitied her when she looked far from her normal self; he knelt on the sofa slipped on arm under her legs and gently began to lift her.

While he carried her upstairs, Andrea hung onto his neck and kissed him which made him smile. Gordon gently lowered her to the floor and when she slowly walked inside the bathroom, he watched saying, "I'll go tidy the bedroom first."

Gordon walked back out onto the landing when Andrea unsteadily walked out and grabbed his arm. Continuing inside his bedroom she asked, "Could I have a shower later?"

"Of course you can, just have a rest first. I'll call up every now and again," he replied then kissed her. Gordon waited until Andrea lay down then pulled the quilt over her, and waited again until she was settled before set off.

She smiled had been in here before, however, like downstairs it seemed the room had changed and couldn't figure out how. Andrea smiled could occasionally feel a waft of warm air blowing across her arms. She smiled with contentment and also the fact that Gordon fussed her.

With two sales that morning, after closed the shop for lunch, Gordon made some sandwiches, put them on a tray with a cup of tea and took them upstairs. "You are spoiling me," said Andrea, was still laid on top of the bed.

"Of course, and you could have got in bed properly," he said while sat with her.

"Maybe later," she said before took a sandwich.

"Will it be alright to send Tracy to the fish shop when she returns home from school?" he asked before had a drink.

"She'll manage alright; she's run up and down after me something rotten."

"She's not a bad girl," said Gordon before picked up a sandwich.

Andrea raised her eyebrows saying, "I know this much, she thinks the world of you."

"And I do, that's both of you," he replied, leant forward and kissed her. After finished his sandwich, Gordon stood up saying, "It's time for the afternoon shift now, see you later love" and smiled before set off downstairs.

Gordon was in his element having quickly made another two sales after lunch, and at tea time after Tracy returned home from school he asked, "Will you do me a favour please my love. Go change first then go to the fish shop for us, I'll organize something better for dinner tomorrow."

"Of course," she replied, and when Tracy walked passed him she smirked saying, "I do love that painting of mum."

Gordon had to smile, suddenly turned when the shop door opened he asked, "Hello and what may I do for you?"

With another sale of a set of draws and luckily every one took their order with them, at quarter past five when Tracy returned from the fish shop, Gordon closed the shop door and turned off the lights. In the kitchen, he shared out their meal, placed them on a tray before carried them upstairs.

Tracy followed and sat on the bed opposite Gordon and began to explain to her mum what she had done at school. Gordon noticed Andrea only ate half her meal, and understood saying, "Sorry my love I ought to have known they would be a bit greasy."

"They are lovely but sorry I can't manage them all," she said, rest back watching Tracy wolf hers down.

Gordon also noticed asked, "Have you any homework?"

"Yes just a bit," replied Tracy.

"After that then go get it done," said Gordon, and smiled noticed she never even left a scrap.

Later in the kitchen, Gordon sat with Tracy at the table while she did her homework. Deciding to do the books, Gordon thought if he left her on her own her mind would wander. "Do you do those every day?" She asked.

"No, I just thought I'd keep you company."

While frowning she asked, "Gordon is my mum going to be alright?"

"Of course," he replied, and smiled to reassure her.

"The thing is, if anything should happen to her, like, well, you know, would you look after me?" she asked.

"Of course I would," he replied then reassuringly smiled.

Staring at him she asked, "But why?"

"Because I love you both," he replied, however, slightly blushed.

Tracy stared then began quizzing asked, "Well if you do love us, why did you walk out that day?"

"Because it was over a silly disagreement, your mum and I had not really got to know each other well enough. We didn't fall out were just unsure of each other that's all," he replied but thought, *you little bugger, you are saying all this on purpose to embarrass me.*

"So when you get married I can call you dad then?" she asked then grinned.

"That is up to you. I know you can remember your proper father and please don't ever forget him, but I will be a stand in dad if you want me to be."

"Oh thanks," she said, and carried in writing.

Andrea was at the top of the landing listening and had to smile. When they went quiet she carried on into the bathroom had decided to have a shower. When Gordon heard the boiler start, he put down his pen saying, "I won't be long," then set off upstairs.

Hearing the shower running he waited outside, and when it switched off, asked, "Are you alright Andrea?"

"In one of those bags there is a clean nightie, could you pass me it please?" she shouted.

Gordon rummaged through the bags, and eventually found one. When he took it to her, Andrea walked out had a towel round her and smiling took it. She slowly continued into the bedroom and with her back to him slipped it over her head, "Feeling any better?" he asked.

Andrea sat on the bed, swung her legs up and lay down. Smiling at him she replied, "I am and that shower was lovely."

Gordon sat on the bed, and not looking at her asked, "Is your rent paid for this week?"

Frowning she asked, "Yes and why?"

"Because I want you to live here permanent here with me from now on," he replied, turned and stared straight into her eyes.

Smiling she asked, "Oh do you indeed?"

"Andrea, you know I love you, and I hope you feel the same about me, although I must say this, you have never said so. If you live here I can look after you here and keep an eye on you," said Gordon but had to smile noticed she looked comfortable.

"What's Tracy doing?" she asked while tried to get comfy.

"Her homework," he replied then smiled when her eyes sparkled.

"Have you made her do it?" she asked while settled down.

"No, I sort of did the books to keep her company and then she knows learning is essential part of any business."

Smiling Andrea asked, "Please could you do me a favour Gordon? I could murder a cup of tea."

"Coming up," he replied, stood up and set off downstairs.

Soon as he entered the kitchen, "Do we have to learn this algebra Gordon? Is it really necessary?" moaned Tracy while pulled a face of disgust.

"Yes you do," he replied while filled the kettle.

Staring at him she asked, "Why for? It's so stupid."

"Because when you have learned how it works, working other problems out becomes easier."

Frowning she moaned, "But why mix letters with numbers? It's utterly balmy to me."

"It's all about life. Everything is not as simple as it looks. When you have learned that you can put certain things into perspective better. Honestly it makes things easier to work out," he replied then looked away hoped she understood.

"How's mum?" she asked, to change the subject.

"Better for being here," he replied, and was now relived he had brought her.

Tracy looked serious at him asking, "Gordon, do you mind if I ask you a personal question? Well two really."

"No, and go on," he replied while leant on the sink.

"First, do you love my mum and second, why are we here?"

"Because I love you both, and because I want to look after you both," he replied, turned, and began to prepare the cups thought, *you fishing little bugger.*

"That's what I thought," she said, bowed her head and carried on writing.

Chapter 23

The following Wednesday morning, Andrea was looking much better. The doctor called after breakfast, examined her, gave her the all clear and said he was very pleased with her progress. The only trouble was Gordon was the chief cook and bottle washer. Attending to sales in the shop and in between, dashed into the kitchen preparing meals so was generally run off his feet.

Another thing new to him was shopping, and after closing the shop Friday teatime he took Tracy with him to the supermarket. However, when she advised him what to buy, "Good grief," he moaned at certain commodities then moaned even more when paid at the checkout."

Tracy smirked while packed their goods in carrier bags asking, "What's the matter?"

"This bloody lot," he moaned when picked them up.

Arriving home, after put away the shopping, Tracy made them a cup of tea. Carefully she carried two cups into the front room before handed one to

Gordon then her mum. "Thanks love," said Andrea, and patted the sofa to sit with her.

"Going to finish my homework first," she replied then returned to the kitchen.

After a sip of her tea, "I must thank you for all you have done Gordon," said Andrea, had now put on a little weight and looked better for it.

"You are most welcome my love you know that," he replied before had a drink.

"And I must say this, while you were out, I had a wander round because you have altered this place since I was last here," and looked at him thought she might have done wrong.

"I've had some rooms knocked into one to make them bigger," he replied then smiled really felt cozy and relaxed.

Andrea knew it saying, "I also wandered into the shop and noticed a painting of me."

"Err, oh sorry, I did it from memory," he replied then frowned thought he might be in trouble.

"Don't do that, it's good," she said, reached out and placed her cup on the coffee table.

Smiling he asked, "Oh, do you like it then?"

"Yes, and so does Tracy," she replied when settled back.

"Oh hell, I never thought," he said then smirked.

"So if you like painting nudes, what about doing one of yourself? Or is it always with women you have been with," she asked then purposely raised her eyebrows.

"I beg your pardon? I paint with emotion and I can assure you yours was done with love," he replied staring at her.

"If that's the case, can I go home tomorrow?" she asked.

"No, and this is the first time I am being adamant, I want you to stay here with me now," he replied then finished his tea.

Staring at him she asked, "What for?"

Smirking he replied, "If you don't know now you never will."

Andrea did know, and smiling asked, "Will you sleep with me tonight, I mean under the bedclothes for a change?"

"Only if you want me to," he replied.

Tracy walked in saying, "Goodnight you two."

"Goodnight love," said Gordon.

Andrea never said anything, watched when he waved to her and smiled when he brought his arm down round her neck. When she snuggled up to him, Gordon asked, "So then, what's brought all this on?"

"Tell you later," she replied then hugged him.

Later that night in bed, with her back to him, Gordon snuggled up to Andrea and slipped his arms around her. Her nakedness felt good and she felt the same so didn't spoil the occasion, and both drifted off to sleep.

Next morning a knock on the door woke them, heard Tracy shout, "Breakfast is ready."

"Right love," shouted Gordon, but disturbed Andrea.

Looking at him she smiled saying, "She's playing matchmaker you know that don't you?"

"I know," he replied, lay on his back and looked up at the ceiling.

Andrea slid her hand across his chest asking, "However can I repay you for your kindness?"

"I should think marry me don't you," replied Gordon, desperately wanted to use the toilet, threw back the quilt, was about of get out of bed when Andrea threw her arms around his neck and pulled him back down.

While pinning him down she beamed a smile asking, "Are- you serious?"

"Oh no, I always go round asking women to marry me," replied Gordon, turned, and half laid on her.

"Oh do you?" she asked before kissed him.

That afternoon, Gordon allowed Tracy to serve in the shop while he prepared dinner and was delighted when made a sale, had sold a mirror. "Look at all this," she said handing him thirty pounds.

"Right, as of from now you are on commission, let's say ten percent," said Gordon then noticed her eyes light up.

"So that's three pounds already," she said then giggled.

While paying her, "And here you are."

Three weeks later, Andrea was fully recovered and with Tracy at school she sat in the kitchen with Gordon eating lunch. Looking at him she quietly said, "I think it's time to be going home now."

Gordon smiled before replied, "You know what I think about that."

"Look Gordon. Yes I have fallen in love with you, but as of yet I'm not ready to marry," said Andrea, and not wanting to offend him bowed her head.

Smiling he replied, "So let's leave it until you are."

Staring at him she snapped, "I just don't want to give up my house yet. What happens if we fall out? You could still kick us out, couldn't you?"

"As if I would, you don't think for one moment. Oh sorry, but we are getting at cross purposes here."

"Sit down please? We have to talk, and now is the right time," she asked then moaned, "I've gone through all this once before. I didn't think I would want to again and my emotions are spinning like crazy."

Gordon sat down and slowly bowed his head with disappointment. "If you want to go I'll take you after tea."

"The trouble is I don't. It's just the wrench leaving my house. It's like going on holiday and for some inexplicable reason not being able to return home," she said staring at him.

"You just said you love me and that's the first time you have said it, but do you love my company as well?" he asked then stared into her eyes.

Andrea with mixed emotions, suddenly sighed before replied, "You know I do, and I know Tracy's happy as well, but it's a completely different world for her here."

With disappointment, Gordon leant on the table then sighed said, "I can understand you not wanting to marry me, that's obvious and really I can about leaving your house. If there is anything in it you want to keep you could bring here."

Frowning she said, "There is one or two things, the rest is really rubbish."

Gordon smiled and stood up saying, "Have a good think about it, I know it's been on your mind."

Andrea smiled, watched Gordon continue into the shop, decided to have another drink of tea and poured it out. Holding the cup in her hands and knowing she loved Gordon, had a drink and rest back. Studying her future and recent illness which rendered her helpless, Andrea had to smile now realized Tracy was capable to look after herself.

It was the thought of being trapped, had never been in this position before and never thought she ever would, however, with the obvious trappings of living with Gordon would she lose her independence?

Later, while prepared their tea for when Tracy arrived home; Andrea made up her mind to stay, and smiled heard Gordon in the shop serving a customer. Helping him carry out a flat pack computer desk to his car, but with relief, and with a sweat on, once inside he laid it across the back seat.

Gordon gave him a receipt, his thanks then waved before returned inside the shop. Going straight upstairs into his studio he glanced round, chose two paintings and took them downstairs to fill gaps on the walls from recent sales.

Not having done much painting of late, he decided to do some that night after dinner, suddenly smiled when considered using photos of his mum and dad with David and Doreen. Having decided to paint both couples stood outside the shop door Gordon thought it would make a great scene for the future.

After hung the paintings, he turned round when the shop door opened. A smiling Tracy walked in saying, "Hello Gordon."

"Hello love and had a good day?" he asked before glanced at his watch.

"So so, we had maths this afternoon and it's not sinking in, again," she moaned while continued into the kitchen.

"It takes time my love," he said watching her.

At five o'clock Andrea called him for his tea. "Right love," shouted Gordon, and after a quick look round, locked the shop door before turned off the lights. When Gordon walked into the kitchen, he noticed a serious expression on Andrea's face and instantly feared the worse, now thought she really did want to return home.

While washing his hands Gordon heard Tracy asking, "Are we alright for shopping mum?"

Gordon quickly dried them, glanced round then took a plate from Andrea. Looking at him she joked, "That's something else I've missed, going shopping." Waiting until Gordon sat down and put his plate down. Andrea waited and put hers on the table before sat down. As if knew there was something wrong, Gordon and Tracy were staring at Andrea, when she suddenly asked, "Tracy, would you like to live here permanent?"

"It would be very nice," she replied while carried on eating. Gordon watched her, knew she really could have said anything, especially when he was sleeping with her mum.

"So you're not really bothered?" asked Andrea while picked up her knife and fork.

Looking at her she asked, "Of course I am, but it's not up to me is it? It all depends if you two are getting on. If you are, fair enough, if not why are we here?"

You little sod, thought Andrea, began to cut up her pork chop, turned, looked at Gordon and smiling asked, "Can I leave her with you?"

"Where you go I do as well," said Tracy, and nonchalantly carried on eating.

"Right then, tonight Gordon will you run us home please?" asked Andrea was trying not to smile.

"No mum," snapped Tracy, and quickly stood up looking defiant.

"Sit down you bugger and finish your tea," said Gordon, but smiled. Turning to Andrea he winked then suddenly noticed she looked exceptionally well, even glowing.

Gordon relaxed now knew they were staying, he carried on eating and they finished their tea in silence. However, with her body language, Tracy made it quite apparent she was angry. Gordon did his best trying not to smile but in the end, stood up began to clear the table. While he washed up, when he heard them whispering he asked, "Come and dry Tracy please?"

When she did he noticed Andrea smirking behind her back but after Tracy dried the last plate, while cleaning round he said, "Right then, while you are putting those away, I'll go get out coats."

Gordon winked at Andrea while dried his hands, and when walked out, "Bring mine as well love," she asked but had to turn away didn't want Tracy to see her face.

Ten minutes later, in the car on their way to Andrea's house, it hadn't dawned on Tracy they had left their clothes behind. When Gordon pulled up, Andrea quickly got out of the car walked up the path, unlocked and opened the front door.

Gordon followed Tracy and when they went inside; Andrea turned on the light before continued into the kitchen. Tracy bent down and picked up some letters from the floor moaning, "It's very cold here mum," and after glanced at them, placed them on the windowsill as if not important before continued upstairs.

Andrea turned on the kitchen light, and Gordon smiled walked towards her. She sat at the table, and looking round asked, "Gordon, if I move back in here will you still visit us?"

"Of course I will," he replied then suddenly grimaced thought he had misread her body language.

Andrea stood up saying, "With this week I'll owe four weeks rent. I'd better get the rent book," When noticed Gordon looking out of the window she walked up behind him, and slipped her arms round his waist asking, "Go upstairs and tell her to pack some more clothes? I think I've upset her."

"You have me as well," he said, turned and faced her but now had a relieved look on his face.

"Right then and I know you might think me a funny bugger but I'll give it a go. But I'll tell you this, any falling out and you will have to find me somewhere to live," she said then smirking kissed him.

"I thought as much," said Gordon before wrapped his arms around her.

Half an hour later, sat on the back seat surrounded with bags and boxes, Tracy had a big smile on her face while they travelled back to Gordon's. Reaching there, they all carried them inside and with her mum, began to sort out the washing. "If you don't mind, can I go up and have a couple of hours painting?"

"Why ask me," said Andrea then winked.

"I'll bring you up a cup of tea soon," said Tracy, while filled the washer.

At nine o'clock, Andrea took him a cup of tea, and stood in the doorway watched him. Gordon sensed her, and smiling said, "I know your there."

Andrea walked inside and glanced round before put his cup on the table. Standing back she squinted asking, "Who is that?"

"You must be a poor mother not to recognize your own daughter," he replied then laughed.

"Is it Tracy?" she asked before had a closer look.

"You can't tell just yet but you will when there's more detail," he replied while put down his brush.

Andrea tried to visualize the painting saying, "Gordon, there's still time to back down you know. If you have any regrets, you can fill the car up and take me home."

"Go bugger off Andrea, oh sorry I didn't mean it like that, oh you know what I mean," he said then quickly leant forward and kissed her.

"So Monday morning, I will go to the council offices, pay the rent and give in my notice. And if you don't mind, on my way back I'll call round my old neighbors and give them what furniture they want," said Andrea while continued to the door.

"Hang on, you can bring round here what you want to keep you know," he said while picked up his cup.

"No Gordon, I haven't much, but it's better than what most of the young ones on the estate have. There are odd bits and pieces I want to keep, so would you run me round tomorrow for them?"

Winking he replied, "Of course my love."

The following Friday evening, with all bills paid and her house empty, Andrea had one last look round, before locked the front door. When she continued to the car and got inside. "Any regrets?" asked Gordon watched her close the door.

"Well, obviously part of my life was lived in there, and the experiences will come in handy. Memories are different you never forget them, now tomorrow that is the future, so let's get on with it."

Gordon admired her words as he felt that in a way they were a warning, but accepting Andrea's statement as fact said, "Right then madam, we'll call at the council offices now and you can post those keys then it's all done with," started the engine and had to smile noticed her staring at the house as if were recalling memories.

Tracy had stayed at Gordon's to do her homework, didn't want to go with them and when nearly finished the phone rang. Picking up the receiver she said, "Hello Mathews Furnishers."

"Oh hello, I'm trying to contact a Gordon Mathews," said, what sounded like a young man.

"He's not in right now, he's out with mum."

"Never mind then and thanks," he said then replaced the receiver.

"Soon as she replaced the receiver, it rang again. Tracy picked it up saying, "Hello Mathews furnishers."

"Is Gordon there? This is the auction house," asked a chap, rather snappy.

"He's out at the moment," replied Tracy beginning to feel nervous when it sounded important.

"Will you tell him I'll call on Wednesday morning about ten please," he said, now sounding really impatient

"Will do," she replied, and when he quickly replaced the receiver looked round for a piece of paper to make a note.

On their way back home Gordon called to the off-license, bought some wine, cans of pop and crisps.

Putting them in the boot he said, "That might keep her quiet for an hour."

"That's what you think," said Andrea smiling.

Arriving home, Tracy informed him about the auction house, then studied saying, "Oh yes, it sounded like a young lad that called and he asked for you."

"Did you ask him his name?" asked Gordon while placed bottles on the kitchen worktop.

"No he didn't give me chance, he just said he was trying to contact you," she replied while eyed the wine.

Gordon noticed, and smiling asked, "Go get a glass then."

Later that evening when they all sat in the front room watching TV and drinking wine. "That's enough, no more," said Andrea, watching Tracy top up her glass.

"Oh mum," she moaned.

"Do as you are told," said Gordon winking at her.

Andrea smiled while they sat together on the sofa, and Tracy was sat on the floor leant on her. This cozy and warm atmosphere she liked very much when it was years since it last happened. Although tried to recall when she was ill and Gordon looking after her, could only remember parts through haziness of the drugs she took.

Andrea had never said, but being seriously ill was the worst thing that had happened to her since losing her husband and having to deal with death had really frightened her. Never having any thoughts of taking up with another man, when Gordon came into her life it was like being in another world and she was really thankful when he said he loved her, because she did him.

Half an hour after Tracy went up to bed they followed. Andrea looked in on her and as normal left the door ajar. In their bedroom, she undressed, smiled at Gordon already in, and if it was the wine or not, she began to make amends about the uncertainty she gave him.

At one o'clock in the morning and as quiet as Gordon could be he went to the toilet. Returning he slipped into bed, and when Andrea wrapped her arms around him he asked, "Does that mean we are staying together now?"

"Oh yes, and I've told you once before to be careful, we are too old to be parents now," she replied then laughed.

"You bugger," he moaned, knelt up over her and bit her neck made her squirm.

"Get out you daft sod, if Tracy sees a love bite on my neck we will both get some stick off her," she moaned and pushed him up. Andrea wrapped her arms around his neck and kissed him. She came up for breath, and stared into his eyes whispered, "I do love you Gordon."

"And I love you too," he replied then hugged her.

Next morning, they did get some stick from Tracy, when she cheekily ribbed them about walking her up during the night. "You must have been dreaming," said Andrea then looked away smirking.

"I don't think so," replied Tracy then winked at Gordon.

"Right, first thing some washing, come on let's get started," said Andrea, mainly to change the subject.

When she began to sort it out, "Do we have to mum?" moaned Tracy while pulled a face of disgust.

"Yes, and on Sunday, we can all go shopping, let's try that new supermarket," said Gordon.

"Oh cool," she said then instantly helped.

As promised, Sunday after breakfast Gordon drove them to the new supermarket and not having been in one for ages, was amazed at what was on sale. Tracy pushed a trolley while eyed CDs and clothes. Gordon noticed saying, "Listen a minute, you can have twenty pounds to spend and that's all."

"That's too much Gordon," said Andrea but saw her face light up.

"No she's earned it, just so long as she continues to look after the shop when I'm busy," he replied before winked.

Andrea seemed impatient asked, "Can I have a quiet word please?"

"No because I know what you are going to say, so you can have fifty," he replied then laughed.

Tracy, moaned, "How come she gets more than me?"

"Because she bigger for a start," said Gordon then suddenly cringed.

"Thanks very much," snapped Andrea, and to tease him, stood with her hands on her hips purposely frowned.

Gordon frowned then moaned, "Oh good God, I didn't mean it like that, you know getting bigger I meant it because you're her mum."

"I know I've put a little weight on," said Andrea, and jokingly looked down.

"Why the hell do I always put my foot in it, honest, it was just a slip of the tongue," said Gordon watching her.

"If you say so love," said Andrea, and smiled took hold of his arm.

Fifteen minutes later, Tracy didn't need any encouragement to spend her money, but Andrea did. "Look love you get what you want for yourself and besides I've seen some shirts, and lets be fair I need some desperate," said Gordon, while ushered her towards the ladies section.

Andrea needed a lot of persuasion and in the end gave up when Gordon and Tracy pestered her. At the checkout, when her bill came to sixty pounds she froze looked aghast. "No problem," said Gordon then paid.

"Are you sure?" she asked but pulled a face was unsure.

"Can I go over with my money?" asked Tracy, tried to push her luck.

"No," replied Gordon, and laughed.

On the way home, Andrea was over the moon with her new clothes, because she hadn't bought any for years had always put Tracy first. However, Tracy had bought three new CDs of her favorite pop star and couldn't wait to get home to play them.

When they did arrive home, after parked the car, Gordon closed the gates, smiled and followed them inside the house. Suddenly he grinned when Andrea, kissed him saying, "I'm going up to try these on first."

"And I'm going up to hear these," said Tracy then set off.

"Thanks a lot. I'll make my own tea then," moaned Gordon while filled the kettle.

"I'll have one as well love," shouted Andrea.

"And me," shouted Tracy.

"And what about my dinner?" he asked staring at the stairs.

Andrea beamed a smile replied, "Oh there's plenty of time for that," winked and closed the door behind her.

Chapter 24

Over the next five years and because of David's failing health, Gordon reluctantly asked if he wanted to retire permanently. Assuring him he could call in the shop anytime, David seemed relieved and agreed. Throughout these years the shop just maintained a profit and unfortunately it was not a fantastic amount. There would have been sufficient to keep Gordon, but not to maintain a family.

Luckily what he had in the bank was being topped up with occasional sales from paintings and even though Gordon gradually managed to build up a catalogue, he looked forward to having another sale.

Tracy had grown into a fine young woman, and with Gordon's help progressed well at school. With many more students and their parents, she was disappointed when the education system changed dramatically. O level standard had been dropped, however, Tracy was well pleased when found out she had attained nine GCSE's.

On Sunday, after treating them to a celebration lunch for attaining her results and seventeenth birthday, Gordon carried on to the supermarket.

This had become a weekly outing and when they returned home, after unloaded the car, he made a drink of tea while Andrea prepared a light tea.

Later, sat in the front room, Gordon studied, recalled he hadn't seen or heard from his sister for years and when the phone rang, he suddenly winced when an old customer informed him David was very poorly. When he rang David and received no answer, Gordon rang Barbara and found out he was now living permanent with her and her husband. However, when eventually spoke with David; he informed Gordon he was selling his house to live with them.

That evening, while painting, Gordon recalled his mum saying their Tracy was getting married, didn't know if she had or not and didn't really care. His relationship with Andrea had blossomed, and realty that was all he was bothered about.

With Andrea's Tracy, he had all the family he wanted, however, Gordon had behaved and was careful, knew she didn't want any more children. As time marched on and unfortunately more quickly as you get older, Gordon dismissed the fact he would ever be a proper father, suddenly remembered Caroline and never hearing anything from her never knew whether or not she had his child. What he didn't know was, his mum had eventually contacted her and promised not to inform him the result. So not letting on, Jessie had unfortunately taken it to her grave.

Through boredom and wanting to earn their keep, Andrea now worked in the shop and loved it. During a quiet period she explained to Gordon it would be better if they sold vases, lampshades, including wicker furniture and drapes. Gordon agreed knew wicker furniture was all the rage at the moment was used in extensions or conservatories.

Often smiling when heard Andrea chatting with customers knew she enjoyed being involved and while he continued painting for the auction house, which had become haphazard but he always agreed, knowing extra trade generated more income.

Occasionally and mainly at the weekend, Tracy helped her mum in the shop, had the effect of more customers coming in, were the younger end and male. Gordon would often smile listened to them chatting her up. However, this allowed him more spare time, and up to date had finished twenty paintings.

Hanging some in the shop he always kept the best upstairs towards another sale. Gordon really didn't have the heart to ask the auction house for another display seeing as they never asked him and often wondered why when his first one went well.

His objective was to have thirty of his best paintings ready then enquire and looked forward to it. Seeing as private commissions had dropped off, hadn't done any for years and would now refuse them anyway, because at this moment in time everything was rosy.

Andrea, being financially sound for the first time in her life and because it wasn't her nature, never asked for anything for herself. She didn't even know the shop finances but did know when Gordon had sold a painting, when he always informed her with enthusiasm which made her smile.

Always maintaining a display of ten paintings hanging in the shop, including the one of Tracy, which had a permanent sold sign on it because it wasn't for sale, however, every time she passed it, Tracy always moaned, "It reminds me of a school photo, I look like an infant with my hair like that.."

"Nonsense, it's beautiful," said Andrea, always knew she wouldn't like it as she grew up.

Gordon brought them a cup of tea and heard her. Always tormenting her he would snap, "You can moan as much as you like young lady it's staying there."

"It's a showing up, what will my mates think?" she asked, and pulled a face of disgust while took a cup.

Smiling her mum said, "Tracy, you should be thankful, not everybody gets painted."

"Well, that's true, I suppose," she moaned, before set off upstairs.

Friday morning Andrea was in the shop serving an elderly woman. Gordon returned from upstairs noticed her chatting, continued into the kitchen and prepared them a cup of tea. When the customer left had bought a vase, Andrea walked in saying, "That was Mrs Collins, and according to her, Tracy is going to the pictures with her son tomorrow night."

"Oh, is she indeed?" he replied while passed her a cup.

Frowning while sat down Andrea moaned, "I suppose she had to start courting sometime."

Gordon heard the shop door open, and smiled saying, "Won't be a moment love." Setting off when inside he noticed a young chap carried a small case with a hold-all slung over his shoulder. Smiling Gordon asked, "Yes and how may I help you?"

"I'm looking for Gordon Mathews," he replied, while leaning forward to inspect a painting.

Gordon smiled asking, "And what for?"

"Just to have a chat," he replied turned and continued towards him.

Gordon stood with him noticed he was about his height and same hair coloring asked, "A painter, are you?"

"Sort off, I've just been kicked out of art college, and mainly for not trying," he replied then grinned.

Gordon grinned had always thought that would have happened to him asked, "So what do you want to see Gordon for."

"Oh sorry, my name is Graham Mathews, I'm his son," he replied while held out his hand.

Gordon stared at him gasped, "Pardon."

Graham smiled saying, "If you go get him I will explain."

"I am he, and I think you better had, right now" said Gordon then gulped.

Andrea popped her head round the door asking, "Want a hand love?"

"I'm afraid I need a big one," replied Gordon was staring in amazement.

"What's the matter love?" she asked, walked up to them took hold of his arm and stared into his eyes thought he was ill.

"Well, according to this lad, he says he is my son," he replied, now looked bewildered.

"Please, can I can explain all?" said Graham, and seemed a little nervous while took off his hold-all.

"Just a minute, I'll go lock the shop up. I think we had all better go into the kitchen," said Gordon, turned and stared at Andrea before set off to the door.

Andrea returned into the kitchen filled the kettle and began to make some tea. Not trying to smile when Gordon entered with Graham, who now looked very serious? They slowly sat down either side of the table staring at each other. Gordon could see a resemblance asked, "Right then, in your own time and you had better start from the beginning."

"Well, my mother, that's Caroline Blakemore unfortunately she died two years ago," said Graham then bowed his head.

"She's what?" gasped Gordon, and stared at him couldn't believe his words.

Andrea stared at Gordon, and placed two cups on the table asked, "Do you want me to go?"

"Do I hell, please sit down love," he replied, and when she did placed her cup on the table, Gordon turned to Graham asked, "Go on then?"

"Mum developed a heart murmur, I think I was about three then. She just lived with it and carried on did her best, but as I grew older I found out the consequences of her condition. You could see it affected her badly. She just got slower and slower. My aunt Janice helped her all she could, but when she died I had to take over. I hadn't been at Art College all that long and I knew then that's when all the problems would start," said Graham before had a drink.

"And in what way?" asked Andrea, didn't understand.

"Well, before I went there I could get home from school at lunchtime and see to mum, but travelling home from college would be impossible," he replied.

"Which college did you attend?" asked Gordon, was desperately thinking of questions to ask.

"Up here at Leeds," he replied, leant on the table and nodded the direction.

"Where were you born then? More to the point where did you live? Oh, wasn't it near Nottingham?" asked Gordon, was feeling a little unsure about him.

Feeling Andrea staring at him he guessed she knew he was quizzing Graham so picked up his cup and had a drink of tea.

"No Sheffield. According to form mum was living around here then returned with my aunt Janice. They lived with a relation, put in for a house and was granted one," he replied before carefully picked up his cup and had a drink.

Gordon looked at Andrea for help because he didn't know how to continue their conversation. As if knew, she smiled asking, "Have you any identification Graham, sorry, that's not that I don't believe you?"

"Of course," he replied, leant down and opened his hold-all. Taking out two envelopes, he passed one to Andrea, she took it, opened it and smiled while read his birth certificate had his name on it.

Andrea returned it to the envelope, handed it back, and looked at Gordon saying, "It has your name on as father."

"Mum said I had to give you this if anything happened to her," said Graham, swapped envelopes and handed Gordon the other one.

Taking it he said, "Thanks." Gordon tore it open, noticed a hand written letter, and resting back in his chair began to read it.

Caroline apologized for leaving the area and stated her health was fading fast. She asked if he would look after Graham, who was hell bent on being an artist. She had never informed him who his dad was until it was necessary and luckily because the letter was basic, after he read it, passed it to Andrea.

Graham smiled saying, "Mum had opened a bank account for me before I was born and put ten thousand pounds in it. She told me it was for when I grew up and I could have it when I was eighteen."

"And how old are you now?" asked Gordon, had tried to reckon up the years and failed.

"Seventeen, mum said she did it because of her benefits or something, anyway according to form she used to have a shop and it was from when she sold it," he replied then finished his tea.

Andrea asked, "Where are you staying now?"

Slowly he sheepishly bowed his head saying, "Nowhere."

"Exactly when did your mum die?" asked Gordon, and stared at him as if waiting for him to work it out.

"Two years ago later this month, she asked to be cremated and her ashes were scattered over her mum and dad's grave. I had this done and then our house was taken by the council just because I was living in student accommodation in Leeds. Hang on a minute I have the receipt from the undertaker somewhere," he replied, and leant down to his hold-all.

"No it's alright," said Gordon, and quickly stood up.

Andrea watched him and smiled knew he was in a predicament. She stood up asking, "Shall we go into the shop a moment love?"

"Please love, you stay here a moment Graham," replied Gordon then set off.

Andrea followed noticed Graham examine his empty cup. In the shop, she turned to Gordon asking, "What are you going to do?"

Shrugging his shoulders he replied. "I haven't a clue."

"You can't kick him out when everything looks in order, he even looks like you," said Andrea then smirked.

Staring at her he moaned, "What about us though?"

"How do you mean us?" she asked, and placed her hand on his arm when he glanced towards the shop door. Andrea didn't want it sound like they were arguing over Graham before asked, "Keep your voice down."

Gordon looked at her and pulling a face quietly asked, "Well… will it affect us?"

"Don't be so silly. I have a past and now yours has caught up with you, the only trouble is explaining it all to Tracy," she replied, was going to laugh thought better of it so just grinned.

Taking hold of her hand he moaned, "Oh good God, what a time for this to happen."

"Why? What difference does it make? To be honest I think you should go in and get better acquainted.

I'll keep out of the way and get dinner on," replied Andrea before patted his hand.

Leading him back into the kitchen, Gordon let go, and sat down saying, "Well Graham... you have really put me on the spot. I really don't know what to say."

"Will you stay for dinner Graham?" asked Andrea.

"If you don't mind," he replied, did look in need of a good meal.

"So why did you get kicked out of college?" asked Gordon.

"Basically because I wanted to paint my way and be taught how I could improve it. All our tutor would say was, you learn my way or not at all," he replied.

Gordon thought that's what he would have done, and smiling asked, "So what do you like painting best?"

"Well, really anything that catches my eye. I have done the town hall in Leeds, including a crowd scene in the city square and also portraits of a couple of fellow students."

"But have you sold any of them?"

"Oh yes, that's the only way you can afford to live. The grant I receive pays for my accommodation and leaves me with about three pounds a week pocket money, a brilliant way to learn is it?" he replied, and sickly smiled.

Andrea peeled some potatoes, while glanced at the clock asked, "Is there anything you don't like to eat?"

Looking sheepish Graham replied, "No."

"I don't know what the hell to do," moaned Gordon then stood up.

"For a start, go open the shop," said Andrea, and laughed.

Gordon looked bewildered, turned to Graham, and nodded for him to follow asked, "Come on then." Graham slowly stood up and sheepishly followed him inside the shop. After Gordon unlocked the door, when he turned, noticed Graham inspecting one of his paintings he sauntered up to him asking, "What do you think then?"

"I know you are a painter I've read all about you, and if you painted these it would be foolish to give you my candid opinion because I might insult you," he replied, turned and began to inspect another.

Gordon seemed impatient, and shaking his head snapped, "There is no wonder your tutor kicked you out. As an artist you must have an opinion and give it candid. If you don't stamp your authority when asked for an opinion you can't do it with your own work. That is the difference between a winner and a loser."

Graham turned asking, "So really you wouldn't mind then?"

Gordon smiled saying, "Oh I'm sorry lad; I know it must be difficult for you as it is for me, I know your only trying to be polite."

"I am, and really I know you were well respected for your work because mum saved press clipping of you. I knew who you were soon as I walked in your shop," he replied, and nervously laughed.

Gordon stared at him, and had to smile when he had the same laugh. "Go on then, give me your opinion of this one?" and pointed to the painting of Tracy.

"Well, for a start little girls are very hard to paint," he replied, then looked round when the shop door opened.

When Tracy walked inside, Gordon smiled at her asked, "Just a minute love?"

"The trouble is when children grow up they look nothing like their early years. It's like a photograph, timeless and nothing like the end product. I would have painted her looking slightly older and wearing plain clothes, they never go out of style," said Graham while studied.

"That's what I think as well," said Tracy, was now stood behind them.

Graham turned, and smiling at her asked, "Do you?"

Gordon interrupted asking, "Go on then, what else?"

"This backdrop is far too old fashioned; it complicates the scene and should have been plain. Sat at a piano as if playing would have looked very good," he replied then gestured the position at the painting.

"I like your style," said Tracy, and grinned before set off into the kitchen.

When Graham watched her, Gordon noticed saying, "I'll explain all later. Now what do you think of this one?" while pointed to the painting of his parents.

"That I really like," he replied, smiled then examined it closer.

"You should do, if you are who you say you are those are your grandparents," said Gordon smiling.

"Oh, well, you can tell you painted it with care as those brush strokes are perfectly equally, and the colours in tone. It is excellent, no brilliant, and please forgive me for asking this, are they still alive?" he asked.

"Unfortunately not," replied Gordon, and frowned however, of late had greatly missed his mum for advice.

"Oh, unfortunately that is another part of my family I shall not meet," said Graham then sighed.

Gordon stared at him asking, "Does it matter?"

"In a way yes because I've always been a loner. Of course I had mates when I was young but it always seemed strange when I used to visit their relations and I never had any," he replied then quickly turned to another painting.

Gordon suddenly turned when Tracy walked up to them asking, "Do you both want a cup of tea?"

Noticing her smiling at Graham, Gordon replied, "Please love," and tried not to smile, now knew Andrea had informed her about their visitor.

Unawares, Graham stood back, and seemed engrossed saying, "I'm not keen on this somehow."

"Neither am I, it was a rush job because I was fed up of the damn thing," said Gordon then laughed.

Tracy smiled, spun round and continued into the kitchen. "How are they going on?" asked Andrea, while checked the grill.

"They seem to be talking okay, just looking at those paintings, chatting and laughing," she replied, picked up and began to fill the kettle.

"Keep an eye on these and make the tea love, I'll just go in for five in case someone comes in the shop," said her mum while wiped her hands on a tea towel.

Andrea had timed it right, had just walked inside when the shop door opened. Looking at Gordon, she smiled saying, "I'll get it love."

Gordon watched when Andrea continued towards a customer then quickly turned when Graham asked, "Have you any more ready in the pipeline?"

"I have a studio upstairs, maybe later we'll have a walk up, unfortunately Andrea might want a hand soon," he replied while eyed her.

She did and while wrote out a receipt, Gordon helped a chap fold down and then carry out a dining table and four chairs to his car. Graham watched was going to ask if he needed any help when Tracy walked up behind him, and cheekily asked, "How have you got on then?"

Smiling he replied, "Oh hello and…I don't really know. I suppose it's the shock, you know after all these years."

"Gordon is a nice chap really. So then, what's brought you here?" she asked, and stared into his eyes had learned a long time ago from her mum how to read them for the truth.

"To be honest I've nowhere else to go. I wasn't going to call at all, you know, it's all in the past and leave well alone, but I've hit rock bottom and don't know who the hell to turn to."

Believe you me I know what that feels like and its soul destroying, anyway come on in the kitchen now I've poured out some tea," said Tracy, was satisfied with his reply and spun round.

Graham followed and sat at the table with her. After had a drink, he held the cup in his hands asked, "Right where were we?"

"Oh sorry Graham but I don't know if anyone has explained my presence yet but Gordon isn't my real dad. They aren't married either just live together mind you I don't know why they don't. Who knows, maybe they will in time," replied Tracy, and smirked, recalled dropping many hints but in the end had given up.

Andrea waited outside the door for Gordon to return. She had ear wigged their conversation and grinned. When he did, she asked, "Are you locking up now love? We might as well have an early dinner."

"Go on then," he replied, and glanced at his watch while returned into the shop.

Not interrupting Graham and Tracy but straining to overhear their conversation, now mainly about music and college. Gordon gave Andrea a hand to finish preparing their meal. When he placed Tracy's and Graham's plate on the table, Andrea was about to pass him his, so he sat down.

Andrea placed her plate on the table before sat with them. She smiled saying, "Right then after this we'll start to make some arrangements."

Gordon looked at her but didn't say anything, although had an idea what she meant. Taking it that she approved of Graham's presence and in a way he did, when he not only looked like him also had his mannerisms. Tracy broke the silence asking, "So could you go back to college?"

Half-smiling Graham quietly replied, "Well, unfortunately I let rip and made a fool of myself before I stormed out."

Gordon stared at him asking, "In what way?"

"In the way I told my tutor to stick his brush up his backside because he was useless bugger," replied Graham then grimaced because expected another telling off from Gordon.

"Oh, and are your fee's paid? Or I should say up to date," asked Gordon while placed his knife with his fork on his plate.

"No they ran out last week."

"Oh," said Gordon, and glanced at Andrea thought, *one way or another while you are here you will have to earn your keep my lad.*

Chapter 25

When they finished dinner, "Shall we go into the front room now?" asked Andrea then stood up.

"Graham and me will wash up," said Tracy, stood up and picked up her plate.

"Oh, of course," said Graham, slowly stood up and did the same.

Gordon smiled at Andrea saying, "I can't refuse then."

In the front room, while sat on the sofa discussing what to do and while heard chattering in the kitchen, Andrea asked, "Are you going to let him stay?"

"To be honest love, I really don't know what to do," replied Gordon then rest his head back seemed bewildered.

"Everything looks in order and you can't say he doesn't look like you because he does. Graham even has your ways," she said then smirked when he had never asked what they were.

"Go on then, what do I do?" he asked raising his eyebrows.

Andrea patted his arm saying, "Tell you later, shush I think they are coming in now."

Tracy popped her head round the door asking, "Shall I open a bottle of wine mum?"

"Go on then," replied Andrea then winked at Gordon.

Five minutes later, Graham walked in carried a tray had four glasses on it and a bottle already opened. After placed it on the coffee table he stood with Tracy in front of the fireplace. Gordon noticed he seemed uneasy, and gestured asked, "Please, sit down lad."

Andrea leant forward and poured out the wine. She glanced at Tracy when she sat of the floor next to Gordon, and craftily smiled but quietly said, "This is a nice family gathering."

With a hint of uncertainty in his voice Gordon asked, "Graham what are your intentions from now. You have turned up here unannounced and to be fair your future looks very bleak. I don't mind feeding you because you look undernourished, however, I would like to hear your future plans?"

"Well, I did ring you a few years ago," he replied, before sheepishly picked up a glass then carefully sat in a chair.

Gordon eyed him asked, "Did you indeed?"

"Yes, it was when mum told me all. She was very poorly at the time. After she explained her upbringing and where she had worked she gave me some documents and stressed I had not to bother you. To be honest I thought she was going to die then so later that afternoon I panicked and rang you," replied Graham and looking upset bowed his head.

"She recovered then?" asked Gordon, but not knowing what to make of his actions leant forward and picked up a glass.

"In a way, that evening when the doctor called he took me to one side and explained fully about her condition. I was only young at the time and he suggested I might have to be taken into care."

Gordon noticed Andrea staring at him as if telepathically saying; leave off, so he said, "Oh."

"I think he did very well, studying and looking after his mum," said Tracy, as if sticking up for Graham.

"So do I," said Andrea before had a drink.

Gordon did the same but studied. Holding the glass in his hand he asked, "How many GCSE's did you get?"

"Nine," replied Graham.

Smiling with enthusiasm, "Same as me," said Tracy.

"Concerning your scholarship, exactly what aspects of art did you want to learn?" asked Gordon but eyed him, wanted to measure his enthusiasm.

Graham sat up and seemed to relish the question. "According to mum I was always drawing or painting when I was a kid. It sort of grabbed me when I was about ten. I painted my aunt Janice in oils that she bought me for Christmas, and when I showed it to mum she cried."

"And why?" asked Gordon before had a sip of wine.

"She never said, and I regret not having painted mum now, although I might when I've chance," he replied, and had a sip of wine.

Gordon recalled the one he did of Caroline then the fact he had sold them all. He didn't regret it just knew he had to move on and look towards the future. Gordon also knew time goes by so quickly and things you should have done when had the chance, now knocking on in years they become well passed your capabilities. Glancing at Tracy he cringed when she was now a woman, suddenly smiled when recalled picking her up and kissing her goodnight.

Gordon had a drink and listening to silence thought of his parents and knew he could no longer ask them for advice. Now with wisps of gray hair and a receding hairline, same as his dad, Gordon made up his mind saying, "Right then, you can stay here tonight. I suppose Tracy will show you to the spare room, its only small but comfortable."

"Thank you, and however can I repay you?" asked Graham, looked sheepish.

Gordon nodded towards his case saying, "We'll sort all that out tomorrow, and is everything you own in there?"

Graham smiled at Tracy before said, "Yes, including my brushes and oils. To be honest I was going into

Leeds tomorrow and sketch in the city square, you know try and earn a few pounds that way."

"Go take him up to his room," said Andrea smiling at Tracy.

"Come on then," she replied, and quickly stood up.

Soon as they walked out of the room, Andrea confidently smiled saying, "I think you've done the best thing."

"To be honest love, I haven't a clue what to do. I just hope he is who he says he is but I'll find out tomorrow," replied Gordon, while poured out the rest of the wine.

Andrea had noticed Graham never mentioned Gordon's name in conversation, put it down to nerves, meeting his dad for the first time. It looked like they had one thing in common though, painting, and when she snuggled up to him, Gordon slipped his arm around her asking, "What do you think love?"

"I think you'll have to do twice as many paintings to keep us all now," she replied then giggled.

Next morning, Gordon and Andrea prepared breakfast when Tracy and Graham walked in the kitchen together and also said good morning together. "Good morning all and hurry up don't miss your bus," said Andrea while passed Tracy a plate.

"Here you are," said Gordon, and passed Graham a plate, turned then picked up his own.

Graham seemed nervous when he continued over towards the table but not sitting down said. "If you don't mind when I've eaten this I'll be off out of your way," said Graham before ate his toast.

Andrea carried a plate, and sitting down asked, "Please, just sit down for now?" She turned and gestured to Tracy asked, "Oh hell I forgot, pass the tea love."

Gordon frowned before saying, "Tracy, don't miss your bus."

"Your nothing but a slave driver," she moaned, and smirked before set off. With still six months to go at college, Tracy was unsure about her future. Designing clothes she liked and wished to expand her ideas, unfortunately didn't have the money to attend university and didn't have the heart to ask Gordon to finance her.

However, one thing she was going to ask him was that if she bought a sewing machine, would design clothes then make them, and would he allow her to try and sell them in the shop just to see if she could earn a living.

Thirty minutes later, Andrea opened the shop, had left Gordon and Graham in the kitchen drinking the last of the tea. She did it on purpose just to allow them to sort out their future and when she began to dust the furniture, suddenly smiled knew Tracy had taken a shine to Graham.

"Right then, you have a birth certificate, letters from home and have you a student union card?" asked Gordon frowning at him.

Graham knew he was still unsure replied, "Yes everything's all here in my wallet."

Gordon waited until he passed him the relevant documents, inspected them then gave everything back. Resting back in his chair Gordon seemed to study before said, "Right then, first let's get you back in college. We can't have two in the family without any qualifications."

Graham recalled last night's conversation then his eyes suddenly lit up before asked, "Does that mean as a painter, you are completely self-taught?"

"I rebelled, same as you did, however, that doesn't mean to say there isn't time for you to make amends. First though I want to know had your mum anymore relations in Sheffield," asked Gordon then stood up.

While he began to fill the kettle, Graham replied, "I don't think so. She never mentioned any nor did my aunt."

Gordon began to pour out some tea then turned when Andrea entered the kitchen. Smiling she said, "I'm just in time."

"As ever," said Gordon turned and leant on the worktop looking at Graham asking, "Do you want to return to college?"

"Not really, but by the look on your face it seems I have to," replied Graham, and sighed when took a cup from Andrea.

"It really is up to you," said Andrea, carried hers and sat down at the table.

"No, it isn't," snapped Gordon, carried his cup, walked over and sat with them. Looking straight at Graham he said, "It is a matter of finance. If you return to college to study with your grant you can live here and pay board. I'm sorry but at the moment our finances are just ticking over. Four living here will definitely over strain the budget."

"I understand," said Graham looking disappointed.

Andrea stood up and smiling said, "Unfortunately Gordon is right. I must say this though and please don't make the same mistake as him. Learn all you can now because it's free, later on in life you will have to pay dear for it."

Gordon studied thought her advice sound and smiled when she patted him on the shoulder before carried on into the shop. As it was the first time Andrea had so boldly made a statement, Gordon decided to back it up saying, "My father kept me twenty years before I considered myself good enough. Oh sorry Graham I shouldn't have said that."

"I do know what you mean. It's just that with my painting I feel I'm lacking quality but don't know where? Oh yes I can do it, it's just that in my mind I'm always questioning have I done it right?" said Graham staring at him.

Since Gordon had gone through the same uncertainty himself, he leant on the table and decided to speak his mind about painting raised his hands saying, "These are the main culprits. The brain knows what to do and your eyes must determine the picture. However, these hands must be good enough to portray it on canvas."

"I know that but what I mean is I need somebody to tell me where I am going wrong, it's the finer details," moaned Graham and frowned as if couldn't comprehend.

"In other words when you go to college bloody well listen to your tutor instead of moaning like a kid," snapped Gordon had purposely chastised him to make the point.

"Oh I, and listen to a little weasel with ginger hair going on about the Yorkshire dales with ten thousand different shades of green. He'd watch you, laugh then say, and don't forget to add a few cows," moaned Graham then quickly stood up.

"Where are you going to?" asked Gordon trying not to smile was now positive he couldn't take criticism and lacked discipline.

"I don't know," replied Graham, quickly sat down and bowed his head.

Feeling slightly unnerved because at that age he was exactly the same, Gordon trying not to smile asked, "Right lad, let's go upstairs to my studio and get you a style. And while we are at it, knock your attitude into shape, because by God have you one hell of a chip on your shoulder."

That evening and now over the moon working with an expert, Graham painted with enthusiasm. Gordon had given him a piece of work to copy and while he sat on the sofa reading, occasionally watched him. Gordon reflected back at the chap from the auction house in Leeds and smiled when never knew his name, however, suddenly frowned when without reason he had stopped calling.

All that commotion he caused about displaying my work and he hasn't been near for years thought Gordon, suddenly turned and gave the thumbs up when Graham asked what he thought.

Even though his painting had suffered was now a hit and miss affair, over the last few years and although had never classed himself as an expert, Gordon had always underestimated his expertise. Others hadn't, however, being out of the limelight for nearly ten years he didn't know he was still dinner conversation where he had worked on commission.

Watching Graham paint, Gordon had to smile when he gave very good accuracy to detail. His style was similar to himself even down to the way he stood, but what gave him the most satisfaction was

Graham's perception of light and he used it to great advantage.

Gordon was mesmerized while educating Graham with the do's and don'ts, especially when he seemed to absorb every little bit of information given to him. This of course helped them build a relationship. At first Graham wouldn't risk questioning Gordon's advice, however, when didn't understand anything, politely asked.

Over the following two weeks Graham began to question more. On one or two points, Gordon did relent especially when Graham used his perception of light to great effect even more so with skin tone, so deliberately gave praise.

"Let's hope my tutor will be in the same frame of mind on Monday morning," said Graham then grimaced didn't fancy the prospect of meeting him again, however, had liked the compliment from Gordon while took a painting off the easel.

"Oh he will I can assure you because I'm coming with you," said Gordon then laughed.

Graham turned and staring at him asked, "You are never?"

"Oh yes. I never did like anyone tearing my style apart and even more so when it affects part of my family," said Gordon, took the painting from him and inspected it closely.

"Graham watched, and smirked said, "Right dad."

"And don't call me dad I'm not used to it and by the way clean those brushes before you come down," moaned Gordon while leant the painting against the wall but had to smirk when he continued downstairs.

Chapter 26

Waiting while the Whitsuntide holidays had finished, but on the Sunday evening, forms were filled in, addresses changed, and when Gordon gave Graham a cheque to pay his fees for the rest of the year, Graham did his best to deter Gordon attending college with him the next day. On the other hand, he was very pleased and proud when he did. His tutor was ten years younger than Gordon and fully aware of his work after explained that as a student he attended his exhibition in Leeds with his parents and would be honored if he would stay and assess his class.

In the seminar, Gordon blushed slightly when he was introduced, smiled and nodded to everyone while continued to the rear of the class. Purposely sitting at the back out of their way, but still listened with interest, he observed the class of eight women and seven men. However, took notice one of one young woman, a tall leggy brunette aged early twenties, especially when she enthusiastically made room for Graham to sit next to her. Throughout the lesson she was smiling continuously at him and always trying to make conversation. In other words made it obvious she fancied him.

It annoyed Gordon and he had to smile didn't know why but the one thing he was most impressed about was, while listening to the tutor it also refreshed his memory so occasionally winced when recalled his bad habits.

When they broke for lunch, after Gordon gave praise for his method of teaching, while shaking hands with the tutor he asked to be excused. After slapped Graham on the arm, Gordon told him not to be late home and waved to everyone to everyone before walked out of the seminar.

Feeling slightly relieved mainly because sometimes the tutor did waffle on too much, while driving home Gordon began to study about the brunette hanging round Graham and knew Tracy had her eye on him. Knowing they were going to the university dance in Leeds on Saturday night he decided to keep quiet about her, smiled then suddenly gasped for breath. Twitching in his seat feeling his heart racing for no apparent reason, Gordon didn't understand so stared to panic, sat upright and grasped the steering wheel when his vision blurred.

Shaking with nerves, Gordon quickly pulled into a bus lay-by and yanked on the handbrake. After opened the window for air he slacked his tie before slipped his hand into his pocket and took out a hanky. Wiping sweat from his brow he gasped, "Bloody hell," began to think to what he had eaten or drank and thought the milk must have been off in the college canteen.

Hearing a loud horn behind him, Gordon glanced in the mirror and winced noticed a bus behind him. Setting off slowly he left the window open and the fresh air soon revived him.

Graham, however, was in completely different spirits while eating lunch now surrounded by his fellow students all wanting him to confirm that Gordon was his dad. When he did and liking the celebrity status, he also liked the fact while returning to the seminar the leggy brunette had her arm in his. Most important to him, his tutor had now come down to their level, when on a more friendlier basis he began to explain in greater detail so seemed to assess his pupils more logically.

Eventually Gordon reached home safe and sat in the kitchen began to explain to Andrea what had happened in the car. She eyed him before made him go rest on the bed and stressed that no way was he picking Graham up at five. "No I'll go I promised, besides if the traffic is light then so I'll pick up Tracy as well," he said, then kissed her as if to reassure her before set off upstairs.

Later, and feeling refreshed after a nap, Andrea was in the shop serving when Gordon waved and said he was setting off. "Right love," she replied, and waved. In actual fact Andrea was rather proud of her accomplishments when turnover in the shop had risen each year she had been looking after it.

Her suggestion of selling soft furnishings had done well, and as she now did the books and ordering this gave Gordon more free time. With her mind fully occupied, Andrea felt this was the most enjoyable part of her life. It showed when she looked picture of health and unfortunately sighed when Gordon didn't.

Gordon picked up Graham, however, missed Tracy and both waited for her at the bus-stop. When she did arrive soon as she got into the car, closed the door, turned and asked Graham about his day. "It wasn't too bad but a lot better when he set off home," he replied while cheekily nodded towards Gordon.

"Don't forget you are all on the bus tomorrow," said Gordon pulling up outside the rear of the shop.

When they all entered the house, Andrea was making dinner, suddenly smiled when Gordon kissed her before sat down. Tracy did the same before continued upstairs. "I've had a good day as well," said Graham, and kissed her on the cheek.

Graham was about to go upstairs when, "Just a minute. While we are on our own about that brunette sat next to you in college, she looks bad news to me," said Gordon frowning at him.

"She sure is, and don't worry in that department I'm no beginner," said Graham, and smiled carried on.

Andrea stared at Gordon, and not only wondered what was going on because knew Graham was taking Tracy out that evening so she wanted an explanation. After making a pan safe so it wouldn't burn, sitting down she asked, "I want to know what all that was about please?"

"It's nothing really love. Well, It's just that I noticed one of the women students in Graham's class giving him the eye, you know what I mean," said Gordon then stood up.

"Please, sit back down because I have some more news for you," said Andrea, reached over, and switched off the oven. When she looked back at Gordon who thought she was acting very much like his mum when she asked, "Did you know that tonight Graham is taking Tracy out to Leeds?"

Smiling he replied, "I know all about it."

"And tomorrow," she replied.

"Oh, I thought she said just tonight, said Gordon then frowned.

"And also did you know one of them has been sneaking into the others bedroom late at night?" she asked then raised her eyebrows.

"No I bloody well didn't," he replied, looked serious and leant on the table rubbed his brow.

"One of us has to put their foot down," said Andrea, stood up then bent down to open the oven door.

"No, both of us will," said Gordon, and frowned didn't relish doing it on his own.

Fifteen minutes later, all sat round the table, Gordon patiently waited until everyone had finished eating. "I'll just wash up," said Graham then stood up.

"No you won't lad just sit back down a minute," said Gordon then looked at Andrea blank as if undecided what to say.

"What's the matter?" asked Tracy, could tell something was wrong by the tone of his voice.

Andrea, looking very angry snapped, "Just this, seeing as your bedrooms are next to each other you are not at liberty to go flitting from one to another during the night."

"Pardon," said Graham, and stared gob smacked at her.

"What are you on about mum?" asked Tracy seemed bewildered.

"Please listen to me, you know I think the world of you Tracy, mind you on the other hand you know full well I am not your dad. However, while living here, will you please give you mum and me some decorum, and especially you Graham," said Gordon then turned to him but unfortunately saw a blank expression on his face and listening to silence made him angry.

Graham suddenly stood up snapped, "Gordon, just because I am taking Tracy out tonight and tomorrow, if you don't agree with it just say so."

Gordon wiped his brow with the back of his hand and thought it was over hot in the kitchen. When he glanced across at Andrea for support, she guessed he was in a dilemma, quickly turned to Tracy asking, "You can sit there and honestly say to me that nothing has been going on?"

"No mum, and thanks for the accusations. A quiet word would have been much better," said Tracy, quickly stood up and marched upstairs.

"Gordon, your sweating," gasped Andrea staring at him.

Graham looked very serious, stood up saying, "It must be with lack of sleep, laying awake all night trying to pin something on us, and you are absolutely wrong."

"Are you alright love?" asked Andrea, stood up walked round to Gordon and slipped her arm around his shoulder.

"I'll be alright love," he replied, and shakily stood up. Gordon tried to smile and kissed her on the cheek before unsteadily and for the first time used the handrail, slowly continued upstairs.

At the top, Gordon noticed Tracy leaving the bathroom and took a deep breath before asked, "Go give your mum a hand to wash up love please?"

"Sure will," she replied, and dashed downstairs.

Gordon continued into his studio could hear Graham whistling in his bedroom. Stood in the middle of the room, he glanced round at his paintings and smiled because any could have been done by either of them. His style had taken him years to perfect and now Graham had appeared on the scene as if had all his qualities built in.

Having not felt well all day, Gordon was about to return downstairs suddenly felt dizzy; he stopped and in panic stretched his arms to lean on the wall. Suddenly a violent pain came to his right shoulder, surging across his chest then it went black and he groaned out. Taking his breath so not able to speak, when it became too much, he gasped out for someone to hear him then it turned into a gurgle rendering him unconscious.

Hearing a loud crash Andrea dashed out of the kitchen, stared at Gordon, laid on his back at the foot of the stairs and screamed out. Graham dashed down and when Tracy followed, he pointed towards the kitchen shouting, "Go phone for an ambulance quick."

Tears streamed from Andrea's face while she carefully knelt down at the side of Gordon and sobbed while cradled his head. She quickly turned, glanced up at Tracy noticed tears streaming from her eyes and blurted out, "How long will they be?"

"They are on their way," she replied, continued, unlocked and opened the shop door. After glanced outside, she turned and stared at her mum and Gordon. Shaking with nerves, Tracy was thankful for Graham's presence when he dashed into the kitchen, made it safe and after locked the back door returned into the shop.

Graham knelt down, checked Gordon was breathing properly, but grimaced at Andrea who looked devastated and then all waited impatiently for the ambulance to arrive.

Soon after it did a paramedic team set about Gordon who after checked his condition laid him on a stretcher. Ten minutes later, watching through tears and gripped with apprehension, everyone remained silent while on the way to the hospital. Tracy held onto her mums arm while watched one of the ambulance team carry out various tests on Gordon then occasionally write notes on a clipboard.

Arriving at the hospital, the ambulance doors suddenly opened and they all watched in horror when Gordon was quickly taken out and had to nearly run to follow when he was whisked through a large door and then down a corridor. All stopped dead when their entrance was barred by a nurse. Looking impatient and nervous, Graham, Andrea, and Tracy were escorted into a side ward.

One hour of purgatory passed when suddenly a Doctor entered, glanced round and nervously introduced himself. After stating that Gordon had a stroke it was not as big as at first thought however, they couldn't determine the outcome until he woke up.

Escorting them into a ward and seeing Gordon wired up to a monitor, with tears streaming down Tracy and Andrea's faces, Graham sighed at their concern. It had also upset him and tears came to his eyes when he hugged them now realized he was an essential part of Gordon's family. "He looks so peaceful," said Tracy, while took hold of Graham's hand and sobbed.

"Come on dad, you can't leave us yet, we have some paintings to sell," said Graham, and squeezed her hand while reached out with his other and patted Gordon's arm.

Andrea noticed and began to reflect back on the uncertainty at the start of their relationship. Gordon had always been the positive one, however, always thoughtful not pushy. Forever thankful to him for her own health she now seemed helpless with his, however, later that night when he seemed to regain conscious and moan out, she instantly broke down in tears and thanked God.

Gordon began drifting in and out of consciousness but before opened his eyes and then knowing he was in a bed, decided first to assess who was with him. Listening while he glide his tongue over his bone dry lips, when realized it was his family he began to test his senses. Hearing a regular beep, he squinted and although his eyelids flickered, realized he was in a hospital.

 Wriggling his toes, Gordon tried to feel anything against them and couldn't. Not having the strength to raise his arms, he did the same with his fingers, couldn't feel anything and shuddered with the consequences. While laid quiet, and as they say, your past life flashes by, it didn't, and when Gordon only recalled the bad things he had done, didn't like it

Listening to voices and hearing the word, 'Stroke,' Gordon grimaced with apprehension. Having heard the word quietly mentioned by his parents and thought some of his family had died because of them, it had always been in the back of his mind if he would ever have one.

Being a believer of hereditary conditions and thinking now the inevitable had happened, and because of the pumped into him, while listening to an uncanny silence, Gordon's mind began to wander. *Good God I feel weak* he thought when tried to open his eyes and failed but managed to slowly turn his head. Andrea noticed, instantly sat up, tried to smile and wiped his brow with a damp cloth said, "Hello my love," but felt disappointed when he lay motionless.

Fifteen minutes later, a middle aged lady consultant wearing a white smock entered the ward and sounding rather posh, introduced herself. Before gave them the results of their tests, she stated Gordon did have a stroke and subject to further tests in the morning, this would determine when he could go home. Of course this also determined what future medication and treatment he could receive, however, Andrea couldn't grasp her words, turned, stared at Gordon, who was seemingly laid peaceful, and she grimaced when it remind her of seeing her husband Jack.

Andrea would never forget being accompanied by a police constable when she entered the ward and stared at Jack's body was in a terrible mess. The doctor stated he was barely alive and all he wanted to do was turn off the ventilator, but Andrea was in two minds to allow it. Adding more pressure, the nurses repeatedly made it appear everything was in short supply. Stating they would have to dash because they were short of staff, short of this that and the other then always mentioned was drastically short of beds.

In the end she agreed for them to turn off the ventilator but a few days later wished she hadn't when it preyed on her mind, had she done right, or had she been swayed by the hospital staff, when now had the feeling patients were simply on a conveyor belt.

Now knowing Gordon's life was not in immediate danger, when the consultant left, the relief of Andrea's face was that much she fell into Tracy's arms and cried her eyes out. Graham realized the love between them, glanced at Gordon sleeping peacefully moaned, "Bloody hellfire. All the help he's given me, and now I feel so stupidly helpless."

Slipping out of dreamland and back into reality, with his senses returning, Gordon had heard, didn't open his eyes, and quietly whispered, "You'll bloody pay for it eventually."

Andrea gasped out; she stared at Gordon, suddenly leant down and kissed him. Noticing his eyes closed, quietly she asked, "How do you feel my love?"

"I feel numb," he replied, and after a moment slowly opened his eyes. They flickered as if focusing then he turned his head slowly looking at her. Gordon moaned, "I feel so strange, completely relaxed but uncannily weak."

"That'll be the drugs," said Graham, and half-smiled at Tracy as she wiped tears from her eyes.

"That is something you had better not take else I'll break your neck," said Gordon, and suddenly winced as if in pain.

They all looked round when the lady consultant returned. Walking up to them she smiled, glanced over at Gordon saying, "Oh right then, nice to see you are with us Mr. Mathews." She looked round for a chair, saw one in the corner, picked it up and noisily placed it at the side of the bed.

When she sat down, Graham, asked, "If he's had a stroke, how serious was it?" and suddenly frowned knew Gordon could hear.

As I said slight, he needs to be up on his feet and exercising soon as possible," she replied then began to read her notes. Looking up she asked, "If you are his son? You must be prepared to help. Physically and in such short a time, my assessment mentally is that Mr. Mathews is what I class as unlucky," she replied smiling.

Quietly, Gordon asked, "Could you please explain?"

"Sorry, I didn't know you were fully awake Mr. Mathews. Well now, what has happened to you is just one of those things, it happens to some and not others. It isn't as if strokes run in your family because they don't," she replied, looked down and began to thumb through and then read her notes.

Now smirking Gordon said, "I could never do anything right."

"Pardon me?" asked Andrea, and with tears streaming from her eyes, leant down and kissed him.

The consultant stood up saying, "If you wish to stay the night you can, although it would be awkward with all three of you."

"We will have to go home and look after the shop," said Tracy, turned and looked at Graham.

This time is was Andrea who began to lay down the rules. Because it seemed Gordon was not in any immediate danger, she turned to Tracy, and purposely raised her voice said, "I will say this once. No funny business else you will be both out on the street."

The consultant stared at Andrea and realized her statement was obviously a family matter. She coughed before said, "Mr. Mathews should be ready to go home in a few days time. However, it is his rehabilitation I am concerned about. First it must be in a completely stress free environment and secondly diet and exercise must be rigidly adhered to."

Although Andrea's mind was drifting in and out of past experience, she pulled herself together stressed,

"I can assure you that my...Gordon will be well looked after at home."

"And we will help all we can," said Graham half-smiling.

After checking a list of do's and don'ts and explaining the contents in detail, the consultant passed them to Andrea before she left. Gordon had heard and understood their conversations, however, during which he began to ascertain his own physical state. While trying to move his legs, he sighed with relief when now could feel the sheets rubbing over them and felt the same when he raised his left arm. Unfortunately this was not the case with his right arm for as much as he tried, could not raise it.

Chapter 27

One hour later, while Gordon was drifting in and out of consciousness, after more instructions from Andrea including giving them some money for a taxi home, with the keys for the house and shop, Tracy and Graham decided to leave. Understanding Andrea had to stay with Gordon, they both agreed when she asked them to ring her first thing in the morning.

Knowing alterations had to be made to the house and thought Gordon would probably need a bed downstairs. However, before they set off, she gave them that motherly scowl, as if meant, you had better behave yourselves else end up in hot water.

Soon as they were out of site, Andrea had to smile knew they were getting on like a house on fire. She sauntered over towards the window and glanced out tried to see them, didn't have time when Gordon asked, "Have they gone home?"

"Yes love," she replied, quickly walked over and sat at his side. Andrea smiled mainly with relief now knew Gordon was alright. She didn't care what condition he was in provided he lived and was also aware that now due to disabilities, at the first opportunity they had to have a family meeting to discuss their futures.

Although Gordon had always treated Tracy as his daughter he had never officially adopted her. It had repeatedly crossed Andrea's mind that if she married Gordon and then if Tracy and Graham married, although their surnames were different, she thought it wouldn't look right. Gordon turned and noticed her daydreaming asked, "What are you thinking about?"

"Oh sorry love and funnily enough I were dreaming about something we haven't spoken about for years," replied Andrea then smiled.

Gordon licked his lips, and opened his eyes asked, "Could I have a drink please love?" Having realized what she meant he said, "Only this time I think we ought to as well."

"Oh, a mind reader are we?" asked Andrea while held a beaker to his lips.

Gordon had a sip, then smacked his lips moaned, "That was good." When he settled, Andrea noticed he seemed to relish being looked after. She suddenly stared, when he smiled said, "I dreamt Tracy and Graham got married but I think we ought to let them first before we do."

"Oh do you, and after all this time, should we indeed?" asked Andrea then smirked.

"Well, I don't think this is going to be a long job really. I'll tell you this as well, to celebrate the shop being open fifty years mum always wanted a party for all her past customers," said Gordon then wriggled to get more comfortable.

"She never said anything to me," said Andrea then studied.

"She did me. You know the sort of thing, sherry, tea coffee and sandwiches. Mind you the shop would have to be stocked up first so they could look round and browse," he said while grinned.

"I suppose we could arrange something," said Andrea, and studied. Gordon had never mentioned this before, and Andrea could not recall his parents mentioning it so she asked, "So when did your mum mention it last?"

"Oh come on love, it was only last week. I thought you had heard her but obviously not," said Gordon before closed his eyes.

"Oh, yes I recall it now," said Andrea, and smiled. She patted his arm knew his mind had been wandering, suddenly turned when a nurse entered carrying a tray. She had brought a sandwich and a cup of tea and Andrea smiled took it from her and politely kept out of the way while she dealt with Gordon. After tidied his bedclothes and administered his medication, "There that's done," said the nurse, and smiled before checked the monitor.

"Is everything okay?" asked Andrea, before had a drink.

Smiling she replied, "Oh yes, he's doing remarkably well. The doctor was thinking it was more on the lines of hardening of the arteries than a stroke."

Keeping her voice quiet so he wouldn't hear, Andrea, said, "Gordon's mind has been wandering. He's mentioned his mum and she's been dead quite a while."

"Don't worry about that it is very common. A lot of it is due to medication, most of the drugs administered are to relax you and that's when your mind works overtime. Anyway I must go now, more to do so see you later," said the nurse, and smiled before walked out.

"Thanks," said Andrea then studied

Arriving at the shop, Graham paid their fare while Tracy unlocked the back door. Inside the kitchen, first Graham checked the shop, continued throughout the house and when he returned, smiled at Tracy when she had made them a cup of tea. They sat at the table began to work out a rota for the shop and as instructed not forgetting next morning when they were to ring the hospital at nine o'clock.

Now alone in the house, that night they did sleep together, however, with respects to their parents and Gordon's incapacity that's all they did. Although because she couldn't sleep, Tracy woke Graham, and to pass time, between them they worked out what might be best for all concerned.

Graham said he would paint more to his dad's instructions, while Tracy, with what she had saved, was going to buy a new sewing machine, planned to design more, create new clothes and if Gordon would allow her, then soon as possible sell them in the shop.

"That's sound great, and if I can sell a few paintings we could try and build up some savings," said Graham smiling with enthusiasm.

"The main thing is Graham; we should inform our parents about us first. I think mum knows but we owe a lot to Gordon. Being here with you is beautiful but wrong because we are taking advantage. I think it is about time to come clean," said Tracy staring at him.

Graham, kissed her, and smiling said, "Let's make sure dad has fully recovered before dropping it on them. Mind you I think he's a lot tougher than what you think."

"That's not the point he's ill and needs looking after. The shop is paramount; it feeds us all so we all must rally round to maintain it," said Tracy, and frowned to make the point before lay her head on his chest.

The following morning, Graham woke first and showered before dressed. About to go downstairs, he heard Tracy do the same, continued into the kitchen and filled a bucket of water. His first job was to wash the shop windows and sills, and while he did, answered enquiries about Gordon from folk on their way to work.

Now nine o'clock, and inside the shop, Graham dusted round could hear Tracy in the kitchen. He had just finished when she popped her head round the door, and smiled said, "Breakfasts ready."

While eating, more plans were made, and keeping one eye on the clock, Tracy said, "I'll ring at half past," suddenly leant past Graham when heard the shop door open.

"I'll get it love," said Graham, and set off approached an elderly gentleman wearing a brown trilby hat and tawny raincoat and asked, "Yes sir and how could I help you?"

"I'm looking for Gordon? Is he about?" he asked, and as if had a stiff neck slowly glanced round.

"He's incapacitated at the moment," replied Graham smiled at him.

"Oh that's a shame. I haven't called for quite a number of years and I wondered if he would like to restore some paintings again for us? He's very good and he used to do in the past," he said then squinted at one painting.

Graham seized the opportunity to earn some pocket money, and smiling asked, "I'm sure he will. Next-time you pass just drop them in someone will be around."

"I've brought them with me, they are in the car," he said, spun round and opened the shop door.

After he left, in Gordon's studio, Graham eyed the paintings propped up against the wall. Tracy entered saying, "I've rung and mum say's Gordon's doing fine and they think he might be home tomorrow afternoon."

"Very good," said Graham while seemed to be engrossed.

"She told me we have to stay here look after the shop but when we go to the hospital tonight she needs some clothes, you know the sort of thing," said Tracy, quickly turned when the shop door opened saying, "I'll go get it."

Taking it turns to serve, because Graham began work on a painting that needed the least work doing to it, Tracy made their dinner and while ate were interrupted with sales. The only drawback was they had to wait for a customer to return with a mates van to pick up the last second hand chest of draws on display, however, during the day, had discussed and planned what to do and say that evening to their parents.

When the van arrived, Graham helped him to load it, and soon as he set off, locked up while Tracy phoned for a taxi. Using money from sales, forty minutes later, he paid the driver and both entered the hospital. In the ward, Tracy gasped when Gordon, looking rather well, was sat up in bed with her mum leant on it holding his hand.

She kissed him, them her mum, gave her a carrier bag contained clothes, then turned saying, "Thanks," when Graham passed her a chair.

"Right then, so come on how was your day?" asked Gordon but had to smirk.

Andrea stared, not with astonishment but interest while between them, after informed them their daily duties, Graham and Tracy outlined their future plans. Gordon noticed excitement in their eyes, as if ready to take on the world, and their body language had changed dramatically. They were now leaning towards each other, patiently waiting, not interrupting and unfortunately, both their heads bowed simultaneously when Andrea asked, "I trust you slept in separate beds?"

"No," replied Graham.

"I thought as much, anyway we can deal with that problem later. As for you Graham, I want to see what you have done with that painting first before you proceed with any more," said Gordon, then wriggled trying to get more comfortable.

"What about college?" asked Andrea, and frowned knew Gordon had paid his course.

"And I want to pack in now," said Tracy, looking soulful at her mum saying, "I think it's time to earn a wage mum don't you. I have to start putting something in; you can't keep taking out forever."

Craftily smiling Gordon asked, "Why didn't you tell that chap from the auction house I was poorly?"

"Because I want a chance to prove myself, I realize now there is only you that can help me expand my painting career. With Tracy's help we want to build our future together, and that's starting from now," replied Graham then suddenly felt assured noticed Andrea slightly smiling.

"Right you two, thanks for what you have done, and keep the shop money in your pocket until I get home. Really I think the best thing to do is when I do return home we'll discuss it further," said Gordon while winked at Andrea.

It looks like having to move round a bit of furniture love? Mind you we will have a bedroom extra," said Andrea, and tried not to laugh.

Tracy stared gasped, "Mum."

"And that's what you will be if you don't watch what you are doing," replied Andrea smirking.

"Steady on you lot because now I will put my foot down. My life from now on is supposed to be stress free so please, as I am supposed to be a second hand man, no more complications," said Gordon then grimaced.

"I don't know how you have cheek to ask that, and as for being a second hand man, that you have never been," gasped Andrea but had a smirk on her face while stared at him.

"What's up now?" asked Graham, and frowned didn't understand.

"I think she means life is supposed to flow by interrupted on a daily basis. Whereas we are so good at creating our own complications within it and do so regularly," said Gordon then smirked.

"Too true mate and you are number one at making most of them," said Andrea then laughed.